LOCUS

LOCUS

LOCUS

LOCUS

to

fiction

to 57
戀人版中英詞典
A Concise Chinese-English Dictionary for Lovers
作者：郭小櫓 （Xiaolu Guo）
譯者：郭品潔
責任編輯：丘光　校對：柳淑惠
法律顧問：董安丹律師、顧慕堯律師
出版者：大塊文化出版股份有限公司
台北市105南京東路四段25號11樓
www.locuspublishing.com
讀者服務專線：**0800-006689**
TEL：(02) 87123898　FAX：(02) 87123897
郵撥帳號：18955675　　戶名：大塊文化出版股份有限公司
版權所有‧翻印必究

A Concise Chinese-English Dictionary for Lovers by Xiaolu Guo
Copyright © 2007 by Xiaolu Guo
First published in Great Britain by Chatto & Windus, February 2007
Complex Chinese translation copyright © 2008 by Locus Publishing Company
This translation published by agreement with Chatto and Windus
through the Chinese Connection Agency, a division of The Yao Enterprises, LLC
All rights reserved.

總經銷：大和書報圖書股份有限公司
地址：新北市新莊區五工五路2號
TEL：(02) 89902588　　FAX：(02) 22901628
排版：天翼電腦排版印刷有限公司　　製版：瑞豐實業股份有限公司
初版一刷：2008年4月
初版六刷：2017年6月

定價：新台幣360元
Printed in Taiwan

國家圖書館出版品預行編目資料

戀人版中英詞典 / 郭小櫓(Xiaolu Guo)著；郭品潔譯.
-- 初版. -- 臺北市：大塊文化, 2008.04
544面；14x20公分. -- (to ; 57)
譯自：A Concise Chinese-English Dictionary for Lovers
ISBN 978-986-213-041-4 (平裝)

873.57　　　　　　　97000900

A Concise Chinese-English Dictionary for Lovers
戀人版中英詞典

郭小櫓　著
郭品潔　譯

For the man who lost my manuscript in Copenhagen airport,

and knows how a woman lost her language.

獻給哥本哈根機場遺失我手稿的那個男人，
　　　只有他知道一個女人是如何遺失她的語言的。

Nothing in this book is true,

except for the love between her and him.

Sorry of my english

本書內容全屬虛構，
　　　　除了她和他之間的愛。

抱歉我的英語

Contents

目次

BEFORE

prologue

n. 1. an introductory section or screen in a book, play, or musical work; 2. an event or action leading to another.

Now.

Beijing time 12 clock midnight.

London time 5 clock afternoon.

But I at neither time zone. I on airplane. Sitting on 25,000 km above to earth and trying remember all English I learning in school.

I not met you yet. You in future.

Looking outside the massive sky. Thinking air staffs need to set a special time-zone for long-distance airplanes, or passengers like me very confusing about time. When a body floating in air, which country she belonging to?

People's Republic of China passport bending in my pocket.

Passport type	**P**
Passport No.	**G00350124**
Name in full	**Zhuang Xiao Qiao**
Sex	**Female**
Date of birth	**23 JULY 1979**
Place of birth	**Zhe Jiang, P. R. China**

I worry bending passport bring trouble to immigration offi-

【序幕】

〈名詞〉**1.** 序言，開場白；書本、戲劇或音樂作品的開頭部分；**2.** 發端的事件或行動。

　　此刻。

　　北京時間午夜十二點。

　　倫敦時間下午五點。

　　但我不在這兩個時區。我人在飛機上。離地兩萬五千公尺的高空坐著，拚命回想學校教過的所有英語。

　　我還沒遇見你。未來的日子才會有你。

　　窗外望去，天空廣袤無際。想想看，機組員得替長途客機或像我這樣搞不清時間的旅客設定時區。當人的身體浮游高空時，哪個國家算她的歸屬所在？

　　中華人民共和國的護照摺疊在我口袋。

護照類型	P
護照號碼	G00350124
全名	莊小喬
性別	女
生日	1979 年 7 月 23 日
出生地	中華人民共和國浙江省

　　我擔心這本摺疊的護照讓移民官看見會有麻煩，搞不好他

cer, he might doubting passport is fake and refusing me into the UK, even with noble word on the page:

The Ministry of Foreign Affairs of the People's Republic of China requests all civil and military authorities of foreign countries to allow the bearer of this passport to pass freely and afford assistance in case of need.

China further and further, disappearing behind clouds. Below is ocean. I from desert town. Is the first time my life I see sea. It look like a dream.

As I far away from China, I asking me why I coming to West. Why I must to study English like parents wish? Why I must to get diploma from West? I not knowing what I needing. Sometimes I not even caring what I needing. I not caring if I speaking English or not. Mother only speaking in village dialect and even not speaking official Mandarin, but she becoming rich with my father, from making shoes in our little town. Life OK. Why they want changing my life?

And how I living in strange country West alone? I never been to West. Only Western I seeing is man working in Beijing British Embassy behind tiny window. He stamp visa on brand new passport.

What else I knowing about West? American TV series dubbing into Chinese, showing us big houses in suburb, wife by window cooking and car arriving in front house. Husband back work. Husband say Honey I home, then little childrens running to him, see if he bringing gift.

But that not my life. That nothing to do with my life. I not having life in West. I not having home in West. I scared.

I no speaking English.

I fearing future.

懷疑護照是假的，拒絕讓我入境英國，儘管上頭印著堂皇的字眼：

中華人民共和國外交部請各國軍政機關對持照人予以通行的便利和必要的協助。

　　中國愈來愈遠，消失在重重雲幕之後。底下是大海。我從沙漠一樣的小鎮來，這輩子頭一回見到海。它看起來恍如一夢。

　　遠離中國，我問自己為什麼要到西方來。為什麼我非得照爸媽的希望學習英語？為什麼我必須跑到西方來拿文憑？我不清楚自己到底需要什麼？有時甚至我也不在乎自己要什麼。我不在乎自己說不說得了英語。媽媽一輩子只能說家鄉話，國語開都開不了口，可她跟我父親在家鄉那小地方靠製鞋也攢了好多錢。日子過得挺好的。怎麼他們就想要改變我的人生？

　　而且自己一個人，怎麼在一個陌生的國家過活？我從沒到過西方，唯一見過的西方人只有北京英國大使館窄小窗口後頭當班的那個男人。他負責在簇新的護照上頭蓋簽證。

　　關於西方世界，我還懂個什麼？配上國語發音的美國電視劇，展示郊區的大別墅，太太在窗邊做晚餐，轎車直接開進屋前。丈夫上班回家。先生對太太說：親愛的我回來了，然後小鬼頭連蹦帶跳，纏著看父親帶禮物回來沒有。

　　但那些電視劇不屬於我的生活。它們跟我的人生沒有關係。我不是他們，我在西方沒有家。我害怕。

　　我的英語開不了口。

　　我害怕往後的日子。

　　我害怕。

February

alien

adj. **1.** foreign; **2.** repugnant (to); **3.** from another world. *n.* **1.** foreigner; **2.** being from another world.

Is unbelievable, I arriving London, "Heathlow Airport". Every single name very difficult remembering, because just not "London Airport" simple way like we simple way call "Beijing Airport". Everything very confuse way here, passengers is separating in two queues.

Sign in front of queue say: ALIEN and NON ALIEN.

I am alien, like Hollywood film *Alien*, I live in another planet, with funny looking and strange language.

I standing in most longly and slowly queue with all aliens waiting for visa checking. I feel little criminal but I doing nothing wrong so far. My English so bad. How to do?

In my text book I study back China, it says English peoples talk like this:

"*How are you?*"

"*I am very well. How are you?*"

"*I am very well.*"

Question and answer exactly the same!

Old saying in China: "*Birds have their bird language, beasts have their beast talk*". English they totally another species.

Immigration officer holding my passport behind his accounter, my heart hanging on high sky. Finally he stamping on my visa. My heart touching down like air plane. Ah. Wo.

【外國人】

〈形容詞〉**1.** 外國的；**2.** 格格不入的；**3.** 來自其他世界的。〈名詞〉**1.** 外國人；**2.** 來自其他世界的生物。

　　不敢相信，我人到了倫敦，「希斯洛機場」。好拗口的名字，怎不直接叫「倫敦機場」，像我們那兒叫「北京機場」多省事。這裡樣樣讓人摸不著腦袋，旅客被分開排成兩條人龍。

　　人龍前頭分別標示：「外國」，「非外國」。

　　我是個外國人，像好萊塢片子《異形》當中的外星人──長相荒誕，言語怪異。

　　站在漫長的隊伍裡，我跟所有的「外星人」一道等著查驗簽證。我感覺我是他們國家的罪犯嫌疑人，雖然我可沒犯什麼錯。麻煩的是：我的英語詞不達意。怎辦？

　　記得以前在中國，課本上教我們，英國人這麼講話：

　　「**你好嗎？**」

　　「**我很好。你好嗎？**」

　　「**我很好。**」

　　問話跟回話沒半點分別！

　　中國的老話說：「**鳥有鳥語，獸有獸言。**」英國人他們說的不是鳥語就是獸言。

　　櫃檯後邊的移民官員接過護照，我一顆心吊在半空。過了幾十秒，終於他將一顆大印按上去，我心頭一落，像飛機安然著陸。哦。噢。喔。哈。提起行李，現在我可是個合法的外國

Ho. Ha. Picking up my luggage, now I a legal foreigner. Because legal foreigner from Communism region, I must re-educate, must match this capitalism freedom and Western democracy.

All I know is: I not understanding what people say to me at all. From now on, I go with *Concise Chinese-English Dictionary* at all times. It is red cover, look just like *Little Red Book*. I carrying important book, even go to the toilet, in case I not knowing the words for some advanced machine and need checking out in dictionary. Dictionary is most important thing from China. *Concise meaning simple and clean.*

人。不過因爲來自共產國家，我必須接受再教育，我得努力跟上這西方資本主義自由民主的腳步。

　　現實擺在眼前：我聽不懂別人開口講的話。從現在起，我身邊隨時得準備**簡明中英辭典**。這本辭典紅彤彤的封皮，看起來跟毛語錄一樣。連上洗手間都不能馬虎，我怕他們的先進設施不時出現害人茫茫然的字眼，不靠它查個明白哪行。從中國帶來的東西沒一樣比得上中英辭典那麼重要。

　　「Concise Dictionary」，我查了「concise」的中文意思：**簡單明瞭**。

hostel

n. building providing accommodation at a low cost for a specific group of people such as students, travellers, homeless people, etc.

First night in "hostel". Little *Concise Chinese-English Dictionary* hostel explaining: a place for "people such as students, travellers and homeless people" to stay. Sometimes my dictionary absolute right. I am student and I am homeless looking for place to stay. How they knowing my situation *precisely*?

Thousands of additional words and phrases reflect scientific and techno-logical innovations, as well as changes in politics, culture, and society. In particular, many new words and expressions as well as new usages and meanings which have entered the Chinese language as a result of China's open-door policy over the last decade have been included in the Chinese-English section of the dictionary.

That is sentence in *Preface*. All sentence in preface long like this, very in-understandable. But I must learning this stylish English because it high-standard English from authority. Is parents" command on me: studying how speak and write English in England, then coming back China, leaving job in government work unit and making lots money for their shoes factory by big international business relations. Parents belief their life is dog's life, but with money they save from last sev-

【住宿處】

〈名詞〉為特定人士如學生、旅者、遊民等提供便宜膳宿的場所。

　　頭一晚待在「住宿處」。袖珍本的**簡明中英辭典**，住宿處的解釋：「給學生、旅者或沒有家的人過夜的地方」。有時候我的字典完全正確。我是學生，我沒有家，想找個地方過夜。怎麼這本中英辭典能夠準確無誤地知道我的**處境**？

「在這本中英-英中簡明辭典裡，新增的幾千條詞彙和片語反映了世界科技方面的創新，以及政治、文化、社會方面的諸多變遷。特別是，許多新字和詞句伴隨著新的用法和意義出現在中國語言中作為近十年來中國改革開放政策的結果業已收錄於本中英辭典當中。」

　　那是我的辭典「前言」裡頭的英文句子。前言裡所有的句子都是這種語言風格，冗長而費解。但我要學的便是這種所謂「漂亮」的英語，出自語言權威的「高水平」英語。爸媽對我出國的最高指示便是：到英國學會說寫英語，然後回到中國，辭掉政府單位的工作，和國際大企業拉上關係，幫他們的鞋廠賺大錢。爸媽覺得他們一輩子過得跟狗似的，還好過去幾十年來辛苦攢了點錢，可以供我到西方接受教育，改善往後的生活。

eral years, I make better life through Western education.

Anyway, *hostel* called "Nuttington House" in Brown Street, nearby Edward Road and Baker Street. I write all the names careful in notebook. No lost. Brown Street seem really brown with brick buildings everywhere. Prison looking. Sixteen pounds for per bed per day. With sixteen pounds, I live in top hotel in China with private bathroom. Now I must learn counting the money and being mean to myself and others.

First night in England is headache.

Pulling large man-made-in-China-suitcase into hostel, second wheel fall off by time I open the door. (First wheel already fall off when I get suitcase from airport's luggage bell.) Is typical suitcase produced by any factory in Wen Zhou, my hometown. My hometown China's biggest home-products industry town, our government says. Coat hangers, plastic washbasins, clothes, leather belts and nearly-leather bags, computer components etc, we make there. Every family in my town is factory. Big factories export their products to everywhere in the world, just like my parents get order from Japan, Singapore and Israel. But anyway, one over-the-sea trip and I lost all the wheels. I swear I never buy any products made from home town again.

Standing middle of the room, I feeling strange. This is *The West*. By window, there hanging old red curtain with holes. Under feet, old blood-red carpet has suspicions dirty spots. Beddings, they covering by old red blanket too. Everything is dirty blood red.

Room smelling old, rotten. Suddenly my body feeling old too. "English people respect history, not like us," teachers say

這間住宿處叫「Nuttington House」，什麼意思？我不明白。位於布朗街，靠近艾德華路和貝克街。附近所有街道的名稱，我一字不漏地寫進英文學習筆記本裡。布朗街成排褐色的磚頭房子，像是關犯人的地方。十六英鎊，換來一張床住一天。花十六鎊，在中國我想我能住進一間像樣的飯店，有自己的洗澡間。現在可好，我得學著計算支出，對自己對別人得學著吝嗇點。

在英國的第一個夜晚就讓我頭疼不已。

拖著中國製的大皮箱進到住宿處，才一開門第二個滾輪就掉了。（從機場行李輸送帶拿到箱子時，第一個滾輪早已失蹤。）這是一般常見的行李箱，我家鄉溫州的每家工廠都能製造。據我們政府的官方資料，溫州是中國規模最大的家庭工業生產重鎮。掛衣架，塑膠臉盆，衣服，皮腰帶，仿皮提袋，電腦零件，林林總總，我們那兒都有生產。城裡每戶人家都是工廠。規模大一點的能把產品出口到世界各國，像我爸媽的訂單就來自日本、新加坡和以色列。不過呢，提著老家生產的行李箱，跨海出個遠門，滾輪全部掉光。我發誓絕不再買老家做的任何產品了。

站在房間中央，感覺好陌生。這就是所謂的「西方世界」嗎？在中國我們只從電影裡見識過高貴的西方。比起眼前的現實，電影根本在瞎掰。房間窗邊掛著老舊的紅布簾，好幾個地方抽絲穿孔。腳底下，年代久遠的腥紅地毯，凌亂的髒印子不知怎麼來的。床上，是類似的紅色陳年毛毯。每樣東西都是一片骯髒腥紅。

房間的味道好不到哪裡，同樣陳舊，腐敗。霎時間我的身

to us in schools. Is true. In China now, all buildings is no more than 10 years old and they already old enough to be demolished.

With my enormous curiosity, walking down to the night street. First night I away home in my entirely twenty-three years life, everything scare me. Is cold, late winter. Windy and chilli. I feeling I can die for all kinds of situation in every second. No safety in this country, I think unsafe feeling come from I knowing nothing about this country. I scared I in a big danger.

I scared by cars because they seems coming from any possible directing. I scared by long hair black man passing because I think he beating me up just like in films. I scared by a dog. Actually chained with old lady but I thinking dog maybe have mad-dog-illness and it suddenly bite me and then I in hospital then I have no money to pay and then I sent back to China.

Walking around like a ghost, I see two rough mans in corner suspicionly smoke and exchange something. Ill-legal, I have to run — maybe they desperate drug addictors robbing my money. Even when I see a beggar sleeping in a sleep bag I am scared. Eyes wide open in darkness staring at me like angry cat. What he doing here? I am taught everybody in West has social security and medical insurance, so, why he needs begging?

I going back quickly to Nuttington House. Red old carpet, red old curtain, red old blanket. Better switch off light.

Night long and lonely, staying nervously in tacky room. London should be like emperor's city. But I cannot feel it. Noise coming from other room. Laughing in drunkenly way.

體似乎也老了。「英國人尊重歷史，不像我們總希望日新月異，」學校的老師這樣告訴我們。這倒是真的。現在的中國，建築物的屋齡很少超過十年，而且就已經算是老舊到可以拆除的了。

滿腹好奇，我不願意早早上床休息，離開房間，下來住宿處，走進夜裡的街道。好冷的冬夜，寒風刺骨。活了二十三年，第一個離家的夜晚，每樣東西都讓我害怕，感覺自己隨時會遭遇危險的狀況。這國家好不安全，我想會有這種感覺是因為我對這地方懵懂無知。我怕自己身處險境還不曉得警覺。

我被車子嚇著，它們似乎從四面八方橫衝直撞。我被旁邊走過的長髮黑人嚇著，怕他會攻擊我就像美國電影演的那樣。我被一隻狗嚇著，其實有個老太太牽著，但我害怕那狗或許有狂犬病，搞不好突然咬我，害我進了醫院但卻沒錢付帳，結果被遣送回去中國。

我像鬼魂般漫遊在大街上，我看見街角兩個神色可疑的傢伙在抽菸，手邊不知拿什麼東西交換著。肯定正從事非法行為，我得快跑——或許他們是凶險的毒蟲專門搶人家錢的。即使看見一個乞丐躺在睡袋我也害怕。他眼珠睜大黑暗裡瞪著我像隻瘋貓。他在這兒做什麼？國內的宣傳教我說西方人人都有社會安全保障和醫療保險，如果是這樣的話，幹嘛他還要當乞丐？

我快步走回「Nuttington House」（納廷頓之家）。紅色舊地毯，紅色舊窗簾，紅色舊毛毯。快把燈關了罷。

夜晚漫長孤單，窩在寒酸的房間裡焦慮不安。倫敦應該像伊莉莎白女王的宮殿。但我一點感覺也沒有。喧鬧聲從其他房間傳來。有人大概酒喝多了，狂笑不止。樓上的電視新聞熱烈

Upstairs TV news speaking intensely nonsense. Often the man shouting like mad in the street. I worry. I worry I getting lost and nobody in China can find me anymore. How I finding important places including Buckingham Palace, or Big Stupid Clock? I looking everywhere but not seeing big posters of David Beckham, Spicy Girls or President Margaret Thatcher. In China we hanging them everywhere. English person not respect their heroes or what?

No sleeping. Switching on the light again. Everything turning red. Bloody new world. I study little red dictionary. English words made only from twenty-six characters? Are English a bit lazy or what? We have fifty thousand characters in Chinese.

Starting at page one:

A

Abacus: (meaning a wooden machine used for counting)
Abandon: (meaning to leave or throw away)
Abashed: (meaning to feel embrassed or regretful),
Abattoir: (meaning a place to kill the animals)
Abbess: (meaning the boss of woman monk's house)
Abbey: (meaning a temple)
Abbot: (meaning the boss of a temple)
Abbreviate: (meaning to write a word quickly)
Abduct: (meaning to tie somebody up and take away to somewhere)

Words becoming blurred and no meaning. The first night I falling into darkness with the jet-lag tiredness.

播放「鳥語」，我一句也聽不明白。街上不時有人咆哮像瘋子。我擔心，我擔心自己萬一走丟了，中國那邊豈不是沒有人知道。白金漢宮，大笨鐘，這些有名的地方在哪兒？奇怪，怎麼到處都見不到貝克漢的大海報，辣妹合唱團或「總統柴契爾夫人」的也沒看見。在中國我們掛得到處都是。英國人沒有偶像崇拜嗎？他們是不在乎自己國家的英雄人物還是怎樣？

睡不著。燈一打開，窗簾，地毯，毛毯，樣樣東西變回紅色。歡迎光臨血色新世界。無事可做，我只好讀起小紅辭典來。英文字怎麼只有二十六個字母？英國人是有點懶還是怎樣？中國文化起碼有五萬個字哪。

從辭典第一頁開始：

A

Abacus:　　　　（意指一種木製器物用來算數）

Abandon:　　　　（意指遺棄或丟棄）

Abashed:　　　　（意指感到尷尬或羞愧）

Abattoir:　　　　（意指屠宰動物的地方）

Abbess:　　　　（意指尼庵住持）

Abbey:　　　　（意指大寺院）

Abbot:　　　　（意指大寺院男住持）

Abbreviate:　　　（意指簡寫或縮寫）

Abduct:　　　　（意指綁架劫持）

字與字的邊緣逐漸模糊，它們的意義也在我的腦海中逐漸消失。頭一夜我帶著時差疲乏沉入黑暗當中。

full english breakfast

1. Builder's Super Platter: double egg, beans, bacon, sausage, bubble, mushroom, tomato, 2 toast, tea or coffee included.

2. Vegetarian Breakfast: double egg, bubble, mushroom, beans, veggie sausage, hash browns, tea or coffee included.

"Talk doesn't cook rice," say Chinese. Only thing I care in life is eating. And I learning English by food first, of course. Is most practical way.

Getting up early, I have free *Full English Breakfast* from my *hostel*. English so proud they not just say hotel, they say *Bed and Breakfast*, because breakfast so importantly to English situation. Even say "B and B" everyone know what thinking about. Breakfast more important than Bed.

I never seeing a *breakfast* like that. Is big lunch for construction worker! I not believe every morning, my *hostel offering* everybody this meal, lasting three hours, from 7 clock to 10 clock. Food like messy scrumpled eggs, very salty bacons, burned bread, very thick milk, sweet bean in orange sauce, coffee, tea, milk, juice. Church or temple should be like this, giving the generosity to normal people. But 8.30 in the morning I refuse accepting two oily sausage, whatever it made by pork or by vegetables, is just too fat for a little Chinese.

What is this "baked beans"? White colour beans, in orange sticky sweet sauce. I see some baked bean tins in shop when I arrive to London yesterday. Tin food is very expensive to China. Also we not knowing how to open it. So I never ever try tin food. Here, right in front of me, this baked beans must

【全套英式早餐】

1. 招牌超級餐盤：雙蛋，燉豆子，培根，香腸，包心菜煎馬鈴薯，蘑菇，番茄，吐司兩片，附茶或咖啡。
2. 素食早餐：雙蛋，包心菜煎馬鈴薯，蘑菇，燉豆子，素香腸，煎薯餅，附茶或咖啡。

「**光說煮不了飯**」，中國人的說法。吃飯是我人生第一要務。自然而然，我學習英語也從吃的東西開始。這個辦法對中國人來說最實際不過。

早早起床，住宿處提供我免費的「**全套英式早餐**」。英國人自豪得很，他們住宿的地方不會只說「**旅社**」，他們說「**供宿兼早餐**」，早餐對英國人而言再重要不過。「B and B」人人一聽就懂。早餐供應可比住宿重要多了。

我從沒見過這種「**早餐**」。好像給飢餓的建築工人吃的午餐分量。每天早上，七點到十點，連續三個鐘頭我的「住宿處」供應這種餐點給房客。食物未免也豐盛過頭了，有費工的炒蛋，鹹培根，烤麵包，非常稠的牛奶，橙子醬燒甜豆，咖啡，茶，牛奶，果汁。教堂或寺廟像這樣該多好，餵飽無依無靠的老百姓。不過到了八點半我不行了，對於再來兩條油膩膩的香腸敬謝不敏，不管裡頭葷也好，素也好，總之，對一個中國小姑娘來說實在太油了。

不過這「燉豆子」到底是什麼名堂？豆子白白的，混在黏答答的甜橙醬裡面。昨天抵達倫敦的時候經過商店，我看見店裡有賣這種燉豆罐頭。在中國鄉下罐頭是名貴東西，我們連打開也不曉得怎麼弄，所以我根本沒機會嘗試。這會兒，在我眼

九

be very expensive. Delicacy is baked beans. Only problem is, tastes like somebody put beans into mouth but spit out and back into plate.

Sitting on breakfast table, my belly is never so full. Still two pieces of bread and several "baked tomatoes" on my plate. I can't chew more. Feeling guilty and wasty, I take out little Concise Chinese-English Dictionary from my pocket, start study English. My language school not starting yet, so I have to learn by myself first. Old Chinese saying: "the stupid bird should fly first before other birds start to fly".

When I am studying the word *Accommodate*, woman come clean table, and tell me I must leave. She must hate me that I eat too much food here. But not my fault.

First morning, I steal white coffee cup from table. Second morning, I steal glass. So now in my room I can having tea or water. After breakfast I steal breads and boiled eggs for lunch, so I don't spending extra money on food. I even saving bacons for supper. So I saving bit money from my parents and using for cinema or buying books.

Ill-legal. I know. Only in this country three days and I already become thief. I never steal piece of paper in own country. Now I studying hard on English, soon I stealing their language too.

Nobody know my name here. Even they read the spelling of my name: *Zhuang Xiao Qiao*, they have no idea how saying it. When they see my name starts from "Z", stop trying. I unpronouncable Ms Z.

First three days in this country, wherever I walk, the voice from my parents echo my ears:

前，「名貴」的燉豆子這麼擺著，好高檔的美食哪。唯一的問題是，嚐起來好像有人把豆子放進嘴裡含過又吐回餐盤。

坐在早餐桌旁，我的肚子從沒這麼撐過。盤裡還剩兩塊麵包和幾片「烤番茄」。我一口也吃不下了。罪過啊，糟蹋食物，我從口袋掏出袖珍簡明中英辭典開始學習。語言學校還沒開學，我得先自我學習。中國有句老話說得好：「笨鳥先飛」。

等我讀到「Accommodate（適應）」這個字的時候，有個女的來清理桌子，跟我說我該離開了。她一定是有點嫌棄我，覺得我愛占便宜，一個人吃掉那麼多食物。對不起，我不是故意的。

頭一個早上，我從桌上偷了個白色咖啡杯。第二個早上，我偷了個玻璃杯。所以我可以在自己的房間喝茶或水了。早餐過後我偷了點麵包和水煮蛋當做午餐，這樣就不必額外花錢買食物。我甚至省下培根當晚餐。我可以省下一點爸媽給的錢，拿來看個電影或者買書。

非法行為。我知道。才來到這國家三天，我已經學會當賊。在中國我可連一張紙也沒偷過。這會兒我學習英語這麼起勁，遲早會連他們的語言一併偷走。

這裡沒有人認得我的名字。就算西方人讀出我姓名的拼音：莊小喬（Zhuang-Xiao-Qiao），合起來還是不會唸。他們乾脆不試了，直接叫我名字的開頭——「Z」。我成了名字沒辦法發音的Z小姐。

來這國家的前三天，不管走到哪兒，爸媽的聲音在我耳朵迴響：

「別跟陌生人講話。」

"*No talking strangers.*"

"*No talking where you live.*"

"*No talking how much money you have.*"

"*And most important thing: no trusting anybody.*"

That my past life. Life before in China. The warns speaking in my mother's harsh local dialect, of course, translation into English by *Concise Chinese-English Dictionary*.

「別說你住在哪兒。」

「別說你有好多錢。」

「最重要的一點：別相信任何人。」

這些警告來自我過去的人生。過去在中國的人生。不消說，這些警告是母親用她嚴厲的家鄉話講出來的，「簡明中英辭典」再幫我譯成英語。

properly

proper adj. **1.** real or genuine; **2.** suited to a particular purpose; **3.** correct in behaviour, excessively moral. *properly adv.* **1.** in a proper way; **2.** in the precise sense.

Today my first time taking taxi. How I find important place with bus and tube? Is impossibility. Tube map is like plate of noodles. Bus route is in-understandable. In my home town everyone take cheap taxi, but in London is very expensive and taxi is like the Loyal family look down to me.

Driver say: "Please shut the door properly!"

I already shut the door, but taxi don't moving.

Driver shout me again: "Shut the door properly!" in a *concisely* manner.

I am bit scared. I not understanding what is this "properly".

"I beg your pardon?" I ask. "What is *properly*?"

"Shut the door properly!" Taxi driver turns around his big head and neck nearly break because of anger.

"But what is "properly", Sir?" I so frightened that I not daring ask it once more again.

Driver coming out from taxi, and walking to door. I think he going kill me.

He opens door again, smashing it back to me hardly.

"Properly!" he shout.

Later, I go in bookshop and check "properly" in *Collins English Dictionary* ("THE AUTHORITY ON CURRENT

【妥當】

〈形容詞〉**1.** 妥當的，真的；**2.** 適合特定目的的；**3.** 行為正確的，嚴守規矩的。〈副詞〉**1.** 妥當地；**2.** 嚴格地。

今天我第一次搭計程車。搭巴士和地鐵的話我怎麼找得到目的地？這沒辦法。地鐵行車圖看上去像一盤麵條，巴士路線怎麼也沒辦法弄懂。在我家鄉人人搭便宜的計程車，但倫敦貴死了，而且計程車像皇室成員般輕視我。

司機說：「請把門關 properly！」

我已經關上車門了，但計程車動也不動。

司機又吼我：「把門關 properly！」不肯**多說一句**的樣子。

我有點膽怯。我不懂什麼是「*properly*」。

「對不起？」我問他。「什麼是 *properly*？」

「把門 properly 關好！」計程車司機轉過來氣到差點扭斷那顆大頭和粗脖子。

「可是什麼是『properly』，先生？」我怕得要命不敢再多問一句。

司機下車，走到門邊。我想他會宰了我。

他打開車門，向我重重摔了回去。

「Properly！」他吼道。

稍晚，我來到書店，翻開《**柯林斯英文辭典**》（「當代英語

一二

ENGLISH"). *Properly* means "correct behaviour". I think of my behaviour with the taxi driver ten minutes ago. Why incorrect? I go to accounter buy little *Collins* for my pocket

My small *Concise Chinese-English Dictionary* not having "properly" meaning. In China we never think of "correct behaviour" because every behaviour correct.

I want write these newly learned words everyday, make my own dictionary. So I learn English fast. I write down here and now, in every second and every minute when I hear a new noise from an English's mouth.

權威」)。「*properly*」（妥當）代表「正確的行為」。我回想自己十分鐘前對計程車司機的行為。哪裡不正確了？我去櫃檯付錢買下袖珍本**柯林斯**好放口袋。

我小本的**簡明中英辭典**沒有「妥當」的解釋。也許我們中國人不會去計較什麼「正確的行為」，因為隨便哪個行為都是正確的。

有了這番經驗，我想把每天學到的新字寫下來，自己弄一本辭典。這樣可以加快英語學習的速度。我應該現在就寫下來，才好隨時準備應付哪個英國人又對我動口發出怪音。

fog

n. a mass of condensed water vapour in the lower air, often greatly reducing visibility.

"London is the Capital of fog." It saying in middle school textbook. We studying chapter from Charles Dickens's novel *Foggy City Orphan*. Everybody know Oliver Twist living in city with bad fog. Is very popular novel in China.

As soon as I arriving London, I look around the sky but no any fogs. "Excuse me, where I seeing the fogs?" I ask policeman in street.

"Sorry?" he says.

"I waiting two days already, but no fogs," I say.

He just look at me, he must no understanding of my English.

When I return Nuttington House from my tourism visiting, reception lady tell me: "Very cold today, isn't it?" But why she tell me? I know this information, and now is too late, because I finish my tourism visiting, and I wet and freezing.

Today I reading not allowed to stay more than one week in hostel. I not understanding hostel's policy. "Money can buy everything in capitalism country" we told in China. My parents always saying if you have money you can make the devil push your grind stone.

But here you not staying even if you pay. My parents wrong.

I checking all cheap flats on LOOT in Zone 1 and 2 of

【霧】

〈名詞〉低空彌漫的凝結水汽團，容易導致能見度降低。

「倫敦以霧都聞名。」中學課本上如此說道。我們讀過狄更斯《霧都孤兒》（編按：台譯《孤雛淚》）的小說選摘。這本書在中國名氣大得很，人人曉得主角奧利佛住的地方霧害不是普通的嚴重。

這會兒真的來到倫敦，四下張望卻見不到半點霧。「不好意思，請問哪兒看得到霧？」我問街頭的值勤員警。

「什麼？」他說。

「我已經等了兩天，都沒有霧，」我說。

他直盯著我瞧，一定是聽不懂我的英語吧。

出門走馬看花回到「納廷頓之家」，接待處的女士跟我說：「今天好冷，是不是？」幹嘛這樣說，這我已經曉得了，現在講有什麼用，我剛從外面觀光回來，早就凍到不行了。

今天我才讀到，住宿處不許居留超過一個禮拜。我不懂這算什麼規矩。在中國聽人家說「資本主義國家金錢萬能」。還有我爸媽老愛講的，有錢能使鬼推磨。

怎麼這地方付錢也不讓人家待下去。爸媽的話不準了。

我上網查看倫敦第一和第二區便宜的租房，抄下電話打給仲介公司。接電話的先生聲音聽起來全像來自阿拉伯國家，而且名字全叫阿里。他們的英語也是勉強湊合而已。一位阿里負

London and ringing agents. All agents sound like from Arabic countries and all called Ali. Their English no good too. One Ali charges Marble Arch area; one Ali charges Baker Street area. But I meet different Alis at Oxford Circus tube station, and see those houses. I dare not to move in. Places dirty and dim and smelly. How I live there?

London, by appearance, so noble, respectable, but when I follow these Alis, I find London a refuge camp.

責雲石拱門區，一位阿里負責貝克街區。不過我挑了牛津圓環地鐵站附近，請另外一位阿里先生帶我去看房子。結果連走進門都有問題。地方髒、光線差不說，還有濃厚的異味。我哪有膽搬過去住？

倫敦表面光鮮，堂皇，然而這些阿里帶我探過究竟之後，才曉得原來倫敦也有難民營般的所在。

beginner

n. a person who has just started learning to do something.

Holborn. First day studying my language school. Very very frustrating.

"My name is Margaret Wilkinson, but please call me Margaret," my grammar teach tells in front blackboard. But I must give respect, not just call Margaret. I will call Mrs. Margaret.

"What is grammar? Grammar is the study of the mechanics and dynamics of language," Mrs. Margaret says in the classroom.

I not understanding what she saying. Mrs. Margaret have a neatly cut pale blonde hair, with very serious clothes. Top and her bottom always same colour. She not telling her age, but I guessing she from 31 to 56. She wearing womans style shoes, high heel black leather, very possible her shoes are all made in home town Wen Zhou, by my parents. She should know it, one day I tell her. So she not so proud in front of us.

Chinese, we not having grammar. We saying things simple way. No verb-change usage, no tense differences, no gender changes. We bosses of our language. But, English language is boss of English user.

Mrs. Margaret teaching us about nouns. I discovering English is very scientific. She saying nouns have two types —

【初學者】

〈名詞〉剛要開始學習某樣東西的人。

在霍爾本。第一天上語言學校。結果徹底被打敗。

「我的名字是瑪格麗特・韋金生，請叫我瑪格麗特，」我的文法老師在黑板前面自我介紹。但我不能隨便，不能直呼瑪格麗特。我得叫她瑪格麗特小姐。

「什麼是文法？文法專門研究語言的技巧和動態變化，」瑪格麗特小姐在課堂上講解。

我聽不懂她教的東西。瑪格麗特小姐一頭修剪整齊的淡色金髮，儀容一絲不苟，上下服裝永遠成套配色。她是沒提自己的年齡，不過我猜介於三十一至五十六之間。她足登黑色皮質高跟鞋，看起來女人味十足。搞不好她的鞋子有可能全部都出自溫州老家我爸媽的巧手。找一天可以把這件事告訴她，讓她在我們面前別老是這麼神氣。

我們中國人沒這麼多文法講究。我們講話多簡單，沒有五花八門的動詞用法，沒有時態區別，沒有性別差異。我們自己就是語言的主人，不像講英語的時候被語言牽著鼻子走。

瑪格麗特小姐教我們名詞。這才發現英語真的相當科學。她說名詞分兩種——可數與不可數。

「你可以說一輛車，不能說一粒米，」她說。不過在我看來，滿街橫衝直撞的汽車才不可數，反倒是碗裡的米，只要肯

countable and uncountable.

"You can say a car, but not a rice," she says. But to me, cars are really uncountable in the street, and we can count the rice if we pay great attention to a rice bowl.

Mrs. Margaret also explaining nouns is plural and singular.

"Jeans are pairs," she says. But, everybody know jeans or trousers always one thing, you can't wear many jean or plural trouser. Four years old baby know that. Why waste ink adding "s"? She also saying nouns is three different gender: masculine, feminine, and neuter.

"A table is neuter," she says.

But, who cares a table is neuter? Everything English so scientific and problematic. Unlucky for me because my science always very bad in school, and I never understanding mathematics. First day, already know I am loser.

After lunch breaking, Mrs. Margaret introducing us little about verbs. Gosh, verb is just crazy. Verb has verbs, verbed and verb-ing. And verbs has three types of mood too: indicative, imperative, subjunctive. Why so moody? "Don't be too frustrated. You will all soon be speaking the Queen's English." Mrs. Margaret smiles to me.

花功夫，一顆顆都能數得清清楚楚。

　　瑪格麗特小姐又解釋名詞有複數和單數的差別。

　　「牛仔褲要用複數，」她說。可是，誰不曉得牛仔褲或褲子都是一件一件的，你哪能穿上複數的牛仔褲或褲子。這道理四歲小娃也懂，幹嘛還要浪費墨水加上「s」？她還說名詞分三種性別：男性、女性、中性。

　　「一張桌子是中性，」她說。

　　奇怪，誰會在乎桌子中不中性？英語這麼多科學名堂，偏偏我學校裡的科學成績一塌糊塗，數學更是頭痛無解。才上課頭一天，我就已經注定要當失敗者了。

　　午餐休息過後，瑪格麗特小姐幫我們稍微介紹了一下動詞。原來真正要命的在這裡。動詞分現在式、過去式、現在進行式。另外動詞還有三種語氣：直接語氣、祈使語氣、假設語氣。這麼變化多端到底作用何在？「別嚇著了。你們很快就能說上一口英國女王般的道地英語。」瑪格麗特小姐對著我微笑。

pronoun

n. a word, such as *she* or *it*, used to replace a noun.

First week in language school, I speaking like this:

"Who is her name?"

"It costing I three pounds buying this disgusting sandwich."

"Sally telling I that her just having coffee."

"Me having fried rice today."

"Me watching TV when me in China."

"Our should do things together with the people."

Always the same, the people laughing as long as I open my mouth.

"Ms Zh-u-ang, you have to learn when to use I as the subject, and when to use *me* as the object!"

Mrs. Margaret speaking Queen's English to me.

So I have two *mes*? According to Mrs. Margaret, one is subject I one is object I? But I only one I. Unless Mrs. Margaret talking about incarnation or after life.

She also telling me I disorder when speaking English. Chinese we starting sentence from concept of time or place. Order like this:

Last autumn on the Great Wall we eat barbecue.

So time and space always bigger than little human in our country. Is not like order in English sentence, "I", or "Jake" or "Mary" by front of everything, supposing be most important

【代名詞】

〈名詞〉一個字，比如她或它，用以代替某個名詞。

　　頭一個禮拜在語言學校裡，我講的英語如此這般：

　　「誰是她的名字？」

　　「它花我三鎊錢買了這難吃的三明治。」

　　「莎麗告訴我她剛剛有在喝咖啡。」

　　「我吃炒飯今天。」

　　「我看電視當我在中國。」

　　「我們應該一起做事跟大家。」

　　屢試不爽，我一開口便惹人發笑。

　　「莊小姐，你得注意什麼時候用 I 當主詞，什麼時候用 me 當受詞！」

　　瑪格麗特小姐嚴肅糾正我。

　　所以我有兩個我，照瑪格麗特小姐教的，一個我是主詞，另一個我是受詞。可是我明明只有一個啊。除非瑪格麗特小姐指的是分身或下輩子的我。

　　她也指出我講話的順序不對。我們中國句子多半從時間或地點開頭。順序像這一句：

　　去年秋天在長城我們一起烤肉吃。

　　跟我們中國的時空一比，渺小的人物只能乖乖讓位。但英文句子的順序就大異其趣，「我」、「傑克」或「瑪莉」搶在其

thing to whole sentence.

English a sexist language. In Chinese no "gender definition" in sentence. For example, Mrs. Margaret says these in class:

"Everyone must do *his* best."

"If a pupil can't attend the class, he should let his teacher know."

"We need to vote for a chairman for the student union."

Always talking about mans, no womans!

Mrs. Margaret later telling verb most difficult thing for our oriental people. Is not only "difficult", is "impossibility"! I not understanding why verb can always changing.

One day I find a poetry by William Shakespeare on school's library shelf. I studying hard. I even not stopping for lunch. I open little Concise Dictionary more 40 times checking new words. After looking some Shakespeare poetry, I will can return back my China home, teaching everyone about Shakespeare. Even my father know Shakespeare big dude, because our in our local government evening classes they telling everyones Shakespeare most famous person from Britain.

One thing, even Shakespeare write bad English. For example, he says "*Where go thou?*". If I speak like that Mrs Margaret will tell me wrongly. Also I finding poem of him call "An Outcry Upon Opportunity":

'Tis thou that execut'st the traitor's treason;
Thou sett'st the wolf where he the lamb may get

19

他東西前面，占據整個句子的首要地位。

此外，英語性別歧視的情形還真令人大開眼界。還好我們中文句子裡面沒有「性別定義」的問題。比方說，瑪格麗特小姐在課堂上講：

「每個人要盡他的努力。」

「如果學生有事不能到課，他應該知會他的老師。」

「我們必須投票選出學生會的主席先生。」

用的字眼永遠是男性，我們女人在哪兒？

瑪格麗特小姐稍後提到，我們東方人往往覺得最困難的莫過於動詞。要摸清楚豈止「困難」而已，根本就「不可能」！我怎麼也沒辦法明白動詞為何老是變化無窮。

有一天，在學校圖書架上，我找到一本莎士比亞詩集。我讀個不停，連午餐時間也不休息。我翻開袖珍簡明辭典查看生字，前後起碼超過四十次。讀過莎士比亞的大作，將來回到中國老家，我可以教大家見識一下莎士比亞。連我爸爸也曉得莎士比亞是個大文豪，因為連我們老家地方政府辦的夜校也有提到，歷史上最最出名的英國人就是莎士比亞。

真有意思，連莎士比亞也會寫出拙劣的英文。比如他說「何往汝？」要是從我口裡講出這句，一定躲不過瑪格麗特小姐的糾正。我還讀到他一首詩叫〈慨嘆機運〉：

奸賊的叛逆陰謀，有了你才能得逞；

是你把豺狼引向攫獲羔羊的路徑；

I not understanding at all. What this "*'tis*", "*execut'st*" and "*sett'st*"? Shakespeare can writing that, my spelling not too bad then.

After grammar class, I sit on bus and have deep thought about my new language. Person as dominate subject, is main thing in an English sentence. Does it mean West culture respecting individuals more? In China, you open daily newspaper, title on top is "OUR HISTORY DECIDE IT IS TIME TO GET RICH" or "THE GREAT COMMUNIST PARTY HAVE THIRD MEETING" or "THE 2008 OLYMPICS NEED CITIZENS PLANT MORE GREENS". Look, no subjects here are mans or womans. Maybe Chinese too shaming putting their name first, because that not modest way to be.

我完全看不懂。這是什麼字，「'tis」（it is），「execut'st」（execute），「sett'st」（set）？莎士比亞有辦法寫成這樣，那我的拼字也不算太糟嘛。

　　上完文法課，我搭乘公車，一路尋思今天學到的課程內容。英文句子裡，最主要的就是看哪號人物在前面當主詞。這表示西方文化比較重視個人？如果翻開中國的報紙，頭條標題不外乎像是「我們的歷史決定富強的時刻已經到來」，或「偉大的共產黨召開第三次會議」，或「二○○八年奧運需要市民加強綠化工作」。看見沒，標題的主詞不會是男人或女人。或許中國人生性害羞，不肯把名字放在第一位，那可太招搖了。

slogan

n. a catchword or phrase used in politics or advertising.

I go in bookshop buy the English version of Little Red Book. Not easy read but very useful argue with English using Chairman Mao slogans. English version is without translator name on cover. Yes, no second name can be shared on Mao's work. Chairman Mao

has inherited, defended and developed Marxism-Leninism with genius, creatively and comprehensively and has brought it to a higher and completely new stage.

The English translators of this book, they are like feather compare with Tai Mountain.

In West, Mao's words work for me, though they not work in China now. Example, today big confusion in streets. Everywhere people marching to say no to war in Iraq.

"No war for oil!"

"Listen to your people!"

The demon-strators from everywhere in Britain, socialists, Communists, teachers, students, housewifes, labour workers, Muslim womans covered under the scarf with their children... They marching to the Hyde park. I am in march because I not finding way to hostel. So no choice except following. I search

【口號】

〈名詞〉用於政治或廣告宣傳的口號或標語。

　　我去書店買了本英文版的毛語錄。讀起來是有些吃力，然而跟英國人爭辯時，毛主席的口號特別有用。英文版的封面上沒寫翻譯者是誰。這就對了，毛主席的著作豈有他人名字容身之地。要知道他老人家

以天才創造性及全面性地繼承、捍衛和發展馬克斯列寧主義，並且將它帶往一個更高更完整的新階段。

　　這本書的英譯者和毛主席相較之下，可謂鴻毛之於泰山。
　　儘管這年頭，在中國已經引不起多少興趣，但毛主席的金句對身處西方世界的我居然特別受用。比如像今天，街頭出現混亂的狀況。四處可見人們聚眾遊街抗議伊拉克戰爭。
　　「反對石油戰爭！」
　　「聽從人民心聲！」
　　示威者來自英國各地，有社會主義人士，共產黨人，教師，學生，家庭主婦，勞工，牽著小孩、蒙覆頭巾的穆斯林婦人……他們往海德公園方向遊行集結。我找不到路避開回住宿處，只好也跟著人群走。我在遊行隊伍當中搜尋中國臉孔，幾乎見不到半個。這也難怪，人家在外賣餐館都忙不過來了，應

Chinese faces in the march team. Very few. Maybe they busy and desperately earning money in those Chinese Takeaways.

People in march seems really happy. Many smiles. They feel happy in sunshine. Like having weekend family picnic. When finish everyone rush drink beers in pubs and ladies gather in tea houses, rub their sore foots.

Can this kind of demon-stration stop war?

From Mao's little red book, I learning in school:

A revolution is not a dinner party, or writing an essay, or painting a picture, or doing embroidery; it cannot be so refined, so leisurely and gentle, so temperate, kind, courteous, restrained and magnanimous. A revolution is an insurrection, an act of violence with which one class overthrows another.

Probably Communist love war more than anybody. From Mao's opinion, war able be "Just" although it is bloody. (But blood happen everyday anyway . . .) He say:

Oppose unjust war with just war, whenever possible.

So if people here want to against war in Iraq, they needing have civil war with their Tony Blair here, or their Bush. If more people bleeding in native country, then those mens not making war in other place.

該沒這種閒工夫。

　　參加遊行的群眾看起來興致高昂，大家笑瞇瞇的，陽光下快活得很，好像週末家人一起外出野餐團聚。遊行剛一結束，人人湧進酒吧搶啤酒喝，小姐太太們則占領茶館，按摩舒展痠疼的腳板。

　　這種示威活動有能耐阻擋戰爭？

　　我學過，毛語錄裡面講得直接了當：

革命不是請客吃飯，不是做文章，不是繪畫繡花，不能那樣雅致，那樣從容不迫，文質彬彬，那樣溫良恭儉讓。革命是暴動，是一個階級推翻另一個階級的暴烈的行動。

　　或許，共產黨比任何人都愛打仗。依毛主席之見，戰爭可以實現「正義」，雖然流血難免。（不過反正每天都會有人流血……）他說：

只要有可能，就用戰爭反對戰爭，用正義戰爭反對非正義戰爭。

　　所以，如果英國的老百姓真有想要阻止伊拉克戰爭，他們必須發動內戰打倒托尼·布萊爾，或是連小布希一併打倒。如果有更多的老百姓在自己的國家裡面流血犧牲，那些傢伙就不會跑到別人的地盤撒野開戰。

weather

n. the state of the atmosphere at a place and time in terms of temperature, wind, rain, etc. *v.* (cause to) be affected by the weather; come safely
through.

Carrying meat ball and pork slice from supermarket, now I
am in place calling *Ye Olde English Tea Shop*. What is this
"Ye"? Why "Olde" not "Old"? Wrong spelling.

Tea house like Qing dynasty old style building waiting for
being demolish. Everything looking really old here, especial
wood stick beam in middle of house, supporting roof. Old carpet under the foot is very complication flower pattern, like
something from emperor mother house.

"Where would you like to sit?", "What can I get you?", "A
table for one person?", "Are you alone?". Smiling waiter ask
so many questions. He making me feel bit lonely. In China I
not have loneliness concept. Always we with family or crowd.
But England, always alone, and even waiter always remind
you you are alone...

Everybody listening the weather at this moment in tea
house. All time in London, I hearing weather report from
radios. It tells weather situation like emergency typhoon coming. But no emergency coming here. I checking *Concise
Chinese-English Dictionary*. It saying all English *under the
weather*, and all English is *weather beaten*, means uncomfortable. Is reasonable, of course. England everybody beaten by
the weather. Always doubt or choice about weather. Weather it

【天氣】

〈名詞〉某一時地的氣候狀態，包括溫度、風力、降雨情形等等。〈動詞〉承受天氣的影響；平安度過。

　　從超級市場買了肉丸子和豬肉片，我來到一處叫「咦老的英國茶館」的地方。什麼叫「咦老的」（Ye Olde）？怎不直接叫「老」（Old）英國茶館就好？拼錯字了吧！

　　茶館像清朝遺留下來的老式建築，隨時準備拆除。這裡每樣東西看起來歷史悠久，特別是房屋中央的老舊木樑，居然還有辦法支撐屋頂，真不簡單。還有，腳下鋪的地毯花樣精細繁複，像是皇太后寢宮流出的寶貝。

　　「你想坐哪個位子？」，「要我拿點什麼給你？」，「一張桌子一個人？」，「你自己一個？」。服務生笑臉問題接二連三，害我覺得有些寂寞。在中國我可連寂寞的概念都沒出現過。我們總是一家子或一群人在一起。可是來到英國之後，不論去哪兒都是自己一個，連服務生都要提醒你，你怎麼一個人孤孤單單……

　　這會兒，茶館裡每個人都在聽氣象。倫敦不管哪個時辰，我老從收音機裡聽到氣象報告。它播報起來好像颱風已經緊急逼近。結果呢，什麼緊急狀況也沒有。我翻了翻**簡明中英辭典**。裡頭說英國人全都**處在天氣底下**，他們全都被**天氣敲打**，原來這是形容他們人不舒坦的狀況。當然啦，這還用說。在英國，人人沒兩下就會被天氣打敗。他們隨時都在猜測懷疑天氣

rain or weather it sunshine, you just not know.

Weather report also very difficult understand. The weather man not saying "rain" or "sunny" because they speaking in complication and big drama way. He reporting weather like reporting big war: "Unfortunately... Hopefully...". I listen two hours radio I meet twice weather report. Do they think British Empire as big China that it need to report at any time? Or clouds in this country changing every single minute? Yes, look at the clouds now, they are so suspicious! Not like my home town, often several weeks without one piece cloud in sky and weather man has nothing more to say. Some days he just saying "It is Yin", which mean weather is negative.

走勢如何。究竟會下雨，還是出太陽，有人知道才怪。

　　氣象報告要聽懂也不簡單。氣象員的用詞不是「下雨」或「出太陽」，他們講的可複雜了，好像上演什麼大戲似的。他報起氣象有如大戰爆發：「很不幸的……有希望地……」。我聽收音機，兩個小時遇上兩回合氣象報告。難不成他們以為大英帝國像中國一樣遼闊，任何時間都需要報告掌握。還是這國家的雲朵每一分鐘都在變化。這倒是，你看現在的雲層，一副靠不住的模樣！不像我老家，常常幾個禮拜天空見不到一片雲，氣象員根本沒什麼好報的。一連幾天他只會說個「天氣陰」，意思指天氣是負的，不怎麼樣。

confusion

confuse *v.* mix up; perplex, disconcert; make unclear. confusion *n.* **1.** the state of being confused; **2.** a situation of panic or disorder; **3.** the mistaking of one person or thing for another.

English food very confusing. They eating and drinking strange things. I think even Confucius have great confusion if he studying English.

It is already afternoon about 3 o"clock and I so hungry. What can I eat, I asking waiter. He offering "Afternoon Tea". What? Eat afternoon tea?

So he showing me blackboard, where is a menu:

Ye Olde English Tea
2 scones, jam, whipped cream, pot of tea £3.75

Whatever, I must to eat whatever they have or I faint. Three minutes later my thing arrives: "scones" hot and thick and dry, cream is unbelieveable, butter is greasy, and jam are three kinds: raspberry, cramberry and strawberry. A white tea pot with a white tea cup.

I confusing again when I look at "whipped cream" on little blackboard. What is that mean? How people whip the cream? I see a poster somewhere near Chinatown. On poster naked woman only wears leather boots and leather pants, and she whipping naked man kneeling down under legs. So a English chef also whipping in kitchen?

【困惑】

〈動詞〉拌和；弄糊塗，擾亂；使含混。〈名詞〉**1.** 混亂狀況；**2.** 恐慌或騷亂狀態；**3.** 把人或物搞錯混淆。

　　英國食物處處令人困惑，他們吃的喝的常教人摸不著頭緒。就算讓孔老夫子來學這些英語，肯定也會成了空腦夫子。

　　已經下午三點，肚子餓扁了。我問服務生能吃點什麼。他推薦「下午茶」。什麼？吃下午茶？

　　他指一塊小黑板給我看，上面寫著菜單：

「咦老的英國茶」
司康兩個，果醬，鞭打奶油，茶一壺　　3.75鎊

　　隨便，有東西吃就好，反正我已經餓昏了。三分鐘後東西送來：「司康」是熱的，厚厚乾乾一塊，奶油很誇張，又稠又油，果醬有三種口味：覆盆子、小紅莓和草莓。一個白磁壺配一只白茶杯。

　　看那小黑板寫的「鞭打奶油」（編按：台灣稱「打發的鮮奶油」），我又糊塗了。什麼意思？奶油怎麼鞭打？我見過中國城附近有張海報，上頭印個只穿皮靴皮褲的裸女，她舉鞭抽打跪在腳邊的裸男。難不成英國大廚也在廚房裡揮舞皮鞭？

　　我將司康塞進嘴巴，急匆匆灌茶下去。旁邊聽見有人點「起泡的咖啡」。

I put scones into mouth, and drink tea like horse. Next door me, I hearing somebody wanting "frothy coffee".

A lady with a young man. She say: "Can I have a frothy coffee, please? And my friend will have a black coffee, with skimmed milk."

It must be big work making something "skimmed", and "frothy", and "whipped". Why drinking become so complicating and need so much work?

And water are even more complicating here. Maybe raining everyday here and too much water so English making lots kind water.

I thirsty from eating dry scones.

Waiter asks me: "What would you like? Still water, or filthy water?"

"What? Filthy water?" I am shocked.

"OK, filthy water." He leave and fetch bottle of water.

I so curious about strange water. I opening bottle, immediately lots bubbles coming out. How they putting bubbles in water? Must be highly technicaled. I drinking it. Taste bitter, very filthy, not natural at all, like poison.

是位女士和一位年輕先生。她說：「請給我一杯起泡的咖啡。我朋友一杯黑咖啡，脫除（脂）牛奶。」

真是工程浩大，東西得經過「脫除」，「起泡」，加上「鞭打」。喝個東西有必要如此工程浩大？

這裡想喝個水甚至更麻煩。或許雨下太多，水多到英國人有辦法生出千百種飲用水。

司康乾巴巴的，越嚼越渴。

服務生問我：「你要哪一種？自來水還是汙水？」

「什麼？汙水？」我嚇壞了。（編按：氣泡水 fizzy water 被聽成了汙水 filthy water）

「汙水，馬上來。」他走去拿了瓶水過來。

我很好奇這是什麼怪水。瓶蓋打開，立刻冒起一陣陣泡泡。他們怎麼把泡泡裝在水裡面的？一定是高科技。我喝了一口，苦苦的，髒死了，一點也不天然，好像毒藥。

homesick

adj. sad because missing one's home or family.

In my language school, Mrs. Margaret ask me:

"Would you like some tea?"

"No," I say.

She looking at me, her face suddenly frozen. Then she asking me again:

"Would you like some coffee then?"

"No. I don't want."

"Are you sure you don't want anything?"

"No. I don't want anything wet," I saying loudly, precisely.

Mrs. Margaret looking very upset.

But why she asking me again and again? I already answer her from first time.

"Oh, dear." Mrs. Margaret sigh heavy. Then she standing up, and starting make her own tea. She drink it in very thirsty way, like angry camel in the desert. I am confusing. Am I make tea for her before she asking me? But how do I know she thirsty if she not telling me directly? All this manners very complication. China not have *politeness* in same way.

And how to learn be *polite* if I not getting chance talk people? I am always alone, talking in my notebook, or wandering here and there like invisible ghost. Nobody speak to me and I not dare open my mouth first because when I start talking, I

【想家】

〈形容詞〉因為思念家鄉或家人而難受。

在語言學校，瑪格麗特小姐問我：

「想不想喝點茶？」

「不用，」我說。

她看著我，臉僵住了。然後又再問：

「那要不要來點咖啡？」

「不用。我不想。」

「你確定什麼都不要？」

「不用。我不想喝東西，」我大聲、明確地回答。

瑪格麗特小姐看起來很挫折。

可是她幹嘛問我一遍又一遍？我一開始就回答她了不是嗎？

「噢，親愛的。」瑪格麗特小姐深嘆口氣，然後起身去泡她的茶。她喝茶的模樣渴得要命，像沙漠裡氣壞的駱駝。我只是困惑，我應該在她發問之前就先把茶泡好嗎？但她不直說的話我怎麼知道她口在渴？這些規矩好複雜。中國的禮貌客氣可差得遠了。

而且，連跟別人講話的機會都沒有，我上哪兒去學禮貌？我老是一個人，自言自語給我的筆記本聽，東晃西晃像不見影的鬼魂。沒有人要跟我講話，我也沒那個膽先開口，因為一開

asking the rude questions.

"Excuse me, you know there are some red spots on your face?"

"Are you a bit fatter than me?"

"I don't believe we same age. You look much older than me."

"I think you are a very normal person. Not a special person."

"The food you cook is disgusting. Why nobody tell you?"

I already have very famous reputation in my language school. They say: "You know that Chinese girl..." "Which one?" "That rude one of course!". I hear it several times. Maybe I need get trained from "Manners International Etiquette Workshop", which is advertisement I read on Chinese newspaper. It say:

Manners International custom tailors each etiquette program to the specific requirements of each individual, business/corporation, organization, school, Girl Scout Troop, or family.

I think I am exactly that "individual" needing to be taught there, if fee is not too expensive. Re-education is always important.

Mrs Margaret look at me in sad way. "You must be very *homesick*," she says.

Actually not missing family at all, and not missing boring little hometown also. I happy I not needing think about stinking shoes with anyhow the same style on showroom shelfs in parent factory. I glad I not having go work every day at work

口就會出狀況。

「對不起，你臉上有紅點你曉得嗎？」

「你是不是比我胖一點？」

「我不信我們兩個年紀一樣。你看起來比我老多了。」

「我覺得你這個人蠻普通的，沒什麼特別。」

「你煮的東西實在很難吃。都沒人跟你說？」

我的粗魯在語言學校裡已經聲名遠播。他們說：「那個中國女孩子你知道……」「哪一個？」「還有哪個！」我聽過好幾次了。或許我該去受訓受訓，我讀中文報紙看見一則「國際禮儀工作坊」的廣告，上面說：

國際禮儀為您量身規劃各種專屬禮儀課程，不管您是個人，公司行號，部門組織，學校，女童軍團，家庭等等，均可提供服務。

如果費用不會太高，我想我是正好符合需要去那兒接受指導的「個人」。再教育是很重要的。

瑪格麗特小姐幽幽看著我。「妳一定很想家，」她說。

其實，我一點也不想家，一點也不想那個無聊的小鎮。真高興自己不用掛念那些難聞的鞋子，款式千篇一律擺在爸媽工廠的展示架上。真高興我不用每天趕去單位上班。唯一我會朝思暮想的就是食物。烤鴨，熱鍋裡的鮮羊肉，香辣魚……一想到這些吃的，我就覺得離開中國錯得離譜。

英國對我而言，等於全新的世界。我在此地沒有過去。到目前為止談不上什麼回憶，沒有傷心，沒有喜悅，有的只是訊息，每天害我暈頭轉向的千百種信息。

unit. Only thing I missing is food. Roasted ducks, fresh cut lamb meat in boiling hot pot, and red chilli spicy fish . . . When thinking of food, I feel I make big mistake by leaving China.

This country to me, this a new world. I not having past in this country. No memory being builded here so far, no sadness or happiness so far, only information, hundreds and thousands of information, which confuse me everyday.

Except my English class every morning, I so bored of being alone. I always alone, and talking to myself. When sky become dark, I want grab something warm in this cold country. I want find friend teach me about this strange country. Maybe I want find man can love me. A man in this country save me, take me, adopt me, be my family, be my home. Every night, when I write diary, I feeling troubled. Am I writing in Chinese or in English? I trying express me, but confusing—I see other little me try expressing me in other language.

Maybe I not need feeling lonely, because I always can talk to other "me". Is like seeing my two pieces of lips speaking in two languages at same time. Yes, I not lonely, because I with another me. Like Austin Power with his Mini Me.

每天，除了早上的英語課，我都是自己無聊一個人。我老是一個人，自己跟自己講話。天色暗下來的時候，我想抓住些溫暖的什麼，這地方可真冷。我想找找看有誰能當朋友，教我認識這奇怪的國家。或許，我想找個可以愛我的男人。這男人可以在這陌生的國家拯救我，帶領我，接納我，當我的家人，我的依靠。每天晚上，寫日記的時候我很困擾。到底要寫中文還是英文？我想表達自己，令人困惑的是──我看見另一個小小的我用另一種語言在表達自己。

或許我不用覺得寂寞，因為我有另一個「我」可以傾訴。彷彿可以看見我的兩瓣唇肉同時說著兩種語言。沒錯，我不孤單，有另一個我陪伴著我。就像《王牌大間諜》的奧斯丁‧包爾有他的「迷你我」相依相隨。

progressive tenses

(Also called 'Continuous Tenses') Progressive tenses are made with TO BE + -ING. The mose common use of the progressive form is to talk about an action or situation that is already going on at a particular moment we are thinking about. But the 'going to' structure and the present progressive can also be used to talk about the future.

People say "I'm going to go to the cinema . . ."
Why there two go for one sentence? Why not enough to say one *go* to *go*?

I am going to go to the supermarket to buy some porks?
You are going to go to the Oxford circus to buy clothes?
He is going to go to the park for a walk?

"I go" is enough to expressing "I am going to go..." Really.

This afternoon, I am going to go to cinema watch double bill —*Breakfast at Tiffiny's* and *Some Like it Hot*. Double bill, they letting people pay one time but twice of the bill, how clever the business here! Cinema is my paradise. When a person not having any idea about real life, just walk into cinema choosing a film to see. In China, I seeing some American films, like *Titanic*, and *Rush Hours*, but of course Hollywood stars speaking Mandarin to us, and I can sing soundtrack from *Titanic*, "My heart goes on and on", only in Chinese translation.

American films strange in London. People at Language School tell me use student card, I can have cheap cinema tick-

【進行時態】

又稱連續時態，進行時態由 TO BE 與動詞的現在分詞連用所構成。最常見的進行式為敘述者言談當下正在進行的活動或狀態。而「going to」結構加上現在進行式可用於談論未來事件。

人們說「我現在要來去看電影去……」

為什麼一句話要有兩個去字？用一個去就好了不是嗎？

我現在要去超級市場去買點豬肉？

你現在要去牛津圓環去買衣服？

他現在要去公園去走一走？

「我去」不就已經足以表達「我現在要去」的意思了，真是的。

今天下午，我要來去戲院去看同場加映的電影———《第凡內早餐》和《熱情如火》。同場加映，付一張票的錢可以看兩部片子，真有生意頭腦！戲院就是我的天堂。一個人現實生活沒辦法作主的時候，只管走進戲院選部電影來看。我在中國看過好些美國片，像《鐵達尼號》，《尖峰時刻》，當然，螢幕上好萊塢影星講的是國語，我還會唱《鐵達尼號》的電影主題曲，《我心永不止息》，不過是中文翻譯的版本。

倫敦放映的美國電影好怪異。語言學校的人教我利用學生證，可以買到便宜的電影票。上禮拜我去中國城的查爾斯王子

et. Last week I go Prince Charles in Chinatown. They say is cheapest cinema in London. Two films screening: *Moholland Driver*, and *Blue Velvet*. All together is more than 4 hours. Perfect for my lonely night. So I buy tickets and get in.

What crazy films! I not understanding very much the English speakings, but I understand I must never walk in highway at night alone. The world scary and strange like deep dark dream. Leaving cinema, trembling, I try find bus to home, but some mean kids teasing at each other on bus stop. Shouting and swearing bit like terrorist. Old man drunk in street and walk to me saying words I not understanding. Maybe he think I prostitute. England is hopeless country, but people having everything here: Queen, Buckingham Place, Loyal Family, oldest and slowest tube, BBC, Channel 4, W.H. Smith, Marx & Spencer, Tesco, Soho, millennium bridge, Tate Modern, Oxford Circus, London Tower, Cider and ale, even Chinatown.

Anyway, after *Breakfast at Tiffany* where posh woman dressing like prostitute and *Some Like It Hot* where mans dressing like womans, I go back my new home which have cheap renting 65 pounds per week. It is ugly place. It smelling pee in every corner of street. Nearby tube station called Tottenham Hale.

House is two floors, lived by Cantonese family: housewife, husband who work as chef in Chinatown, and 16-year-old British-accent son. Is like one child policy still carried on here. The garden is concrete, no any green things. Very often little wild grass growing and come out between the concretes, but housewife pull and kill grass immediately. She is grass killer.

戲院，人家說倫敦最便宜的就是這間。當時放映的片子：《穆荷蘭大道》和《藍絲絨》。兩部加起來片長超過四個鐘頭。晚上無聊打發時間正好，我買了票進場。

好瘋狂的電影！電影對白聽不太懂，但我曉得自己絕對不可以一個人半夜溜上公路。電影裡面的世界詭異嚇人，像黑沉沉的夢境。離開戲院，打著哆嗦，我想搭公車回家。不過公車站有幾個壞孩子打打鬧鬧，叫囂咒罵，像恐怖分子。街上有個老頭醉醺醺走近我，嘴裡不知嘟囔什麼。搞不好他還以為我是賣的。英國這國家沒救了，儘管這裡的百姓什麼都不缺：女王，白金漢宮，皇室家族，老爺地鐵，英國廣播公司，瑪莎百貨公司，特易購量販店，蘇活區，千禧橋，泰特現代美術館，倫敦塔，蘋果酒和麥酒，甚至連中國城都有。

看完電影——《第凡內早餐》窮女人裝得像公主，《熱情如火》大男人假扮女裝——我回去新的住處，每週六十五鎊便宜租來的。挺醜陋的地方，街角尿騷味終日不散。不過幾步路就到地鐵多特哈姆哈爾站。

房子有兩層，住了戶廣東人家：太太，中國城當廚師的先生，十六歲英語很溜的兒子。一胎化政策好像在這兒也奉行不逾。房子的庭園只見光禿禿的水泥，沒半點綠意。雜草不時從地縫冒出頭，但馬上逃不過房東太太的法眼。她是綠草殺手。隔壁鄰居繁茂的枝葉老想踰越鐵鏽圍籬，但沒有任何玩意足以動搖這戶水泥人家。這地方活像中國的廉價工廠，勞動者死命掙錢，沒有生活，沒有綠意，沒有愛。

這一家子講的是廣東話，聽也聽不懂。牆壁懸掛中國的農民曆。還有炒菜鍋，筷子，麻將，第四台的中國節目……屋子

The lush next doors trees trying come through rusty iron fence, but nothing getting in this concrete family. This house like factory place in China, just for cheap labours earning money, no life, no green, and no love.

Family speaks Cantonese so I not understanding them. Chinese moon calendar is on wall. Wok, chopsticks, Mah Jong, Chinese cable TV programmes... everything inside house is traditional. Not much fun. Outside, view is rough. Old rusty railway leading to maybe more interesting place. Walking along railway I see nearby shopping centre, a McDonalds, a KFC, a Burger King, a petrol station called "Shell", a sad looking Tottenham Hale tube station.

Every night I coming out Tottenham Hale tube station and walking home shivering. I scared to pass each single dark corner. In this place, crazy mans or sporty kids throwing stones to you or shouting to you without reasons. Also, the robbers robbing the peoples even poorer than them. In China we believe "rob the rich to feed the poor". But robbers here have no poetry.

"Dare to struggle and dare to win." Chairman Mao's words like long time no see friend coming to me. I need somebody protect me, accompany me, but not staring at me in darkness. I longing for smile from man, longing for smile even only remaining several seconds.

裡看見的都是傳統玩意。屋外的景致也高明不到哪裡。積鏽的舊鐵道或許能帶人前往多點歡樂的所在。沿著鐵路漫步，我看見附近的購物中心，一家麥當勞，一家肯德基，一家漢堡王，一座加油站掛著「殼牌」，然後難看的多特哈姆哈爾地鐵站出現了。

　　每天晚上，我從多特哈姆哈爾站出來，提心吊膽走回住處。每經過一處暗角我就緊張。這地方有瘋漢，有調皮的小鬼，無緣無故石頭就飛過來，還一陣鬼吼鬼叫。更過分的是，還有惡棍專門打劫，連比他們處境更慘的人也不放過。在中國，「劫富濟貧」是江湖不成文的規矩。倫敦的歹徒真沒詩意。

　　「**勇於鬥爭，勇於求勝**。」毛主席的金句讓我如見故人。我需要有人可以守護我，陪伴我，驅趕黑暗中窺探的眼睛。我渴望男人對我微笑，幾秒鐘的微笑就好。

homosexual

n., adj. (person) sexually attracted to members of the same sex.

I meet you in the cinema. It is film called *Fear Eats Soul*, from German director Rainer Werner Fassbinder. Programme say Fassbinder *is homosexual*. What is it? Now I have this *Collins English Dictionary*—THE AUTHORITY ON CURRENT ENGLISH. It tells me what is *Homosexual*. Strange word, I cannot imagine it.

It is the Ciné-Lumiere, near South Kensington. 7 o'clock Monday, raining. Not over ten people, half are old couple with white hair. Then there you are.

You are alone. You sit almost beside me. Two seats between us. Your face quite pale in the dim light, but beautiful. I too am alone in the cinema. I always alone in the cinema before I meet you. I am bit confused whether if cinema make me less lonely or even more lonely.

On the screen, old German woman dancing with young black man in a pub. All the peoples in pub watching. Old woman she has humble smile. She has hard life. Then I see your smile in the dark light. Why I can see your smile while I am watching the film? You turn your face and understand I am looking at you. You smile again, but very gentle, and very little. You look back the screen.

You have warm smile. Is like a baby's smile. Nobody smile

【同性戀】

〈名詞〉〈形容詞〉對同性產生性慾者。

　　我在戲院和你相遇。電影叫《恐懼吞噬心靈》，德國導演雷納・韋納・法斯賓達。節目單說法斯賓達是同性戀。什麼意思？我翻開袖珍柯林斯英文辭典——當代英語權威。上頭解釋了同性戀。好怪的字，我沒辦法想像。

　　南肯辛頓附近，「盧米耶戲院」。星期一晚上七點，雨。觀眾不會超過十個，多半是上了年紀的伴侶。你在那裡。

　　你一個人，幾乎就坐我旁邊，只隔兩個空位。弱光下你的臉色蒼白，不過很美。戲院裡我也是自己一個。遇見你之前，我來戲院都是自己一個。我有點迷糊，電影院究竟減輕，還是讓我更加寂寞。

　　螢幕上，德國老婦人和黑人青年在酒吧裡跳舞。全部酒客看著他們兩個。老婦人臉上的笑容卑微。她過慣了苦日子。暗亮中我看見你露出微笑。我看電影的時候怎麼還能看見你的微笑？你臉動了一下，知道我在看你。你又笑了，非常輕柔，似有若無。你專心回到螢幕上。

　　你的笑容很溫暖，嬰兒般的笑容。這冰冷的國家之前沒有人這樣對我笑過。黑暗中，我在想你應該人很親切。這部電影表現白人老婦和黑人青年之間不可能的愛。跟「同性戀」半點關係也沒有。

to me before like you in this cold country. In the darkness, I am thinking you must be kind man.

It is a film shows impossible love between old white woman and young black man. But nothing to do with "*homosexual*".

After film, we walk to exit. Our bodies so close. Out from cinema, road lights finally light up our faces.

Then, with gentle smile, you ask me:

"Did you like the film?"

I nod head.

Is like the uncomfortable English weather have some sun-shine suddenly.

You ask my name. I say name start from Z, "But please no worry to remember," I say, "my name too long pronounce." You tell me your name, but how I remember English name? Western name are un-rememberable, like all Western look the same. But I want remember you, want remember the difference you with others. I look at your face. Brown eyes, transparent. Thick brown hair, like colour of leafs in autumn. Your voice gentle, but solid. It sound safe.

We walk from South Kensington towards Hyde Park. A long way for feets. What we talk about? I tell you of famous English creamy tea. You say prefer French Patisserie.

"Patty surly?"

"No *patisserie*."

"How spell?"

"P-a-t-i-s-s-e-r-i-e." You speak slowly with slowly moving lips, like Mrs Margaret.

"What is it?" I not bring dictionary tonight.

You stop in front very fashionable "French Patisserie" shop.

電影演完，我們朝出口處移動。兩個人的身體如此貼近。出了戲院，街燈終於亮出我們的臉孔。

帶著溫柔的笑意，你問我：

「喜歡這部電影？」

我點頭。

像英國沉悶的天氣突然出現陽光。

你問了我的名字。我說名字的開頭是Z，「不過很麻煩的你別記，」我說，「我名字太長了不好唸。」你跟我講了你的名字，但我哪記得了英國名字？西方人的名字，跟他們的長相一樣難記。不過，我想要記住你，想要記住你和別人不同的樣子。我注視你的臉。棕色眼珠，透著光。濃密的棕髮，色澤如秋葉。你的聲音溫柔，堅定。聽起來令人安心。

我們從南肯辛頓信步走向海德公園。好一段考驗腳力的路程。我們都談了些什麼？我提到赫赫有名的英式奶茶。你倒比較喜歡法式糕點。

「法式什麼？」

「法式糕點。」

「字怎麼拼？」

「P-a-t-i-s-s-e-r-i-e。」你嘴唇輕啓一個字一個字慢慢唸，像瑪格麗特小姐那樣。

「什麼意思？」今晚我忘了帶辭典。

你在一家非常時髦的「法式糕點」店鋪前面停下腳步。這麼晚了還沒關門。櫥窗裡滿是誘人的美麗蛋糕。

「妳喜歡哪一個？」你看著我。

我怕價錢不知多貴。

「我不知道，」我說。這些軟綿綿的玩意我哪清楚？

Still open at late time. Beautiful cakes waiting inside window.

"Which one would you like?" You look at me.

I worried of price.

"I don't know," I say. How I know about these soft stuffs?

"Then I"ll choose one for you."

You give me a piece of creamy thing.

"What is it?" I hold it on my hand carefully.

"c-h-o-c-o-l-a-t-e e-c-l-a-i-r."

"OK."

I bite it, but immediately cream squeeze out, falling on street.

I look at white cream drop on dirty street.

You look at white cream drop on dirty street.

"Oh well, never mind," you say.

So we talk, and talk, and talk, through Hyde Park, then to West End, then Islington, walk towards my place. Nearly four hours walking. My legs is so sore, and my throat so dry, but I enjoying it. Is first time a person walking beside me through chilly night. Is also first time a person being patience listen my nonsense English, and learning me bad language. You much better than Mrs Margaret. She never let us talk freely.

When I arriving back, is already deep night.

In front of house, you kiss my two cheeks, and watch me go in door.

"Good meeting you," you say.

Everything happen in very gentle way.

I want go immediately my room think about English man who smile and kiss me like lover, but I see Chinese landlord

「我來選好了。」

你給我一塊奶油夾心的東西。

「這什麼？」我小心翼翼捧在手心。

「巧-克-力-閃-電-泡-芙。」

「真好。」

我咬了一口，不料奶油擠出來，掉落地面。

我看著白色奶油落在骯髒的街道。

你看著白色奶油落在骯髒的街道。

「噢，沒關係，沒關係，」你說。

我們一路談著，談著，談著，穿過海德公園，經過西區，經過伊士靈頓，一路走回我住的地方。幾乎整整走了四個鐘頭。我兩條腿痠得要命，喉嚨又乾又渴，然而我很快活。這是第一次有人陪我走過刺骨的寒夜。也是第一次有人耐心聽我那一口爛英語。你比瑪格麗特小姐好多了，她從來就不肯讓我們自由發言。

最後到家的時候，夜已經深了。

你在屋子前面親吻我臉頰，看著我進門。

「很高興遇見妳，」你說。

每件事發生都那麼溫柔。

我得馬上回到房間，仔細想一想這微笑的英國男人，他親了我，像愛人一樣。但我的中國房東還在廚房裡看電視，他在等我。他呵欠連連，擔心我這麼晚還沒回家。同時間，房東太太也從樓上臥室下來，身上披著睡袍。

「我們替妳擔心死了！我們從沒像妳這麼晚回來過！」

憂慮的聲音讓我想起母親。她對我講話一向是這種口氣。

sitting on kitchen, watching TV and waiting for me. He is yawning. He worried my late back. At same time wife come down from upstairs bedroom in sleeping robe:

"We were so worried about you! We never come back as late as you do!"

Nervous voice remind me of my mother. My mother always talk to me like that.

I say I OK. Don't worry.

Wife look at me seriously: "It is dangerous at night and also you are a young girl."

I take off my guilty shoes.

"Next time if you are late, phone my husband and he can come and pick you up. This is England not China. Men easily get drunk in the pub!"

With last yawn, husband turn off TV. He look cross and tired.

I feel good after I close my bedroom's door. My heart hold a secret to make me warm at night.

The leafs blow outside. The street lights shine on my window. I am thinking I am only person to be awake in the world. I am thinking of China, thinking of old German lady dancing, thinking of your smile. I fall to sleep with sweet feelings inside my body.

我說我沒事，不用替我擔心。

房東太太正經八百看著我：「晚上外面多危險，妳這麼年輕的小姐。」

我脫下犯了罪的鞋子。

「下次要這麼晚回來，打電話給我先生，叫他去接妳。這裡是英國不是中國。酒吧裡一堆醉漢！」

最後一聲呵欠，先生關上電視。他看起來又氣又累。

我闔上房門，忍不住歡喜。我心裡有個祕密，寒夜升起暖意。

外頭樹葉吹響。街燈映照我的窗口。我直想著我是全世界唯一清醒的人。我想著中國，想著德國老婦人跳舞，想著你的微笑。我睡著了，睡夢中身體仍有甜蜜的感覺。

guest

n. **1.** person entertained at another's house or at another's expense; **2.** invited performer or speaker; **3.** customer at a hotel or restaurant.

A new day. You call me. At once I know your voice. You ask if I want visit Kew Gardens.

"Queue Gardens?"

"Meet me at Richmond tube station," you say. "R-i-ch-m-o-n-d."

Is beautiful weather. What a surprise. And so peaceful in the grassy space. So green. Cherry blossoms is just coming out and you tell me about your favourite snowdrops. We see there is different small gardens with different theme. Africa garden are palm trees. North America garden are rocks. South America garden are cactus. And there is too Asia gardens. I so happy Manager not forgetting Asia gardens.

But I so disappointing after we walk in. Lotuses and bamboos is growing in India garden, plum trees and stone bridge is growing in Japanese garden. Where is my Chinese garden?

"Doesn't look like they''ve made a Chinese garden," you say to me.

"But that very unfair," I say in angry voice. "Bamboos belongs to China. Panda eats bamboos leafs in China, you must hear, no?"

You laugh. You say you agree. They should move some plants from India and Japan garden to make Chinese garden.

【客人】

〈名詞〉**1.** 到別人家裡作客或接受他人款待的人；**2.** 應邀表演或演講的人；
3. 飯店或餐館的顧客。

嶄新的一天。你打電話給我。我馬上認出你的聲音。你邀
請我去參觀裘園。

「裘園？」

「到瑞奇蒙地鐵站和我碰頭，」你說。「瑞-奇-蒙。」

多好的天氣。真是難得。四處綠油油的一片，多寧靜的地
方。櫻桃樹含苞待放，你為我介紹了心愛的雪花蓮。我們看見
那地方按不同的主題闢建了許多小花園。非洲花園的主題是棕
櫚樹。北美洲花園是大岩石。南美洲花園是仙人掌。還有亞洲
花園也在那兒。我真高興管事的人沒有漏掉亞洲花園。

不過進去一看令人好生失望。蓮花和竹子長在印度花園，
梅樹和石拱橋長在日本花園。我的中國花園在哪兒？

「看起來他們好像漏掉了中國花園，」你對我說。

「太不公平了，」我氣著說。「竹子屬於中國。熊貓在中
國吃的就是竹葉，你一定聽過，對不？」

你笑出聲來。你說你同意。他們應該從印度和日本花園移
出幾樣植物好好建個中國花園。

草地邀請我們兩個躺下來。我們並肩躺在一塊。我從來沒
有跟一個男人這樣靠近過。青草的汁液沾溼我的白襯衫。天空
蔚藍，飛機低低越過我們頭頂，好清晰。我看著草地上移動的

The meadow asking us to lie. We rest beside each other. I never do that with a man. Juice from grass wetting my white shirt. My heart melting. Sky is blue and airplane flying above us, low and clear. I see moving shadows of the plane on the meadow.

"I want see where you live," I say.

You look in my eyes. "Be my guest."

飛機身影。

　　「我想看看你住的地方，」我說。

　　你直直看進我的眼睛。「那就當我的客人。」

misunderstanding

misunderstand *v*. fail to understand properly. misunderstanding *n*. *informal* a disagreement, argument, or fight.

That's how all start. From a misunderstanding. When you say "guest" I think you meaning I can stay in your house. A week later, I move out from Chinese landlord.

I not really have anything, only big wheel-missing suitcase. The husband helping me suitcase. The wife opening door. Your white van waiting outside, you with hands on wheel.

Husband puts wheel-missing suitcase on your van, you smile to landlord and turn engine key.

I want ask something to my landlord that I always wanting ask, so I put my head out of window:

"Why you not plant plants in your garden?"

Wife is hesitate: "Why? It is not easy to grow plants in this country. No sun."

For last time I look the concrete garden. Is same no story, same way as before. Like little piece of Gobi desert. What a life! Or maybe all the immigrants here living like that?

White van starting up, I respond to wife:

"Not true. Everywhere green in this country. How you say not easy growing plant here?"

We leave house behind. The couple is waving hands to me.

I say: "Chinese strange sometimes."

You smile: "I don't understand you Chinese at all. But I

【誤會】

〈動詞〉未能恰當地理解。〈名詞〉通俗的口語用法，指雙方意見不一致，起爭議，或爭吵。

　　原來這全都是起於一個誤會。當你說出「客人」一詞，我以為這表示我可以住進你的房子當「房客」。一個星期之後，我就真的搬離中國房東。

　　其實我沒多少家當，一只滾輪失蹤的大皮箱就處理完畢。先生替我搬箱子。太太幫忙開門。白色小貨車等在屋外，方向盤上你的兩隻手擱著。

　　先生將滾輪失蹤的行李箱抬上貨車，你對著房東笑笑，鑰匙一扭發動引擎。

　　好想問房東一個心裡憋了很久的問題，我把頭伸出車窗：

　　「你們院子裡為什麼都不種點東西？」

　　太太愣了愣：「幹嘛種？這地方東西長不成的。沒太陽。」

　　我掃了這塊水泥院落最後一眼。還是一樣，沒有任何細節值得留戀。像一小塊迷你的戈壁沙漠。這算什麼生活！還是所有移民到此地的人都這麼過日子？

　　白色小貨車起步，我回房東太太：

　　「沒這回事。這地方到處綠地。怎麼妳說樹會長不成？」

　　我們駛離那棟房屋。房東夫婦不停向我揮別。

　　我說：「中國人有時候很怪。」

would like to get to know you."

We driving in high street. My suitcase lie down obediently at back. Is so easy move house like this in West? I happy I leave my grey and no fun Tottenham Hale, heading to a better area, I think. But streets becoming more and more rough. Lots of black kids shouting outside. Beggars sitting on corner with dogs, smoking, and murmuring.

"Where your house?" I ask.

"Hackney."

"How is Hackney?"

"Hackney is Hackney," you say.

你笑了：「你們中國人我完全不懂。不過我倒是很想好好認識妳。」

　　我們駛上大馬路。我的皮箱默不作聲躺在後頭。搬個家在西方如此輕鬆愉快？我很高興能夠搬離沉悶無趣的多特哈姆哈爾，心想終於可以開往高明一點的地區。可是兩旁駛過的街道越來越不對勁。成群的黑人小孩呼嘯嬉鬧。狗狗圍著乞丐坐在角落，他們抽菸，嘴裡不知喃喃些什麼。

　　「你住的地方在哪兒？」我問。

　　「哈克尼。」

　　「哈克尼什麼樣子？」

　　「就哈克尼那樣，」你說。

bachelor

n. **1.** an unmarried man; **2.** a person who holds the lowest university or college degree.

Your house is old house standing lonely between ugly new buildings for poor people. Front, it lemon yellow painted. Both side of house is bricks covered by mosses and jasmine leafs. Through leafs I see house very damp and damaged. Must have lots of stories happened inside this house.

And you are really *bachelor*. Your bed is single bed. Made by several piece of big wood, with wooden boxes underneath. Old bedding sheets cover it. Must be very hard for sleep, like Chinese peasants *kang* bed. In kitchen, teacups is everywhere. Every cup different with other, big or small, half new or broken . . . So everything single, no company, no partner, no pair.

First day I arrive, our conversation like this:

I say: "*I eat. Do you eat?*"

You correct me in proper way: "*I want to eat. Would you like to eat something with me?*"

You ask: "*Would you like some coffee?*"

I say: "*I don't want coffee. I want tea.*"

You change it: "*A cup of tea would be delightful.*"

Then you laughing at my confusing face, and you change your saying: "*I would love a cup of tea, please.*"

I ask: "*How you use word 'love' on tea?*"

41

【單身漢】

〈名詞〉**1.** 單身漢；**2.** 大學學士。

　　你的房子很老舊，被安頓貧民的醜陋新建物夾在中間，一派孤伶伶的模樣。房屋正面漆上檸檬黃，兩邊的磚牆被青苔和茉莉葉遮覆，但掩不住底下的斑駁與風霜。可以想見屋子裡經歷過多少前塵往事。

　　你是不折不扣的單身漢。一張單人床。幾片床板拼湊起來，底下墊著木箱，簡單鋪上老舊床單。睡起來一定硬邦邦的，像中國的土炕。廚房裡到處是茶杯，每個長相都不一樣，有大有小，半新或缺了口……所以樣樣東西都是單獨一件，沒有同伴，沒有搭檔，沒有配對成雙。

　　頭一天來到這裡，我們的對話如下：

　　我說：「我吃。你要吃嗎？」

　　你更正我的措詞：「我想吃點什麼。你願意跟我一起吃點東西嗎？」

　　你問：「妳想來點咖啡嗎？」

　　我說：「我不想要咖啡。我想要茶。」

　　你修正：「一杯茶會讓人非常愉快。」

　　你看著我困惑的神情笑出聲來，你又換一種說法：「我很愛來一杯茶，請。」

　　我問：「你怎麼用『愛』這個字在茶上面？」

First time you make food for me it is some raw leafs with two boiled eggs. Eggy Salad. Is that all? Is that what English people offer in their homes? In China, cold food for guest is bad, only beggars no complain cold food. Maybe you don't know how cook, because you are a bachelor.

I sit down on your kitchen table, eat silently. Lampshade is on top of my head, tap is dripping in sink. So quiet. Scarily. I never ate such a quiet food in China. Always with many of family members, everybody shouting and screaming while eating. Here only the noise is from me using the forks and knife. I drop the knife two times so I decide only use one fork in my right hand.

Chewing. Chewing. No conversation.

You look at me eating, patiently.

Finally you ask: "*So, do you like the food?*"

I nod, put another leaf into my mouth. I remember me is bad speak with food full of my mouth. You wait. But patience maybe running out, so you answer your question in my voice:

"*Yes, I like the food very much. It is delicious. It is yami.*"

第一次你弄東西給我吃，幾片生菜葉配兩顆水煮蛋。雞蛋沙拉，沒別的了？英國人在自己家裡準備的就是這種東西？在中國，沒有人會招待客人冷掉的食物，只有乞丐才沒得抱怨吃冷食。或許是你不懂得燒飯，單身漢嘛，難怪。

　　我餐桌邊坐著，默默地吃。頂上一盞燈罩，水槽裡龍頭滴答。好安靜。怪怕人的。我在中國從沒這麼安靜吃飯過。總是全家大小，你一言我一語，邊鬧邊用餐。這地方唯一出聲的只有我手中的刀和叉。掉了兩次餐刀之後，我決定只拿右手的叉子就好。

　　嚼。嚼。嚼。沒有人講話。

　　你一直看著我吃東西，真有耐性。

　　最後你問：「怎麼樣，食物還好嗎？」

　　我點頭，又塞了片菜葉進嘴巴。我知道自己嘴裡有食物的時候不太會講話。你等著我回應。不過耐心可能跑掉了，你模仿我的腔調自問自答：

　　「是的，我非常喜歡食物。真是美味極了。」

The memory becomes so uncertain.

The memory keeps a portrait about you. An abstract portrait like pictures I saw in Tate Modern, blur details and sketchy lines. I start draw this picture, but my memory about you keep changing, and I have to change the picture.

記憶變得如此隱晦不明。

記憶留存一幅你的肖像。那肖像如同我在泰特現代美術館所見的抽象人物畫，細節朦朧，線條簡潔。我著手描繪這圖像，然而對你的記憶閃爍不定，我描繪的圖像也隨之改變。

green fingers

pl. n. Brit. informal skill in gardening.

Our first night. First time we make love. First time in my life doing this.

I think you are beautiful. You are beautiful smiles, and beautiful face, and beautiful language. You speak slowly. I almost hear every single word because you speak so slowly, only sometime I not understanding what you mean. But I understanding you more than anybody else I meet in England.

Then you are taking off clothes.

I look at you. Man's body seems ugly. Hair, bones, muscles, skins, more hair. I smell at you. Strong smell. Smell animal. Smell is from your hair, your chest, your neck, your armpit, your skin, your every single little bit in body.

Strong smell and strong soul. I even can feel it and touch it. And I think your body maybe beautiful also. Is the home of your soul.

I ask how old are you, is first question Chinese people ask to stranger. You say forty-four. Older than me twenty years. Forty-four in my Chinese think is old, is really old. Leaves far behind away from youth. I say age sound old, but you look young. You say thanks, and you don't say more.

I say I think you beautiful, ignoring the age. I think you too beautiful for me, and I don't deserve of you.

【綠手指】

〈名詞複數形〉（英國非正式用語）搞園藝的技能。

　　我們的初夜。我們第一次做愛。我生平第一次做愛。

　　我覺得你很美。你有美麗的微笑，美麗的臉，美麗的語言。你講話慢慢的。你放慢速度，幾乎每個字我都能聽進去，只偶爾我會沒辦法理解你的意思。可是你已經比我在英國遇到的任何人都更能讓我理解。

　　然後你脫掉衣服。

　　我盯著你看。男人的身體不怎麼好看。毛髮，骨頭，肌肉，皮膚，更多的毛髮。我嗅著你。體味濃烈。動物的味道。味道源自你的頭髮，你的胸膛，你的脖頸，你的胳肢窩，你的皮膚，你身體的每一處毛孔。

　　強烈的味道，強烈的靈魂。我幾乎可以感覺到，碰觸到。我在想你的身體或許也是美麗，是你靈魂的家屋。

　　我問你年紀多大了，這是中國人習慣問陌生人的第一個問題。你說四十四。比我大二十歲。四十四在我的中國觀念裡算老了，真的老了。距離年輕已經有好長一段歲月。我說年紀聽起來老了，不過你看起來很年輕。你說謝謝，然後不再多說一句。

　　我說我覺得你很美，年紀姑且不管。我說你太美了，我配你不上。

Very early morning. You are sleeping, with gentle breathe. I look through bedroom's window. Sky turning dim into bright. I see small dried up old grapes hang under vines by window. Their shapes are become clear and clear in cold spring morning light. Garden is messy and lush. Your clothes and socks hanging in washing line. Your gardening machines everywhere on soil.

You are man, handy and physical. This is man's garden.

You make me feel fragile. Love makes me feel fragile, because I am not beautiful, I never being told I am beautiful. My mother always telling me I am ugly. "You are ugly peasant girl. You have to know this." Mother tells this to me for all twenty-three years. Maybe why I not never having boyfriend like other Chinese girls my age. When I badly communicating with others, my mother's words becomes loud in my eardrum. I am ugly peasant girl. I am ugly peasant girl.

"My body is crying for you," you say.

Most beautiful sentence I heard in my life.

My bad English don't match your beautiful language.

I think I fall in love with you, but my love cannot match your beauty.

And then daytime. Sun puts light through garden to our bed. Birds are singing on roof. I think how sunlight must make people much happier in this dark country and then I watch you wake up. We see each other naked, without distance. In light of reality. "Good morning," you say. "You look even more lovely than yesterday." And we make love again in the morning.

清晨時間還很早。你在睡夢中，呼吸均勻。我從臥室窗戶往外看。暗淡的天色轉趨微明。我看見臨窗的藤枝底下掛著乾縮的小葡萄。冷春的晨光中，它們的形狀越來越清明。庭院一片雜亂蒼翠。你的衣服和襪子吊在曬衣繩上。土地上你的園藝用具任意擺放。

　　你是男人，靈巧，強壯。這是男人的庭院。

　　你讓我覺得脆弱。愛讓我覺得脆弱，因為我不美，從來沒有人說我美。我母親老是講我長得醜。「你是個鄉下醜姑娘。你自己要認命。」媽媽這樣對我唸了二十三年。或許就為這緣故，我不像其他同齡的中國女孩多半結交過男友。當我蠢兮兮地和別人往來時，母親的話語響徹耳膜。我是鄉下醜姑娘。我是鄉下醜姑娘。

　　「我的身體好渴望有你，」你說。

　　我這輩子聽過最美的句子。

　　我的爛英語配不上你優美的語言。

　　我想我愛上你了，但我的愛配不上你的美。

　　然後白天降臨。太陽將光線穿過庭院送達我們床上。屋頂上有鳥啼唱。我在想，陽光應該可以讓這陰暗國家的人民快樂一些，然後你就醒了。我們赤裸裸看著彼此，沒有距離。在真實的光線裡。「早安，」你說。「妳怎麼看起來比昨天更可愛。」晨光中我們再度做愛。

fertilise

v. **1.** to provide (an animal or plant) with sperm or pollen to bring about fertilisation; **2.** to supply (soil) with nutrients.

You take me to garden. Is very small, maybe ten square metres. One by one, you introduce me all the plants you have put there. Sixteen different plants in a ten square metres garden. In my home town in China, there only one plant in fields: rice.

You know every single plant's name, like they your family and you try tell me but I not remember English names so you write them down:

Potato, Daffodil, Lavender, Mint, Spinach, Thyme, Dill, Apple tree, Green beans, Wisteria, Grape vine, Bay tree, Geranium, Beetroot, Sweet corn, Fig tree

Then I tell you all these plants have very different names and meanings in Chinese. So I write down names in Chinese, and explain every word at you.

Potato	*earth bean*
Daffodil	*fairy maiden from the water*
Lavender	*clothes perfuming weeds*
Mint	*light lotus*
Spinach	*watery vegetable*

【下種】

〈動詞〉**1.** 提供（動物或植物）精子或花粉使之產生授精作用；**2.** 供給（土壤）養分。

　　你帶我到庭院。面積很小，不會超過十平方公尺。一樣接著一樣，你為我介紹院子裡栽種的全部植物。十平方公尺的庭院總共有十六種植栽。哪像我中國老家，田裡只有一樣作物：稻米。

　　你認得每樣植物的名稱，它們像是你家庭的成員，你講的英語名稱我記不住，所以你拿筆為我寫下來：

　　土豆（編按：台稱馬鈴薯），水仙，薰衣草，薄荷，菠菜，百里香，蒔蘿，蘋果樹，豆子，紫藤，葡萄，月桂樹，天竺葵，甜菜，玉米，無花果樹

　　接著我告訴你，這些植物在中國的名稱和意義和你寫的截然不同。我將它們的中國名字一一寫出來，附上說明。

土豆	泥土豆子
水仙	來自水中的仙女
薰衣草	衣服香草
薄荷	輕微的荷花
菠菜	水波蔬菜

Thyme	*one hundred miles fragrant*
Dill	*the herb of time*
Apple tree	*clover fern fruit tree*
Green beans	*son of beans*
Wisteria	*purple vines*
Grape vine	*crawling plant*
Bay tree	*moon laurel*
Geranium	*sky bamboo flower*
Beetroot	*sweet vegetable*
Sweet corn	*jade rice*
Fig tree	*the fruit tree without flowers*

You laughing when you hear the names. "I never knew flutes grew on trees," you say. It seems I am big comedy to you. I not understand why so funny. "You can't say your Rs. It's *fruit* not *flute*," you explain me. "A *flute* is a musical instrument. But your Chinese name seems just right: a fig tree really is a fruit tree without flowers."

"How a tree can just have fruit without having flower first?" I ask.

Like teacher, you describe how insect climbs into fruit to fertilise seed.

What "fertilise"? I need looking in *Concise Chinese-English Dictionary*.

"Fertilise" make me think Chairman Mao. He likes fertiliser. Was big Mao thing increase productivity, increase plants. Maybe that why China, biggest peasants population country, still alive and become stronger after using fertiliser on the soil.

I ask: "How long a fig tree has figs after insects fertilising

百里香	一百里芳香
蒔蘿	時間藥草
蘋果樹	首蓿蕨果樹
豆子	豆的兒子
紫藤	紫色藤蔓
葡萄	爬行植物
月桂樹	月亮桂冠
天竺葵	天空竹子花
甜菜	甜蜜蔬菜
玉米	碧玉稻米
無花果樹	沒有花的果樹

你聽到這些中文名稱失聲而笑。「我沒想到樹上也能長出長笛，」你說。好像我在你面前上演了爆笑片。可我搞不懂自己哪裡好笑。「你沒有發 r 的音。應該唸 fruit，不是 flute，」你解釋給我聽。「flute 是一種樂器。不過你講的中國名字倒滿正確的：無花果樹的確是一種沒有花的果樹。」

「怎麼會有樹不先開花就能結果？」我問。如同老師上課般，你描述昆蟲如何爬進果子裡面下種。

什麼是「下種」？我得查一查簡明中英辭典。

「下種」這個詞讓我想起毛主席。他最喜歡下種。毛主席喜歡大手筆增加產能，提高農作。或許正因如此，中國這個擁有最多農村人口的國家，歷經土地反覆施肥利用後，猶能存活而且日趨強大。

我問：「昆蟲下種之後，無花果樹多久能長出果子？像女人那樣得懷孕十個月嗎？」

it? Like woman have ten months pregnant?"

You look at me, like look at *alien*.

"Why ten months? I thought it took nine months," you say.

"Chinese we say *shi yue huai tai*（十月懷胎）. It means giving the birth after ten months pregnant."

"That's strange." You seem like want to laugh again. "Which day do you start to count the pregnancy in China?" you ask seriously. But how I know? We never being taught this *properly* in school. Too shameful to teach and to study for our Chinese.

Standing under your fruit tree without flowers, I pick up piece of leaf, and put on my palm. A single leaf, but large. I touch the surface and feel hairy.

"Have you read the Bible?" you ask.

"No." Of course not, not in China.

You fetch a big huge black book from room. You open the pages. "Actually the fig tree is the oldest of mankind's symbols." You point at beginning of book:

And the eyes of them both were opened, and they knew that they were naked, and they sewed fig leaves together, and made themselves aprons.

"What is that?" I am curious.

"It is about Adam and Eve. They used fig leaves to cover their naked bodies."

"They clever. They knowing fig leaves bigger than other leafs," I say.

You laugh again.

Your gardening machines everywhere in disorder.

你瞪著我，像看到外星人一樣。

「爲什麼要十個月？我知道應該是九個月罷，」你說。

「我們中國人都說十月懷胎。懷孕十個月之後小孩才會出生。」

「那就怪了。」你似乎又想發笑。

「你們中國從哪一天開始起算孕期？」你問得很認眞。但我哪會知道？學校裡根本沒有人教過我們。這種事太丟人了，怎麼學怎麼教？

站在你那株沒有花的果樹底下，我撿起葉子，攤在掌心。只有一片，但葉子好大。我摸了摸葉面，毛茸茸的。

「妳讀過聖經嗎？」你問。

「沒有。」當然沒有，在中國沒有。

你從屋內取來厚厚一本黑皮書，翻開書頁。「其實無花果樹是最古老的人類象徵。」你指著書本的開頭。

他們二人眼睛就明亮了，纔知道自己是赤身露體，便拿無花果樹的葉子，爲自己編作裙子。

「那是寫什麼？」我很好奇。

「那是亞當和夏娃的故事。他們用無花果樹的葉子遮掩赤裸的身體。」

「他們好聰明，還曉得無花果的葉子比其他樹葉大片，」我說。

你又笑了。

你的園藝用具零落散置。

Spade	*For cutting the soil*
Fork	*For soften the soil*
Rake	*For scratching the grass*

Suddenly I bit shocked, stop. There are some nudity in your garden.

"What this?" I ask.

"Those are my sculptures," you say.

Sculptures? A naked man no head, facing to ground of the garden. Body twisted, with enormous hands and enormous feet. Close to ground, between the legs, two beautiful eggs, like two half of apples. In the middle of apples, a penis like little wounded bird. I walk to him and touch. Is made of plaster. I amazed by this body, is huge, looks suffered. I remember picture from Michelangelo's David on your bookshelf, a very healthy and balanced body. But yours, yours far different.

Beside this body statue, some other smalls clay sculptures. Ear, big like basin, in brown. Shape of that ear spread like a big flower. Then more ears, different shape, different size. They lie on the grass quietly, listening us.

Under fig tree another penis made from clay, gentle, innocent. Then another one, looks harder, lies down beside honeysuckle roots, in soil colour. Little clay sculptures there, like they live with plants hundred years.

The noisy London being stopped by brick wall. The grey city kept away by this garden. Plants and sculptures on sunshine. Glamorous, like you. Maybe all mans in London green fingers. Maybe this country too cold and too dim, so plants and garden can showing imagination the spring, the sun, the

49

鏟子　　　用來挖土

叉子　　　用來鬆土

耙子　　　用來耙草

　　突然間我眼前錯愕，不敢移動半分。你的庭院裡居然出現一些裸體的東西。

　　「這什麼東西？」我問。

　　「我的雕塑，」你說。

　　雕塑？一個光溜溜的男人沒有頭，朝向庭院地面。身體歪扭，巨大的手和腳。靠近地面，兩腿之間，兩顆美麗的蛋，像一對剖半的蘋果。蘋果中央，有根陽具像受了傷的小鳥。我走近他，伸手觸摸。原來是石膏做的。令人驚異的軀體，厚實，看起來正在承受痛苦。我想起你書架上，米開蘭基羅的大衛像圖片，非常健壯，骨肉均勻的身軀。然而你的，你的雕像截然不同。

　　除了這具身體雕像，還有其他比較小件的黏土雕塑。耳朵，臉盆大小，棕色的。那隻耳朵舒展的形狀有如一朵巨花。還有其他的耳朵，形狀各異，尺寸有別。它們草地上靜躺著，聆聽我們倆。

　　無花果樹底下另有一根黏土陽具，溫和，無邪。接著又有一根，堅挺一些，靠著忍冬樹根部臥躺著，泥土的色澤。小件的黏土雕塑分布在那兒，彷彿已經和植物們共存了百年之久。

　　倫敦的喧囂於磚牆前止步。灰濛濛的城市被這方庭園阻隔在外。植物和雕塑浸潤於陽光，令人神往，你也是。或許倫敦所有的男人都是綠手指。或許這國家太過寒冷，太過暗淡，植物和庭園反倒更能突顯春天的嚮往，嚮往那陽光和溫暖。植物

warmth. And plants and garden giving love like womans warm mans life.

When I stand in garden with sixteen different plants, I think of Chinese mans. Chinese city-mans not plant-lover at all. Shameful for Chinese city-mans pour passion onto those leafs. He be considered a loser, no position in society. But you, you different. Who are you?

和庭園散發愛意，像女人偎暖男人的生命。

　　站在這十六種植栽生長的庭園，我想起了中國的男人。在中國，城市裡的男人絕對不可能愛好栽種。中國的都會男子愛弄花花草草的話，面子馬上掛不住。他會被人家視為缺乏雄心壯志，在社會沒辦法立足。可是你，你不一樣。你究竟是何等人物？

instruction

n. **1.** order to do something; **2.** teaching- *pl.* information on how to do or use something.

We have so much sex. We make love every day and every night. Morning, noon, afternoon, late afternoon, evening, early night, late night, midnight, even in the dreams. We make love in sun, we make love in grey afternoon, and we make love at raining night. We make love on narrow bench of garden, under fig tree, on hammock covered by the grape leafs, by kitchen sink, on dinner table, on anywhere we feel like to make love. I feel scared towards your huge energy. You come into me strong like a storm blowing a wooden house in the forest, and you come into me deep like a hammer beating the nail on the wall. You ask me if it feels good, and I say it make me feel comfortable.

"Only *comfortable*!?"

"Yes," I tell you. "I find your body is very comfortable, like nothing else I find in this uncomfortable country."

Do I feel shame about sex? Yes, I do, in beginning. A lot. Is such taboo in China. I never really know what is sex before. Now I naked everyday in the house, and I can see clearly my desire. Recent I dream few times that I am naked in street, in market, and even on highway. I run through busy street fast as I can to get home. But still, everybody in street surprising to see I am naked.

【使用說明】

〈名詞〉1. 命令，指示；2.（複數）使用說明，操作指南。

　　我們性事頻仍異常。我們沒日沒夜的做愛。早晨，中午，下午，晚午，傍晚，入夜，夜深，午夜，甚至是睡夢中。陽光和煦我們做愛，午後陰灰我們做愛，夜雨綿綿我們做愛。我們在庭院狹窄的長椅上做，在無花果樹下做，在葡萄樹葉庇蔭的吊床上做，扶著廚房水槽做，餐桌上做，隨便哪兒，我們想做就做。你旺盛的精力令我驚懼。你猛力進入我像暴風狂掃林中的木屋，你深深搗入我如同榔頭鎚釘入牆。你問我感覺是否滿足，我說我覺得舒服。

　　「才舒服而已!?」

　　「對，」我告訴你。「我發覺你的身體很舒服，在這個不舒服的國家裡面沒有任何其他東西比得上。」

　　對於性我是否害羞？沒錯，我害羞，一開始的時候。害羞得要命。在中國這可是大禁忌。以前，我對性事連一知半解都談不上。如今在家裡每天光著屁股，我可以清楚看見自己的慾念。最近幾回，我夢見自己脫光光在街上，在菜市場，甚至在公路上。我全速跑過熱鬧的街頭一路往家裡衝。不過呢，街上每個人還是被一絲不掛的我嚇到了。

　　這種夢代表什麼？

　　你說，這種夢顯示因為害怕曝露而產生的羞恥或恐懼。每

What this dream about?

You say this dream about shame or fear of being exposed.

Every time we make love you produce so much sperm on my skin like the spring on the Trafagar Square, you are worried sometimes that maybe I get pregnant. We only want have each other and we don't want let the third person take over our love.

You say we need use the condom.

In our long-shabby-Hackney-Road, there no any "*Boots*" (*Boots* is a shop represent civilisation to me), although *Cost Cutter* sells condom sometimes. But shopkeeper in *Cost Cutter* know us just like he know niece or nephew. And he is serious Muslim, he might anti condom user. So we have go to Brick Lane, where the Bangladeshi shopkeepers are kind and messy, and they can't remembering every single customer face whom from Hackney Road.

PLEASE READ THESE INSTRUCTIONS CAREFULLY, as it say on the box. I open box, unfold notes, then start read. I never read condom instruction before. I think people maybe only read condom instruction when the first time they try to sex. Anyway I new to this.

Tear along one side of the foil, removing the condom carefully. Condoms are strong but can be torn by sharp fingernails or jewellery.

"What is *jewellery*?" I ask.

"Sparkly stuff women love to wear," you say, without emotion.

一回我們做愛，你在我肌膚上製造大量的精液，有如特拉法加廣場的噴泉。有時你會擔心我因此而懷孕。此刻我們只想彼此擁有，容不下第三者占據我們的愛。

你說我們需要保險套。

在我們這條寒酸的哈克尼路上，長路漫漫就是找不到一間「博姿」（博姿藥妝店在我眼中代表文明水準），雖然「省錢王」其實就有在賣保險套。不過「省錢王」的老板跟我們已經熟到不行。人家可是個正經八百的穆斯林，搞不好鄙視保險套使用者。所以我們得轉移陣地到東區的紅磚巷，那兒開店的孟加拉老闆比較和氣，馬虎，他們也不可能記住每個來自哈克尼路的客人長相。

請詳閱使用說明，包裝盒上這樣說。我打開盒子，攤開紙條，讀了起來。我從沒讀過保險套使用說明。我猜大家或許都只在第一次使用準備性交的時候讀過。反正我是新手就對了。

沿著包裝箔邊線撕開，小心取出保險套。保險套雖夠強韌，仍可能被尖銳的指甲或 jewellery 劃破。

「*jewellery* 是什麼？」我問。

「亮晶晶的玩意，女人喜歡戴在身上，」你沒勁地說。

當陰莖勃起準備和您的伴侶接觸時才戴上保險套。此舉幫助防止 STDs 及懷孕。

「什麼是 *STD*？」

「性接觸傳染疾病，」你隨問即答，彷彿這種事家常便飯，如你每天不可或缺的薄荷茶。

Only put the condom on when the penis is erect and before contact with your partner's body. This helps prevent STDs and pregnancy.

"What is STD?"

"Sexually Transmitted Disease," you reply quickly, as if is thing you are familiar as your every day's mint tea.

Now place the condom over the end of the penis with the roll on the outside. With one hand pinch the teat of the condom to expel any trapped air, this will make space for the sperm.

I being stopped by these word:

one hand pinch the teat of the condom to expel any trapped air

. . . I needing several seconds to imagine that scene. Is like pornography. We cannot have words like this in Chinese. We too ashamed. Westerner has nothing too ashamed. You can do anything in this country.

Using the other hand, roll the condom down the length of the penis to its base. Withdraw the penis soon after ejaculation whilst still erect, holding the condom firmly in place at the base of the penis. Wait until the penis is completely withdrawn before removing the condom. Keep the penis and condom away from the vagina to avoid any contact with sperm . . .

I can't continuing reading. I am totally lost these words. But you laughing.

將保險套放置陰莖前端，捲邊朝外。一手捏緊保險套前緣小袋將多餘空氣擠出，此設計為精液儲存空間。

我的注意力停在這行字上：

一手捏緊保險套前緣小袋將多餘空氣擠出

　　……我得花幾秒鐘想像一下那個畫面。好像黃色小說。我們在中國可不能看到這種字眼，太丟人了。哪像西方人不曉得害羞。你在這國家愛幹什麼都行。

使用另一隻手，順著陰莖長度捲覆保險套直至陰莖根部。射精後趁陰莖仍處勃起狀態立即抽出，抽出陰莖時需由根部握緊保險套。陰莖未完全抽出之前不可除去保險套。勿使陰莖和保險套靠近陰道以避免任何精液接觸……

　　我看不下去了。這幾行字看得我眼花撩亂。你一直笑。

本保險套乃為陰道性交設計，其他用途會增加破損風險。

　　我停下：「這什麼意思？」

　　「這是暗語。這表示你不能把它放進屁屁。」你回答，非常明確，但已經顯得不耐煩了，開始讀起你的《週末衛報》。

　　使用說明的另一面我也翻過來讀了，內容比較沒那麼重要。例如，

即使您並未計畫性交活動，隨身攜帶保險套乃明智之舉，有備無患。

　　隨時攜帶保險套乃明智之舉？西方人隨時有機會性交，哪怕他們只是去購物，等公車，等火車的時候。性在這國家等於

Condoms are intended for vaginal intercourse, other uses can increase the potential for breakage.

I stop: "What's that mean?"

"It is a hint. It means you shouldn't put it into the arse." You answer, very precise, but no more patience, as you start reading your *Guardian Weekend*.

I read other bits of instruction on other side as well, and they less important. For example,

Even if you are not planning on having sexual intercourse, it's sensible to carry condoms with you, just in case.

Sensible to carry condoms all the time? Westerner can always have sex whenever they go shopping, or waiting for bus or train. Sex in this country is like brush the hair or the teeth.

Words on the instruction are more exciting than sexy magazines on shelfs of corner shop in our street.

梳頭刷牙般尋常。

　　使用說明上頭的文字簡直比我們街角書報攤的成人雜誌還讓人臉紅心跳。

charm

n. **1.** attractive quality; **2.** trinket worn on a bracelet; **3.** magic spell. *v.*
1. attract, delight; **2.** influence by personal charm; **3.** protect or influence
as if by magic.

From first day we being together, until next two and three
days, our skins being non stop together, not separating even a
hour. You talk to me about everything. But I not understand
completely. You say:

*"I used to try to love men. For most of the last twenty years I
have been out with men."*
I think is good try love men. World better place. But go out
where?

*"When I was a squatter, I made a lot of sculptures. They"d
fill the houses."*
What *squat*? I take out dictionary. Says "to sit with the
knees bent and the heels close to the bottom or thighs." Very
difficult position, I imagine.
What kind houses you squatted there? Don't lonely sit with
the knees bent without chair on the floor?

*"I used to plant potatoes and beans on a farm, and I looked
after my goats. I loved doing that, more than anything else."*
So you a peasant? How come you also such a city man?

【魅力】

〈名詞〉**1.** 迷人的特質；**2.** 鐲子上的小飾物；**3.** 符咒，護身符。〈動詞〉**1.** 吸引，使高興；**2.** 令人陶醉；**3.** 施加魔法保護或控制。

從我們同居的第一天開始，接下來一連兩三天，我們的肌膚交纏不休，連一個鐘頭的空檔都沒有。你凡事都對我吐露，可惜我未能百分之百理解。你說：

「從前我想要去愛人。過去二十年大部分的時間我一直跟人出去。」

我覺得想要去愛人是很棒的事。世界會變得更加美好。不過都出去哪兒？

「那時候我是 squatter（編按：違建居民或強占空屋的非法住民），做了好多好多雕塑。整間屋子堆得滿滿都是。」

什麼是 *squat*？我取出辭典。上面寫說「屈膝而坐，腳後跟靠抵臀部或大腿」。好辛苦的姿勢，我可以想像。

你那時候蹲的地方是什麼樣的房子？沒有椅子屈膝蹲在地上不會孤單無聊嗎？

「我以前在田裡種馬鈴薯和豆子，還得照顧我的山羊。我喜歡幹活，比什麼都喜歡。」

原來你是鄉下人？可你根本就像都市人啊？

"*I love old things. I love second-hand things. I hate new things. I don't want to buy new things any more.*"

But old things rotten, dying. How you feel alively and active with daily life if only live with old things?

Every sentence you said, I put into my own dictionary. Next day I look at and think every single word. I am entering into your brain. Although my world so far away from your, I think I be able understand you. I think you absolutely *charming*. Thing around you fascinating.

I feel a concentrate of love for you, farmer, sculptor, lover of men, stranger. Noble man.

In China we say hundreds of reincarnations bring two peoples to same boat. Maybe you are that people for me to be same boat. I never met mans like you before. I think we perfect: You quite Yin, and I very Yang. You earthy, and I metal. You bit damp, and I a little dry. You cool, and I hot. You windy, and I firey. We join. There is mutualism. And we can benefit each other. And all these makes us efficient lover.

「我喜歡老東西。我喜歡二手舊貨。我討厭新的東西。我再也不想買新的東西了。」

可是老東西破破爛爛，壽命已盡。如果只跟老東西住在一起，你每天日子要怎麼過得新鮮，過得起勁呢？

你講的每個句子，我一一寫進我自己的「詞典」。隔天又拿出來看，仔細推敲每一個字。我鑽進你的腦袋。儘管我的世界離你那般遙遠，我還是覺得自己有辦法了解你。我覺得你真是魅力無窮。你周遭的一切特別吸引人。

我感到全心全意只想愛你，愛你這個農夫，雕塑家，愛人者，陌生人。高貴的男人。

在中國我們說百世修得同船渡。或許你就是那個注定跟我同船的人。我從沒遇過像你這樣的男人。我認為我們倆是絕配：你偏陰，我偏陽。你屬土，我屬金。你有點溼，我有點乾。你冷，我熱。你生風，我起火。我們結合，正好產生互補作用，對彼此有利。這些加總起來，我們剛好天生一對。

vegetarian

n. a person who eats no meat or fish for moral, religious, or health reasons. *adj.* suitable for a vegetarian.

One problem between us and that is food.

Chop Chop, local Chinese restaurant in Hackney. I make you go there even though you say you never go Chinese restaurants.

Restaurant has very plain looking. White plastic table and plastic chairs and white fluorescent lamp. Just like normal government work unit in China. Waiter unhappy when cleans table, not looking anybody. Woman with pony tails behind counter she even more mean. A plastic panda-savings-tin sitting on top of counter. None of them can speak Mandarin.

"No. Sit there. No, no, not this table. Sit at that table."

Waiter commands like we is his soldiers.

"What you want? . . . We don't have tap water, you have to order something from the menu . . . We don't do pots of green tea, only cups."

I hate them. I swear I never been so rude Chinese restaurant in my entirely life. Why Chinese people becoming so mean in the West? I feel bit guilty for horrible service. Because I bring you, and you maybe thinking my culture just like this. Maybe that why some English look down of our Chinese. I am shameful for being a Chinese here.

But we still have to eat. Especially me, starving like the

【素食者】

〈名詞〉基於道德、宗教、或健康因素而不吃肉或魚的人。〈形容詞〉素食者可用的。

我們之間有個麻煩，食物。

「**手腳快**」──哈克尼當地的中國館子。我把你拖去那兒，雖然你已經表明從來不上中國餐館。

館子陳設很簡單。白色塑膠桌椅，白色螢光燈。看起來活像標準的中國政府單位。跑堂的不情不願擦了擦桌面，頭也不抬。櫃檯小姐紮著馬尾，態度更冷。櫃面擺了個塑膠熊貓存錢筒。這裡沒有人會說國語。

「不。坐那兒。不對，不對，不是這張桌子。坐那邊那張。」

跑堂的指揮部隊般下達命令。

「你們要什麼？……我們不供應開水，你們要從菜單裡自己選……我們沒有壺泡的茶水，只有杯子裝的。」

我討厭他們這些人。我發誓這輩子還沒到過這麼粗魯的中國餐館。怎麼中國人到了西方變得如此小氣巴拉。服務態度糟糕到我有點內疚。因為是我帶你來的，或許你會以為我們的文化就是這副德性。難怪有些英國人瞧不起我們中國人。在這地方身為中國人我直想找個洞來鑽。

不過東西還是要吃。尤其是我，餓死鬼投胎。我老是喊餓。就算剛剛才填飽肚子，一兩個鐘頭馬上又餓了。以前我們

Ghost of Hunger. I always hungry. Even after big meal, later by one or two hours I feel hungry again. My family always very poor until several years ago. We used eat very small, barely had meat. After my parents started shoes factory, and left the poor peasants background behind, changed. But still I think foods all the time.

You not know nothing about Chinese food so I quickly order: duck, pork, fried tofu with beefs.

Meal comes to table, and I digging fastly my chopsticks into dishes like having a snowstorm. But you don't have any action at all. You just look me, like looking a Beijing opera.

"Why you not eat?" I ask, busy chewing my pork in my mouth.

"I am not very hungry," you say.

"You use chopsticks?" I think maybe that's the reason.

"Yes. Don't worry." You raise your chopsticks and perform to me.

"But you waste the food. Not like Chinese food?"

"I am a vegetarian," you say picking up little bit rice. "This menu is a zoo."

I am surprised. I try find my dictionary. Damn, is not with me this time. I remember film English Patient I watch on pirate DVD in China to education me about British people. "What that word? Word describe a people fall asleep for long long time, like living dying?"

"You mean coma?" You are confused.

"Yes, that is the word! You are not like that, do you?"

You put chopsticks down. Maybe you angry now.

"I presume you are thinking of the persistent vegetative

58

家窮得很，吃不起東西，飯桌上幾乎沒瞧過肉。這幾年爸媽開了製鞋工廠，脫離貧農背景之後，情況才慢慢有了改善。可我還是動不動就嘴饞想吃東西。

你對中國食物一竅不通，我很快就點好東西：鴨肉，豬肉，牛肉燴豆腐。東西一送上桌，我迅速舉筷，暴風雪般狂掃盤中。但你半點動靜也沒有。你只是看我一個人表演，好像在觀賞京戲。

「你怎麼不吃？」我問，嘴裡猛嚼豬肉。

「我肚子不太餓。」你說。

「你會用筷子吧？」我想會不會是這原因。

「會啊，沒問題。」你拿起筷子表演給我看。

「可是你不吃多浪費。怎麼，不喜歡中國菜？」

「我是個素食者，」你說著，挑起幾粒米飯。「這裡菜單跟動物園沒兩樣。」

我很意外，想拿我的辭典。去，結果這回沒帶身上。我記得在中國的時候，為了訓練自己認識英國人，我看過盜版的《英倫情人》DVD。「有個字怎麼說去了？就說有人一直睡一直睡醒不過來，好像死了那樣。」

「妳是說昏迷？」你搞不清楚。

「對，就那個字！你不會是像那樣吧？」

你放下筷子。或許生氣了。

「我猜妳在想的是植物人狀態，」你說。「素食者的意思是不吃肉。」

「喔，對不起，」我說，嚥下滿嘴的豆腐和牛肉。

這下我明白為何家裡從來沒出現過肉類了。本來還以為是你沒錢的關係。

state," you say. "Vegetarian means you don't eat meat."

"Oh, I am sorry," I say, swallowing big mouthful tofu and beefs.

Now I understand why never buy piece of meat. I thought it is because you poor.

"Why don't eat meat? Meat very nutritious."

". . ." You have no comments.

"Also you be depression if you don"t eating meat."

". . ." You still have no comments.

"My parents beaten me if I don't eating meat or any food on table in a meal. My parents curse me being picky and spoiled. Because others dying without any food to eat."

". . ." Still don't say anything.

"How come man is vegetarian? Unless he is monk," I say.

Still no words from you, but laughing.

You watch me eating all of meal. I try finish the duck, and the tofu and the beefs. My stomach painful. There are still porks left, and I order to take them away.

While I eating, you write top ten favorite food on a napkin:

avocado, asparagus, lentils, spinach, lettuce, pumpkin, radish, broccoli, aubergine, carrot

But, is this list will be the menu in our kitchen for rest of life? Is terrible! What about my meatball, my mutton, my beefs in black bean sauce? Who will be in charge of kitchen?

「爲什麼不吃肉？肉不是很有營養？」

「……」你不作聲。

「你如果都不吃肉人會沒精神。」

「……」你依舊不作聲。

「我爸爸媽媽會修理人，如果我不吃肉或飯桌上的任何東西。他們會罵我挑嘴，說我被慣壞了。好多人快餓死了都還沒東西吃呢。」

「……」你不說就是不說。

「人怎麼會想要吃素？除非他要當和尚，」我說。

你還是不講話，不過臉笑開了。

你看著我一個人包辦全部的東西。我努力解決鴨肉，還有豆腐和牛肉。我肚子撐死了。結果豬肉沒辦法，我請他們打包。

趁我吃的時候，你把十樣最喜歡的食物寫在餐巾紙上：

酪梨、蘆筍、扁豆、菠菜、萵苣、南瓜、蘿蔔、甘藍、茄子、葫蘆

唔，這張單子不會就是我們往後這輩子的廚房菜單罷？嚇壞我了！怎麼辦，我的肉丸子，我的羊肉，我的豆豉牛肉？廚房裡到底誰來當家？

noble

adj. showing or having high moral qualities; of the nobility; impressive and magnificent.

Sunday. I want do shopping. I say we need buy some toilet paper, some candle, some garlic, some ginger, some greens. (I not say meat, but actually that what I want buy after eating vegetables with you every day.)

"I want go to Sainsbury." After saying that, I realising I need practise my English manner, so I ask you again: "Shall we go to Sainsbury?"

You not look happy.

"Hmm, right. Let's worship in Sainsbury's every Sunday."

"What worship?"

"Worship? It's how the Chinese feel about Mao."

I don't know what say. Don't you know now we worship America?

"I don't like Sainsbury's," you say. "I like the rubbish market. They have much more interesting things there."

"Which rubbish market?"

You take me to the Brick Lane market. Is really a rubbish market. All kind of second-hand or third-hand radios, old CDs, used furniture, broken television set (who want buy a broken TV set?), old bicycles, tyres, nails, drilling machines, dusty shoes, pirate DVDs, cheap biscakes . . . I wonder if all these things made in China.

【高貴】

〈形容詞〉展現或擁有高尚的道德品質；貴族出身的；威嚴宏偉的。

　　禮拜天。我想去採買東西。已經察看過了，我們需要補充
衛生紙，蠟燭，蒜頭，薑，幾樣青菜。（我沒提肉類，不過跟
你接連幾天吃素下來，我最想買的就是肉。）

　　「我要去聖伯利生鮮超市。」話一出口，我就知道自己的
英語禮貌有待加強，我又重問一次：「我們去聖伯利好嗎？」

　　你看起來臉色不太好。

　　「哼，很好。我們每個禮拜天都去聖伯利朝拜算了。」

　　「什麼朝拜？」

　　「朝拜？就你們中國人對毛的態度那樣。」

　　我不會回答。莫非你不曉得我們現在朝拜的對象換成美
國？

　　「我不喜歡聖伯利超市，」你說。「我喜歡去垃圾市場，
那裡的東西有意思多了。」

　　「哪一個垃圾市場？」

　　你帶我到紅磚巷市場。還真的是垃圾市場。各式各樣的二
手或三手收音機，舊CD，舊家具，破掉的電視機（破掉的電
視機誰有興趣？），舊腳踏車，輪胎，鐵釘，鑽孔機，積灰的
鞋子，盜版DVD，便宜糕餅……我好奇這些東西會不會全都
出自中國製造。你跨步走進垃圾市場，身穿咖啡色老皮夾克和

You walk in the rubbish market with your old brown leather jacket and your dirty old leather shoes. The jacket is so old that the sleeves are wore out and the bottom is pieces. But you look great with these rubbish costumes in the rubbish market.

I think you are a noble man with noble words. I am not noble. I am humble. And I speak humble English. I from poor town in south China. We never see noble.

髒兮兮的舊皮鞋。那件皮夾克年代久遠，袖口磨穿了，下襬也已經綻裂。稀奇的是，你這身破舊裝扮配上垃圾市場，看起來居然出色得很。

我覺得你是個貴族，講的是貴族語言。我就跟高貴完全無緣。我很卑微，我講的英語也很卑微。我出身中國南方窮困的小鎮。我們沒見過高貴人士。

April

surprise

n. **1.** an unexpected event; **2.** amazement and wonder. *v.* **1.** to cause to feel amazement or wonder; **2.** to come upon, attack, or catch suddenly and unexpectedly.

Suddenly another thing else new and unexpected: "I need to leave London for a few days." You pack clothes. "For what? For where?" It is too out in blue for me. "To see my friend Jack, in Devon." "Who is Jack? I never heard you talk about him." "Well, I have lots of friends." "I come with you." I starting open wardrobe to take some clothes out. "No. You don't have to." "I want to." "No, I'm going on my own." "Why?" "I just don't think it's the right time for you to come." "Why not?" "Well, I have my own life. . . ." I don't understand you mean: "But we go together. We lovers!" I upset. Your decision destroying image of perfectness. "Come next time," you say. I stop. Don't know what do. "How many days away? I will feel lonely." "Just three or four."

【意外】

〈名詞〉1. 意外之事；2. 驚奇，詫異。〈動詞〉1. 使吃驚；2. 出其不意的遇見，攻擊，或逮住。

　　突然間又一件事出乎我的意料之外：

　　「我要離開倫敦幾天的時間。」你收拾衣物。

　　「爲什麼？要去哪兒？」我又是青天霹靂。

　　「去看我朋友傑克，在德文郡。」

　　「誰是傑克？從來都沒聽你提過他。」

　　「嗯，我朋友很多。」

　　「我跟你一起去。」我打開衣櫃開始拿衣服。

　　「不。妳不用跟我去。」

　　「可是我想去。」

　　「不用，我自己去就好。」

　　「爲什麼？」

　　「我覺得妳現在去時間不太合適。」

　　「爲什麼不合適？」

　　「唔，我有自己的日子要……」

　　我不懂你的意思：「可是我們一起去嘛。我們是男女朋友！」

　　我心煩意亂。你的決定破壞了我的完美想像。

　　「下一次再帶妳去，」你說。

　　我頓住。不知如何是好。

I can't say anything. But what I am do without you here in house? I even don't knowing where electricity box, and how answer telephone in proper way.

"You know, you"ve got to go out and make some friends," you say, "so you"re not always dependent on me. What about those girls from your language school?"

"Don't need another friends. I don't want. I only want be with you."

You pack some your stuffs. You walk to the back room. Five seconds, you pushing blue bicycle out.

"This is for you. I bought it in Brick Lane. Look, you can wear a skirt—there's no bar in between."

"Try it," you say.

I don't care the bicycle. I walk and hug you tightly. I put my head into your old leather jacket.

Finally, you leave. White van stays outside. You take bus and then you will take train. England is small country compare China, but still, I feel you leaving me somewhere far away, somewhere unknown, somewhere I don't involve at all.

I thought we together, we will spend time together and our lifes will never separated. I thought I don't needing go these double-bill screenings to kill raining nights. I thought I will not scared to live in this country alone, because now I having you, and you my family, my home. But I wrong. You doesn't promise anything solid.

So now I go out into the world on my alone . . . with that blue bicycle. And remind me to ride on left side at all times.

「要去幾天？我會很寂寞。」

「就三四天而已。」

我想不出話說。你走了我一個人在家怎麼辦？我連電箱在哪兒都不清楚，而且有人打電話來的話我要怎麼應對。

「說真的，妳應該到外面多走一走，交點朋友，」你說，「那妳就不用老是依賴著我。妳語言學校不是有幾個女同學嗎？」

「不用其他朋友。我不想要。我只要跟你在一起就好。」

你把幾樣東西收拾好，走到後面房間，五秒鐘後，牽了一輛藍色腳踏車出來。

「這個給妳。我在紅磚巷買的。瞧，妳穿著裙子也可以騎——中間沒有車槓。」

「試一下看看，」你說。

我才不管腳踏車。我走過去緊緊擁住你，一頭死命鑽進你破舊的皮夾克裡。

最後，你還是走了。白貨車停在屋外。你搭巴士，再轉火車。英國跟中國一比只是個小小的島國，不過，我覺得你前去的地方離我好遙遠，那個未知的地方我連半點邊都沾不上。

本來以為我們已經在一起，不論何時何地永不分離。我本來以為再也毋須跑到同場加映的戲院去謀殺漫漫雨夜。我以為不用害怕在這國家孤孤單單過日子，因為我現在已經有你，你是我的家人，我的庇護依靠。但我錯了。你根本沒有具體承諾任何東西。

此刻，我得一個人面對外面的世界……踩著那輛藍色腳踏車。記得提醒我隨時要注意靠左邊騎。

pub

n. a building with a bar licensed to sell alcoholic drinks.

Park my bicycle outside from Dirty Dick's, nearby Liverpool Street Station. Dirty Dick? That normal name for English pub? Anyway, it is first time I came into *building with a bar licensed to sell alcoholic drinks.* I hope you will take me into pub, but you went away somewhere unknown instead.

I sit in pub alone, trying feel involving in the conversation. It seem place of middle-aged-mans culture. I smell a kind of dying, although it still struggling. While I sitting here, many singles, desperately mans coming up saying, "Hello darling". But I not your darling. Where your darling? 7 o'clock in the evening, your darling must be cooking baked bean in orange sauce for you at home . . . Why not just go home spending time with your darling?

But mans here just keep buying pint of beer one after another. Some is drinking huge pint Lager, is like pee. Others buying glass of very dark liquid, looks like Chinese medicine. They watching football and shout together, without having food. In corner some tables with foods. Make me feel very hungry. See the food is biggest reason I am deciding go to pub. But everyone pretending food not there. Like is invisible or just for the good show. I take out my *Concise Chinese-English Dictionary,* start to study. I trying not thinking of the food too much.

【酒吧】

〈名詞〉領有酒吧執照可以供應酒精飲料的場所。

　　我將腳踏車停在「下流迪克」店外，靠近利物浦街地鐵站。下流迪克？英國酒吧取這種店名算正常？這是我頭一遭來到這種領有執照可以供應酒精飲料的場所。我原本希望你能帶我來酒吧，結果你扔下我自己不知跑到哪兒去了。

　　我在酒吧裡獨坐，試著想要融入周遭的對話。這裡似乎屬於中年男子的地盤。空氣中有股人生塵埃落定、然而猶想掙扎的氣味。獨坐的過程當中，陸續有幾個肆無忌憚的男客過來攀談，「哈囉達令。」我可不是你的達令。你的達令在哪兒？晚上七點鐘，你的達令一定在家為你準備橙醬燉豆子……幹嘛不回家陪你的達令共度良宵？

　　可是吧裡的男人光耗著，啤酒一品脫喝過一品脫。有的灌著巨杯的貯藏啤酒，看起來跟尿沒什麼兩樣。有的杯裡裝的顏色好深，彎像中國人熬煎的藥湯。他們眼睛猛盯電視播放的足球，彼此大呼小叫，光喝酒都不用配東西。角落邊有幾張桌子擺了食物在那兒，害我猛吞口水。這些食物是引誘我走進酒吧的罪魁禍首。但奇怪好像人人都假裝沒注意到有食物存在。莫非東西全都隱形或只是擺著好看的。我取出**簡明中英辭典**，開始專研，藉此分散食物的誘惑。

　　我坐的桌子前面，有五個大塊頭全部抽著雪茄；倫敦之霧

In front of my table, five big mans all smoking cigarettes; this is the *fog* of London. After some times, mans come to my lonely table and ask something.

The way I am talking in English make everybody laugh. They must like me.

A young man buy me beer. He is the only good looking one.

I say: "I feel so delightful drinking with you. Your face and words are very noble."

The man surprised and happy. He stops his drinking.

"Noble, eh?"

"Yes," I say, "because when you start talk then you look very proud. I like the confidence. I don't have."

The man holding his big pint listens careful but not sure about what I mean.

A while, he says: "Love, you only think my words are noble because I can speak English properly"—oh *properly*, that word again!—"but it is my mother tongue, you know. It's not that hard. But anyway, thank you for the compliment."

"You deserving it." I answer seriously.

But the man calls me "Love"! Love is cheap object in London.

My eyes looking towards delicious feast on side table. Everything ready waiting but no action.

I think the man gets hint from me, so he introduces me to English food system in pub calling *Buffet*, is meaning same word for "self service".

"Why two words for same food system?" I ask him.

He laughs: "Because one is the English word and one is the French word. The French word is more *noble*."

出現了。過了一陣子，他們擠到我這張孤單的桌子問東問西。

我講的英語引發眾人呵呵大笑。他們顯然喜歡我。

一個年輕人請我喝啤酒。他是眾人當中唯一長得順眼的。

我說：「我很高興能夠和你一起喝東西。你的長相和談吐都非常高貴。」

那男的驚訝又高興。他放下杯子。

「高貴，嘎？」

「沒錯，」我說，「因為你一開口講話顯得十分豪邁。我喜歡你很有自信。我就沒有辦法那樣。」

那男的手持大啤酒杯聽得很專注，但顯然不確定我意指為何。

停了半晌，他說：「親愛的，妳光聽我能講出妥當的英語就覺得高貴」——噢妥當，這個字又來了！——「但這本來就是我的母語，妳曉得。沒什麼好困難的。不過，還是多謝妳的恭維。」

「你太客氣了，」我正經回答。

那男的竟叫我「親愛的」！愛情在倫敦真不值錢。

我的眼神飄向角落邊的美味佳餚。萬事俱備，只欠開動。

我想那男的接收到我的暗示，為我介紹英國酒吧的用餐規矩，叫「**吧肥**」，其實就等於「自助式」的意思。

「同一套用餐規矩幹嘛還要分兩種說法？」我不解。

他笑了：「因為一個是英國話，一個是法國話。法國話比較**高貴**。」

全部老傢伙都笑開了。

吧肥。我把這高貴的生字記住。

盤子裡疊了些白白黏黏的玩意，樣子像豆腐，聞起來很

All old mans laughing.

Buffet. Now I remember this noble word.

There are some white sticky stuffs on the plate. It looks like Tofu, but smells bad.

"What is this?" I ask bar man.

"That is goat's cheese, darling. Would you like to try some?"

In China we not have cheese. We not like drinking milk, until last ten years maybe. I feel very surprise. I thought goat is too skinny make cheese.

"No. Thanks. What that? That Blue stuff?"

"It's another cheese. Stilton."

"Another stinking cheese with different names?" So many different cheeses! Like our Tofu system!

"Is this made by cow?" I ask.

"That's right, love," the barman laughs loudly. "Handmade by Communist cows."

"What?" I am confused.

"Sorry to tease you, sweetheart. What you"re trying to ask is "Is it made *from* cow's milk?" English is a bloody nightmare, isn't it?"

Back home I write list my new learnings for Mrs Margaret: *made by, made from.*

嗯。

「這什麼東西？」我問酒保。

「那是山羊的起司，達令。要不要嚐一點？」

我們中國沒有起司這種東西。我們不愛喝牛奶，或許最近十年才有點改變。我覺得很訝異，原本以為山羊瘦愣愣的做不了起司。

「不用了，謝謝。那個呢？那個藍色的？」

「那是另一種起司。斯提爾頓乳酪。」

「又一種難聞的起司，但名稱不同？」起司的種類真多！像我們的豆腐也是！

「這東西是母牛製造的嗎？」我問。

「答對了，親愛的，」酒保笑聲響亮。「共產主義母牛手工精製。」

「什麼？」我迷糊了。

「抱歉逗妳玩的，甜心。妳要問的是『這東西是用牛奶做的嗎？』英語真他媽的難搞，對不？」

回到家，我寫下新學到的英語範例，準備給瑪格麗特小姐過目：*made by*（由某某製造），*made from*（用某物製成）。

drifter

n. **1.** a person who moves aimlessly from place to place or job to job; **2.** a fishing boat equipped with drift nets.

Third day you are away. Feels like you are gone for a month. Before, I never be alone living in this house. Now, I realise this your house. Everything yours, and everything in this place *made by* you. Very little to do with me. But this place completely take over my life. I am a little alone teacup belonging to your cupboard.

I wandering in your house, silently, lonely, like cat without master.

On your dusty books shelf, I take out photo album. There is picture of you, arms around big tree, like lover. You naked in the picture. Very young and with a brown skin. You smiling at the person with camera. Must be your lover.

Another picture, you on boat. Is old black and white photo, so sea looks totally brown. You only wear shorts, and your muscles are strong. You smile to camera, holding the boat's paddle.

Who with you on that boat? Which sea it is?

Another old picture, you are with a man, a young man. You both are naked, standing on rock by the sea. The waves coming up on your legs. Man beside you is handsome. Who is person taking this photo? Man or woman? You must be three very intimate, very close friend, if you both naked in front the cam-

【漂泊者】

〈名詞〉**1.** 漫無目標，四處流浪或換工作的人；**2.** 配置漂網之漁船。

　　你不在的第三天。感覺好像你已經離開了個把月。之前，我從未單獨在這棟房子裡面生活。此刻，我明白這房子是屬於你的。每樣東西都是你的，而且樣樣出自你的巧手打造，跟我幾乎毫無關聯。不過這地方已經全面接管我的人生。我是單獨一只小茶杯，臣屬於你的櫥櫃。

　　我在你房子裡面遊走，無聲，孤單，猶如少了主人的貓咪。

　　從你蒙塵的書架上，我抽出相簿來看。

　　有你的照片，張臂環抱著大樹，像戀人。照片裡的你全身赤裸，非常年輕，膚色黝黑。你望著手持鏡頭的人笑得很燦爛。一定是你愛人。

　　另一張照片，你在小船上。老式的黑白照片，海的顏色極深。你只著短褲，肌肉結實。你看著鏡頭笑，手持船槳。

　　誰跟你在那艘船上？那是哪裡的海？

　　又一張老照片，你跟一個男的，一個年輕人。你們兩個全身脫光，站在海邊的岩塊上，浪頭湧過腿間。你旁邊的那個男的模樣很俊。誰幫你們拍的照片？男的還是女的。你們三個一定交情深厚，否則你們兩個怎會在鏡頭前全身扒光。

　　將相簿歸回原位，我很忌妒，我嚐到妒意帶來的痛苦。

era.

Putting back photo album, I am jealous, and I feel the pain from my jealousy.

I open one of your old boxes on top the books shelf. Some letters inside. I think they are love letters. Letters you wrote and being returned from somebody in a one big package. You said in one letter:

Of course I am committed to you, and always will be. But I can never see myself in a couple. Yes, you are my lover, but you are also my friend, and we will always feel sperical together. Friendship always endures longrt than romance.

Romance not to be found in my *Concise Chinese-English Dictionary.*

Some your old diaries in box too, from 1970s and 1980s. A long time ago. When I was really little. Gosh, this is the man really older than me twenty years. Twenty years of extra life. You from such a different world.

Something is very important about this word *drifter.* I meet it in your letters, or the letters somebody wrote to you, or in diary with broken pages; I meet it everywhere in your long-ago past, but I never understand what it mean.

I have to learning this word first, then to learning something about you.

Open your old *Roget's* Thesaurus on your shelf (*Thesaurus*! More strange word! In Chinese, we not having a second word to replace "dictionary"!) On the cover: *first published 1852.* Gosh! 1852. That an old dictionary. In China there is very old

將你擱在書架頂層的舊盒子打開。裡面有信。我想一定是情書。你跟某人魚雁往返的信札厚厚一疊。其中一封你寫說：

　　我對你當然是認真的，而且我會認真到底。不過我沒辦法想像自己和他人結合。是的，你是我的愛人，不過你也是我的摯友，我們兩個的關係感受永遠特別。友誼總是比羅曼史更經得起時間考驗。

　　我的**簡明中英辭典**找不到**羅曼史**。

　　盒子裡還有幾本你的舊日記，從一九七〇年代到八〇年代。真是年代久遠。那時候我真的還很小。這個男人居然真的比我大了二十歲，整整多出二十年的人生。你的世界離我何其遙遠。

　　drifter 這個字顯然非常非常重要。你那些信裡出現這個字，別人給你的信裡寫到這個字，日記的殘頁裡也有這個字；你久遠的光陰中這個字無所不在，但我一直沒能看懂它究竟是什麼意思。

　　我必須先把這個字學會，接下來才能進一步瞭解你。

　　翻開你書架上的舊版《羅傑索引典》（**索引典**！多怪的字！在中國，我們哪會想出別的字眼來取代「辭典」！）封面上寫著：**第一版 1852**。一八五二！好老的辭典。中國也有一七〇〇年間康熙時代非常古老的辭典，裡面我認識的字不會超過一半。

　　查了《索引典》只有讓我更迷糊。drifter 像捕魚的小船？drifter 乘坐漁船去捕魚？還是說漁船航行海面的情形就好比drifter 的處境。

Character Dictionary from 1700s Kang Xi era but I only know not half of the characters.

Thesaurus only make me more confusing. Drifter like fishing boat? Drifter goes fishing on a fishing boat? Or situation of a fishing boat swing in the sea is like situation of drifter?

I think of that picture you are on the boat wearing the shorts, holding the paddle, smiling the camera. Behind you is brown colour sea. You a drifter, I believe.

In your diary, you describing your father a drifter. He is bus driver, and he doesn't like stay at home. Don't know why. One day he leave you and mother and sisters and never came back. You say you learned your father travels anywhere hot and anywhere can have sex. Gosh, I can't believe what I read. Your mother decide buy piece of farm in Cornwall. Farm has a name called Lower End Farm. She live with sheep and goats and cows. Without any mans around.

You grow up, feeling cold from your family. You feel womans so dull and womans not interesting. You wanting something exciting and something desirable. So you decide leave find a place far away from that cold farm, a place cannot reach your mother and your tough sisters. You love the sea and you want see the world.

When nineteen you go to long voyage with man from your hometown. From your diary, I think he called John. Boat belonging to John's. You young and you write diary because you think that is your historic time in life.

The first page of your sailing diary:

February 6th, 1978

我想像那個畫面，你在船上穿條短褲，手持船槳，對著鏡頭微笑。你身後是深色的海洋。你是個漂泊男兒，我想一定是。

　　日記裡，你描述你父親是漂泊者。他當公車司機，不喜歡待在家裡。原因天曉得。有一天他拋下你和母親和姊妹們，頭也不回。你說你後來得知你父親四海為家，哪裡氣候炎熱，哪裡上床容易就往哪裡窩。我不敢相信眼前讀到的情節。你母親決定在康瓦耳郡買下一塊農地。那塊地有個名字，叫低尾農場。她終日與綿羊、山羊和母牛為伴。周遭見不到一個男人。

　　你長大成人，跟家裡關係冷淡。你覺得女人又蠢又無聊。你想要體驗刺激好玩的東西。你決定找個地方遠離那塊冰冷的農場，遠離你母親，遠離難纏的姊姊妹妹。你愛的是汪洋大海，你想多多見識這個世界。

　　十九歲的時候，你和同鄉一個男的結伴出海遠航。根據你的日記，我想他的名字叫約翰。那艘船是約翰的。年輕的你自覺來到人生的歷史關卡，於是提筆寫下日記。

　　你航海日記的第一頁：

1978，2月6日
我們全都渴望快點出航，不過眼前的準備工作已經把我們搞得七葷八素。我想這趟航行一定很刺激，大伙兒一定可以學到許多東西。

　　在那天的結尾，簿頁底下，你用大寫字母寫了這麼一行：

「浪漫的愛爾蘭已經死去」──W.B. 葉慈

We are all lookinf forward to sailing but at the moment we" er blindea by
the work and preparation needed before we can set out. I think it's going to
be a realy exciting trip during which much will be learnt by everyone.

At the end of that day, underneath the page, you wrote a line
in capital:

"ROMANTIC IRELAND'S DEAD AND GONE" − −W.B. YEATS

Another page, words is soaked by water. Difficult read:

Sunday IIth February
We have eventually left amidst cheers from our friends on the quayside. . .
We were all pleased to get away from what was beginning to become a
stale atmosphere where no one could do anything without consulting
someone else. At first pure excitement, but later when the open sea was
below us, I started feeling sick. Our watch began

The writing start becoming very messy and un-readable.

I open last page on diary and find out you spend nine
months on boat all together. From February 1978 to 4
November 1978. How a person can do for so long without his
feet stand on soil? I imagine you must be suffered from storms.
Sometimes you must be burning by sun. Were you ill on boat
in all nine months? Did you wish you be anywhere but not on
boat?

You saying in your journey sometimes you feel life exciting
because you are on enormous sea, sailing and sailing for ever,
but sometime you really bored in every single minute because
you are always on boundless sea, sailing and sailing for ever. I

翻過另一頁，字跡泡過水，辨讀不易：

2月11日，禮拜天
我們最後終於在擠滿碼頭的友人歡呼聲中出發……
大家都很高興能夠脫離已經開始沉悶的氣氛，沒經過他人
指點的話，什麼事也做不了。起初我感到無比的興奮，但
後來無邊的大海在我們底下搖晃，我開始反胃。我們開始
值班

　　底下的字跡凌亂，沒辦法讀。
　　我翻到日記最後一頁，發現你總共在船上待了九個月。從
一九七八年二月到一九七八年十一月四號。一個人怎麼有辦法
兩腳脫離土地如此之久？我可以想像你一定飽受風暴之苦。有
時你免不了烈日灼身。你整整九個月都在暈船嗎？你可曾但願
自己選擇了那艘船以外的任何地方？
　　你說船途中有時你感到生命激昂，因為身處無垠的大海，
航行，無止境的航行，但有時你每一分鐘都厭煩難耐，因為無
邊的大海永遠包圍著你，航行，無止境的航行。我嘗試想像分
分秒秒大海就在眼前，但我不能。我甚至連海邊都沒摸近，只
有從飛機上眺望過。

1978，6月7日
早餐：金槍魚。晚餐：金槍魚，我儘量設法多吃綠色蔬
菜，不過電冰箱被看守得很緊（昨天有顆番茄不見了）。
巴拿馬，哥斯大黎加，尼加拉瓜，薩爾瓦多，瓜地馬拉。
我們航行經過這些中美洲國家，有幾個我們根本連影子都

try imagine to watch sea every single minute but can't. I never even been close sea. Only watched from plane.

7th June, 1978
Breakfast: tuna. Supper: tuna, I try to eat as much green veg as I can, but the fridge is well guardea (a tomato went missing yesterday)
Panama, Costa Rica, Nicaragua, El Salvador, Guatemala. These are the central American countries which we have passed, although some we have not seen becaues the boat has been too far out to sea.

Next page, you arrive San Diego and San Francisco.

You not really write about love. Was love not in your nine-teen-year-old life? Is really only blue sea in your brown eyes at that time? What about your dreams?

After that long voyage, you longing for something you can do with your hands. Twenty years old, you go art school. You studying sculptures there by making your hands dirty. A photo between the pages. I guess was that the sculpture you made. Enormous naked man, lying down and taking over whole floor of big studio. A giant, but naked giant. That the main subject of your sculptures. Then you writing you have sex with several boys in that art school.

First I think I reading wrong and you mean girls not boys, but then I look again. Matt, Dan, Peter. These are boys names.

"*I don't feel any real love in my heart,*" you write.

When you move London, you go squat in old houses and meet mans in street every night. You talk to the strangers in the park and you go to home together. You say you feel warm by

看不到，因為船實在離岸邊太遠了。

下一頁，你們抵達聖地牙哥和舊金山。

你一直沒寫到跟愛情相關的東西。難道愛情在你十九歲的生命當中並不存在？那時候你棕色的眼珠裡真的只有藍色汪洋？你夜裡都夢見些什麼？

經過那次長途遠航，你渴望找到一些雙手能夠掌握的東西。二十歲，你進了藝術學校。你主修雕塑，兩手隨時弄得髒兮兮。簿頁中夾了張照片。我猜是你那時候完成的雕塑作品。巨大的裸男，躺在地上占據了工作室的全部面積。巨人，赤條條的巨人。那是你雕塑創作的主題。然後你寫到跟那間藝術學校的幾個男孩子上床。

起初我以為自己眼花，你指的是女孩子，不是男孩，但我又看了一次。麥特，丹，彼得。這是那幾個男孩的名字。

「我心中沒有感受到任何真愛，」你寫道。

後來你搬到倫敦，找了間老房子蹲，每天夜裡上街找男人。你在公園向陌生人搭訕，然後一起回家。你說撫摸別的身體，找男人上床給你帶來溫暖。你認為自己是同性戀，你說那叫**同志**。可是第二天你連面孔和名字都沒辦法記住。

接著又一本日記。時間是幾年之後。你對獵逐男孩的生涯感到空虛，你搖身成為社會運動者，一個示威抗議人士。你投入運動對抗資本主義，對抗麥當勞的擴張，你跑到印度阻撓探礦公司的投資案。你和其他年輕的示威團體跑遍各地，新德里，加爾各答，墨西哥，洛杉磯……永遠漂泊不定。不過我想，或許你根本不清楚自己的人生目標為何。你不曉得自己為

touching other's body, by having sex with mans. You think you a homosexual, you call it *Gay*. But you even can't remember faces and names the second day.

Then there is another diary. Is some years later. You feel empty that kind of hunting-boy-life, so you become campaigner, a demon-strator. You for campaign against the capitalism, against the McDonald developing, and you go India stopping mining companies doing developmenting there. You go with young demon-strater group to everywhere, Delhi, Calcutta, Mexico, Los Angeles . . . Always drifting around. But I thinking maybe you not know what want to do in your life. Or why you travel so much? In those squatter's days, the sculpture you made are all destroyed. Nothing left. You don't have a woman lover being with you (or maybe you never want to?), and you don't have a man lover being with you either. Only thing you had, you wrote, is "*sex and seduction*".

You wrote about days you work as youth worker. I didn't understand what this job about. You wrote about holiday trips with children. There photos between pages: you with teenagers laughing in front of camera. You love those teenage boys. You work that for ten years. But how come you stop a job which you really like? I don't understand. Maybe because your *gay* life? Maybe kind of scandal as homosexual teacher. I never know . . . Anyway you left your job, and what happening next?

My eyes becoming sore. I am tired of reading, all these words, my brain is just too full by your past. Everywhere is you, and you are everywhere, every sentence, every page.

I put back all these old diaries, old letters. My hand covered

什麼老是來來去去？那段時間裡，你創作的雕塑全部毀掉了，什麼也沒留下。沒有女性愛侶陪在你身邊（或許你從來不想？），同樣的，也沒有男性愛侶陪在你身邊。唯一擁有的，你寫道，就是「**性和誘惑**」。

你寫下關於擔任青少年社工的日子。我不懂這工作的內容為何。你寫到假日帶孩子出遊。簿頁裡有幾張照片：你和幾個少年在鏡頭前笑得開懷。你愛那些少年郎。這工作你幹了十年。後來你怎會離開如此喜愛的工作？我不明白。難道是因為你的同志生活？或許身為同性戀教師引發了醜聞。我不得而知……反正你離開了這份工作，接下來發生的又是什麼？

我的眼睛好累。我讀不下去了，全部這些字句，我的腦袋裝載太多你的塵封往事。這裡，那裡，到處是你，每一句，每一頁。

我把全部這些舊日記和舊信放了回去。我的手沾滿塵埃。我在冰涼的自來水下將手洗過。我想你自己不知已經多久沒有讀過這些東西。搞不好我是二十年來第一個打開這些盒子的人。

夜好漫長。外頭靜悄悄。偶爾有汽車駛過。我坐在你的椅子上，感覺有些沉重，呼吸有點困難。

我單獨睡在你床上，搬進來之後我們每晚一起睡在這裡。其實這張床僅供一人容身。我再度意識到這件事。我醒著。我想為你畫一張圖，一張標示出你人生往事的地圖。然而太困難了。我看著屋外的晨光穿透庭院，穿透無花果樹。這是你離家的第四天，你將於今天歸來。你說抵達的時間是早上，大約十點半左右。

by dust. I wash my hand, under cold tap water. I thinking probably you never read these things for long time. Maybe I am first person opening these boxes in last twenty years.

Night is long. Quiet outside. Cars passing sometimes. I sit on your chair. I feel bit heavy. I feel bit difficult to breathe.

I sleep on your bed alone, which we slept every night together since I move in. Actually is single bed supposed be for one person. I realise this again. I am awake. I trying draw map of you, map of your past. But is difficult. I see the morning lights outside through the garden, through fruit tree without flowers. Is fourth day you away and is the day you will be return. You said you be here in the morning, about half past ten.

Nine o'clock now. I get up, and I brush my teeth, and I make some tea. I put my cold hand on teapot to get warm. I wait for you to return. But now I scared about you to return. You will drift with your Chinese woman, in boat on the ocean. No seashore in distance. She floating away and passing in your life like piece of wood on the sea.

One hour going by, and waiting is painful. I try study *singular* and plural from textbook which Mrs Margaret give to us.

child—children	ox—oxen
mouse—mice	fairy—fairies
tooth—teeth	thief—thieves
goose—geese	foot—feet
wolf—wolves	larva—larvae

I don't like plural, because they not stable. I don't like nouns too, as they change all the time like verbs. I like only

已經九點鐘了。我起身，刷了牙，沖好茶。我把僵冷的手按在茶壺上取暖，等著你回來。但這一刻我竟害怕你的歸來。你將帶著你的中國女人漂泊，乘風破浪航行。海岸遙不可及。她穿越你的生命漂流而去，如汪洋中的一截浮木。

一個小時過去了，等待令人痛苦難挨。我拿起瑪格麗特小姐交待的課本學習名詞的單數形和複數形。

child—children（兒童）　　ox—oxen（牛）

mouse—mice（老鼠）　　fairy—fairies（仙女）

tooth—teeth（牙齒）　　thief—thieves（賊）

goose—geese（鵝）　　foot—feet（腳）

wolf—wolves（狼）　　larva—larvae（幼蟲）

我不喜歡複數，它們都不固定。我也不喜歡名詞，它們像動詞一樣老是變來變去。我只喜歡形容詞和副詞。它們固定不變。可以的話，我真想只說形容詞和副詞就好。

十一點過一刻，你開門隨一道寒風進來。你放下滿是風塵的行囊然後親我，抱住我。看到我你很開心。我問起你的朋友如何，你說一切安好。你微笑，興奮起來，想要做愛。好像一切如常，什麼都沒發生。你說你想念我。可我怎能為一個來去如此輕易的人牽腸掛肚？

「這幾天過得還好嗎？」你問。

「不好。」

「怎麼了？妳沒有去外面認識一些朋友？」

「沒有。我不想認識什麼朋友。」

「那妳都做些什麼？」

adjectives, and adverbs. They don't change. If I can, I will only speak adjectives and adverbs.

A quarter past eleven, you come back with a cold wind through door. You put down dusty bag on floor then you kiss me, you hug me. You are pleased to see me. I ask how is your friend, you say everything is fine. You smile and you are excited and you want make love. Like nothing happened. You say you miss me. But how I can miss someone easy coming easy going?

"Did you have a nice time?" you ask.

"No."

"Why not? Did you go out to see people and make friends?"

"No. I don't want make friends."

"So what did you do?"

What to say? I feel the sea inside me too big, too never-ending to speak.

該怎麼啓齒？我感覺內心的汪洋太過廣闊無邊，吞沒了我的言語。

bisexual

adj. sexually attracted to both men and women.

I am a woman and you are a bisexual. Both love beautiful mans so much. But beautiful young mans is always living in our imagination. He is daily life's fantasy. The reality about him so fragile that is easy to be broken, like delicate Chinese vase.

You have so many books to do with naked mans. On your shelf: *The Nude Male, Gay Writings From India, The Penguin Book Of International Gay Writing, Fully Exposed—the Male Nude in Photography* . . . How I know you not going to go with the beautiful gay man again and ruin my life? How I trust you stay with me? Maybe I ruin rest of my life to be with you.

Is there lots of free love in gay's world because they not produce children? No children then no serious weight. They not need considering responsibilities of next generation, and they not need worry about the pregnancy/abortion. But how that work if far-east foreign woman fall in love with West gay man?

When we see beautiful mans in street, or when we talk to beautiful mans in pub, we have very different view. You always wondering how he will look like when naked, just like you look at good painting carefully with magnifying glass. But my first question to that man more practical: will he possible become my husband? If so, will he having stable incomes and be able buy house for his family?

【雙性戀】

〈形容詞〉同時對女人和男人產生性慾的。

　　我是女人而你是雙性戀。我們兩個都愛標緻的男人。標緻的年輕男子總是存在我們的想像裡。他是日常生活幻想的一部分。一碰觸到現實，他變得如此脆弱，像纖細的中國花瓶一碰就碎。

　　你有好多關於裸男的書籍，擺在書架上：《男性裸體》，《印度同志書寫》，《企鵝版國際同志書寫》，《完全暴露：男性裸體照片》……我怎麼曉得你不會再去勾搭漂亮的男同志，害我毀掉人生？我怎能相信你會跟我在一起？搞不好跟你這樣走下去我的人生只會完蛋而已。

　　同志的世界，愛慾如此自由是否由於他們無須生兒育女？沒有小孩就沒有沉重的包袱。他們不用去考慮教養下一代的責任問題，也沒有懷孕／墮胎的麻煩需要煩惱。一個遠東的外國女子愛上一個西方男同志，這種事行得通嗎？

　　看見街頭的標緻男人，或者在酒吧和美男子談天，我們兩個人的眼光角度截然不同。你總是好奇想看他剝光的樣子，就像你拿放大鏡審視精美的畫作。而我首要的考量就實際多了：他有可能成為我的丈夫嗎？如果是的話，他的收入是否穩定，是否有能力購屋安頓家人？

chinese cabbage + english slug

cabbage *n.* a vegetable with a large head of green leaves. slug *n.* **1.** a land snail with no shell; **2.** a bullet; **3.** a mouthful of an alcoholic drink.

Hardly days is absolutely sunny, sunny until sun falling to the west. Sky in England always look suspicious, untrustful, like today's. You see me sad but don't understand why.

Standing in the garden, you ask me: "Do you want to have your own little plants in this garden? I think it should be a woman's garden as well."

"Yes. I want. I want plant Chinese cabbages, some water lily, some plum tree, and maybe some bamboos, and maybe some Chinese chives as well. . . ."

I immediately image picture of tradition Chinese garden.

"No, honey, it's too small for so many Chinese plants."

Then, Sunday, we went to Columbia Road Flower Market. It my favourite market. We brought the small little sprouts of Chinese cabbage at home. Eight little sprouts all together.

We plant all these little things. Digging the soil, and putting every single sprout into the hole. You are fast than me. So you finished planting five, and I only putting third one in the little hole.

We watering Chinese cabbage sprouts every morning, loyal and faithful, like every morning we never forgetting brushing our teeth. Seeing tiny sprouts come out, my heart feel happy. Is our love. We plant it.

【中國甘藍菜＋英國蛞蝓】

甘藍菜〈名詞〉一種有大顆結球的綠葉蔬菜。蛞蝓〈名詞〉**1.** 一種無殼陸生蝸牛；**2.** 子彈；**3.** 喝一大口酒精飲料。

幾乎難得遇上整天放晴，陽光普照直到日落西斜。英國的天空永遠令人猜疑，無法信賴，像今天就是。你看我不開心但不知道為了什麼。

站在院子裡，你問我：「妳自己想不想在院子裡種點東西？我在想這庭院應當也有女人的空間。」

「好啊，我想種。我想種中國甘藍菜，種荷花，幾株梅樹，或者是竹子，或者像中國青蔥也可以……」

我心裡即刻浮現一幅中國老式庭院的畫面。

「不好吧，親愛的，這地方容不下那麼多中國植物。」

於是，星期天，我們前往哥倫比亞路花卉市場。這是我最喜歡的市場。我們帶著中國甘藍的小顆球芽回家。一共有八顆小小的球芽。

我們把這些小東西全種下去。先挖好土，一顆一顆放進洞裡。你的手腳比我快。有五顆是你種的，我只放了三顆在小洞裡。

每日清早我們幫中國甘藍小球芽澆水，既忠心又可靠，就像每天早上我們不會忘記刷牙一般。看著小球芽冒出頭來，我滿心的喜悅。這是我們的愛。我們兩個一起種的。

你說：

You say:

"Growing a vegetable and seeing it grow is more interesting than anything else. It's magic. Don't you agree?"

Yes. Is interesting. But in China, is just for peasant. Every person can do this, nothing special for growing food. Why so different here?

Then we see some little leafs come out but are bitten by the slug.

"It's dangerous that the slugs keep eating the small sprouts. They can die really easily," you tell me.

Carrying with torch, every night, around 11 o"clock, you sneek into garden and check the slug. They are always several slug hidden behind the young leafs. Enjoying the delicious meal under the moonlight. You taking them out from the leafs, one by one. You putting these slug together in one glass bottle. Soon glass bottle becomes a slug-zoo.

"What your favourite words? Give me ten," I say when we are sitting in garden. I want learn most beautiful English words because you are beautiful. I even not care whether if useful.

A piece of blank paper, a pen.

You writing it down, one by one.

"*Sea, breath, sun, body, seeds, bumble bee, insects.*" You stop: "How many are there now?"

"Seven," I say.

"Hm . . . *blood* . . ." you continue.

"Why you like blood?"

"I don't know. I feel blood is beautiful."

"Really? But blood violence, and pain."

「把青菜種下去看它生長比其他任何事都有意思多了。它有魔力。妳說對不對？」

沒錯。好有意思。可是在中國，只有農夫會這麼想。種菜這誰都會，沒什麼特別的。怎麼這裡的感受就是不一樣？

然後我們看見小嫩葉抽長出來，馬上被蛞蝓吃掉了。

「不妙，蛞蝓一直在吃小球芽，沒兩下它們就會死光光，」你告訴我。

帶著手電筒，每天晚上，十一點左右，你潛進院子察看蛞蝓。每次總有幾隻躲在嫩葉後面。月光下享用著佳餚。一隻接一隻，你把它們全捉起來，統統放進一只玻璃瓶中。玻璃瓶馬上淪為蛞蝓動物園。

「你最喜歡的字有哪些？講十個來聽，」我們院子裡坐的時候我說。我想學會最美麗的英國字彙，因為你是如此美麗。我不在乎這些字能否派上用場。

一張白紙，一枝筆。

你一個字一個字寫下來。

「海，呼吸，太陽，身體，種子，大黃蜂，昆蟲。」你筆停住：「現在幾個了？」

「七個，」我說。

「唔……血……」你繼續。

「你怎麼會喜歡血？」

「我不知道。我覺得血很美。」

「真的？可是血好暴力，而且會痛。」

「不。不盡然。血賜給你生命，使你強壯。」你的語氣很認真。

"No. Not always. Blood gives you life. It makes you strong." You speaking with surely voice.

You see things from such different perspective from me. I wonder if we change perspective one day.

"And why *breath*, then?"

"Because that's where everything is from and how everything starts."

You are right.

"So, what else? Last favourite word?" I say.

"*Suddenly.*"

"*Suddenly*! Why you like *suddenly*? Suddenly not even noun." You a strange brain, I think.

"Well, I just like it," you say. "So what are your favorite ten words?"

I write down one by one:

"*Fear, belief, heart, root, challenge, fight, peace, misery, future, solitude. . . .*"

"Why *solitude*?"

"Because a song from Louis Armstrong calling 'Solitude'. It is so beautiful." I hear song in my ear now.

"Where did you hear that song?" you ask.

"On your shelfs. A CD, from Louis Armstrong."

"Really? I didn't even know I had that CD." You frown.

"Yes, is covering the dust, and look very old."

"So, you''ve been through all my CDs?"

"Of course," I say. "I read your letters and diaries as well."

"What?"

"And looked your photo."

"What? You''ve looked through all my stuff?"You seeming

你看東西的觀點跟我截然不同。我好奇是否有天我們會互換觀點。

「那為什麼會寫呼吸？」

「因為萬物從呼吸來，也從呼吸開始。」

你說的對。

「那，還有什麼？最後一個字？」我說。

「突然。」

「突然！怎麼會喜歡突然？突然根本不是名詞。」你腦袋少根筋，我想。

「嗯，我就是喜歡，」你說。「那妳呢，你喜歡哪十個字？」

我依次寫下來：

「害怕，信念，心，根，挑戰，奮戰，和平，苦難，未來，孤獨……」

「為什麼是孤獨？」

「因為路易‧阿姆斯壯有首歌就叫〈孤獨〉。美得不得了。」我現在耳中就能聽見這首歌。

「妳在哪裡聽到這首歌？」你問。

「你的書架上。一塊CD，路易‧阿姆斯壯的。」

「真的？我都不曉得自己有這塊CD。」你皺起眉頭。

「有啊，上面灰塵很厚，看起來好舊了。」

「所以我全部的CD妳已經巡過一遍？」

「當然，」我說。「你的信和日記我也讀了。」

「什麼？」

「我還看到你的照片。」

「什麼？妳把我全部的東西都看了？」你似乎像突然間聽

like suddenly hear the alien from Mars attack the Earth.

"Not all. Parts that diary are make me sad. I can't sleep at night," I say.

到來自火星的異形攻打地球。

　　「沒有全部。那些日記有的部分讓我好難過，害我晚上睡不著，」我說。

privacy

n. **1.** the state of being alone or undisturbed; **2.** freedom from interference or public attention.

"You"ve invaded my privacy! You can't do that!" First time, you shout to me, like a lion.

"What privacy? But we living together! No privacy if we are lovers!"

"Of course there is! Everybody has privacy!"

But why people need privacy? Why privacy is important? In China, every family live together, grandparents, parents, daughter, son, and their relatives too. Eat together and share everything, talk about everything. Privacy make people lonely. Privacy make family fallen apart.

When I arguing about privacy, you just listen and not say anything. I know you disagree me, and you not want live inside of my life, because you a "private" person. A private person doesn't share life.

"When I read your past, when I read those letters you wrote, I think you are *drifter*."

"What do you mean by that?"

"You know what is drifter, do you? You come and leave, you not care about future."

"To me, to live life is to live in the present."

"OK, live in present, and which direction you leading then?"

【隱私】

〈名詞〉**1.** 獨處或不受打擾的狀態；**2.** 免受干預或公共注目的自由。

「妳侵犯了我的隱私！妳不可以這樣！」第一次，你對我吼叫，像頭猛獅。

「什麼隱私？可是我們住在一起！我們是愛人不該有隱私！」

「當然要有！每個人都需要隱私！」

可是人要隱私做什麼？隱私有什麼重要？我們中國，每個人都是全家住在一起，爺爺姥姥，爸爸媽媽，女兒，兒子，加上其他親戚。大家一起吃一起用，沒有事不能談的。隱私會讓人孤單，搞得全家分裂不和。

我對隱私發表意見的時候，你只是聽，不發一語。我明白你不同意，而且你不打算參與我的生命經驗，因為你是個「孤僻」的人。孤僻的人不願分享人生。

「讀了你的往事，讀了你寫的那些信之後，我知道你是個**漂泊者**。」

「妳說這句話什麼意思？」

「漂泊者你知道的，對不對？你來來去去，你不在乎未來。」

「對我而言，生命就是活在當下。」

「好，活在當下，接下來你要往哪個方向走？」

"What are you talking about?"

"I mean, you don't have plan for tomorrow, for next year?"

"Well, we are talking about different things. I don't think you understand what I am saying. To me the future is about moving on, to some new place. I don't know where I am going. It's like I am riding a horse through the desert, and the horse just carries me somewhere, maybe with an oasis, but I don't know."

Suddenly the air being frozen. Feeling cold. I not know what to say anymore. You older than me twenty years. You must understand life better than me?

You look at me and you say: "It's like the way you came into my life. I feel as if I am not naked anymore."

I feel as if I am not naked anymore. That a beautiful sentence.

I listen, I wait. I feel it something you not finish in your sentence, but you not want say it.

So I help you: "Ok, I come into your life, but you not know if you wanting carry on this with me all the times. You will want to break it and see what can make you move on. . . ."

"We will see." You stop me, and take me into your arms.

"It's important to be able to live with uncertainty."

「妳是在講什麼？」

「我是說，你沒有計畫想到明天，明年的事？」

「嗯，我們兩個講的東西不一樣。我想妳不了解我說的意思。對我而言，未來就是繼續前進，走到新的地方去。我不知道那個地方會是哪裡。這情形好比我騎著馬橫越沙漠，馬會載我到某處，或許有綠洲的地方，但我沒辦法事先預料。」

突然間空氣凝結。感覺冰冷。我不知道還能開口講什麼。你比我大上二十歲，應該比我了解人生何物。

你看著我開口說道：「現在妳像是走進了我的生命，我感覺自己似乎再也不是全身赤裸。」

我感覺自己似乎再也不是全身赤裸。那是個美麗的句子。

我聆聽，等待著。我感覺你話裡還有東西沒有講完，但你不願再說。

所以我幫你講完：「好，我現在走進你的生命，但你沒把握自己是否願意一直這樣跟我走下去。你會想要打破它，看有什麼東西可以讓你繼續往前……」

「到時候再說吧。」你攔住我的話，將我擁入懷中。

「重點是要能夠和悠悠無定的人生共處。」

intimate

adj. **1.** having a close personal relationship; **2.** personal or private; **3.** (of knowledge) extensive and detailed; **4.** (foll by with) euphemistic having a sexual relationship (with); **5.** having a friendly quiet atmosphere.
n. close friend.

How can *intimate* live with privacy?

We have lived together after first week we met. You said you never lived so closely with another person before. You always avoided intimate with the other person. You said to have your friends more important than your lovers. That's so different with my Chinese love—family means everything.

Maybe people here have problems being intimate with each other. People keep distance because they want independence, so lovers don't live with together, instead they only see each other at weekend or sleep together twice a week. A family doesn't live with together therefore the intimate inside of a family disappeared. Maybe that why Westerners much more separated, lonely, and have more Old People's House. Maybe also why newspapers always report cases of peterfiles and perverts.

We are in your old white van. You want to show me somewhere special called the Burnham Beach.

"Is it the British ocean?" I ask, excited to visit sea for first time. You are laughing.

"B-e-e-c-h, not b-e-a-c-h. In English, a beech is a type of tree, not an ocean. I''ll take you to the sea another time."

How I ever understand your complicated language—not

【親密】

〈形容詞〉**1.** 擁有親密的人際關係；**2.** 個人的，私人的；**3.**（和知識相關）精通的，詳細的；**4.**（+with）有性關係的委婉用語；**5.** 怡人、融洽的氣氛。〈名詞〉密友，至交。

　　兩個人親密生活如何保有隱私。

　　我們認識一個禮拜之後便住在一起。你說之前從未和別人如此親密生活。你說，當你的朋友比當愛人重要。那和我的中國式愛情觀念天差地遠──家庭代表了一切。

　　或許西方人彼此親密有困難。大家儘量保持距離，免得失去獨立，所以相愛的人也不住在一起，他們選擇只在週末的時候相聚，或者一個禮拜睡覺兩次。家人分開住的結果導致家庭親密感喪失。或許正因如此，西方人較常見到隔閡，孤單，老人院一堆。或許，這也是報紙不時出現「彼得檔案」（成年男子沉迷於手淫給女人觀看）和性變態報導的原因。

　　我們在你的白色老貨車裡。你想帶我去一個特別的地方，柏翰海灘。

　　「是英國的海嗎？」我問，想到第一次造訪大海就興奮。你咧開嘴笑。

　　「B-e-e-c-h，不是 b-e-a-c-h。在英國，beech 是一種樹，不是海。我下次再帶妳去海邊。」

　　我哪有辦法分辨你們複雜的語言──那不像我們中國光是腔調變化而已。我們有四種聲調，聲調不同字就不同。比如：

even any change in accent like we have in Chinese. We have four intonations, so every tone means different word. Like:

mi in first tone means to close eyes.

mí in second tone means to fancy something.

mǐ in third tone means rice.

mì in fourth tone means honey.

Anyway, on the highway of M40, I have my dictionaries to check out what exactly that beach/beech is. Collins tells me that is a European tree, but when I look my little Concise dictionary, says it is a tree called "Shan Mao Ju", which grows everywhere in China. We cut those trees for lighting fires in kitchen. We used to carry baskets and collect their nutty seeds when we were little.

The woods are dark, lush, and wet. Trees are huge, tall, and solid.

The whole woods are growing silently and secretly. The whole woods are decay. On way to woods it was a beautiful day, but inside woods the climate is totally different. Is chilly and rainy. Rain drops from those hundred-year-old greyish branches and leafs, and the rain fills the ponds stuffed by weeds.

In the muddy and greeny pond, lotus gently floats, and the dragonfly dashes. You hold me and caress me. We are in each other's arm. You lift my denim skirt, and you touch my garden. My garden is warm and moist. You stroke my hip, and I unzip your jean. We make love. We make love. We make love under the silent beech tree. So quiet, so quiet. We can hear children on the football field in the distance are yelling. Only the rain drops, fall on our hair, our skin. Rain drops on the cowslip flower by our feet, without disturbing us.

ㄇㄧ 一聲代表眯。

ㄇㄧˊ 二聲代表迷。

ㄇㄧˇ 三聲代表米。

ㄇㄧˋ 四聲代表蜜。

　　車子在M40公路上跑，我拿出辭典想把beach/beech查個究竟。柯林斯跟我說那是一種歐洲樹木，可是看我的小本簡明辭典，說是一種樹叫「山毛櫸」，中國到處可見。這種樹我們砍來當廚房材薪燒。我們拿它來挑籮筐，小時候我們還採過山毛櫸結的堅果。

　　森林黝暗，茂密，潮溼。林木巨大，參天，堅實。

　　整片森林默默地暗自生長。整片森林腐朽。到森林的路上天氣極美，進了林子氣候不變。又溼又冷。雨珠從百年的灰色枝幹和葉面墜落，雨水填滿雜草叢生的小水塘。

　　渾濁青綠的水塘裡，蓮花自在漂浮，蜻蜓俯衝。你抓住我，愛撫我。我們緊緊相擁。你撩起我的牛仔裙，撫摸我的花園。花園溫暖，溼潤。你揉捏我的臀股，我扯下你牛仔褲的拉鍊。我們做愛。我們做愛。我們在沉默的山毛櫸樹下做愛。如此靜。如此靜。我們可以聽見遠處足球場上小孩子又吼又叫。只有雨水滴落，落在我們的頭髮，我們的肌膚。雨水滴落在我們腳邊的櫻草花上，沒有干擾到我們兩個。

free world

esp. US hist. non-Communist countries.

You say:

"I feel incredibly lucky to be with you. We"re going to have loads of exciting adventures together. Our first big adventure will be in west Wales. I"ll show you the sea. I"ll teach you to swim because it is shameful that a peasant girl cannot swim. I"ll show you the dolphins in the sea, and the seals with their babies. I want you to experience the beauty of the peace and quiet in a Welsh cottage. I think you will love it there."

You also say:

"Then I want to take you to Spain and France. I know that you"ll love them. But we"ll have to wait for a while. We need to earn some money. I"ll have to get more work doing deliveries in the van to boring rich people. Can you put up with me being so boring—or do you think you"ll get fed up with me after a while?"

Later you say:

"I feel so good about the love that you and I have with each other because it happened so quickly and spontaneously, like a forest fire."

And you say:

"I just love the way you are."

Everything good so far, but from one thing—you don't

【自由世界】

（美國特定歷史用語）非共產國家。

你說：

「我覺得能夠跟妳在一起真是幸運到不行。我們可以一起四處去冒險犯難。第一次歷險可以選西威爾斯。我會帶妳去看海。我會教妳游泳，像妳這樣農家出身的女生不會游泳真的說不過去。我會帶妳去看海豚，還有海豹媽媽帶著小海豹。我想讓妳體驗住在威爾斯小農舍那種靜謐的美感。我相信妳會愛上哪裡的。」

你又說：

「接下來我打算帶妳去西班牙和法國。我知道妳會喜歡那些地方。我希望我們可以在那裡住上一陣子。」

過一會兒你說：

「我覺得妳和我能夠相愛真是太棒了，這一切發生得如此迅速，自然，好像森林燎火。」

你還說：

「我就喜歡妳這個樣子。」

目前為止一切美好，除開一件事——你不明白我拿的簽證有其限制。我是來自中國大陸土生土長的中國人。我不屬於自由世界的成員。我在這裡只有一年的學生簽證。我沒資格就這麼撇下倫敦的英國語言學校，隨性跑到有樹有海的地方，就算

understand my visa limited situation. I am native Chinese from mainland of China. I am not of free world. And I only have student visa for a year here. I not able just leave London English language school and go live somewhere only have trees and sea, although is beautiful. And I can't travel to Spain and France just to fun—I need show these embassy officer my bank account to apply my Europe visa. And my bank statements is never qualify for them. You a free man of free world. I am not free, like you.

那兒再美也不成。而且我不能跟你到西班牙和法國去旅行逍遙
──我必須先讓他們大使館的官員檢視我的銀行戶頭才能申請
歐洲簽證。而我的銀行報告單根本不夠資格提出申請。你是自
由世界的自由人士。我沒資格像你那樣自由自在。

custom

n. **1.** a long-established activity or action; **2.** usual habit; **3.** regular use of a shop or business.

The café is name greasy spoon, Seven Seas. All windows is foggy from the steam. You order tea as soon as you walk into. Noisy. Babies. Mothers. Couples. Lonely old man. You are opening the newspaper and start drink thick English Breakfast milky tea. And me being quiet.

I want talk to you. But you are reading paper. I have to respect your hobby.

"So where are you from?" I ask handsome waiter in white suit.

"Cyprus." He smiles.

"Are these chefs also from Cyprus?"

"Yes."

"So your Cyprus chefs cook English breakfast for English?"

"Yes, we Cypriots cook breakfast for the English because they can't cook."

I see from open kitchen that sausages are sizzling on the pan. And mushrooms, and scrambled eggs, they are all waiting for being devoured.

I love these old oily cafes around Hackney. Because you can see the smokes and steams coming out from the coffee machine or kitchen all day long. That means life is being blessed.

【習俗】

〈名詞〉**1.** 由來已久的習俗，慣例；**2.** 個人習慣；**3.** 對某家店或行業經常的惠顧。

　　那家平價咖啡館的店名叫「七海」。全部窗戶被水汽蒸得霧茫茫的。你一進門便點了茶。好吵喔。小嬰兒，媽媽們，情侶，孤單老頭。你報紙一攤，喝起濃郁的英式早餐奶茶。而我悶聲不響。

　　我想和你講講話。可你正讀著報紙，我該尊重你的癖好才對。

　　「你是哪裡人？」我問那一身白的帥氣侍者。

　　「賽普勒斯。」他面帶笑容。

　　「你們店的師傅也是賽普勒斯來的？」

　　「是的。」

　　「所以你們賽普勒斯的師傅幫英國人做英式早餐？」

　　「沒錯，我們賽普勒斯人幫英國人做早餐，因為他們不善烹調。」

　　我看見開放式廚房裡香腸躺在平底鍋滋滋作響。還有磨菇，炒蛋，全等著填進肚囊。

　　我愛死哈克尼這些油汪汪的老咖啡店。你可以全天候欣賞到咖啡機和廚房煙霧蒸騰的景象。那代表生命受到照料的愉悅。

　　這家店裡，眾人頭頂上有架電視機。電視機有開，可是看

In this café, there is a television set above everybody's head. The TV on but doesn't have any images, only can hear BBC news speaking scrambly from the white snow screen. It is a little disturbing for me, but it seem everybody in this place enjoy it. Nobody here suggest fix the TV.

Suddenly white-snow-screen changes to green-snowscreen, and the BBC voice continues. A man nearby eating some bacons with the Daily Mirror says to the chef:

"That's an improvement."

"Yes, Sir," replies the chef. "Well, at least you don't have to eat your breakfast, read the paper and watch the TV all at the same time."

"That's true." The man chew his bacons and concentrates on page with picture of half naked blonde smiling.

I want to talk. I can't help stop talking. I have to stop you reading.

"You know what? I came this café before, sit here whole afternoon," I say.

"Doing what?" you put down the paper, annoyed.

"I read a porn magazine called *Pet House* for three hours, because I studied English from those stories. Checking the dictionary really took lots of time."

You are surprised. "I don't think you should read porn mags in a café. People will be shocked."

"I don't care."

"But you can't do that. You"ll make other people feel embarrassed."

"Then why they sell these magazines in every little corner shop? Is also even sold in the big supermarket."

不到任何影像，只聽見雪花白的螢幕傳出BBC新聞零落的聲音。我被攪得有點心神不寧，其他顧客倒是一副老神在在的模樣，沒有人提議電視該修理了。

突然間雪花白的螢幕轉成青花白，BBC的聲音繼續。近旁有個享用培根配《每日鏡報》的男顧客對廚師說：

「有改善了。」

「是的，先生，」師傅回答。「最起碼，您不用同時忙著應付吃早餐、讀報紙和看電視。」

「那倒是真的。」男顧客嚼著他的培根，全副精神回到清涼照那一頁，半裸的金髮美女笑臉迎人。

我想說話。我沒辦法忍耐不說。我得讓你暫停讀報。

「你曉不曉得，我之前來過這家咖啡店，在這裡坐了整個下午，」我說。

「來做什麼？」你放下報紙，快快的。

「我讀一本叫《寵物之家》的成人雜誌（編按：指《閣樓》（Penthouse）雜誌，英文拼法有別），讀了三個鐘頭，我從裡面寫的那些故事學習英語。光查字典就耗掉我大半的時間。」

你很驚訝。「我想妳最好別在咖啡店裡讀成人雜誌。別人會被妳嚇到。」

「我才不管。」

「可是妳不該這樣。妳會害別的客人很難為情。」

「那他們幹嘛每個轉角小店賣這種雜誌？甚至大型超市也都有賣？」

我以為和性有關的每樣東西在西方都沒什麼好丟臉的。

我們隔壁座的男的已經吃完培根，大胸脯的清涼裸女圖片依然毫無遮掩。

I believe everything to do with the sexuality is not shameful in West. Do what you like.

The man next to us finishes his bacons, half naked woman photo with huge breasts still being exposed.

"I think I go now buy another porn magazine," I say, standing up.

"OK, you do whatever you want," you say shaking head. "This is Hackney after all. People will forgive you for not being *au fait* with the nuances of British customs."

You dry up your cup of tea.

「我現在又想去買本成人雜誌來看，」我說，作勢要起身。

　　「好吧，妳想幹嘛就幹嘛，」你搖搖頭說。「反正這裡是哈克尼。妳不擅長分辨英國習俗的微妙差異人家也不會怪妳。」

　　你將杯裡的茶一飲而盡。

fart

vulgar slang n. emission of gas from the anus. *v.* emit gas from the anus.

Suddenly the man next table reading newspaper with naked-breast-woman made a huge noise.

"What is that noise name?" I ask you.

You cannot understand what I mean. Too much involving in looking house property advertisement on the newspaper.

I try to explain: "How to say a word which represents a kind of noise from the arse?"

"What?"

"You know that. You know it is a wind comes from between two legs."

"It's called a fart."

Fart?

The old man who reads the newspaper stares at us for several seconds, then buries himself into the paper again.

I never hear English person says anything about fart. They must be too shameful to pronounce that sound. There are lots of words we used in China so often, but here people never use it. Even English dictionary say it is a "taboo".

"屁" is *fart* in Chinese. It is the word made up from two parts. 尸 is a symbol of a body with tail, and underneath that 比 represent two legs. That means fart, a kind of Chi. If a person have that kind of Chi regularly in his daily life that means

【放屁】

（粗俗俚語）〈名詞〉從肛門發射的氣體。〈動詞〉從肛門發射氣體。

　　突然間，鄰桌那個閱讀大胸脯裸女報紙的男顧客發出一聲巨響。

　　「那聲音叫什麼名堂？」我問你。

　　你不懂我所指為何。你太專注研究報上的房地產廣告。

　　我進一步解釋：「哪個字可以表示從屁股發出的聲響？」

　　「什麼？」

　　「你知道我在說什麼。就是從兩腿間放出來的風。」

　　「那叫 fart。」

　　「fart？」

　　那個讀報的老傢伙瞪了我們好幾秒鐘，然後又一頭栽進他的報紙裡。

　　我從沒聽過英國人提到任何跟 fart 有關的東西。他們一定太難為情了，連那個字的發音都不敢出聲。我們中國有成堆的字眼可以交替運用，但這裡的人只會避而不談。即便是英語辭典都說它是「禁忌」。

　　fart 就是我們中國人說的「屁」。這個屁字可以拆解成兩個部分。尸代表人的身體拖著一條尾巴，底下的比代表兩條腿。兩個合起來就是屁，一種氣。如果一個人日常生活有規律地產生這種氣，代表他非常健康。氣，每樣和氣有關的東西對我們

he is very healthy. Chi (氣), everything to do with Chi is very important to us Chinese. We had so many words related to Chi, like Tai-Chi, or Chi-Gong, or Chi-Chang.

Yes, *fart*, I want remember this word. Is the response means you enjoys a good homely cooking, after big meal. Mans in China loves to use this word everyday.

You are still concentrating on your *Guardian*, something serious about the terrorism. I am talking to nobody. The old man next table sees I am fed up, so says to me:

"I'm off, darling. Do you want my paper?"

He leaves the café but turns his head looking at me again.

I pick the newspaper from his table. There is a headline:

LOST FOR WORDS—THE LANGUAGE OF AN
ENDANGERED SPECIES

It is a story about ninety-eight-year-old Chinese woman just died. She is the last speaker of womans-only language: "Nushu". This four-hundred-year-old secret language being used by Chinese womans to express theys innermost feeling. The paper say because no womans practise that secret codes anymore, it marks that language died after her death.

I want create my own "Nushu". Maybe this notebook which I use for putting new English vocabularies is a "Nushu". Then I have my own privacy. You know my body, my everyday's life, but you not know my "Nushu".

中國人相當重要。我們和氣連在一起的字有很多，比如太極，氣功，氣場。

是的，fart，我想記住這個字。屁可當做你開懷大嚼家常美食後表達滿意的利器。中國男人每天特別喜歡用上這個字。

你仍舊專注於你的《衛報》，跟恐怖主義有關的正經事。我沒有人可以交談。隔壁桌的老傢伙看我一臉煩悶，便對我說：

「我要走了，達令。報紙妳要嗎？」

他從咖啡館走出去的時候，還回頭望了我一眼。

我把他桌上的報紙拿過來。上面有個標題：

失落的話語──一個瀕臨消失的語言

這是個享年九十八歲，剛剛過世的中國姥姥的故事。她是最後一個通曉某種女性獨有語言：「女書」的言說者。中國女性使用這種祕密流傳四百年的語言表達內心深邃的情感。報導指出，如今由於這種祕密符碼後繼無人，她的去世同時標誌了此一語言的消亡。

我想創造我自己的「女書」。或許我這本收錄英文生字的筆記本就是「女書」。這樣一來我便擁有自己的隱私。你曉得我的身體，我每天的一舉一動，可你對我的「女書」一無所知。

home

n. **1.** a place where one lives; **2.** an institution for the care of the elderly, orphans, etc. *adj.* **1.** of one's home, birthplace, or native country; **2.** sport played on one's own ground.

"I am going to go to see a family nearby, do you want to come?" you ask me.

"Family? What kind of family? Not your family?"

"No. They are Bengalis."

Is not very normal you want see other family. Because you not really like family concept. You say family against community. You say family is a selfish product.

It seems that you like other's family more than you like your own. In this Bengali family, you know those kids for many years, since you worked as youth worker. In a house, between Brick Lane and Bethnal Green Road, old Bengali mother raises ten children. Is big three-floor house with ten little rooms. Five childrens are from same mother, and another five childrens are from another woman but with the same man. The father, a Bengali married man, came to London twenty-five years ago and remarried to this mother in London. He ran some business between England and Bangladesh. Then he died, left one family in London, one family in Bangladesh. But the five Bangladesh-living children want come to London, so they were brought here living with this London mother. These kids are from three to twenty-four. The youngest one was born in 2000. How strange a child born of that year! He only can say

【家】

〈名詞〉**1.** 人居住的地方；**2.** 收容照料老人或孤兒等等的機構。〈形容詞〉**1.** 家庭的，出生地的，本國的；**2.** 主場，在本地舉行的體育賽事。

「我要去探望附近的一戶家庭，妳要一起來嗎？」你問我。

「家庭？什麼樣的家庭？不會是你的吧？」

「不是。他們是孟加拉人。」

事情不太尋常，你竟會想去探望別人的家。因為你不怎麼欣賞家庭的概念。你說家庭和社群對立。家庭是自私的產物。

看起來，你喜歡別人家庭的程度勝過自己的家。這一戶孟加拉人，你認識他們的小孩已經好多年，從你做青少年工作的時候開始。一間房子，位於紅磚巷和貝思納爾格林路之間，年邁的孟加拉母親撫養十個孩子。三層樓的大房子，共有十個小房間。其中五個小孩出自這老母親，另外五個是別的女士和同一位先生生的。這位父親，一個孟加拉的已婚男子，二十五年前來到倫敦之後，又和這位母親結婚。他在英國和孟加拉之間來來回回經營生意。後來他死了，倫敦和孟加拉兩地各留下一個家庭。可是那五個孟加拉小孩想來倫敦，所以他們被送到此地和這位倫敦母親一起生活。這些孩子的年紀從三歲到二十四歲。最小的生於公元兩千年。好怪，有小孩子真的在那一年出生！他只會說英語的「拜—拜」。年紀最大的孩子剛從倫敦大學金匠學院畢業。他唸政治學，以後想當律師。

"bye-bye" in English. The oldest one just graduated from the Gold Smith College. He studied Politics and he wants become lawyer.

"I not understand how mother can raise ten children without a husband," I say in little voice. "And she doesn't have any job either!"

"That's why I like this family. They just get on with their life without making any fuss. They have a small business making earrings and necklaces from home."

"And two groups of children from different mother, they don't fight at all?"

"No. They enjoy sharing life together, not like other families. I wish my family was like this."

"Do you hate your family?" I ask.

"Well, I don't like them. They are sad people. I broke away from them many years ago."

You go into silent.

I can't imagine what like to break up with my family. Even though my mother very bad temper and make me pain, my life relies on them, and I can't survive without them.

"Do you want have family with me?" I ask.

"Aren't we a family now?" you say.

"No, a real family."

"What is a real family?"

"House, husband and wife, then have some children, then cooking dinner together, then travel together . . ."

"I thought the Chinese were supposed to be Communists."

You seem like making fun. What you mean?

We look at each other, no more discussion on this.

「我不明白一個母親怎有辦法獨立撫養十個小孩，」我壓低聲音。「而且她又沒有工作！」

「所以我才這麼喜歡這一家人。他們過自己的日子，不會怨東怨西。他們想辦法自己做點耳環項鍊之類的小生意。」

「可是兩邊的孩子來自不同的母親，難道他們都不會吵吵鬧鬧？」

「不會。他們樂於共同分擔生活，不像其他的家庭。真希望我家也能像這樣就好了。」

「你討厭你們家人？」我問。

「唔，我不喜歡他們。他們人很可悲。許多年前我就和他們斷絕聯繫了。」

你跌入沉默。

我沒辦法想像和我的家人斷絕聯繫的情景。即使我的母親脾氣很壞，令我痛苦，我的生活衣食還得仰賴他們，我沒辦法靠自己過活。

「你想和我成立家庭嗎？」我問。

「我們現在不就是一個家庭？」你說。

「不，我是說真正的家庭。」

「什麼叫真正的家庭？」

「有房子，丈夫和妻子，然後生幾個小孩，一起煮晚飯，一起出門旅遊……」

「我還以為中國人信的是共產主義。」

你似乎是在說笑。幹嘛這樣講？

我們彼此對看，不再討論下去。

你出聲問候那老母親。她身裏青色的舊莎麗。她的膚色褐黝，臉上爬滿皺紋。她沒受過任何教育，一句英文也不會講。

You say salaam malai coom to the old mother. The mother, she is covered in old green Sari. Her skin is deep brown and lots of wrinkles on her face. She never any education and never speak one word English. She always smiles and very little talking. When her children talks in English loudly in TV room and watching BBC she just sit there, peacefully watching, like she understand they say. Bathroom flush doesn't work and shower doesn't work. There is not money to fix house. But it seem fine for them. It seem their life is not messy at all. They use cold-watershower once a week, and they don't use toilet paper because they always use water to clean then tip bucket down loo.

There are drug dealers doing business outside of their windows, and many drunkens pass by with bottles clunkling every night, but the family not get any harm.

In Chinese, it is the same word "家" (jia) for "home" and "family" and sometimes including "house". To us, family is same thing as house, and this house is their only home too. "家", a roof on top, then some legs and arms inside. When you write this character down, you can feel those legs and arms move around underneath the roof. Home, is a dwelling house for the family to live.

But English, it's different. In *Roget's Thesaurus*, "Family" related to: *subdivision, greed, genealogy, parental, posterity, community, nobility.*

It seems like that "family" doesn't mean a place. Maybe in West people just move round from one house to another house? Always looking for a house, maybe that's the lifelong

她總是面露笑容，幾乎難得開口。她的孩子在電視間看BBC，用英文高談闊論時，她只是坐在一旁，平靜地看著，好像能夠聽懂他們講的每一句話。浴室沖水和淋浴的設備都壞了，沒有錢可以整修房子，但他們似乎怡然自得，生活還是井然有條。他們每個禮拜洗一次冷水澡，上廁所不用衛生紙，習慣先用水清潔，再拿桶子沖洗馬桶。

他們家窗外就有藥頭在交易，夜裡醉漢經過拿酒瓶亂敲，但這一家人安然度日，未受任何傷害。

在中國，一個「家」字可以同時表示「家庭」和「家人」，有時還包括「住所」在內。對我們來說，家人等同於住所，這間住所也是他們唯一的家。「家」，上面有屋頂，裡面有好多條腿和手。當你寫下這個字，可以感受到那些腿和手在屋頂下不停扭動。家，就是給家人安居的住所。

然而，英國的情形就不一樣。根據《羅傑索引典》，和「Family」相關的詞條有：分支，血統，系譜，父母親的，子孫後代，社群，貴族。

看起來「family」似乎沒有住所的意思。或許在西方，人們純粹只是從這間房子換到另一間房子？永遠在尋找下一間房子，或許這是西方人終身的任務。

我不停告訴你我需要一個家。你的臉色越發凝重，似乎為了無法令我快樂而失望。

「但我就是妳的家，」你說。

「沒錯，可是你老是跑東跑西，而且你也不想住在這棟房子。」

「妳說對了。我已經厭倦住在城裡。」你又加上這麼一

job for Westerners.

I keep telling you I need a home. Your face look gloomy, and seem disappointed that you cannot make me happy.

"But I am your home," you say.

"Yes, but you always move around, and you don't want live in this house."

"You"re right. I'm tired of living in the city." Then you add, "I can't see myself getting married either."

"But I like city and like to have marriage. So that mean we can't have a home together," I confirm.

"No, I didn't say that," you say.

You look distant to me.

Love mean home. Or, home mean love?

The fear of without home. Maybe that why I love you? The simple fear?

I am building the Great Wall around you and me because I am too scared to lose the home. I been living in that big fear since my childhood.

You barely ask my childhood. To you it a blind zone. When I look back my childhood I realise how violence of my emotional world was.

We were peasants. My parents worked in rice fields. They not making shoes until I graduated from high school. After they understood they never earn money from their fields, they sold fields cheaply, and start making small business. I always being beaten up by big girls. In village people show their emotion by hitting and shouting to each other. My father hit me sometimes, also my mother. That was normal.

句，「我也沒辦法想像自己走入婚姻。」

「可是我喜歡城市而且想要結婚。所以就是說我們兩個不能擁有共同的家庭，」我強調。

「不，我沒有這樣說，」你說。

你看起來和我距離遙遠。

愛代表家。或者，家代表愛？

害怕沒有家，或許這就是我愛你的原因？單純出於恐懼？

我築起萬里長城將你我包圍，因為不能失去這個家。打從孩提時起我便活在巨大的恐懼當中。

你幾乎沒問過我的童年。對此你毫無所悉。如今回顧，我才明白自己童年的情感世界如何飽受摧折。

我們家是農民背景，父母在田裡耕種稻米。直到我高中畢業他們才改行做起鞋子。一旦認清不可能靠種田攢錢翻身後，他們便把田地便宜賣了，開始投入小生意。我常常被年紀大點的姑娘欺負。鄉下地方，人們表達情感的方式就是互相打罵。我父親有時會打我，我母親也是。這種事稀鬆平常。

我們家很窮，連吃的東西都不夠。每一餐，我都怕自己是不是吃得超過母親允許的分量。偶爾餐桌上出現豬肉，味道聞起來有若天堂。但我根本沒膽量將筷子伸過去，豬肉是專門為父親準備的。理所當然，男人需要吃肉，他們比女人重要多了。我眼巴巴望著豬肉，嘴饞到內心打結。能讓我嚐上一塊的話，誰要什麼我都給他！無奈母親總是緊盯著餐桌。我恨她，可我也她怕得緊。如果我伸向豬肉的話，她鐵定會打落我的筷子。

我母親脾氣壞得跟什麼似的。或許因為我是個不中用的女

We were poor. The food was not enough. We had little meat. I was frightened to eat more than my mother expected in every meal. Occasionally there was some fried porks on the table, and it smelled like heaven. But I dared not to reach my chopsticks to the meat, which prepared only for my father. Man needs meat and man is more important than woman, of course. I looked at pork and my heart was squeezed by the desire. I give away anything for could bite one piece fried pork! My mother always watched out on the table. I hated her, but also frightened by her. She would beat my chopsticks if I reached that pork. I was hungry all the time, because I never can have something I really wanted eat, like meat, any kind meat. That hunger still remains in my stomach until today.

My mother had very bad temper. Maybe she hated me because I was an useless girl. She cannot have the second children because we have one child policy. Maybe that's why she beated me up. For her disappointment. Life to her was unfair too. She was beated up by her mother for marrying my father. She was deprive everything which belonged to her since she married him.

When I grow up from teenage, I couldn't trust anything and anybody. Maybe I even don't have concept of "trust" at all. It not existing in my dictionary. First, I couldn't trust my country. We told that we are proud of thousands of years history but next day we saw beautiful old temples being demolished into ruins. All old things have to be demolished and to be cleaned up. Does that mean our past value nothing anymore?

I need make my own home, a home with my lover. But I don't know how keep that home, all the time, for rest of my

孩子她才如此怨恨。基於一胎化政策的關係，她沒辦法再生一個。或許她是基於失望才打我發洩。她的人生遭遇同樣也不公平。為了嫁給我父親，她被她母親毒打。從嫁給父親開始，原本屬於她的一切統統被剝奪一空。

　　十幾歲長大之後，我從來不相信任何人、任何東西。或許我壓根連「信任」的概念都沒有。我的辭典裡找不到這個字。首先，我就不信任我的國家。人家說，我們應該為千年悠久的歷史感到驕傲，但隔天一瞧，古老的美麗寺院被拆成廢墟。所有的老東西一一拆個精光，連痕跡都沒留下。這豈不表明我們的傳統價值早該扔了？

　　我必須打造自己的家，一個屬於我和愛人的家。但我不知道如何守護那個家，一輩子長長久久的守護。我怕早晚會失去那份愛。這恐懼毒藥般啃噬我內心的每個角落。你受不了的便是這種心理。

　　「妳應該相信我才對。我不會去愛上別人的，」你說。

　　「這誰知道？我可以相信你，不過一旦有人誘惑你的時候我可不相信，」我說。

　　「但妳必須相信我，」你堅持。

　　「話是這樣沒錯，這不代表你就不會愛上別人。你可以信任我，但我或許會去愛上其他人。所以到底什麼才叫信任？」

　　「嗯，如果我們真的愛上了別人，那也只能這樣。那不是我們所能控制的事情。」你看起來有些冷酷。

　　「什麼叫那也只能這樣？你說不是我們所能控制是什麼意思？我們當然可以控制，只要我們願意！」我說，像女鬥士般激昂。

life. I'm scared I will lose that love. The fear is like poison in the every corner in my heart. That what you dislike.

"You should trust me. I'm not going to fall in love with somebody else," you say.

"But who knows? I can trust you, but I don't trust when you are seduced by someone," I say.

"But you have to trust me," you insist.

"Yes, but that doesn't mean you not fall in love with new person. You can trust me, but perhaps I fall in love with the new person. So what is trust really?"

"Well, If we fall in love with a new person, then that's fine. That's not something we can control." You look bit cool.

"What you mean that's fine? What you mean we can't control? We can, if we want!" I say, as strong as woman warrior.

So we change subject. We know we can't go anywhere. Anything else we can talk under one same roof? Apart from the lovely tea, salad, and learning new vocabularies?

"When is your national day?" I ask.

"Why on earth do you want to know that?"

"Not important day for you?"

"Not particularly. We call it St George's Day. It is some time in April or May, I can't remember."

I don't know who is St George. Or maybe he is someone like Chairman Mao. I don't want bother myself to know all these dead people.

So we are speechless again.

"So, when is your birthday?" you ask me.

"July 23, but that's not my real birthday. My mother only

我們只好換一個話題。我們曉得兩個人無處躲避。同一個屋簷下我們可有其他話題可聊？愉悅的茶，沙拉，學習新字彙，除了這些其他還有嗎？

　　「你們國慶日什麼時候？」我問。

　　「妳怎麼會想到這種問題？」

　　「國慶日對你不重要？」

　　「沒什麼特別的。我們叫它聖喬治節。在四月或五月的哪一天，我記不得了。」

　　我不認識誰是聖喬治。或許他跟毛主席一樣是號大人物。但我沒那麼多閒工夫去認識所有的已故人士。

　　我們再度無話可說。

　　「你生日是哪一天？」你問我。

　　「六月二十三，但那不是我真正的生日。我母親只記得我中國陰曆的生日，後來我們社會改成西方的曆法之後，她就忘了。」

　　「妳說真的？」你臉色一亮。

　　「真的，我們家從來沒有生日蛋糕慶祝，那幹嘛還需要記生日？其實只為了政府登記要用。」我說。

　　「那妳的護照怎麼辦？護照上面要寫哪個日子？」

　　「我就大概寫個西元的日子，相關單位就把它印在我的護照上。」瞧你興奮的樣子，這個話題。

　　我繼續：「我父親不曉得自己的生日，他很小的時候父母就死了。我母親知道她的生日在陰曆七月十五日，剛好是我們中國的中元節，餓死鬼放出來的日子。所以她這輩子都在想辦法躲開那餓死鬼的節日。

know my birthday in Chinese moon calendar date and when Western calendar system introduced into our society she forgot."

"Seriously?" Your face is lighted.

"Yes, we never had birthday cake in our family for ceremony so why you need the date of birth? Only because the official registration," I say.

"But what about your passport? What date is written on your passport?"

"I wrote any Western date I think of and authority just print it on my passport." How exciting to you, this subject.

I carry on: "My father doesn't know his birthday, because his parents died when he was little child. My mother know her birthday is on the fifteenth day of seventh moon, is the day of Hungry Ghost Festival. So all her life is about keeping away from that hungry day."

colony

n. **1.** a group of people who settle in a new country but remain under the rule of their homeland; **2.** a territory occupied by a colony; **3.** a group of people or animals of the same kind living together.

The way you make love with me, is totally new experience in my life. Is sex suppose be like this? Penetrating is way for you to enter into my soul. You are so strong. And your strength is overwhelming. For you, I am unprepared. You crush me and press me into your body. Love making is a torture. Love making is a battle. Then I get used it, and I am addicted by it. The way you hold my body is like holding small object, an apple, or a little animal. The force from your arms and your legs and your hip is like force from huge creature living in jungle. The vibrate from your muscle shakes my skins, the beating of your heart also beating my heart.

You are the commander. You kiss my lips, my eyes, my cheek, my ears, my neck, and my silver necklace. It is like my necklace having a special magic on you. And that magic force you devote yourself to my body. Then you kiss my breasts and you suck them. You are like baby who is thirsty for mother's milk. You lick my belly and my legs and my feet. You possess my whole body. They are your farm. Then you come back to my garden. Your lips are wandering in my cave, and in that warm and wet nature you try find something precious, something you always dream about. You wander alone there and love there and want live there. My whole body is your colony.

【殖民地】

〈名詞〉**1.** 殖民者，於宗祖國的操控下治理一個新的國家；**2.** 殖民者操控的地區；**3.** 同一種類的人或動物共同生活的集群。

　　你做愛的方式，是我前所未有的生命經驗。這就是性愛嗎？你插入，有如進入我的靈魂。你體魄強健。你的力量無可抵禦。在你面前，我毫無防備之力。你壓制我，將我擠入你體內。做愛即拷刑。做愛即作戰。我先是習慣，然後上癮。你掌控我的身軀有如探囊取物，我是一只蘋果，一隻小動物。你的臂，你的腿，你的臀迸發的力氣有如叢林巨獸。你肌肉的律動令我的皮膚悚慄，你的心跳敲擊我的心跳。

　　你是指揮官。

　　你親吻我的唇，我的眼，我的臉，我的脖子，我的銀項鍊。我的項鍊彷彿對你施展異樣的魔力，那魔力驅使你對我的肉體獻身。你親吻我的胸乳，吸吮。你像飢渴的嬰兒吸吮母乳。你舌頭舔過我的腹，我的腿，我的足。你占領我全身上下。它們是你的耕地。接著，你回到我的花園。你雙唇流連我的洞穴，那片自然的溫暖和潮溼當中，你賣力搜尋珍寶，搜尋夢寐以求之物。你隻身徘徊，愛上那個地方，打算就此定居。

　　我全身上下是你的殖民地。

prostitute

n. a person who offers sexual intercourse in return for payment. *v.* **1.** to make a prostitute of; **2.** to offer (oneself or one's talents) for unworthy purposes.

I need develop my Western life so I go Charing Cross Road try to find some cooking books. I want know how to make Western food, like pastas, or Yorkshire pudding. I am ended up in Soho Original Bookshop. There are no kitchen books here, apart *How to Make Love and Cook Dinner at the Same Time.* Lots of books here exposing naked body. Prostitute, I read this word from one of photo books. The pictures are shocking. I am standing there and reading the whole book. Bodies, strange costumes, strange positions, more bodies having sex together.

Soho, Berwick Street. My feet can't move away from a sex shop. Some leather bras with two hole in middle, some leather belt, some handcuff. . .

A word loin written on some instructions, which I never studied before. Standing in front of these shelfs, I check my *Collins* dictionary.

> **Loin** *n.* part of the body between the ribs and the
> hips; cut of meat from this part of an animal —
> *pl.* hips and inner thighs
> **loincloth** *n.* piece of cloth covering the loins only.

【賣淫】

〈名詞〉提供性服務換取報酬者。〈動詞〉1. 賣淫；2. 濫用（個人或個人才能）。

　　我需要增長自己的西方生活技能，所以我跑到查令十字路，想找幾本烹飪書籍。我想學點西方菜餚，比如義大利麵，或是約克夏布丁。最後我逛到蘇活區的專門書店。這裡看不到任何烹飪書，除了這本《如何同時做愛並且煮好晚餐》。舉目所見都是裸露身體的書。賣淫，一本攝影集裡我看到這個字眼。照片好震撼。我站在那兒將整本書翻完。肉體，怪裝扮，怪姿勢，更多肉體性交。

　　蘇活區，伯維克街。我的腳步無法移開情趣用品店。皮胸罩，中間挖兩個孔，皮腰帶，幾副手銬……
　　好幾份使用說明都寫著 loin，我以前沒讀過這個字。站在書架前面，翻開我的《柯林斯辭典》。

> **loin**〈名詞〉：肋骨和臀部之
> 間的部分；獸類的腰肉。
> 〈複數形〉臀部和大腿內側。
> **loincloth**〈名詞〉：纏腰布。

沒有進一步的說明。這辭典好討厭。究竟大腿內側在哪

There is no more explanation. I hate this dictionary. Where is an exactly *inner thigh*? And what *loincloth* look like? Do people wear loincloth everyday?

Putting my dictionary back into pocket, I find shopkeeper stares at me like a tiger. And there are two old mans, both are bald, they stare at me too. I leave the shop.

Red light district.

One, two, three, four, five, six . . . I am changing the notes to coins.

I am in peepshow room. It is tiny room for one person to stand, and I can see turning stage through little hole.

I insert the coin of the first pound, and start watching a woman shows her nude.

She is a blonde. Shining hair like golden velvet. She is young. She wears a tight shining top. Her lower body is also covered by piece of shining cloth. Is that the *loin cloth*? Now she uncovers herself. She has a fine round breast, like two summer grapefruits. Her skin is a little dark, like she just coming back from sunny beach.

The peep hole close. I insert second pound. The light turns into red. Now her sex is bathed in redness. She lies down on round stage, which covered by red velvet. The stage is turning, slowly, smoothly.

I insert third pound. She is opening her legs. The legs of white jade. She smiles to everybody; even the place between her legs is smiling. Her garden is flirting with the world around it. She has a rosy garden, which two lips half opened like waiting for the kiss. I never saw other woman's garden before. It

兒？纏腰布長什麼樣子？有人每天裹著纏腰布嗎？

把辭典放回口袋，我發現店家盯著我瞧，像老虎要吞人。還有兩個老禿頭，他們也朝我猛瞧。我趕緊走人。

風化區。

一，二，三，四，五，六……我忙著紙鈔換成硬幣。

我在偷窺秀房裡。這小房間讓一位客人站著，透過小眼洞我可以看見旋轉的舞台。

我投入第一鎊硬幣，開始觀賞一位女郎展現她的胴體。

她是個金髮妞。亮澤的秀髮有如金色絲絨。她很年輕。她穿著閃亮的緊身上衣，下半身圍裹著同樣閃亮的布匹。莫非那就是纏腰布？她寬衣解帶。她的乳房渾圓，像兩顆盛夏的葡萄柚。她的膚色略黑，彷彿剛從日照的海濱歸來。

窺伺孔關閉。我投入第二鎊。燈光轉紅。她的性感沐浴於紅光當中。她躺下，圓形舞台鋪設紅絲絨，台面旋轉，徐徐地，平穩地。

我投入第三鎊。她敞開腿，兩條白膩玉腿。她對每一個人送出輕笑；連兩腿間的部位也有笑意。她的花園挑逗圍觀的人群。她玫瑰色的花園，兩瓣陰唇輕啟，待人親澤。我還沒見過別的女人的花園。這下傻眼。我記得有天你和我做愛，拿了面小鏡子要我照看兩腿間敞開的部位。

「那是你的陰蒂，」你告訴我。

「陰地？」

我從鏡面看見我的性器顏色深褐，以前還真沒想過自己的顏色如何。

我投入第四鎊。她遮掩的部位完全暴露，祕密的丘壑一覽

shocks my eyes. I remember one day when you and me making love, you give me small mirror to reflect the place between my opening legs.

"That's your clitoris," you tell me.

"Liquorice?"

I found there my colour of my sex is brown. I never know the colour of my sex before.

I insert fourth pound. Now her hidden place is totally exposed, showing her secret landscape. Then her right hand caress her valley of the tenderness. Her long slim fingers, reaching her sex, are like a beautiful ballet dancer dancing in her garden. She fondles her valley, up and down, gently, and again and again. Two petals blossom in her wet garden. The petals are fresh like rose. Her bush is dark, like a fertile delta, a delta connecting to a secret path. She looks light heated. But her face disappears, only the desire talks to people.

I insert the fifth pound. Now she lays her back on the stage, raising her two legs high above. 陰道-Yin Dao: the tunnel of darkness, that is Chinese word to say vagina. Her tunnel of darkness is right in front me. Her secret tunnel, winding and curved, is like a maze. Inside of the tunnel is pink and juicy, like an open fig.

The peep hole close off again, and I insert into my last pound. She still there. Her naked body moving on the red velvet. What her name? What her life like? Is there man in her life or lots of mans? Where she from? Serbia? Croatia? Yugoslavia? Russia? Poland?

Same day, same afternoon, same alive sex show spot. I

無遺。她伸出右手撫弄嬌嫩的溪谷，纖長的玉指來回於性器，有如美貌的芭蕾伶娜在她的花園翩然起舞。她撫弄溪谷，上上下下，輕柔地，一次又一次。她潮潤的園地兩瓣花蕾綻放，清新如玫瑰。她深色的灌叢如肥饒的三角洲，連接密徑的三角洲。她看來逐漸興奮。但她的臉消失了，只剩慾望猶在傾訴。

我投入第五鎊。她將後背平放舞台，兩腿高高舉起。陰道：陰暗的通道，女性生殖器的中國字說法。她陰暗的通道正面對著我。她的祕密通道，迂迴曲折，像座迷宮。通道內壁粉嫩欲滴，如剖開的無花果。

窺伺孔再度關閉，我將身上最後一鎊投入。她還在。紅色絲絨上她的裸身游移。她芳名爲何？她過著什麼樣的日子？她有男人嗎？還是很多男人？她來自何方？塞爾維亞？克羅埃西亞？南斯拉夫？俄羅斯？波蘭？

同一天，同一個下午，同樣的眞人春宮秀。我換了更多的硬幣。這回我花了二十鎊，觀賞雙人演出。

舞台上，一個漂亮的年輕人和一位黑髮女郎。

那男的有一副陽剛的體格。他非常結實，金黃的肌膚。他戴了副眼鏡，豐茂的長髮紮起馬尾。他只穿貼身小短褲，兩腿健美。他親吻那女的。她穿著紅色胸罩和銀色迷你裙。她甜美的奶子挺翹，邀引那些饑渴的目光。男的將她的胸罩解開，乳頭迅即硬突，如初夏粉紅的玫瑰芽蕾。他愛撫她的頸項，她的酥胸，她的纖腰，她的嫩臀，她的玉腿。他動作優雅，好一位年輕的紳士。然而他是賣淫的──爲了卑劣的目的出賣自我者，如辭典所言。

站在那兒觀看這一幕，我渴望賣淫。我想要暴露我的身

change more coins. This time I spent twenty pounds, for watching two persons performing.

Now, on the stage, a beautiful young man and a black hair woman. The man has a masculine body. He is very fit, and his skin is golden. He wears pair of glasses. He has the beautiful lush hair tied up to a pony tail. He only wears tight shorts, and his legs are strong. He kisses the woman. The woman wears a red bra and a silver mini skirt. Her sweet breasts bulged upwards, inviting those thirsty eyes. The man unbuttons her bra. Her nipples are immediately blossom, like pink rose bud in early summer. He caresses her neck, her breast, her waist, her hip, and her legs. He is so elegant, a young gentleman. But he is a *prostitute—person who offers himself for unworthy purposes*, like the dictionary says.

While I am standing there watching, I desire become prostitute. I want be able expose my body, to relieve my body, to take my body away from dictionary and grammar and sentences, to let my body break all disciplines. What a relief that prostitute not need speak good English. She also not need to bring a dictionary with her all the time.

Now her turn, her power on him. She seduces him. Her hands with scarlet fingernail fondle his delta, a place like a hill covered by the grass. His bird is growing bigger and stronger. And he cannot help to devour her pink nipples, to kiss her snow white neck, and to whisper into her ears. Her body is a ceremony, a power station, a light house. And the neon lights spread the magic colour on her skin.

He becomes impulsive. He lifts her short silver skirt, then I see her delta. She has very lush bush, like bush growing by the

體，釋放我的身體，帶我的身體脫離辭典，脫離文法和語句，讓我的身體破除所有規矩。賣淫無須講究英語水準，該有多輕鬆。像她就不用帶著辭典隨時準備應付狀況。

換她了，輪到她施展威力。她媚惑他。她猩紅的纖指撫弄他的三角洲，芳草蔓生的小丘。他的鳥逐漸脹大，堅挺。他忍不住吸吮她的乳頭，啃吻雪白的粉頸，在她耳旁細語呢喃。她的身體是一場儀典，一處發電站，一座燈塔。霓虹燈於她的肌膚潑灑奇幻光彩。

他衝動難抑。他撩起她的銀色短裙，我看見那片三角洲。她的灌叢異常茂密，有如熱帶河岸苗長的蔓草。他的手指穿過那片灌叢，沒入她的洞穴。她容光煥發，朱唇半啓。期待，激動。他抽出手指，跪下來，開始親吻她的灌叢，吸舔她的洞穴。她的愛液染亮他的面龐。

無與倫比的墮落令我著迷。

無與倫比的墮落吸磁般媚惑我。

音樂來到最後一章。旋律盛大。近乎擾人。

舞台旋轉當中，男的直立如山。那女的跪下，將他的鳥放進嘴裡。她的雙唇和溪谷一般淫潤。她吸吮。他微微抖顫，身體擺晃。他出力緊握她光裸的肩頭，強忍著。兩具身體黏合成一塊。他沒辦法再握緊她一分。火山爆噴，銀亮的黏液暈染她的容顏。

river in the tropical zone. His fingers travel through her bushes, and disappeared into her cave. Her face now is lighted. Her mouth is half opened. Waiting and arousing. His fingers come out from her cave. He kneels down, starts to kiss her bush and sucks her cave. Her juice is shining on his face.

The great decadence is attracting me.

The great decadence is seducing me like a magnet.

The music goes to the end part. Big melody. Almost disturbing.

On the turning stage, the man stands like a mountain. The woman kneel down and takes his bird into her mouth. Her lips are as wet as her valley. She sucks him. He is slightly shaking, and his body is swinging. He holds her naked shouder strongly and he endures. Two bodies sticks together. Now he cannot hold her any more. The volcano erupts, and the silver liquid covers her face.

heaven

n. **1.** a place believed to be the home of God, where good people go when they die; **2.** a place or state of bliss.

My father said he once dreamed eating some spring sprouts.

My father loves spring sprouts. In that dream his teeth bites the fresh spring sprouts and he clearly hears the crispy sound from his mouth. It is such a beautiful sound. It is just like heaven, he said. But my mother always disagree with him. My mother think there is no sound in the dream. If you hear sound in the dream just because you imagine you hear it.

"The dream is silent, like heaven." That what she said.

Chinese Heaven must have lots of peach trees, lots fairy ladies dressed in silk skirt with long sleeves, like we saw in the martial art films. There is no mans, but only the son of the Heavens lives there, eating peaches everyday, served by beautiful fairy ladies. I don't know if this Heaven where my grandmother prayed and wanted to go after she died. I hope so. But if my grandmother really living there now, then she would ruin the whole fairyland. Because she is ugly.

"Is Heaven really silent?" I once asked my mother, timidly.

"What?! You think Heaven is as noisy as this compound?" she answered.

The compound we lived was crowdy, tiny and messy like war zone. There were about twenty families live with us, and every family had seven or nine children since One Child

【天堂】

〈名詞〉**1.** 咸信乃神之家園，好人死後的歸所；**2.** 極樂之地或狀態。

我父親說他有次夢見自己在吃芽菜。我父親很喜歡芽菜。夢裡他的牙齒嚼著新鮮的芽菜，那爽脆的聲響分外清晰，何其美妙悅耳的聲音。有如天堂一般，他說。但我母親老愛和他唱反調。她認定夢裡不會有聲音。如果你作夢聽見聲音，那鐵定是你自己幻想出來的。

「夢沒有聲音，跟天堂一樣。」這是她的意見。

中國的天堂裡面一定有很多桃樹，很多仙女身穿絲羅裙，長長的水袖，像我們武術片裡看到的那樣。那兒沒有男人，住的只有天之驕子，每天享用仙桃，還有美貌的仙女服侍。不曉得我姥姥衷心祈求，死後想去的所在是否便是這個天堂。但願如此。不過，如果我姥姥此刻當真住在那兒，整個仙境一定被她拖垮。因為，她實在太醜了。

「天堂真的沒有聲音？」有次我怯怯地問母親。

「什麼？你以為天堂會像我們大雜院一樣吵死人？」她答道。

我們住的大雜院又擠又小又亂，活像戰區。那兒連我們起碼住了二十戶人家，每家少不了七或九個小孩，誰叫一胎化政策一九七七年後才開始實施。所以，總共加起來約莫一百五十個小鬼，成天又吼又鬥又哭。到了晚上，就聽那二十來位老奶

Policy only starts from 1977. So there were about 150 children constantly shouting fighting crying everyday. Then there were about twenty grandmothers shouting to at least forty sons and forty daughters-in-laws every evening. So compound is like little village. And we raised roosters and hens everywhere in the compound too. All the time you can hear little chickens snivelling for being stepped when kids ran over them. And fathers would chase kids and beat the kids up. That was the life before my parents start make business. Soon, leather shoes, cloth shoes, sports shoes were piles and piles like hill sitting in our compound yard. At the beginning they worked for some shoes buyers. Five years later my parents opened their own factory, and then everybody from the same compound became their employees.

So you, a Westerner, ask me again: "What do you think Heaven is like? Assuming you think there is one . . ."

I recall what my mother thought of Heaven and what my father thought of spring sprouts. I am confused: "Which Heaven? Chinese Heaven or Western Heaven?"

"Is there a difference?" you laugh.

"There must be different."

"If there are different Heavens, I guess then the different Heavens might fight each other."

"Fighting is good. Makes Heaven more liveable," I say.

You look at me surprisely. You know I like to fight. I am woman warrior. I like to do everything through fighting. I fight for everything. Struggle for everything. We Chinese are used to struggle get everything: food, education, house, freedom, visa, and human rights. If no need struggle then we don't know how to live anymore.

奶教訓至少四十個兒子加上四十個媳婦。這大雜院等於一座小村落。處處有人養著公雞母雞。隨時都可聽見小雞被孩子踩著了發出哀鳴。作父親的便追過去逮人一陣好打。爸媽做生意之前我們家便是這樣過活。沒多久，皮鞋，布鞋，運動鞋疊成小山堆滿我們的院落。起初，他們幫一些鞋商幹活。五年後，我父母自己搞了鞋廠，大雜院裡的男男女女成為他們的夥計。

而你，一個西洋人，又再問我：「妳認為天堂長什麼樣子？假定妳覺得那兒是……」

我回想起母親關於天堂的看法，以及父親對芽菜的感觸。我困惑了：「哪個天堂？中國的天堂還是西洋的天堂？」

「這有差別嗎？」你笑。

「一定有差。」

「如果天堂還有分別，我猜那不同派別的天堂會鬥來鬥去。」

「鬥就鬥，沒什麼不好，這樣天堂住起來才有意思，」我說。

你驚訝地看著我。你知道我喜歡爭鬥。我是女鬥士。我喜歡每件事鬥上那麼一下。我每件事爭，每件事鬥。我們中國人習慣鬥爭贏得一切：食物，教育，住屋，自由，簽證，人權。如果鬥爭派不上用場，我們生活起來反倒手足無措。

romance

n. **1.** a fantasy, fiction, legend, novel, story, tale; **2.** an exaggeration, falsehood, lie; **3.** ballad, idyll, song.

Friendship endures longer than romance. I often think this sentence in your diary, but when I look in *Thesaurus* I see so many possible words for *romance*. Is *romance* love?

"What is exactly *Romance*?" I ask you.

"Romance?"

You are thinking hard. Maybe is first time people askthis question to you.

"Well, it's a complicated word . . . Maybe romance is like a rose . . ."

"Rose? What kind of rose?"

We are in garden so you go back in house fetch book.

"A rose like in this poem," you say, and read me:

All night by the rose, the rose,
All night by the rose I lay.
Dared I not the rose steal,
And yet I bore the flower away.

Poem very beautiful, I want know who wrote it. On book says Anon.

"This Anon very good writer," I say. "I think I prefer to Shakespeare, much easier."

【羅曼史】

〈名詞〉**1.** 幻想，虛構，傳奇，小說，故事，傳說；**2.** 誇張，謬誤，謊言；
3. 浪漫曲，牧歌，情歌。

「友誼總是比羅曼史更經得起時間考驗。」我常常想起你
日記裡的這一句，但是查過《索引典》，我看到和羅曼史相關
的字眼有好多。羅曼史代表愛情嗎？

「羅曼史到底是什麼？」我抓你來問。

「羅曼史？」

看你苦思的樣子。或許頭一遭有人問你這個。

「噢，這個字蠻複雜……或許羅曼史就像玫瑰……」

「玫瑰？哪一種玫瑰？」

我們人在院子，你進去屋裡拿了本書回來。

「像這首詩裡面的玫瑰，」你說，唸給我聽。

整夜玫瑰為伴，玫瑰
整夜玫瑰為伴我躺下
玫瑰竊賊吾不敢為
然我終究攜花而歸

詩非常美，我想知道這誰寫的。書上署名阿儂。

「這位阿儂寫得可真好，」我說。「我覺得他比莎士比亞
簡單多了，我喜歡。」

You laugh. "Yes, and perhaps even more prolific."

"?"

"*Anon* isn't a person. It's just what we say when we don't know who wrote something."

Annoyed about this Anon, I look round in your garden. There is no any rose, let alone Chinese rose.

"How can you never plant any rose in the garden?" I say. "Every *green finger* growing rose in this country, as far as I can see. You should have one."

You agree with me, this time, no any doubts.

So we now have a climbing rose in our garden, against the wall. Is a skinny plant with five green leafs and some annoying thorn. We had argument in flower market because I want buy rose with blossoms, but you rather buy little sprout and wait for its growing.

You use your favourite tool—*spade*—to dig the hole. "The hole must be twice as wide as the root spread, and two-feet deep . . ." You measure the hole with the fingers: "The rose has mainstructural canes and flowering shoots, so the canes must be tied or woven into a support to keep the rose off the ground." You are so scientific. I look at you. Are you romantic farmer?

Then, here, in new world far away from my home, here, under your fruit tree without flowers, you start sing a song, a famous song which I heard somewhere maybe in China before. You voice gentle and almost trembled.

Some say love it is a river
that drowns the tender reed

你笑出聲。「沒錯，或許還更有創造力。」

「？」

「『阿儂』不是個人。這只表示作者是無名氏。」

這阿儂可真煩，我在你的庭院四下打量。半朵玫瑰也無，中國玫瑰（月季）更不用說了。

「你怎麼院子裡從來都不種玫瑰？」我說。「就我所見，這國家的綠手指沒有人不種玫瑰。你應該要種才對。」

這回，你同意我的看法，沒多說一句。

所以呢，如今我們院子裡多出蔓性玫瑰，順牆攀爬。這細瘦的植物帶有五片綠葉和惱人的尖刺。我們在花卉市場時還針鋒相對，我想買已經含苞的玫瑰，你卻只要小嫩枝，慢慢等它長成。

你操作最喜愛的工具——鐵鍬——挖起洞來。「這洞必須比根的範圍寬兩倍，深要有兩呎……」你比著手指丈量：「玫瑰有主體結構的莖部和長花的枝條，所以莖部要綁住或編牢支架，玫瑰才能站起來往上長。」你好科學，我刮目相看。你是浪漫的莊稼漢嗎？

接下來，這個地方，離我家鄉千里遠的嶄新天地，這個地方，在你的無花果樹下，你開口唱歌，這一首名曲我以前哪兒聽過，或許在中國便曾經聽過。你溫柔的歌聲幾乎微微發顫。

有人說愛是條河
漫過柔順的蘆葦
有人說愛是把剃刀
劃過靈魂任你滴血
有人說愛是飢渴

Some say love it is a razor
that leaves your soul to bleed
Some say love it is a hunger
an endless aching need
I say love it is a flower
and you its only seed

It's the heart afraid of breaking
that never learns to dance
It's the dream afraid of waking
that never takes the chance
It's the one who won't be taken
who cannot seem to give
And the soul afraid of dying
that never learns to live

When the night has been too lonely
and the road has been too long
Then you think that love is only
for the lucky and the strong
Just remember in the winter
far beneath the bitter snow
Lies the seed that with the sun's love
in the spring becomes the rose

If people hears this song, and she doesn't feel moved—then I think that people must not human.

I love you. And you know I love you. And you love me as well.

You tell me song is from Bette Midler—your favorite. You say you like the strong, rude women. You say all homosexual like Bette Midler, Mae West and Billie Holiday. But Billie

苦苦索求沒有盡頭
我說愛是綻放的花朵
唯獨你能為它播種
害怕破碎的心
始終學不好舞步
不敢醒來的夢
總讓機會溜走
那難以打動的人
似乎也就不懂付出
畏懼消逝的靈魂
何曾真正活過

當長夜如此孤寂
當路途太過遙遠
你以為愛專屬那
幸運的強者所有
莫忘嚴冬之中
層層冰雪底下
埋藏陽光鍾愛的花種
留待春日化為玫瑰

　　若有人聽見這首歌，她沒有深受感動——那我想此人形同草木。

　　我愛你。你曉得我愛你。而且你也愛我。

　　你告訴我這首歌來自貝蒂・米勒——你的最愛。你說你喜歡硬派、粗線條的女人。你說所有的同性戀者全都喜歡貝蒂・

Holiday not strong—she commit a suicide.

Two days after, you take me watch documentary films double bill. Two crazy women in one night.

Small cinema on Rupert Street. First one about Mae West, an extremely successful Hollywood star, always make audiences happy and laughing. She is a "No. 1" woman without any "competition" in the world, as she said to media. Sexy, always wearing shining jewellery, flirty, confidently. Even in her eighty-seven years old, she dressed a sexy white dazzling fur coat, and all around by young black bodyguards and cameras. And her face still very beautiful and young even in that age. She the tropical sun, nobody can be more brighter than her.

Second film is *Billie on Billie*, right after Mae West documentary. First scene in the film is Billie Holiday standing on the stage sadly singing, "Don't talk about me . . ."—last appearance on TV before she died. She is a extremely sad face, hopeless expression. From the film I learned her struggled by her childhood, her prostitution mother, her sex abuse when she twelve years old, her drug and alcohol, her poor dignity being a black. Billie Holiday, she is not melancholy, she is hopeless.

"I always fear . . ." she says in the film. A strange fruit. I want leave the cinema to cry. I feel her pain in my heart. And later on when I think of Mae West again I find her story is so surreal, like fairy story comes from the moon . . .

I want become Mae West, be her courage, her bravery, her humour, her creativity, her challenging to the world. She live with admiration, rich, and confidence. Men all her slaves; men

米勒，梅・蕙絲以及比莉・哈樂黛。不過比莉・哈樂黛不夠強硬——她自殺了。

過了兩天，你帶我去看同場加映的紀錄片。一晚有兩位瘋狂的女性。

魯拔街的小戲院。第一部演梅・蕙絲，成就非凡的好萊塢大明星，永遠讓觀眾又樂又笑。她是舉世「第一」，沒有「對手」的女人，她對媒體如此宣稱。性感，永遠一身閃亮珠寶，風騷，氣勢凌人。即使年紀來到八十七高齡，依舊披上性感炫目的白色皮草，身邊簇擁年輕的黑人保鑣和開麥拉。她的臉以年紀來說還是非常漂亮，非常年輕。她是熱帶的驕陽，光熱無人能及。

第二部演《比莉談比莉》，接在梅・蕙絲的紀錄片之後。電影第一個鏡頭，比莉哈樂黛站在舞台幽幽唱著，「別談到我……」——她生前最後一次電視演出。她的臉異常悲哀，無望的表情。從電影我得知她童年的掙扎，她賣淫的母親，她十二歲遭受的性虐待，她的藥癮和酒癮，她身為黑人卑微的尊嚴。比莉・哈樂黛，她不是悽涼，她全然絕望。

「我總是害怕……」電影裡她說。一枚奇異的果實。我想逃出戲院痛哭。我感到她的苦刺疼我的心。稍後，再度想起梅・蕙絲的時候，我發現她的故事如此超現實，彷如來自月球的神話故事……

我想當個梅・蕙絲，我想擁有她的膽量，她的勇氣，她的幽默，她的創造力，她對世人的挑釁。她一生飽嚐欽羨，財富，信心滿滿。男人全都成為她的奴隸，任她差遣使喚。我想演出那種角色。但現實裡的我只是個小卒子，連痛苦的比莉都

used by her. I want play that role. But is the reality I am nobody, not even painful Billie, I am just obscure nobody with name starts from Z. Maybe this *romance* with you put some weight into my life.

不能算，我這無名小輩只配被人家叫做Z。或許和你有了羅曼史才能爲我的人生增添些許分量。

July

physical work

physical *adj.* **1.** of the body, as contrasted with the mind or spirit; **2.** of material things or nature; **3.** of physics.

For six days now London really hot. Suddenly people almost nudes in street and sit about on grasses chatting. Mrs Margaret changed to beige suede sandals. I can't concentrate her lessons in the heat.

Hotness make you unhappy because you must drive van like oven.

I see you always disappear with that white van. A very old van with a side door sunken and another side door cannot close *properly*, unless you kick it violently. The front and the back windows always covered by thick dust. It is a peasant van, or a working-class van.

The van is your business method to earn money via delivering goods. You say you can get this job only because you have got a big van.

You drive whole day in that van for delivering. The goods are for somebody's birthday, party, ceremony, wedding, or any day someone has excuse to consume the money.

You drive from 7 o'clock early morning, till late night.

You drive seven days a week. Every day on the road, on those roads towards middle-class big family houses.

You come back home in the dark, without any energy left. Life suddenly becomes bit boring. I find you are a physical

【勞力工作】

勞力〈形容詞〉**1.** 身體的，和心智或精神相對立；**2.** 物質的或自然的；**3.** 物理的。

　　一連六天，倫敦快要熱死人。突然間，街頭的民眾幾乎扒光身體，坐在草地上議論紛紛。瑪格麗特小姐換上米色麂皮涼鞋。熱浪中我實在沒辦法專心聽她講課。

　　高溫讓你很不高興，因為你開的小貨車有如烘爐。

　　我老是看你和那輛白色貨車一起消失。年事已高的老爺車，一邊的車門凹陷，另一邊沒辦法妥當關閉，除非你狠狠賞它一腳。前面和後面的窗戶永遠卡一層厚厚的汙垢。這是一輛農用貨車，或者說工人階級的貨車。

　　你用這輛車幫人送貨賺取生活費。你說全靠這大傢伙你才有辦法弄到這份工作。

　　你整天開著那輛貨車跑。載東載西，看有誰過生日，開派對，舉行儀式，辦婚禮，或隨便哪天有人找到藉口花錢消費便能派上用場。

　　你從清早七點開始幹活，直到夜深。你一週開車七天。每天路上跑個沒完，通往那些中產階級家庭豪宅大院的馬路。

　　你摸黑回到家，往往已經筋疲力盡。忽然間，日子變得有些乏味。我發現你是個賣力氣的人，一個勞動者，赤手空拳掙飯吃。這世界可有好多人指頭往電腦鍵盤這麼敲敲打打便能過活。

man, a labourer, using your hands to survive. While lots people in this world just need use fingers to earn living by clicking computer keyboard.

I never see you sell the sculptures. Nobody want buy a suffered and twisted statue, I guess. If they do, they maybe buy a female nude statue. Once I saw you were making a wooden swimming pool model, as the advertisement for Red Bull company. Another time I saw you were making a huge telephone model for Vodaphone. I heard you saying "it looks ridiculous", "it is so tacky" while you were making these things. But you got paid. Then one day you stop getting these kinds job. I don't know why.

"You always say physical work makes people happier, but you are not happy now." I make some tea and salad for you. It is so late.

"I am too tired. That's why . . ." You sit on the chair, by the kitchen table. You hair is messy, covered by the dust.

"Physical work doesn't do any good," I say.

"But at least you don't worry about living." You sip the tea, the tea is sucking your energy.

"For me mental work better than physical work," I say. "Nobody wants physical work. Only you, and my parents." I put the salad bowl in front of you.

You start to eat salad, and the room goes quiet. The white cabbage is very crunchy, and the red carrots are hard too. Your teeth are trying to grind them into pieces. Your face looks uneasy.

In my hometown, we don't use these two words:

Physical work / mental work

我從沒看你賣過雕塑作品。那種受苦扭曲的雕像誰都不會想要的，我猜。就算要買，人家大概只想找個裸女雕像。有一回，我看你做個木頭的泳池模型，那是紅牛公司廣告要用的。另一次，我看你幫伏得風電信公司做了個好大的電話模型。我聽見你邊做邊唸：「看起來太荒謬了」，「好低級的東西」。然而有人付錢多好。後來你拒絕再接這種案子。真是搞不懂你。

「你一直說勞力工作會給人帶來快樂，可是你現在哪有快樂？」我為你泡茶做沙拉。已經好晚了現在。

「我累壞了。所以……」你坐在椅子上，廚房餐桌旁邊。你頭髮亂糟糟，都是塵土。

「勞力工作沒半點好處，」我說。

「起碼你不用煩惱生活的問題。」你啜了口茶，茶湯吸吮你的精力。

「對我來說，勞心工作比勞力好多了，」我說。「不會有人想幹勞力工作。只有你，還有我爸媽。」我將沙拉碗往你面前一擺。

你低頭吃起沙拉，屋子沉寂下來。高麗菜嘎吱嘎吱，胡蘿蔔也軟不到哪裡去。你牙齒賣力嚼碎沙拉，臉色看來不太舒服。

在我家鄉，我們不用這兩種字眼：

勞力工作／勞心工作

所有的工作都叫做「討生活」——覓食生活。做鞋子，做豆腐，做塑膠提袋，做三明治……這些工作仰賴我們的身體。身體幫我們賺取生活來源。今天我出國學習英語，我得靠腦力來學習。我曉得未來我可以靠腦力來過活。

All the work is called "討生活"—scavenge the living. Making shoes, making tofus, making plastic bags, making switches . . . All these works rely on our bodies. And bodies earn our living back. Now I come to abroad studying English. And I do that with my brain. And I know in the future I earn living from my brain.

You insist physical worker better than intellectual.

"An intellectual can have a big brain, but a very small heart."

I never heard before that. Why you think of that?

"I want a simple life," you say. "I want to go back to the life of a farmer."

Intellectual: "知識分子 " (zhi shi fen zi).

"知識" mean knowledge, "分子" mean molecule. Numerous molecule of knowledge will make up man knowledgeable.

In China, intellectual is everything *noble*. It mean honour, dignity, responsibility, respect, understanding. To be intellectual in China is splendid dream to youth who from peasant background. Nobody blame him, even in Culture Revolution time and seemed these people suffered, but really was time for them having privileged to being re-educated, get to know another different life.

So if you don't want to be intellectual, then you a Red Guard too, like Red Guards who beat up intellectuals during Culture Revolution. A Red Guard who living in the West.

I never thought I would like a Red Guard, but I like you. I am in love with you, even if you say you not intellectual.

I not intellectual either. In the West, in this country, I am barbarian, illiterate peasant girl, a face of third world, and irresponsible foreigner. An alien from another planet.

你堅持勞力工人好過知識分子。

「知識分子可能大腦發達，心胸渺小。」

我從沒聽過這種說法。你怎麼會這樣想？

「我想簡簡單單過日子，」你說。「我想回到農民過的那種日子。」

Intellectual：「知識分子」。

「知識」代表學問，「分子」代表組成分子。許許多多的知識成分組合起來讓人變得很有學問。

在中國，知識分子樣樣高人一等。它意味著光榮，高尚，責任，敬重，聰明。在中國，能夠成為知識分子對農家出身的子弟來說，等於輝煌的夢想。沒有人會責怪他如此夢想，即使文化大革命時期，這些知識分子飽受折磨，但對他們而言，這時期也讓他們有幸接受再教育，體認廣大群眾的生活。

所以，如果你不願成為知識分子，那你也算紅衛兵，像文化大革命對知識分子拳打腳踢的紅衛兵。一個活在西方世界的紅衛兵。

我從沒想過自己會喜歡上一個紅衛兵，但我喜歡你。我愛上了你，即使你口口聲聲說你不是知識分子。

我也不是知識分子。在西方，在這國家，我是野蠻人，目不識丁的鄉下村姑，一副第三世界的臉孔，靠不住的外國人。我是來自外星球的異形。

isolate

v. to place apart or alone; chem obtain (a substance) in uncombined form.

You are not at home again. You have so many social contacts, so many old friends need to see and chat, so many ex-lovers live in the same city as well, and I don't know anybody in this country. I am alone at home. Dictionary checking, checking dictionary . . . I am tired of learning words, more new words, everyday. More exercise on tense, make a sentence on the past participial tense, and make a sentence on past conditional tense . . . So many different tenses, but only one life. Why waste time to study?

The garden outside is quiet. The leafs are breathing and figs are growing. Bees are beeing around the jasmine tree. But I feel lonely. I look that male nude statue under the fig tree. He is still facing down, like always. An enigma. Totally an enigma. Whenever I go to the modern museum, like Tate Modern, I never understand those modern sculptures. I hate them. They seem don't want to communicate with me, but their huge presence disturb me.

The house is empty. Is the loneliness an emptiness?

I remember my grandmother always recite two sentences from the Buddhist sutras:

色不異空，空不異色
色皆是空，空皆是色

【孤立】

〈動詞〉使孤立，隔離；（化學用語）使離析。

　　你又不在家了。你有好多交際應酬，好多老朋友得去拜訪
談心，好多前任愛人同住一座城市，而這地方我誰也不認識。
我自己一個人在家。找辭典，翻辭典……我好煩，學習生字，
每天學習更多的生字。練習時態，用過去分詞造句，用過去條
件式造句……這麼多眼花撩亂的時態，可生命只有一條。幹嘛
浪費時間學這種東西？

　　屋外庭院寂靜。綠葉吐息，無花果脹大。茉莉花叢群蜂嗡
嗡。我分外寂寞。望著無花果樹下那具男裸雕。他的臉依舊朝
下，恆久不變。不解之謎。完全的不解之謎。每次去到當代的
美術館，比如泰特現代美術館，我永遠看不懂那些現代雕塑。
我只覺討厭。他們似乎從沒打算和我溝通，那巨大的存在徒然
令我心煩意亂。

　　這屋子空空的。莫非寂寞也是空的。

　　我想起姥姥老是喜歡引用佛經裡面兩句：

　　　　色不異空，空不異色。
　　　　色皆是空，空皆是色。

　　她解釋這代表空沒有形式，而形式也是空。空不代表空

She explains it means the emptiness is without form, but the form is also the emptiness. The emptiness is not empty, actually it is full. It is the beginning of everything.

So far, I don't see the emptiness is the beginning of everything. It only means loneliness to me. I don't have a family here, and I don't have a house or a job here, and I don't have anything familiar here, and I only can speak low English here. Empty.

I think the loneliness in this country is something very solid, very heavy. It is touchable and reachable, easily.

The loneliness comes to me in certain hours everyday, like a visitor. Like a friend you never expected, a friend you never really want be with, but he always visit you and love you somehow. When the sun leaves the sky, when the enormous darkness swallow the last red strip in the horizon, from that moment, I can see the shape of the loneliness in front of me, then surround my body, my night, my dream.

Something missing, something lost in my life, something which used to fulfill in my China life.

We don't have much the individuality concept in China. We are collective, and we believe in collectivism. Collective Farm, Collective Leadership. Now we have *Group Life Insurance* from the governments as well. When I was in middle school, we studied *Group Dancing*. We danced with 200 students as part of the school lesson. We have to dance exactly the same pace and the same movement in the music. Maybe that's why I never feel lonely in China.

But here, in this place in the West, I lost my reference. And I have to rely on my own sensibility. But my sensibility toward

虛，實際上它本身完滿。它是萬物的源頭。

到目前為止，我看不出何以空是萬物的源頭。空只會讓我寂寞而已。這地方我沒有家，我沒有房子或工作，這地方沒有任何東西讓我感到熟悉，我會講的只有低水平的英語。空。

我想，在這國家，寂寞還真是結結實實的沉重。你可以摸到它，夠著它，輕而易舉。

每日特定時分，寂寞向我襲來，訪客一般。像你未曾預期的友人，你未曾真心往來的友人，但他持續不斷造訪你，而且不知怎地就是喜歡你。當陽光揮別天空，當無邊的黑暗吞沒遠天最後一抹紅霞，從那時刻起，我可以看見寂寞在我眼前成形，包圍我的身軀，包圍我的夜，我的夢。

某種東西消失，從我生命當中消失，從前在中國曾經填滿我生命的東西。

我們中國沒有多少個體的概念。我們屬於集體，我們信的是集體主義。集體農場，集體領導。如今政府還提供我們**集體人壽保險**。唸中學的時候，我們學習集體舞蹈。兩百個學生同步起舞，這是正規課程的一部分。我們必須同時抓準音樂的節拍，動作整齊劃一。或許正因如此，在中國時我從未感到寂寞。

但這裡，來到這西方世界，沒有人讓我參考學習。一切全憑我自己的感覺行事。然而，我對周遭世界的感覺往往混淆不清。我從你書架取來一本書，《芙烈達・卡蘿》。那個墨西哥女藝術家。這本書冊收錄了她的畫作，她的一生，她駭人的病痛，被巴士撞成殘廢。好多幅自畫像。我還以為畫家一輩子留下一幅自畫像便已足夠，就像人死後只需一塊墓碑。然而芙烈達・卡蘿的自畫像有好多，仿佛她這一生死去好多回。其中有

the world is so unclear.

I take out one a book from your shelf, Frida Kahlo. That Mexican woman artist. It is a picture album of her painting, her life, and her terrible illness, being disabled after the bus accidents. So many self-portraits. I thought one painter only does one of these in his life, like one person only have one gravestone. But Frida Kahlo has so many self-portraits, as if she died many many times in her life. There is one called *Self-Portrait with Necklace of Thorns*. She has the sharp and heavy eyebrow like two short knives; her eyes like black shining glass. She has the thick dark hair like a dark forest; the necklace of thorns climbing on her neck. There is a black monkey and black cat sitting on her shoulder.

The impression on her face is so strong. I learn that she had to plant metal in her body so that to support her survive from disable. I feel my heart is being penetrated by the thorns she painted. I feel painful.

When I put down Frida Kahlo, I think of you. You love the heaviness of life. You like to feel the difficulty and the roughness. I think you like to feel the weight of the life. You said you hated IKEA, because furnitures from IKEA are light and smooth.

I walk to the garden, staring at your sculptures again, one by one, carefully, attentively, thinking of you with my new eyes. That naked man, without head, stubbornly faces down towards the ground with twisted huge legs. What makes him so suffering?

一幅題名《佩帶荊棘項鍊的自畫像》。畫中她鋒利的濃眉宛如兩把短刃；眼眸如玻璃珠般黑亮。她濃密的黑髮像黑漆漆的密林；荊棘項鍊於她頸項間攀爬。兩邊的肩頭各據一隻黑猴和黑貓。

那臉龐孕生的印象如此強烈。我知道她殘廢以後，體內必須植入鋼架方能支撐。我感覺她畫上去的荊棘刺穿我的心。我感到痛。

放下芙烈達·卡蘿，我想起了你。你愛生命的沉重。你喜歡感受困苦和艱辛。我想你喜歡感受生命的重荷。你說過你討厭 IKEA，因為 IKEA 的家具一派輕巧平滑。

我走進院子，再度凝視你的雕塑，一個看過一個，仔細地，專注地，帶著新奇的目光對你思索。赤裸的男子，沒有頭，頑強地朝向地面，兩條巨腿扭曲交纏。令他如此痛苦的到底是什麼？

humour

n. **1.** an ability to say or perceive things that are amusing; **2.** an amusing quality in a situation, film, etc; **3.** a state of mind, mood; **4.** *old-fashioned* fluid in the body. *v.* to be kind and indulgent.

Yesterday at home we celebrate my birthday. I turn to 24. OK I don't know when is my real birthday, but passport birthday can be great excuse to have a big Chinese meal.

It is the year of goat. My animal sign is goat too. It is my second twelth year after the year of my birth, which means I am having my most important year in my life, because it is a year I meet my destiny. My mother will say that.

We are having a hotpot birthday party. You say you never eat hotpot meal before. You say it is interesting to see people sitting around a big table and cook food from a steaming pot in the middle.

So there is about six or seven people all together. Some are your friends. Two of them from my English language school. One is from Japan called Yoko. Yoko has very slim cat eyes, and neat cut fringe covered her forehead like a hat. Her hairs has lots different colours like red and green and blue. She looks like punk, or maybe she is real punk. Another one is from Korea called Kim Yan Zhen. Kim has very pale face, and she looks whiter than any white people. These two are famous in our language school because their English is impossible. Mrs Margaret say my English even is better than them. I think maybe because when Japanese girl speaks English, people

【幽默】

〈名詞〉**1.** 表達或感受有趣事物的能力；**2.** 某個情境或電影所包含的趣味性質；**3.** 心情，情緒；**4.** （舊式用語）人體內基本的體液。〈動詞〉迎合，遷就。

　　昨天，我們在家裡慶祝我的生日。我二十四歲了。對啦，我不清楚自己確切的生日，但護照上的日期也足以提供藉口來一頓中國大餐。

　　今年是羊年。我的生肖正好也是羊年。這是我出生後第二輪的十二年，這表示我來到此生最重要的年份，因為這是我的本命年。我母親一定會這麼說。

　　我們舉辦火鍋生日派對。你說以前從沒吃過火鍋。你說好有趣，一群人圍坐，從餐桌中間熱騰騰的鍋子煮東西吃。

　　全部加起來總共六七個人。其中有你的朋友，兩個我語言學校的同學。一位來自日本，叫洋子。洋子有對細長的貓眼，修剪整齊的瀏海覆蓋前額，像頂小帽。她頭髮的顏色雜陳，有紅有青有藍，看起來像龐克，搞不好還真的就是龐克。另一位來自韓國的叫金妍珍。金的臉色十分白皙，她長得比白人還要白。這兩位在我們語言學校名頭響亮，因為她們的英語能力凡人無法擋。瑪格麗特小姐說我的英語甚至還在她們之上。我在想，或許因為日本小姐開口說英語時，人家還以為她在講日語。而韓國小姐說英語時，一味地點頭欠身表示客氣，無奈嘴巴聲音就是出不來。不過呢，她們總歸都算我的同黨，儘管韓國人討厭日本人，而日本人一向與中國人不對盤。但重要的

would think she is speaking Japanese. And when Korea girl speaks English, she keeps nod her head and bow her back to show the modest, but without giving anything verbal. But anyhow, they are kind of my comrades, although Korea hates Japanese, and Japanese were not friendly with Chinese. Most important thing, they use very simple words. Yoko sits down and say, "Are we eat?"; Kim Yan Zhen looks at the hotpot and asks, "Cook, you?" I like that. I like people speak that way. So we understand each other easily.

It is a meal between East and West, though three Orientals only can speak foreign language to communicate.

It is *worship* of eating, is the exactly word to describe this.

I make spicy red chilli soup for the hotpot, by putting in gingers, garlic, spring onions, leeks, dried mushroom and chillis to stew the soup. After the soup becomes boiling I put in tofu and lamb. With hotpot, lamb is essential for the soup. It gives the form content. Otherwise hotpot is the interesting form of meaningless. Is a pity that you are *vegetarian*, and all of your friends are also vegetarians in this room.

While I am cooking the lamb in the pot, you and your friend just look at it, and put the uncooked carrots straight into the mouth. In Chinese, we say the way you cut the meat reflects the way you live. They must be timid people.

Here is the birthday gift from you. Two book. The first is *The Happy Prince and Other Tales* by Oscar Wilde. You say is good book for me to start with, to understand English writing easily. The second one is *To the Lighthouse* by Virginia Woolf. You say it can be read later on, when my English becomes very good.

是，她們使用的字眼都很簡單。洋子坐下來便說，「煮東西，你？」這我喜歡。我喜歡別人這樣講話。所以我們很容易理解彼此的意思。

這是一場東方對上西方的餐宴，雖然三個東方人只能用異國的語言來溝通。

這是一場大快朵頤的儀式，這個字用來形容這場餐宴再準確不過。

我準備了紅通辛辣的火鍋湯底，裡面加入薑，蒜頭，青蔥，韭菜，乾香菇和辣椒熬製而成。湯頭滾開後，我放進豆腐和羊肉。吃火鍋，羊肉是湯汁的關鍵。它賦予形式以內容。少了羊肉，火鍋便徒具噱頭形式而已。你這個素食者真是太遺憾了，這屋內，你的朋友碰巧還全都是素食者。

我將羊肉放進鍋裡煮的時候，你和你的朋友只是睜眼瞧著，生的胡蘿蔔直接往嘴裡啃。在中國我們說，從一個人切肉的樣子可以看出他如何過活。想必他們都是害羞人士。

這裡有你送的生日禮物。兩本書。第一本是奧斯卡·王爾德的《快樂王子故事集》。你說這本書很適合我這個初學者，裡面的英文很容易懂。第二本是維吉妮亞·吳爾芙的《燈塔行》。你說這本可以慢點再讀，等我英文水平提高之後。

日本小姐洋子給我一個小紙盒。相當精緻，好像香水的包裝盒。盒面上寫著：

防水個人按摩器

中國製

什麼防水的玩意？電池？手錶？盒上有圖示：樣子像小黃

Then Japanese girl Yoko gives me small little box. It is delicate, like perfume box. On the cover it says:

Waterproof Personal Massager
MADE IN CHINA

What's this waterproof? Battery? Watch? There is picture on the cover: it is something looks like small cucumber but slightly bended.

Curiously, I open the box. It comes out a smooth plastic thing look exactly like small cucumber. On the bottom there are some buttons: on/off/fast/slow. Is it toothbrush machine? I put into my mouth, but it not fit easily. A massage machine for facial beauty? Or for back and neck aching? Maybe the instruction will tell me.

I unfold the little piece of instruction.

Natural Contours — it's great to be a woman

Then there is a printed letter:

Dear Customer,

Thank you for purchasing your new natural contours massager. Natural contours is a revolutionary approach to personal relaxation: a massager that's ergonomically designed to fit the contours of a woman's body. It is our goal to offer you personal products that encompass quality, taste, and style to please today's woman.

With the move toward greater self-awareness and exploration for women, we hope this product meets with your expectations and opens up a whole new world of personal relaxation for you.

瓜，有點彎彎的。

　　滿心好奇，我打開紙盒。出來一根光滑的塑膠玩意，看起來正像小黃瓜。底部有幾個按鍵：開／關／快／慢。這可是電動牙刷？我放進嘴裡試試，不太合用。這是臉部按摩美容器？還是舒緩背頸痠疼用的？看了說明書應該就能知道。

　　我將說明書攤開。

自然曲線——樂為女人

　　然後是印刷的文字：

親愛的顧客：

感謝您購買全新一代的自然曲線按摩器。

自然曲線提供革命性的個人紓解之道：本按摩器精心設計貼合女性身體曲線。我們致力提供您結合品質，品味，與格調之個人產品以取悅今日的女性。

為積極促進女性自我覺醒及探索，我們誠摯希望本產品足以滿足您的期盼，並且為您開啟一個自我紓解的嶄新天地。

　　接下來還有詩一般誠摯的廣告語句：

回應高品質個人產品之需求，自然曲線展現無與倫比的成果：高格調按摩器，低噪音馬達提供刺激性震動。精心設計之雅致，耐用的表層完全迎合女性的自然構造。

啟動：轉至「開」的位置

Then there are some sincere advertise on the verse of the page:

Answering the call for quality personal products, natural contours delivers unbeatable performance: a stylish massager with a low noise motor that provides stimulating vibration. The elegant, impact—resistant casing is ergonomically designed to complement a woman's natural shape.

TO OPERATE: SWITCH TO "ON" POSITION

So follow this instruction I switch on the machine. It is beeping. Everybody who eats the hotpot now stops eating and look at me.

You lean to me and whisper in my ear, "It's a vibrator. You put it in your vagina."

Holding the vibrate, my hand is shaking badly. I switch it off. It makes me feel horrified.

Everybody in the party laughs.

"I think Asian people have a great sense of humour," you say.

"No, we don't," I clarify.

"Why not? You and Yoko make everybody laugh all the time."

"No. We Chinese don't understand humour. We look funny just because the culture difference, and we just being too honest," I say.

"Yes, when you say things very honest, people think you are funny. But we stupid," Yoko adds.

"Yes, I agree." Here comes Korea girl Kim Yam Zhen eventually. She barely speaks, but whenever she speaks she impress

遵照指示我轉開機器。它發出嗡鳴。所有人停下吃火鍋看著我。

你俯身在我耳邊低語，「這是震盪器。妳要把它放進妳的陰道。」

握著震盪器，我的手抖得厲害。我關掉它。人整個傻掉了。

派對上所有人都笑了。

「我想亞洲人都很有幽默感，」你說。

「才怪，我們沒有，」我澄清。

「怎麼會？妳和洋子老是逗得大家開心。」

「不。我們中國人不懂幽默這套。我們看起來好玩是因為文化差異的關係，我們人太老實了，」我說。

「沒錯，妳講話很直的時候，人家以為妳很好玩。其實我們是很呆，」洋子附和。

「對，我同意。」韓國小姐金妍珍終於加入。她難得開口，一開口便語驚四座。她嚴肅下斷語：

「幽默是西方人的概念。」

好高檔的英語。我還不曉得金的英語近來如此突飛猛進。

你的朋友看著我們三個東方人，有如看見三隻逃出竹林的熊貓。

我瞧了瞧震盪器，也想來一段評論：「性愛享受也是西方人的概念。」

「胡說八道。全天下的男人都會性愛享受，」韓國小姐金妍珍說。

男人面面相覷。

「不過，我是說，洋子，妳送她震盪器是開玩笑還是正經

everybody. She seriously makes a comment:

"Humour is a Western concept."

Gosh, is super English. I didn't know Kim's English improve so much recently.

Your friends look at us three Orientals, like look at three panda escape from bamboo forest.

I watch the vibrate. I want to make a comment as well: "Enjoy sex is a Western concept too."

"That's rubbish. Mans enjoy the sex everywhere," says Korea girl Kim Yan Zhen.

Mans look at each other.

"But, I mean, Yoko, did you give her the vibrator as a joke or as a serious gift?" you ask.

"Of course serious," answer by Yoko. I know Yoko is serious. Oriental people are serious, even young punks.

"Have you never seen a vibrator before?" one of your friends ask me.

"No. How would I?"

"But it's made in China," the friend says.

"Doesn't mean I see it," I say. "Actually those big international co-op factories run by foreigners. And the managers employ lots cheap labours like peasants, peasants" wives. And those womans they don't really know what is this machine for, but they just make it, by putting every piece of spare parts together. It is like they make computers by putting pieces together, but they never ever use computer."

Why it doesn't say "Dildo" or "automatic sex for woman" on the box? Maybe because it made in China, not allow to say things so clearly. It might become a big scandal if somebody

的？」你問。

「當然是正經的，」洋子回答。我知道洋子是正經的。東方人都很正經，就算當了龐克也一樣。

「妳以前沒看過震盪器嗎？」你一位朋友問我。

「沒。我怎麼會看過？」

「但它是中國製造的，」那朋友說。

「那不表示我有看過，」我說。「實際上，那種國際大工廠都是外國人經營的。管理者大量僱用便宜勞力，像農民，農民太太。而且那些女人其實不會曉得這機器是幹嘛用的，她們只管動手，把各個零件組裝起來。這就像她們會組裝電腦，但一輩子也不會去用到電腦一樣。」

奇怪，包裝盒上為何不寫「假陽具」或「女用自動性具」？或許因為產地在中國，不能容許如此明目張膽的標示。要是有人知道他同村的鄰居每天在工廠製造塑膠老二，那事情就真的大條了。搞不好這些工廠其實受到政府的暗中保護。因為中國政府宣稱性工業在中國並不存在。

往火鍋裡多放一些高麗菜，我不禁想像那些女人每日清早起床趕去上班製造震盪器。我可以看見她們放下失業壞脾氣的丈夫和窮孩子，坐在生產線上忙著製造震盪器。那些農村婦女一輩子也用不到震盪器。她們關心的只是今天能賺多少，她們能為家裡省下多少。

我將塑膠小黃瓜塞回盒裡。放到油膩的餐桌上時，我看見盒身的警語：**請用毛巾和柔皂清潔。**

from his village know his neighbour making plastic cocks everyday in a factory. Or maybe these factories are secretly protected by the government. Because Chinese government say there is no sex industry in China.

Putting more white cabbages into the hotpot, I can't help thinking about those womans waking up early every morning to make vibrators. I am seeing them leaving behind their unemployed bad-temper husbands and poor children to sit on production lines and make vibrators. And those peasant womans will never use the vibrator in this life. All they want to know is how much they will earn today and how much money they can save for the family.

I put back this plastic cucumber into the box. When I leave it on the oily table, I see the warning from the side of the box: *Clean with washcloth and mild soap.*

migraine

n. a severe headache, often with nausea and visual disturbances.

Another hot day. You left home in the morning with your old white van. I went to school and I had an exam on vocabulary. The exam went OK. I think I gain more English words since I have been lived with you. Mrs Margaret praises me. She said I a fast learner. She doesn't know I have been living with an English man every day and night. Soon school will end for summer holidays. My parents not expect there be so many holidays when they paid this school.

I come back home in the evening and switch on BBC Radio 4. I know my listening comprehension still bad. I hear *Six O'clock News, then The Party Line: comedy about a frustrated MP.* I don't understand English comedy.

I am waiting for you to be back.

You come back home almost ten. You hug me with a cold wind. You look so frail. You look painful. You say you got two parking tickets today, one is forty pounds, another one is sixty pounds. You say you were fighting with the traffic policeman who is a black. You say why black people they are so kind and friendly in Africa, but are so rude as long as they live in London. You say London is a place sucks. You say London is the place making everybody aggressive.

You say you got strong headache again, and your whole

【偏頭痛】

〈名詞〉嚴重頭痛，經常伴隨噁心和視力阻礙。

又是炎熱的一天。你和白色老貨車早早便出門。我去學校，今天要考單字。結果我考得不錯。和你住在一起之後，我的英語字彙大有進步。瑪格麗特小姐誇獎我，她說我學習能力很快。她不曉得我和一位英國男士朝夕相處。學校快放暑假了，爸媽付錢讓我上學時，可沒料到這所學校這麼愛放假。

傍晚時分，我回到家，轉開BBC電台頻道。我清楚自己的聽力還很爛。我收聽「六點鐘新聞」，接著聽「政黨路線：失意國會議員笑譚」。我聽不懂英語的笑譚。

我等著你回家。

你快十點才回來。你夾帶冷風擁抱我，人看起來好虛弱。你很痛苦。你說今天收到兩張違規停車罰單，一張四十鎊，一張六十鎊。你說你和那個黑人交通警察爭執許久。你說為何黑人在非洲都很親切友善，可是一旦來到倫敦就粗魯不堪。你說倫敦這什麼爛地方。你說倫敦這地方害每個人火氣變大。

你說你的頭又痛得厲害，連帶整個身體都痛起來。

我泡茶給你喝。你最愛喝的薄荷茶（茶包上寫說：產地埃及。我還以為英國人喝的茶是自己生產的）。我將滾燙的水倒入壺內。這是個咖啡色的舊茶壺，模樣很醜。你說這茶壺用了將近十年。十年了，你從沒摔過它。難以置信。

body aches as well.

I make you some tea. Your favourite peppermint tea. (On the tea bag it says: produce of Egypt. I thought English people they produce their own tea.) I poured the boiled water into the pot. It is an old teapot in brown colour. It is ugly. You say you used this teapot for almost ten years. Ten years, you never break it. Is unbelievable.

You drink the tea and you stare at the steam from cup.

I give you a painkiller pill. You take it. But you look worse. You move your body to the bathroom. You throw yourself up.

It is unbearable. I hear your pains, through the closed bathroom. It feels like you are throwing up all the dirts from your body, all the dirts from the sick world.

The running tap is being switched off. You come out from the bathroom, with a pale face.

"I never had headaches before I came to London. My body was so healthy when I lived in the country with my goats, and I was just planting potatoes. Since I moved here I'm struggling all the time. My body is in misery. That's why I hate London. Not only London, all big cities. Big cities are like huge international airports. You can't have one moment of peace here, and you can't find love and keep it."

But what about the love between you and me? It happen in the big city, a very big city, London, a very international place, like airport. Can you keep that love? Can we keep it? I ask myself, in my heart, touching your hair. There is something shaking inside me.

Now you lie down on the bed, your body is hidden in quilt. Your quilt is so heavy, and the texture feels very rough. Not

你喝口茶，望著杯裡冒出的熱氣。

我給你一顆止痛藥，你吞下它，但看起來神色更糟。拖著身體去到浴室，你吐了。

真令人難以忍受。透過緊閉的浴室，我聽見你的痛苦，感覺好像要把體內所有的塵土嘔出來，所有來自病態世界的塵土。

嘩啦啦的水龍頭關上。你從浴室出來，臉無血色。

「我來倫敦之前從沒頭痛過。住鄉下的時候身體好健康，我養山羊，還種番茄。自從搬到這兒，每天都在掙扎，身體一直受罪。所以我討厭倫敦。不只倫敦，所有大城市我都討厭。大城市簡直就像巨大的國際機場，連一分鐘的平靜都沒有，你找不到，也保不住愛。」

可是你和我之間的愛怎麼說？它在大城市裡發生，非常大的城市，倫敦，非常國際化的地方，像機場。你能保住那份愛嗎？我們能夠保住嗎？我捫心自問，撫摸你的頭髮。我的內心有什麼正在動搖。

你躺到床上，身體躲進被窩。你的棉被如此厚重，質料粗糙。大熱天蓋這種東西。它一定跟了你許多許多年，一定是從別人那裡取得——你從來不買寢具的。頭一次見到你的棉被和床單，我明白你一定沒有女人，獨居許久。有女人的屋子少不了柔軟舒適的寢具。

感受你的身體在痛苦中顫抖，我不能放你獨自受苦。我脫掉衣服，在你身邊躺下。

「妳能跟我做嗎？」你問我，聲音虛弱。

「怎麼？你想要？」我很訝異。

「嗯。」

right for this hot weathers. It must be with you for many many years, and it must be from somebody else—you never buy beddings. When I saw your quilt and sheets the first time, I just know you lived long time on your own without a woman. A house has a woman will definitely have a soft and cosy beddings.

Feeling your body is shivering in pain, I can't leave you there. I take off my clothes, and I lie beside you.

"Will you have sex with me?" you ask me, with a weak voice.

"Why? Do you want?" I am very surprised.

"Hmm."

Your hand still presses your head where is the pain from.

"If I come it helps me forget about the pain and fall asleep," you say.

"But what if nobody beside you or you don't have a lover when you are very ill?" I am shocked.

"Then I would do it with my hand. Like I did before you came into my life."

I don't know what to say anymore.

Touching gently your little bird, I move my fingers. I can feel your pain directly. Your pains is like electric current transfer into my finger, then my palm, then my body, then my head. I become shivering with my anticipation, for that I want cure your pain.

You face look relieved, but your breath becoming much heavier. Your little bird gets harder in my fist. I don't feel sexy at all; all I wish is to stop you suffering.

"Are you ready to come?" I am holding you.

你的手依舊按著發疼的頭部。

「讓我出來可以幫我忘記疼痛，比較好入睡，」你說。

「那要是你病得厲害，但身邊沒人或沒有愛人的時候怎麼辦？」我吃驚。

「那我就靠手來了，就像沒有妳跟我一起生活之前那樣。」

我一時語塞。

輕輕撫著你的小鳥，我手指上下抽動。我能直接感受你的疼痛。你的痛電流般傳導至我的指頭，我的掌心，我的身軀，我的腦門。我隨著期待升高而顫抖，只想治好你的疼痛。

你的臉色稍緩，但呼吸變得濁重。你的小鳥在我的拳握裡堅挺。我沒半點性的感覺，只想要你別再受苦。

「你要來了嗎？」我握住你。

「來了⋯⋯」你說，持續忍受高潮的劇痛。

你的身體震顫。精液射出。我的手全溼了。它噴湧，一陣一陣。那奶汁。人受罪成這樣，奶汁一定很苦。它是愛的奶汁，我對你的愛，但也是痛的奶汁，你生命當中的痛。

你的呼吸平息下來，疼痛離開了。

我們躺著不動，紋絲不動。我們倆就像你靜止的雕像。我掌心的精液漸乾。你沉入夢鄉。我可以察覺你手腕每一分脈動，我可以察覺你心房每一記節拍。我呼吸於你的呼吸當中，我一吸你一呼。我們躺在這裡良久像兩具雕像。我看著你的臉，良久。我甚至看見你的死亡。你死亡的形狀。

"Yes . . ." you say, enduring the great pain of climax.

Your body is shaking. Then the sperm comes. My hand is completely wet. It jets, again and again. The milk. It must be bitter milk when a person is suffering. It is the milk of love, my love to you, but it is also the milk of pain, your pain in your life.

Your breath calms down. You are leaving your pain.

We lie still, without moving even for one centimetre. We are just like your still statue. The sperm on my palm is drying. You fall into sleep. I can feel every single pulse on your wrist. I can feel every single beat from your heart. I breathe in your breath. I inhale your exhale. It is being so long that we lie here like two statues. I look at your face, for so long. I even can see your death. The shape of your death.

August

equal

adj. **1.** identical in size, quantity, degree, etc; **2.** having identical rights or status; **3.** evenly balanced. *n.* person or thing equal to another.

Rupert Street, fish restaurant. Saturday evening. Large lobster placed on the window is so seductive that I can't move my feet away. We get in. You order goat cheese, and extra vegetables. I order fish soup and squid BBQ in wine. We agree having two glasses white wine as well. Later, when waiter gives the bill it forty pounds all together. Expensive.

You take out twenty pounds, put on the bill book. I don't move. I look at you, wondering.

"Half!" you say.

"Why? I don't have twenty pounds with me!" I say.

"You've got a debit card."

"But why?"

"I'm always paying for you. In the West, men and women are equal. We should split food and rent."

"But I thought we lovers!" Loudly, I argue.

The old couple next table stops eating, look at me with strange face.

"It's not about that. You are from China, the country with the most equal relationship between men and women. I'd have thought you'd understand what I'm talking about. Why should I pay for everything?"

I say: "Of course you have to pay. You are man. If I pay too,

【平等】

〈形容詞〉**1.** 大小，數量，程度等方面一致；**2.** 擁有相同的權利或地位；**3.** 均衡的。〈名詞〉（地位等）相同的人或相等的事物。

　　魯拔街，海鮮餐廳。週六夜。大隻龍蝦擺在窗前如此誘人，我沒辦法移動腳步。我們進餐廳。你點了山羊起司，配上蔬菜。我則點了魚湯，還有烤烏賊下酒。我們倆同意來兩杯白酒。稍後，侍者拿帳單來，總共四十鎊。貴死了。

　　你掏出二十鎊，放在帳單上。我沒動，眼睛看著你，心裡狐疑。

　　「出一半！」你說。

　　「為什麼？我身上沒有二十鎊！」我說。

　　「妳有轉帳卡。」

　　「可是為什麼？」

　　「我一直在為你付錢。在西方，男人跟女人平等。我們應該分攤食物和房租。」

　　「但我以為我們是愛人！」我高聲爭辯。

　　隔壁桌的老夫婦停止進食，用奇怪的神情看我。

　　「這跟那無關。妳來自中國，你們國家的男女是天底下最平等的。我認為妳應該清楚我在講什麼。為何全部的東西都要我來付？」

　　我說：「當然應該你付。你是男人。如果我也要付錢，那我跟你在一起幹嘛？」

then why I need to be with you?"

Now you are angry: "Are you really saying you"re only with me to pay your living costs?"

"No, not that! You are man and I am woman, and we are live together. When couple is live together, woman loses social life automatically. She only stays at home do cooking and washing. And after she have kids, even worse. So woman can't have any social position at all. She loses . . . what is that word . . . financial independence?" These are what I learned from Radio Four Woman's Hour every morning ten o'clock.

"Really? OK. So, if the woman stays at home all day, like you, why can't she hoover the floor? Why do I have to do the hoovering after I"ve done a whole day's work?"

That's true. I never woover the floor. I only sweep the floor. And my eyesights is very bad, so there are always lots things left on the floor.

"But I wash clothes! And I cook everyday!"

"Thank you, that's very kind of you. But what's wrong with a bit of hoovering?"

"Because I hate that woover. You must pick it from the rubbish place. It is so noisy, and it is so huge. It is like dragon. I just don't like something so big!"

"Come now! You like a big cock, don't you, so why don't you like a big hoover!"

"!"

OK, so woman and man pay half half even when they live together. And woman and man have their own privacy and their own friends. And woman and man have their own separate bank account. Is that why Western couples split up so easi-

你生氣了：「妳的意思是說你跟我在一起全爲了負擔妳的生活費用？」

　　「不，才不是！你是男人我是女人，而且我們住在一起。情侶一旦同居，女人便自動喪失社交生活。她只能家裡待著洗衣燒飯。再來有了小孩，情況更慘。所以女人一點社會地位也沒有。她失去……那個字怎麼說……經濟獨立？」這一套是我從每天早上十點鐘的電台節目「女性天地」聽來的。

　　「眞的？好，那麼，如果女人整天待在家哩，像妳，那爲什麼她不能吸地板？爲什麼我整天外面奔波之後還要吸地？」

　　那倒是眞的。我從沒用過吸塵器。我只會拿掃把掃地而已。而且我眼力很差，所以地上總是有很多漏網之魚。

　　「但我有洗衣服！而且每天煮飯！」

　　「感謝妳，妳做人眞好。可是稍微吸一下地又會怎樣？」

　　「因爲我恨那台吸塵器。你得從垃圾堆把它搬出來。它吵死人，體積又大，像怪龍一樣。我不喜歡東西那麼大！」

　　「少來！大老二你就喜歡，對不，所以吸塵器大怎麼就不喜歡！」

　　「！」

　　好吧，所以男女即使同居還是得平分帳單。女人和男人各有各的隱私和朋友。女人和男人各有各的銀行戶頭。難道是這原因，西方的情侶分手容易，離婚快速？

　　我們一路爭辯回家。打開家門，泡一壺茶，你又吸起地來。

　　好吵，沒兩秒鐘我頭就痛。吸塵器鐵定是男人發明的。我端坐椅子上，免得被巨龍吞掉，我從抽屜拿出毛語錄。毛的言論裡有提到女人和平等。

ly, and divorce so quickly?

We argue all the way back to home. Open the door, make a pot of tea, you start woover the floor again.

So noisy. It makes me headache immediately. The woover must be invented by mans. I sit on chair not let the big dragon swallow me and take out the *Little Red Book* from my drawer. There are some pages about womans and *equal* in Mao's speech:

In order to build a great socialist society it is of the utmost importance to arouse the broad masses of women to join in productive activity. Men and women must receive equal pay for equal work in production.

This must be the original thoughts which became legend "womans hold up half of the sky" in China.

While I am in deep thought about China, you switch off the dragon. You stare at me, and say:

"I wish I'd never given you books. Now all you do is sit there reading and writing. You've become so *bourgeois*."

為了建設偉大的社會主義社會，發動廣大的婦女群眾參加生產活動，具有極大的意義。在生產中，必須實現男女平等。

　　這必定是那句中國人人朗朗上口的「女人撐起半邊天」的原創思維。

　　我陷入中國的沉思當中時，你關掉怪龍，盯著我瞧，開口說：

　　「早知道當初就不要給妳書看。現在可好，光會坐在那邊又讀又寫，根本已經變成資產階級了嘛妳。」

frustration

frustrate *v*. **1.** to upset or anger; **2.** hinder or prevent. frustration *n*. the feeling of being frustrated.

You lie in bath. The water comes to top, and the bubble covers your body. We both always take bath when we feel depressed. Do most English people do that, especially in the long dark winter? I wonder. How many baths we have been taken since we being together? In last six months the bath I had must be more than I did in the last twenty-four years.

Now, you even didn't switch on the radio. You lie there like a nude statue in the water.

"Why you are silent?"

You shrug your shoulders. Have no comments.

You don't want talk. Not at all. Not even one word.

"Have you got headache?"

You shake your head.

"So you don't want talk to me?"

"No."

"Why not?"

"I just want to be on my own to think. You know people sometimes just want to have their own space."

Only your face is on the surface of water. Impression of your face is like the sky being covered by a big piece of dark cloud. You not happy.

"Why you not happy? What have I done wrong to you?"

【挫折】

〈動詞〉**1.** 使心煩或氣憤;**2.** 阻撓或制止。〈名詞〉挫折感。

　　你浴缸裡躺著。水放滿到池邊,泡泡蓋住身體。每逢意志消沉,我們倆便泡起熱水澡。英國人都這樣泡嗎,特別是嚴冬漫漫時節?我納悶。同居之後,我們究竟泡過浴缸多少回?六個月下來,我泡熱水的次數包準打破過去二十四年的加總。

　　此時此刻,你連收音機也不開了,光躺在那兒像具水中的裸體雕像。

　　「你怎麼不講話?」

　　你聳聳肩,連出聲都免了。

　　你不想講話,完全不想,半句話都不肯。

　　「你頭會痛?」

　　你搖搖頭。

　　「所以你是不想跟我講話?」

　　「不想。」

　　「爲什麼不想?」

　　「我只想一個人想一下事情。妳知道人有時候想要擁有自己的空間。」

　　你只剩臉部露出水面以上。你的神情有若烏雲團團遮蔽天空。你不快樂。

　　「幹嘛不高興?我哪裡惹到你了?」

"I just feel tired of you," you say. "Always asking me words, how to spell them, what they mean. I am fed up."

I listen.

"It is too tiring to live like this. I cannot spend my whole time explaining the meaning of words to you, and I can't be questioned by you all day long."

You come out from bath, covering your body with that blue towel. You are so cold to me. You leave me there alone.

I feel like being *abandoned*. The word I learned the first day I arrived London in the bloody red Nuttington House. It is the second word in my *Concise Dictionary*, coming after *Abacus*.

You carry on:

"It is so hard for me. I don't have my own space to think about my sculptures, my things, and my own words. I don't have time to be on my own. Now when I talk to other people, I become slower and slower. I am losing my words."

I listen. Gosh, I am upset to hear this. I have to say something to defend myself.

"If so, that is not my fault. It is just because we live in such different cultures. It is very difficult for both you and I to find the right way to communicate."

You listen, then you say: "You really are starting to speak English *properly*."

After this, the evening we are in the world of silence. I don't want ask you any words anymore, at least not in several hours, and I tell myself I shouldn't talk to you either, at least tonight. You not want talk to me. The air in the house becomes heavy. Finally you say to me: "Come with me to see a film." I take my jacket and I follow you. We are driving the white van to the

「我只是覺得妳很煩,」你說。「一直問一直問,單字要怎麼拼,意思是什麼。我受夠了。」

我聽著。

「這樣生活真的太累了。我不能把全部時間花在幫妳解釋單字的意義,我也不能一天到晚應付妳的問題。」

你跨出浴缸,披上那條藍色浴巾。你對我好冷酷,撇下我自己一個。

我感覺有如被遺棄。來到倫敦頭一天,我在一片血紅的「納廷頓之家」便學到這個字。它是《簡明辭典》裡的第二個字,排在算盤之後。

你還沒完:

「我真的不行了。我沒有自己的空間思考我的雕塑,我的大事小事,還有我的字彙。我沒有時間做我自己。如今和別人交談時,我講話愈來愈慢。我連自己的字彙都不見了。」

我聽著。聽見這種話讓人很不舒服,我得講點什麼自我防衛一番。

「事情如果這樣,那也不是我的過失。只能怪我們兩個活在不同的文化裡面。要找到恰當的溝通方式對你我來說都非常困難。」

你聽著,然後說:「妳還真的已經會說妥當的英語了嘛。」

這番話之後,接下來的夜晚我們處在沉默的世界。我再也不想開口問你任何字詞,至少幾個鐘頭以內休想,而且我告訴自己別和你說話,至少今晚不要。是你不想和我說話的。屋子裡的氣氛異常沉重。最後你先開口:「跟我來去看電影。」我拎起夾克隨你出門。我們開著白色貨車奔往戲院。噢,戲院救

cinema. Oh, cinema saves our life.

Yes, maybe you are right. Words maybe not really the first thing in life. Words are void. Words are dry and distant towards the emotional world.

Maybe I should give up learning words.

Maybe I should give up writing down words every day.

我們一命。

　　是的，你講的或許沒錯。字詞或許並非生命的第一要務。
字是空洞的，字乾巴巴，離感情的世界何其遙遠。
　　或許我該放棄學習單字。
　　或許我該放棄每天寫下單字。

nonsense

n. **1.** something that has or makes no sense; **2.** absurd language; **3.** foolish behaviour.

I am sick of speaking English like this. I am sick of writing English like this. I feel as if I am being tied up, as if I am living in a prison. I am scared that I have become a person who is always very aware of talking, speaking, and I have become a person without confidence, because I can't be me. I have become so small, so tiny, while the English culture surrounding me becomes enormous. It swallows me, and it rapes me. I am dominated by it. I wish I could just forget about all this vocabulary, these verbs, these tenses, and I wish I could just go back to my own language now. But is my own native language simple enough? I still remember the pain of studying Chinese characters when I was a child at school.

Why do we have to study languages? Why do we have to force ourselves to communicate with people? Why is the process of communication so troubled and so painful?

【無意義】

〈名詞〉**1.**無意義的東西；**2.**胡說八道；**3.**胡鬧。

　　我真他媽的厭倦了這樣說英文，這樣寫英文。我厭倦了這樣學英文。我感到全身緊縛，如同牢獄。我害怕從此變成一個小心翼翼的人，沒有自信的人。因為我完全不能做我自己，我變得如此渺小，而與我無關的這個英語文化變得如此巨大。我被它驅使，我被它強暴，我被它消滅。我真想徹底忘記這些單詞，拼法，時態。我真想說回我天生的語言，可是，我天生的語言它是真正天生的嗎？我仍然記得小時候學漢語有同樣的苦工和痛楚。

　　我們為什麼要學習語言？我們為什麼要強迫自己與他人交流？如果交流的過程是如此痛苦？

discord

n. **1.** a lack of agreement or harmony between people; **2.** harsh confused sounds.

Forgot since when, we started to fight.

We fight everyday. We argue everyday. The sound in this house is discord. Fighting for a cup of tea. Fighting for the misunderstanding of a word. Fighting for the ways I like to add the vinegar in the foods but you hate it. Fighting for the freedom as you think it is important more than anything else.

Argument expands onto every possible direction:

Typical argument 1: (On Tibet)

"I remember you saying that Tibet belongs to China. I can't believe you can think that."

"Well . . . You see things from a white English's point of view. Shame that your English failed to colonise Tibet and China," I throw back.

"But now Tibet is colonised by the Chinese!" You raise your volume.

"If Tibetan is not with Chinese, then it ruled by British Empire, or American anyway. Because Tibet never really been economically independent! They always need rely on others, rely on powerful government. Since China and Tibet are in the same piece of land, why we two can't be together?"

【噪音】

〈名詞〉 1.意見不和；2.噪音，喧鬧。

忘了何時開始，我們爭吵不休。

我們天天吵，天天爭。這屋子裡聽到的只有噪音。喝杯茶爭吵，字誤解爭吵，吃東西我喜歡加醋但你討厭。為了你把自由看得比什麼都重要而爭吵。

爭辯的範圍擴大到每件事都有可能：

典型爭辯1：（論西藏）

「我記得妳說西藏屬於中國。我不敢相信妳會這樣想。」

「唔……你這是英國白種人的觀點。真遺憾你們英國人沒本事殖民西藏和中國，」我回敬。

「現在西藏可是被你們中國殖民！」你拉高音量。

「如果不是中國，西藏早被大英帝國或美國人統治去了。因為西藏一直沒辦法經濟獨立！他們必須依靠他人，依靠其他的強權政府。中國和西藏的土地相連，為何我們不能同一國？」

「那要看你的『同一國』是什麼意思！不能把西藏文化拿來當代價。看有多少西藏人被你們殘害……」

「我才沒殘害過西藏人！我這輩子認識的中國人沒有一個

"It depends what you mean by "together"! It can't be at the cost of Tibetan culture. And look how many Tibetans you've killed..."

"I didn't kill any Tibetans! No any other Chinese I know in my life killed any Tibetans! In fact, nobody in China wants go to that desert!"

"But the Chinese government killed Tibetans."

"Yes, of course BBC news only report bad side of China."

Typical argument 2: (On food)

"It is boring eat with you everyday. You only eat vegetable, no wheat, no pasta, no white rice, no bread, only goat cheese, let alone any fish. Hardly any restaurant suits you. And not very much fun for my cooking either. My parents will say you lose the most joyful thing in your life."

"Well, you are the enemy of animals. How many animals do you think you have you killed in your life?" You fight poison with poison.

"Eating animals is the human nature. In the forest, tiger eats rabbit. Lion eats deer. That's how the nature works." That's how my teacher said in my middle school.

"But you Chinese eat anything, even endangered species. I bet if dinosaurs roamed the forests of China, someone would want to see what dinosaur meat tasted like. How come you people have no sense of protecting nature?"

"But what so different of eating plants? Everything has its life. If you are so pure, why not just stop eating? So you can have no shit?"

殺過西藏人！事實上，中國沒有人會想去那種沙漠地區！」

「可是中國政府殘害西藏人。」

「對啦，當然BBC新聞就只會報導中國的負面消息。」

典型爭辯2：（論食物）

「每天跟你吃飯有夠無聊。你只會吃蔬菜，沒有小麥，沒有麵條，沒有白米，沒有麵包，只有山羊起司，魚肉就別提了。幾乎找不到一家餐館適合你去，我煮東西一點成就感也沒有。讓我爸媽知道，準說你白白浪費一生最大的享受。」

「哼，你們才是動物的敵人。想想看你這輩子要害死多少動物？」你以毒攻毒。

「吃動物是人的天性。在森林裡，老虎吃兔子，獅子吃野鹿，自然的運作道理便是如此。」我的中學老師這麼說過。

「可是你們中國人什麼都吃，連瀕臨絕種的也不放過。我敢說如果中國的森林還有恐龍在遊蕩，一定會有人想要嚐嚐看恐龍肉的滋味。你們這些人怎會毫無環境保育的觀念？」

「那你自己吃植物又有什麼不同？每樣東西都有它的生命。如果你真這麼清高，何不乾脆什麼都別吃？連大便都可以省下來多好？」

「妳真是不可理喻！」你站起來。離開餐桌。

典型爭辯3：（論事業）

我說我想在中國人裡面當個出色的英語演講者，我這輩子一定要想辦法功成名就。

"You are impossible to talk to!" You stand up, leaving the dinner table.

Typical argument 3: (On career)

I say I want to be a great English speaker among other Chinese. And I want to do something big in my life and get fame.

"You"re so bloody ambitious. What's the point of fame? Why not just try to be yourself."

"Why ambitious is not a good thing?" I ask.

"Well, for a start, it makes you pretty difficult to live with," you say.

These words hurt me.

"OK, so I have big ambitious, and it ugly. But why you want to show your sculptures to others? You should just make your own thing and never show it to people!"

"I want to show the sculptures to others because I am curious about what they might think. I'm curious about their reactions. I don't care about being someone big. I don't care about fame or money."

"That because you are a white English living in England and you own the property and you have social security. You are boss of yourself, so you have dignity. But I don't have anything here in your country! I have to struggle to get these things!"

I am almost shouting, but I should not shout in your private property. People call policeman to come anytime in this country.

「妳還真他媽的有野心。能夠出名又怎麼樣？何不設法做妳自己就好。」

「有野心又是哪裡不對？」我問。

「嗯，起碼，它一開始便令妳很難和別人相處，」你說。

這話傷了我。

「好，所以我野心太大，令人討厭。那你為何又要把雕塑秀給別人看？你應該做你自己的東西就好，別人管他的！」

「我把雕塑給別人看，是因為我好奇別人看了會有什麼想法。我是對他們的反應感到好奇，我不在乎出人頭地與否，我不在乎名氣跟金錢。」

「那是因為你是住在英國的白種英國人，你有家產，有社會安全保障。你自己就能當家做主，你有尊嚴。但我在你的國家這裡一無所有！我得靠自己奮鬥爭取這一切！」

我幾乎是咆哮了，可我不該在你的私人產業叫囂。這國家的人民隨時會叫警察的。

identity

n. **1.** the state of being a specified person or thing; **2.** individuality or personality; **3.** the state of being the same.

I try to be quiet with you in the house. I have been reading books you gave to me. I quickly finished Oscar Wilde's *The Happy Prince and Other Tales*. I loved the nightingale story. It was so sad. Nightingale's love not being valued by the prince at all. Why beautiful story always is sad? And I loved the selfish giant who has a huge garden too, but the last sentence made me cry. It goes like this: "And when the children ran in that afternoon, they found the Giant lying dead under the tree, all covered with white blossoms." I start reading To *The Lighthouse*. You are right, it is quite difficult for me. On the back it says it is about a middle-aged woman with her eight children in a summer house. Eight children without any husband? Gosh, it must be a hard book. I holding breath while read the first page. I can't breathe freely because there are hardly full stops. Virginia Woolf must be a very wordy person. The writing is so forceful, is nearly painful for me to read. I suddenly understand that you must be suffered a lot from me, because I am so forceful and demanding on words too. And even worse, you are forced to listen my messy English every single moment. You are unlucky to be my lover.

I put down the book and leave it for my future reading.

I am being caught by the word "*identity crisis*" on *The Times*. I write it down into my notebook. I always want to find

【認同】

〈名詞〉**1.** 特定的人或物；**2.** 個人特性或特質；**3.** 一致性。

　　我試著安靜和你共處一屋。一直讀著你送我的書，很快就把奧斯卡‧王爾德的《快樂王子故事集》看完。我喜歡夜鶯的故事，它好悲傷。王子一點也不把夜鶯愛的心血放在眼裡。為何美麗的故事總是悲傷？我也喜歡自私巨人有座大花園的故事，但最後的句子讓我流淚。它這樣寫：「那天下午，孩子們跑進花園時，發現巨人躺在那棵樹底下，死了，身上覆滿白色花朵。」我開始讀《燈塔行》，你的話沒錯，我看得很吃力。封底說這本書寫一個中年婦人帶著八個小孩住在避暑別墅。八個小孩，沒有丈夫？這本書鐵定艱困。我讀第一頁便屏住呼吸，我沒辦法自在呼吸因為幾乎找不到句號。維吉妮亞‧吳爾芙一定嘮叨慣了。迫力十足的書寫，讀起來幾達痛苦地步。突然間，我領悟到你一定被我折磨光了，因為我對字句有同樣的強力渴求。情況甚至更糟，你被迫隨時收聽我亂無章法的英語。你運氣真好讓我當愛人。

　　我放下書本等來日再讀。

　　我被《時代》雜誌上的一個字「認同危機」給攫住，將它寫進我的筆記本。一直想找這個字，現在讓我遇上，這下得好好思考我自己的認同問題，按知識分子的路數來思考。

　　媽媽以前跟我說：「妳皮膚太黑，頭髮太少，看起來一點

this word, now here I encounter it. Now I want think about my own identity, in an *intellectual* way.

My mother told me: "Your skin too dark and your hair too thin. You don't look like me and your father at all. You are like your barbarian grandmother!" She said to me: "Look at your big feet. A real peasant's feet! Nobody will want marry you."

I hated her, and I wished she could die immediately.

But she is right about this: so far nobody really wanted to marry me.

When I was in middle school, my schoolmates always laughed at me. So I spend time on reading to avoid talking to them. I read *Snow White And Seven Dwarfs* in Chinese, and I saw my mother is as evil as that stepmother queen. But I didn't have a snow-white skin and I was just a peasant girl. So there was no prince will come save me and that's my destiny. Being a teenage I was dying to run away from my hometown, the town which my mother always beat me up and blamed me for everything I have done wrong, the place without my dream and my freedom.

The day when I arrived to the West, I suddenly realised I am a Chinese. As long as one has black eyes and black hair, obsessed by rice, and cannot swallow any Western food, and cannot pronounce the difference between "r" and "l", and request people without using *please*—then he or she is a typical Chinese: an ill-legal immigrant, badly treat Tibetans and Taiwanese, good on food but put MSG to poison people, eat dog's meat and drink snakes" guts.

"I want to be a citizen of the world." Recently I learned to say this. I *would* become a citizen of the world, *if* I have a more useful passport. Ah Mrs. Margaret, that conditional again!

都不像我，也不像妳爸爸。妳倒像妳那粗手粗腳的姥姥！」她又說：「瞧妳那雙大腳，標準的村姑腳丫！看以後有誰敢娶妳。」

我恨她，真希望她馬上死掉。

不過，這一點她講對了：目前為止沒有人想要娶我。

唸中學的時候，同學老嘲笑我。我只管讀書，避免和他們講話。我讀到中文的《白雪公主和七矮人》，在我眼中，媽媽跟那繼母皇后一樣邪門。可我沒有雪白的肌膚，不過一個村姑而已。別指望會有王子前來拯救我，早認命早好。到了青春期，我恨不能逃離家鄉，媽媽成天只會打人，每件事都看我不順眼，這地方既沒有夢想又沒有自由。

來到西方世界那天，我隨即明白自己中國人的身分。只要你有黑眼珠黑頭髮，只要你嗜吃米食，嚥不下任何西方食物，「r」跟「l」的發音沒辦法分別，麻煩別人的時候不用請字——凡有這些症狀的他或她便是典型的中國人：一個非法的外來移民，粗暴對待西藏人和台灣人，東西好吃但專放味精毒人，吃狗肉吞蛇膽。

「我想成為世界公民。」最近我學會說這句話。我願意成為世界公民，如果我能拿到更便利好用的護照。噢，瑪格麗特小姐，條件句又來了！

anarchist

n. **1.** a person who advocates the abolition of government; **2.** a person who causes disorder.

"What is *Anarchist*?" I raise my head from *Guardian*.

We are in "First Choice", a cheap greasy spoon, forty pence for a cup of tea. We like this kind of places. They don't ask us leave if consumption less than £1 after one and half hour. I love east London.

You have an earl grey tea, and I have coffee. Liquidish eggs flow everywhere on my plate. Kids nearby are crying — two crying baby with one fat mother, no husband again. Frown gathers on your forehead.

"Anarchists? Anarchists don't believe in government. They think society shouldn't have a ruling government. That everybody should be equal." You answer, slowly.

"Sound like Communist," I say.

"No. Communists believe the working class can control the power of the whole society, but Anarchists don't believe in any power. They are very individualistic, whereas Communists believe in the collective." You stop describing, as some working class man looks at us, stop biting his sausages.

My interests being aroused. I want to discuss more. You are my academy.

"But sounds Anarchist is the end of the Communist, or the advanced Communist. Is target or triumph of the Communism

【安那其】

〈名詞〉**1.** 無政府主義者；**2.** 擾亂分子。

「什麼是安那其？」我從《衛報》上抬起頭。

我們人在「上選」，一家平價小館，一杯茶四十便士。我們喜歡這種地方，就算待上一個半鐘頭叫不到一鎊東西他們也不趕人。我愛死東倫敦。

你喝伯爵茶，我喝咖啡，餐盤被我吃得蛋汁四溢。旁邊有小鬼在哭——兩個哇哇叫的嬰兒和一位胖太太，又是沒有丈夫。

你額頭疊起皺紋。

「安那其？安那其不相信政府，他們認為社會不該由政府來統治，人與人應該充分平等，」你回答，一字一句的。

「聽起來像共產主義者，」我說。

「不對，共產主義相信工人階級掌管整體社會的權力，但安那其不相信任何權力。他們極度個人主義，相反的，共產主義者信仰集體力量。」你停下嘴巴，有位工人階級先生看著我們，香腸都忘了咬。

這下我興趣來了，很想多討教一番，你真是我的良師。

「可是，聽起來安那其就是共產主義者的目的，或者說更先進的共產主義者。共產革命的目標或勝利不就是這樣，透過革命行動掃除階級差異，然後廢除政府統治，消弭國家的界

revolution is that, through the revolution wiping out the difference of the classes and eliminating the ruling government. No country boundaries. So the world can be *equal*. Am I right?"

"Maybe." You open another page of paper.

"So are you an Anarchist?" I am not giving up.

"I was an Anarchist. But not anymore." Now you give up your paper, and answer me seriously. "Most Anarchists are in fact bourgeois. They don't really want to give up any advantages. They can be very selfish. I don't think I am that kind of person now. I want to give up material things, and live the simplest possible life."

The simplest possible life is the most complicated thing to achieve I say to myself.

"So who are you?" This time I really want to know.

"I don't know. Maybe an *atheist*. I don't believe there is a god living in the sky. I don't believe in Capitalism, but I'm also not convinced by Communism, the way it is now."

"So do you believe in anything?" I ask.

"Hm," is your only answer. "What about you?"

"Me? I do believe there is a kind superpower control all our life. It is also the power above the nature. And this superpower human being cannot really do anything to change it."

I look outside of the window, and I am sure right now in this very right moment there is a mysterious superpower above us, above our cheap cafe and above our silly conversation.

You point the ad of *Donnie Darko* in the paper and ask me: "Have you seen this film? The teacher in it says to Donnie: "You are not an *atheist*, you are an *agnostic*." I think you are an *agnostic* too."

限，到最後世界就能平等。我說的可對？」

「或許吧。」你翻開報紙另外一頁。

「你是安那其嗎？」我仍不死心。

「我曾經是安那其，但現在不是了。」你總算放棄報紙，嚴肅回答我。「大部分的安那其骨子裡其實是資產階級，根本沒打算放棄任何既得利益，他們比誰都自私。我現在不會想當那種人了，我只願自己能夠放下物質包袱，儘可能過最簡單的生活。」

我對自己說，儘可能過最簡單的生活其實最複雜，最難達成。

「那麼你到底算哪種人？」這次我是真心想弄明白。

「我不知道，或許無神論者罷。我不相信真有神活在天上。我不相信資本主義，但我也沒辦法信服共產主義，就憑它現在這種表現。」

「那有任何東西你相信嗎？」我問。

「欸，」你只答了這麼一聲。「那妳呢？」

「我？我的確相信有某種超能力掌控我們全部的生命，它的力量超越大自然，而且人類的任何作為都無法改變這種超能力。」

我的視線越過窗外，我確信正當此時此刻，有一種神祕的超能力高居我們之上，高居這平價咖啡館和我們之間愚蠢的對話之上。

你指著報上《恍目驚魂28天》的電影廣告問我說：「這片子看過嗎？裡面那個老師對東尼說：『你不是無神論者，你是不可知論者。』我看妳也是不可知論者。」

「什麼是不可知論者？」我趕緊找出口袋的《袖珍簡明中

"What is *agnostic*?" I am searching my little *Concise Chinese-English Dictionary* in my pocket.

But after we both look at the dictionary up and down there is nowhere we could find the word *agnostic*. Maybe this is the word not important to Chinese. Or there is no *agnostic* in old time of China at all. Or maybe it is a very capitalism word that's why the authority censored it?

"An *agnostic* is someone who believes in a spiritual world, a metaphysical world. But he hasn't found what he should believe in yet..."

"Wait, what is 'metaphysical'?" I open my notebook.

"Metaphysical means not physical, not real..." A pause, you say: "but I think you might be a *sceptic*."

"What?"

Again, I pick up my dictionary and open it immediately. I am in a hurry to learn. I am in a hurry to understand all these words!

While I am burying myself in the sea of words in the dictionary, you say, "Honey, your English is good, but not *that* good. I have to say."

The working class man in the nearby table chews his kidney pie, looking at me with enormous wonder. I think I make his day.

英辭典》。

可是辭典從頭翻到尾，我們就是找不著不可知論者。或許這個字對中國人來說並不重要，或者說中國古早年代沒有不可知論者，又或許這個字太過資本主義，所以被有關單位審查攔截？

「不可知論者是說某人雖相信超自然世界，形上學世界，然而他未能發現足以相信的⋯⋯」

「等等，什麼『形上學』？」我打開筆記本。

「形上學表示非物質的，非現實的⋯⋯」稍作停頓，你說：「不過我想妳可能是懷疑論者。」

「什麼？」

又一次，我拿起辭典迅速翻查，我求知若渴，急著想把這些單字學起來！

正當我埋首於辭典的字海時，你說：「親愛的，妳的英文很棒，但我得說，別棒過頭了。」

隔壁桌的工人階級先生嘴裡咀嚼牛腰派，兩眼望著我滿是好奇，想來我今天讓他很樂。

hero

n. **1.** the principal character in a film, book, etc; **2.** a man greatly admired for his exceptional qualities or achievements.

You feel happy again, your mood is like English weather.

You are in the peace, like the fruit tree without flowers in the garden. You are happy because you start to make a new sculpture. So now dirt and mess everywhere in the house. It is like living in a construction site. Clay and plaster and wax and water. Your happiness is from your own world, from your physical object, from the molded male head, male arms, male leg, male attraction . . . Your happiness is from your masculine world, and in that world you feel everything is under the control.

Your sadness actually is nothing to do with me. Your stress is not really from me. It is from your masculine world, because you don't feel satisfied with your life as a man. And you might think I am an obstacle in your life. You think your sadness caused by our relationship, by love prison. It is not true. Your happiness and your sadness is from the world that you fight with yourself.

My love to you is like a lighthouse, always searching something special about you. And you are special. But I don't know if you think me in the same way. You always say things like these to me:

"How did you burn the rice again? A Chinese woman

【英雄】

〈名詞〉**1.** 小說或電影的男主角，主人翁；**2.** 才賦或成就超群，備受欽讚的英雄人物。

你又感到快活，你的心情就像英國的天氣。

你祥和寧靜，像院子的無花果樹。你高興是因為開始創作新的雕塑。屋子裡到處泥土雜物，凌亂不堪，活像建築工地。舉目盡是黏土，石膏，蠟，水。你的快活源自你的私人世界，源自你的物質對象，源自那些模型，男性頭顱，臂膀，腿腱，男性魅力……你的快活源自你的雄性世界，那世界裡面你每樣東西都有控制感。

你的鬱悶事實上跟我沒有關係，你的壓力並非來自於我，而是從你的雄性世界產生，因為，你生為男人卻不知足。而且，你可能認為我是你生命的絆腳石，你的鬱悶導因於我們的關係，導因於愛的枷鎖。真是鬼扯，快活也好，鬱悶也罷，要怪只能怪你老愛跟自己過不去。

我的愛對你有如燈塔一般，總是搜尋你與眾不同的地方。而你也的確十分特別。但我不曉得你看我是否也是如此，你對我講話總像這樣：

「妳怎麼又把飯燒焦了？一個中國女人不該把飯燒焦，妳天天都在吃飯。」

「我跟妳相處的時間比跟朋友還多，妳怎麼還要抱怨？妳到底要我怎樣？」……

shouldn't burn rice, you eat it everyday"

"I spend more time with you than with my friends. Why do you still complain? What else do you want?" . . .

It seems you don't treat me as a special person in your life. You treat me as one of your friends. And there is a line you draw between you and me. There is a limit, from your heart, from your lifestyle, which makes love feels like a friendship. You live inside of me, but I don't live inside of you.

You said Frida Kahlo is one of your heroes. Of course I knew that. I knew that from your book shelf. I knew that because I knew your heroes are always in pain, and died of young.

In nobody's London Fields, I sit on a chair, and read about Frida Kahlo again. I want understand you, and I want understand your twisted nude lying on the ground of your garden.

Frida, her body falling apart when she was alive. Her bones were being smashed by the bus accident. Death had been eating her everyday until one day nothing is fresh left. Again I see your naked man lying down on the ground. Your twisted statue, how similar to Frida's body in her painting.

In your world, I am losing my world. In your pain, I am losing myself. Everything makes me thinking about you, only about you and your world. I am like a wallpaper stick on the wall of your house, looking at you and decorating your life. "Don't bury me, burn me. I don't want to lie down anymore," Frida lay on the bed and said to her husband. She could not move one inch. A negotiation between her and the devil. My life compare with hers, is nothing.

你對待我似乎不像生命中的特別人物，我只是你眾多友人之一而已。你畫了一條線在你我之間，你的心，你的生活方式有其界限，這讓愛情感覺起來有如友誼。你活在我心裡，但我走不進你的心坎。

你說芙烈達‧卡蘿是你的英雄，這我當然曉得，從你的書架便看得出來。所以我早就明白，你的英雄總是活得痛苦，並且英年早逝。

空蕩無人的倫敦體育場，我坐在椅子上，再一次閱讀《芙烈達‧卡蘿》。我得想辦法了解你，我想了解躺在你庭院泥地上曲扭的裸雕。

芙烈達，她人活著，但軀體散裂。巴士意外撞碎她的骨頭。死亡一天一天啃噬她，直至體無完膚。我又看見你的裸男躺臥地面，你的扭曲人像，和芙烈達畫中描繪的軀體何其相似。

你的世界當中，我的世界遺落。你的痛苦當中，我失去了自我。每件事都讓我想到你，腦中只有你和你的世界。我就像糊在你房屋牆面的壁紙，望著你，為你妝點生活。「別埋葬我，把我燒了。我再也不想躺平，」芙烈達躺在床上對她丈夫說。她一時也無法動彈。連死都得和魔鬼打商量。我的人生和她一比，等於什麼都不是。

freedom

n. **1.** being free; **2.** exemption or immunity, e.g. freedom from hunger; **3.** right or privilege of unlimited access.

I say I love you, but you say you want to have freedom.

Why is freedom more important than love? Without love, freedom is naked. Why can't love live with freedom? Why is love the prison for freedom? How many people live in this prison then?

【自由】

〈名詞〉**1.** 自由；**2.** 免除或豁免，如免於飢餓；**3.** 不受限制進出或取用的權利或特權。

　　我說我愛你，你說你要自由。

　　為什麼自由比愛更重要？沒有愛，自由是赤裸裸的一片世界。為什麼愛情不能是自由的？難道愛情是自由的監獄？那麼多人活在監獄裡頭嗎？

schengen space

The "Schengen space" is the territory constituted by the countries which are members of the Schengen agreements. The following countries are today active members of the Schengen agreements : Austria — Belgium — Denmark — Finland — France — Germany — Greece — Iceland — Italy — Luxembourg — the Netherlands — Norway — Portugal — Spain — Sweden. The aim of the Schengen agreement is to allow free circulation of people within the territory of the member countries.

All foreigners who are legally resident in one of the Schengen member States can make short visits without a visa in any other member State, provided they travel with their valid passport which must be recognized by all the Schengen States and a resident permit issued by the authorities of the country of residency. Since the UK is not a member of the Schengen agreement, nationals who are not exempted from visa requirements by the Schengen member states and who reside permanently or temporarily in the UK need a visa to enter the Schengen Space.

"Have a look at this," you say. "If you got a visa to go to France, you could go and see all these countries."

You pass to me leaflet.

I read carefully terms of the "Schengen Agreement". I don't know where is Luxembourg, where is the Netherlands, Norway or Finland, and I of course don't know where is Greece. I thought Greece is in Rome. After I check the European map, I read it again the terms. I understand wherever I want to go I need visa, but I still don't understand what is "Schengen". Me, a native mainland Communism Chinese, a

【申根地區】

「申根地區」的範圍包括申根協議成員國的全體領土。今日申根協議的有效成員國有：奧地利、比利時、丹麥、芬蘭、法國、德國、希臘、冰島、義大利、盧森堡、荷蘭、挪威、葡萄牙、西班牙、瑞典（編按：至今又新增東歐數國，共有二十四國）。申根協議之宗旨在於准許民眾於成員國境內自由往來。

所有合法居留於任一申根成員國之外籍人士無須簽證即可短期往返其他成員國領土，通行時須持有效護照——所有成員國一體承認，以及居留國當局核發之居留許可。因為英國不屬於申根協議成員國，其國民未能享有簽證豁免，凡英國之永久居民或短期居留人士均須辦理簽證始得進入申根地區。

　　「看一下這個，」你說。「如果拿得到法國的簽證，那這麼多地方妳都能去了。」

　　你把傳單遞給我。

　　我仔細看過「申根協議」這個專有名詞。我搞不清楚盧森堡在哪兒，荷蘭，芬蘭，挪威也是，當然希臘更不用提。原本還以為希臘在羅馬的。查過歐洲地圖之後，又看了遍傳單。這下明白想去那些地方需要簽證，但還是弄不懂何謂「申根」。我，一個來自大陸共產國家的中國人，非歐盟成員，非英國護照。想申請簽證得準備我的醫療保險文件，財務證明

non-EU member and non-British passport. For visa application I need prepare my medical insurance paper, my financial document (thanks that I have a free accommodation here from you, so I save lots of money from my parents prepared for my renting).

"So much trouble, I don't want to go," I say. "I want stay in Hackney with you."

You look serious. "I think you should see a bit of the world without me. After all, you"ve never been to the sea."

"So, you take me."

You only smiling. "I think it's important you go by yourself."

When visa arrive I am still doing research on European map, trying to understand where is where, like Poland is next to Germany, and Romania is above of Bulgaria. But I couldn't find Luxembourg.

"Don't worry. Just buy an unlimited Inter-Rail ticket, then you can take the train to wherever you want in Europe," you say to me, very experienced.

"Unlimited?" I am so excited to know this.

"Yes, you're under twenty-six, so the ticket will be cheap. You'll get to see the whole of the Continent."

"Continent? Where is that?" I ask.

"You'll know where the Continent is when you come back."

You talk to me like I am your child. Maybe I am like idiot in front of you. Maybe you love the idiot.

You take out some old maps from your bookshelfs. There is map of Berlin, map of Amsterdam, map of Cologne, map of

（感謝有你免費住宿提供，省下一大筆爸媽準備給我租房子的費用）。

「麻煩死了，我不想去，」我說。「我跟你一起待在哈克尼就好。」

你一派正經。「我覺得妳該出去見識世界一番，不要讓我綁在身邊。畢竟，妳都還沒去過海邊。」

「那你就帶我去嘛。」

你笑笑的。「我想重點是妳要自己一個人去。」

簽證下來時，我還在研究歐洲地圖，想弄清楚哪兒是哪兒，比如波蘭在德國隔壁，羅馬尼亞在保加利亞上頭。但盧森堡就是找不到。

「別擔心，買張國際鐵路無限通卡，歐洲隨便坐火車想去哪就去哪，」你對我說，箇中老手的樣子。

「無限卡？」我興致勃勃。

「沒錯，妳不到二十六歲，所以票很便宜。妳可以看遍整塊歐陸。」

「歐陸？在哪兒？」我問。

「到時候等妳回來就知道歐陸在哪兒了。」

口吻有如把我當作你的小孩。或許我在你面前像個白痴。或許你愛的就是白痴。

你從書架拿出幾份舊地圖，有柏林地圖，有阿姆斯特丹，有威尼斯，馬德里……你吹去灰塵，將地圖放進我的袋子。

「這下它們又能派上用場，架上擺了這麼多年之後，」你說。

「可是這些地方跟你去的時候一定變化很大，」我說，想

Rome . . . You blow the dusts on these maps, and put in my bag.

"Now they are useful again, after all those years sitting on the shelf," you say.

"But all these places must be changed from the time you went," I say, thinking of map of Beijing every month being changed.

"It's not like China," you say. Then you take a novel called *Intimacy*, author Hanif Kureishi, and put into my bags too. "This is for you to read on the train."

You sit down on the chair, having tea, and looking at me packing.

I already feel lonely when I put my shirts into the rock-sack. Is that all you want? Want me away from you?

到北京的地圖每個月都要改版。

「沒有像中國那樣，」你說。然後拿出一本小說叫《親密關係》，作者是哈尼夫・庫雷西，同樣放進我的袋子。「讓妳坐車的時候看。」

你在椅子上坐下來，喝茶，看我打包行李。

衣服塞進帆布背包，我已經開始感到孤單。這就是你想要的？要我離開你身邊？

September

Paris

Paris is the capital and largest cuty of France, in the north-central part of the country on the Seine River.

I thought English is a strange language. Now I think French is even more strange. In France, their fish is *poisson*, their bread is pain and their pancake is *crêpe*. Pain and poison and crap. That's what they have every day.

"Du pain?"

The man serves me in a small brasserie nearby Les Halles, with some bread on the little basket.

"Non. Je ne veux pas pain!" I answer. I learn this from *French for Beginners* by Michael Thomas.

But one minute later, he comes back with a small basket of pain again, asks me:

"Encore un peu de pain?"

"Ça sufficient!" I say, wiping my mouth, stand up.

No more pain in my life.

Only rice makes me happy.

Journey London-Paris was big let down. When I sit on the comfortable chair in the Eurostar, the French-accent-staff announce the whole journey will take two hours and thirty five minutes. Gosh, two and a half hours I will be in the centre of a new country. Europe is so small, I can't believe it. No wonder that it wants to become a Union. I am so much looking forward

【巴黎】

法國首都，第一大城，位於中北部，濱塞納河。

　　原本以為英語折騰人，現在覺得法語更是詭異到家。在法國，他們的魚叫 poisson，麵包叫 pain，薄煎餅則是 crêpe。疼痛加毒藥加大便，他們每天吃的就是這些玩意。

　　「Du pain（要不要麵包）？」

　　中央市場附近的小餐館裡，跑堂的提了個小籃子裝著麵包。

　　「Non. Je ne veux pas pain（我不想吃麵包）！」我回答。我從麥可・湯瑪士的《法語初體驗》學來這麼一句。

　　但一分鐘後，他又提著麵包籃過來，問我：

　　「Encore un peu de pain（再來點麵包）？」

　　「Ça sufficient（我已經夠了）！」我說，嘴巴一抹，站起身來。

　　這輩子別再給我 pain。

　　來點米飯的話該有多好。

　　倫敦到巴黎一路失望到底。登上歐洲之星舒適的座椅，那法國口音的列車長宣布全部車程兩個小時又三十五分鐘。兩個半鐘頭便能抵達另一個國家的中心。歐洲真小，小到難以置信，難怪它想合起來成立一個聯盟。我等不及想要親眼目睹英

to see English Channel. I remember a Chinese man in 2001 who swam cross this Channel to earn national face for Chinese government, but when he reached French seashore he didn't have visa to arrive. Of course he didn't have visa, because he almost naked. In China, we all thought that French people don't understand Heroism. Hero doesn't need visa. Even a third world hero. Chairman Mao used to swim cross Yang Zi River, biggest river in China, in his very old age. He is of course, a hero.

The train is fast. There are still green fields and white sheeps outside of window. The speaker announce that in five minutes we will be in the tunnel of English Channel. So exciting, I can't wait. Five minutes later I find we are in the absolutely darkness, deep darkness. I thought the tunnel is made of glass, so it is transparent to be able to see the blue seawater. But there is no difference with London underground. In the long darkness, I wonder if those fishes beside us are blocked by the tunnel and will be confused in the sea. Disappointed, I am finding myself come out from the dark tunnel, and arrive to the French side.

Musée D'Orsay, Paris, a place exhibit lots of work from *Impressionists*. I-m-p-r-e-s-s-i-o-n-i-s-t, and I-m-p-r-e-ss-i-o-n-i-s-m. Longest two words I have ever learned so far. Even longer than c-o-m-m-u-n-i-s-t and c-o-m-m-un-i-s-m. There are several paintings from Monet. I stare at these obscure water lilies, obscure gate, and obscure sunrise. The colour and the subject in these paintings are like somebody looking through a dirty window glass. Especially the one about the impression of

吉利海峽。記得二○○一年，有個中國人為了替中國政府爭面子，游泳橫渡這道海峽，結果游到法國岸邊時，他沒有簽證不能上岸。廢話，全身光溜溜的，他哪來的簽證。在中國，我們一致的結論是，法國人不懂得何謂英雄好漢。英雄何須簽證，即使這位英雄來自第三世界。以前，毛主席游過揚子江，中國第一大河，那時他年紀已經很大了。沒話講，毛主席真是英雄好漢。

火車速度極快。大片綠野和雪白綿羊的窗外景色還沒看夠，廣播已經提醒，五分鐘內我們即將駛入英吉利海峽隧道。太棒了，我迫不及待。五分鐘後我們置身全然深沉的黑暗。原本還以為隧道鋪設透明的玻璃，可以看見海水湛藍。這下跟倫敦地鐵有什麼兩樣。漫長的黑暗當中，我猜想身邊可會有魚群被隧道封鎖，在海水中摸不著頭緒。失望通過，我發現自己已然駛出深沉黑暗的隧道，來到法國這頭。

奧賽美術館，巴黎，展示大量的印象派畫作。印─象─派，印─象─主─義。學到目前為止，最長的兩個英文單字。甚至比共─產─黨，共─產─主─義還要冗長。好幾幅莫內的作品。我瞪著那些朦朧的睡蓮，朦朧的柵門，朦朧的日出。好像某人拿骯髒的玻璃片遮眼畫出這些色彩和題材。特別是那幅日出‧印象，描繪海上的日出。景色一片模糊，波浪，海面，日頭，雲朵，全糊在一塊，連色彩也是模糊不清。

夜裡下榻廉價旅店。四十五歐元含早餐。房間很小，給白雪公主七矮人睡的地方就像這樣，不過，法國風味的露台永遠比英國的高明許多。坐在高背椅上，忽然想到，起碼有一千個

sunrise, sunrise on the sea. Everything blurred, the wave, the sea, the sun, the cloud are all blurred. Even the colour is blurred too.

Night in a cheap hotel. Forty-five euro including breakfast. The room is so small, like a place for one of Snow White's seven dwarfs, but the French-style balcony is always better than English one. I sit on the old high-backchair thinking there must be one thousand dead people used to sit on this chair and spent their hotel time doing strange or boring things. Turn on the desk lamp, I start to write you a letter. But my eyes can't see anything clearly today; especially I can't read clearly the trails of my writing. White paper too sharp for eyes, black ink too weak to read. When I look at the dictionary, every word is blurred. The optician in London told me the power of my short eyesight is growing, getting worse. They said I can't do laser surgery because my corneal are too thin. Will my future is a world of blurness?

I look out of the window. I can see the black clouds at the bottom of the dark sky, and I can see the dim lights in somebody's house which is not far away from this hotel, and the shadow of trees by the street light. But that's all, no more details in the street. I remember once you told me about an American eye doctor, who invented Bates Method. He taught those short-eyesight-patients how to use eyes *properly*. He said keep your vision centered. When you regard an object, only one small part should be seen best. This is because only the centre of the retina has the best vision for detail. Rest of retinal area is less able to pick up fine detail. Does this mean I don't

死者曾經坐過這張椅子，以奇妙或無聊的方式消磨旅店時光。扭開桌燈，準備給你寫信。但今天我的眼睛老抓不準東西；特別是自己筆下的撇捺怎麼也看不清。白色紙張刺眼，黑色墨跡太過淺淡。辭典裡，每個字彙都模糊難辨。倫敦的眼科醫生說我的近視加重，惡化。他們說我的眼角膜太薄，不適合動雷射手術。難道我未來的世界注定模糊到底？

往窗外望去，暗沉沉的天空底部有烏雲堆積，離旅店不遠處，某些家屋的燈火吐露微光，街燈周遭可見依稀的樹影。但最多只能看見這些，街道的細節再分明就沒有了。我記得，有次你提到一位美國眼科大夫，他發明了「貝茲鍛鍊法」，教導那些罹患近視的病人如何妥當地運用視力。他說，將你視線的焦點集中。當你凝視一樣東西，只有一小塊部分看得最清晰。原因在於，唯有視網膜的中心點擁有辨認細節的最佳視力，其他區域的辨認功能相對較弱。這樣說來，我豈非缺乏，或未能善用視網膜的中心位置妥當地看清楚事物？我和莫內，梵谷這些印象派畫家患了相同的毛病，眼中的世界模糊不清？

我的視網膜中心點只想看到你，其餘的就讓它模糊。既然眼中只容得下你，天曉得我來到這塊熱鬧的歐洲大陸幹嘛？

or can't use the centre of the retina to see things *properly*? That I like Monet, Van Gogh and all these impressionists, see the world blurred too?

I want to see *you* only at the centre of retina and everything else blurred. What am I doing in this busy Continent when I just want see you?

Amsterdam

Amsterdam is the constitutional capital and largest city of the Netherlands in the western part of the country where the Amstel River is joined by a sluice dam.

I only stop in Amsterdam for one day. I am going to Berlin. I don't know why I don't feel like to stay. I don't know anything about Holland, and I even didn't know *Holland, Dutch, the Netherland* meaning the same place. Why a country have so many different names? Before I thought these three spread somewhere differently in Europe.

There are only two things I know about Holland: first, the Communist Dutch man Joris Ivens made a film called *The 400 Million* about Chinese against Japanese invasion; second, all the tulips in China are said from Holland. About Joris Ivens, I saw a film camera been exhibited in the Museum of the Revolution in Beijing. It is the camera he gave to the Communists army at late 1930s. Maybe that's why Chinese Communists started making films since then.

Amsterdam Central station. A large place. A place for temporary stop and for passing by.

So many people here, but nobody will stay here more than one hour.

From platform 15 to 1, I cannot find a place to sit my bum. No, there is no single chair or bench in this Central Station. The passengers hold their pizza in hand and eat it without a

【阿姆斯特丹】

荷蘭首府及第一大城，地理位置偏西，於阿姆斯特河上築堤壩發展而成。

　　阿姆斯特丹待不到一天，便要動身前往柏林。不知為何，就是不想多作停留。關於荷蘭，我一無所知，甚至連荷蘭有三種稱呼——Holland，Dutch，Netherland——我都懵懵懂懂。何以同一個國家要有好幾種不同的名稱？以前，還以為這是分布歐洲的三個不同的地方。

　　我只曉得荷蘭兩件事情：一，荷蘭共產主義者尤里斯·伊文斯拍過電影《四萬萬人民》，紀錄中國人抵禦日本侵略；二，中國見到的鬱金香全說產自荷蘭。關於尤里斯·伊文斯，我見過北京的革命博物館展出一架電影攝影機，伊文斯於一九三〇年代末期把它送給共產黨軍隊。或許這是中國共產黨從那時候開始拍攝影片的由來。

　　阿姆斯特丹中央車站。碩大無朋。這地方僅容短暫留步，匆匆來去。

　　此地人潮洶湧，但沒有誰會駐留超過一個鐘頭。

　　從十五月台走到第一月台，找不到一個地方讓我的屁股喘口氣。偌大的中央車站，居然連張椅子或長凳都沒有。旅客手拿披薩，站著吃沒地方坐。旅客兩腿直立喝紙杯裝的咖啡，沒地方可坐。有個男的，巨無霸行李箱加上背包，怪腔怪調一直

seat. The passengers stand and drink paper-cup coffee without a seat. A man, with a huge suitcase and a big rocksack, talk in mobile phone in a strange language. A language without any similarity with other language I have heard in my whole life. He keeps talking in the phone and his face is sad. He talks in the phone for so long, and it seems like he is being sucked by the telewave and disappeared in the phone-zone. In that dark phone-zone it is no seats either.

The train to Berlin will be departure at 8:15 p.m. Five hours to wait. I decide go for a walk.

Outside station so much water. And houses like doll house. In front of one house I meet a man drinking coffee on doorsteps. I stopped to look at house because I saw some familiar leaf with special fragrant. Lush wisterias climbing on a big tree. I always love this plant. It is so Chinese. It was growing everywhere behind our house in my home town. And it is growing in your English garden as well. I put down my heavy rocksack and try to have a rest.

Man on doorsteps looks at me and asks in English, "Would you like a cup of coffee before you start walking again?"

"Oh. Is that convenient for you, to make a cup of coffee?"

He smiles. "It's no problem. I've already made a pot. So I just need to fetch a cup for you."

He goes back inside of house. Quite dark inside.

We sit on doorsteps and drink a very bitter coffee without milk. I dare not ask him about milk, thinking maybe Dutch man doesn't use milk.

"I am Peter. And you?"

"Zhuang Xiao Qiao . . . Well, just call me Z, if you want."

講手機。哪一國的語言，和我這輩子聽過的話語沒有任何交集。他手機講個沒完，臉色難看死了。他對著話機喋喋不休，時間久到似乎已經被電波吸入，隱沒於電話特區。那不見天日的電話特區同樣沒有地方可坐。

開往柏林的火車晚間八點十五分出發。還得等上五個鐘頭，我決定出去遛達遛達。

車站外頭，河水四處可見。房子有如娃娃屋般可愛。一棟房屋前面，門階上坐個男的，正在喝咖啡。我停下腳步，打量那房屋，熟悉的枝葉特殊的芬芳蔓延。一棵蒼樹爬滿茂盛的紫藤。一直很喜歡這種植物，十足的中國味道。故鄉老家後園隨處可見，你的英國庭院裡也有紫藤攀爬。我放下沉重的背囊，打算先歇個腳。

門階上那男的看著我，用英語問道：「要不要喝杯咖啡，休息一下再走？」

「噢，這樣不會麻煩嗎，再泡一杯咖啡？」

他露出笑容。「沒問題，我已經煮好一壺，倒一杯給妳就好。」

他回到屋子裡面，怪陰暗的。

我們一起坐在門階，沒加奶的咖啡味道苦澀，我不好意思問他要牛奶，敢情荷蘭人本來就習慣不加。

「我叫彼得，妳呢？」

「莊小喬……唔，你不介意的話，叫我Z就可以。」

「Z？」他失笑。「好奇怪的名字。」

在英國，人家告訴我，如果某人說某件事物「奇怪」，就表示他們不怎麼欣賞。所以我沒接腔。

接著他又問：

"Z?" he laughs. "That's a strange name."

In England, people tell me if somebody says something "strange" means they don't like it. So I don't answer him.

Then he asks me:

"Are you Japanese? Or Philippino? Or maybe Vietnamese? Or Thailandese?" I a little annoyed: "Why I couldn't be a Chinese?"

"Oh, are you?" he says, and looks at me meaningfully.

His smile reminds me of you. A bit different. He wears a black leather jacket.

"Do you like plants?" he asks me, because my eyes were still on the wisteria.

"Yes, I like those vines, wisteria. It is originally from China," I say.

"Oh, really? I didn't know that."

He starts to look at the plants as well.

"My father told me that wisteria is very long-lived," I say. "Some vines surviving 50 years. They climb the trees and they can kill the trees."

"You know a lot about plants." He looks at me: "So why are you running around the world?"

"I don't know."

"China is far away from here. And you don't have anybody travelling with you?"

I nod my head. Not knowing what to say.

People in the street are in a hurry with their bags, they must rush back to have dinner with their family. Everywhere people live in the same way.

"And are you going to the train station now?"

154

「妳是日本人？或者菲律賓人？還是越南人？泰國人？」

我有點惱：「難道我不能是中國人？」

「喔，妳是嗎？」他說，意味深長地看我。

他的笑容令我想起你。約略有些不同。他穿一件黑色皮夾克。

「妳喜歡植物？」他問我，因為我的眼睛直盯著紫藤。

「對，我喜歡那些藤蔓，紫藤。它原產於中國，」我說。

「喔，真的？不說我還不曉得。」

他同時打量起那些爬藤。

「我父親告訴我說紫藤的壽命很長，」我說。「有些甚至可以活超過五十年。它們攀附樹木生長，直到最後樹活不下去。」

「妳很內行嘛。」他轉過來看我：「妳為何世界各地跑來跑去？」

「我不知道。」

「中國離這兒好遠，都沒有人陪妳一起旅行？」

我點點頭，不曉得該說什麼。

街上的人們提著包包行色匆匆，一定是趕著回去和家人共進晚餐。天下之大，人的生活不外乎這些。

「妳現在得趕去車站了嗎？」

「對。」

「妳要去哪裡？」

「柏林。」

「柏林。很棒的城市。以前去過？」

「沒有。」

「柏林很冷。」

"Yes."

"Where are you going?"

"Berlin."

"Berlin. A nice city. Have you been there before?"

"No."

"Berlin is cool."

But I don't want to know about Berlin, I think only of my home. So I ask, "Do you live in this house? Is this your home?"

"Well, not exactly my home. But I rent it."

"Can I ask what do you do here?"

"Me? I just came back from another country. Cuba. I was there for ten years."

Cuba? Why Cuba? Live there for ten years as a Dutch? Is he also a Communist like Joris Ivens?

I start to watch him, instead of watching the people in the street.

His eyes meet my eyes.

I look up his home. It is a beautiful old house.

"Don't you want to change your ticket? Then you could stay with me for a bit until you want to go." He looks at me sincerely. He is very serious, I think.

I shake my head. I put my empty coffee cup on the stone step. I look at my rocksack in front of me. I stand up and ready to go. But suddenly my tears come out without me noticing.

The man is surprised. He doesn't know what to say. He gives me his hand and lets me hold it. I hold his hand, tightly. I don't know him, I don't know him, I tell myself.

但柏林如何與我何干，我心裡想的只有我的家。於是我問：「你住在這棟房子？這是你家？」

　　「噢，不能算是我家，這是租來的房子。」

　　「能不能請教你在這兒做些什麼？」

　　「我？我剛從別的國家回來。古巴。我在那兒待了十年。」

　　古巴？爲什麼是古巴？一個荷蘭人在那兒住了十年？莫非他和尤里斯‧伊文斯同樣是共產主義者？

　　我從街上的行人收回目光，轉而看他。

　　我們兩眼交接。

　　我朝上打量他的家，非常漂亮的老房子。

　　「想不想更改一下車票？妳可以留在我這裡，等到想離開的時候再說。」他眞摯地看著我。他很認眞，我想。

　　我搖搖頭，將空咖啡杯擺在石階上，看了看身前的背包。我起身，準備要走，霎時眼淚不由自主，奪眶而出。

　　那男的楞了一下，不知道如何開口。他將手伸過來給我，我緊緊握住。我不認識他，我不認識他，我心裡對自己默念。

　　月台的大鐘指向二十點零八分，還剩七分鐘。外頭天色桃紅。寂寞的等候。太遲了，已經沒有時間返回市中心。

　　龐大的車站分外蕭索。這地方遠比倫敦任何車站都要巨大。滑鐵盧車站，國王十字車站，和這一比都算小兒科。單獨旅行，看到這雙雙對對牽手耐心候車令人格外難受。

　　飄浮的微塵，地球上一個小小的漂泊者在上帝眼中想必便是如此。

　　我覺得少了你異常艱辛。我變得語言殘缺，周遭的世界理解起來困難重重。我需要你。

Now the big clock on platform shows 20:08. There are seven minutes left. Sky is pink outside. Waiting and feeling lonely. Now there is no time I can go back to the centre of city.

A big train station is a bleak place. This station is bigger than any station in London. Waterloo Station, King Cross Station are just too normal compare with this one. Travel alone, makes me feel sad when I see all these couples hold each other's hand and wait patiently.

A floating dust, that must be how God see a little human *drifting* on the Earth.

I feel difficult without you. I become language handicapped. I got so many problems to understand this world around me. I need you.

Holding the ticket to Berlin, but I don't feel like to go. There is no one I can meet in Berlin, and there is nothing I know about Germany. I just want go back to London, to my lover.

Home is everything. Home is not sex but also about it. Home is not a delicious meal but is also about it. Home is not a lighted bedroom but is also about it. Home is not a hot bath in the winter but it is also about it.

The speaker on the platform renounces something loudly. It is 20:09. The train will leave in four minutes. I look around and ready to get on train. Suddenly, somebody is running towards me. It's him. The man offered me coffee in front of his doorsteps. He is running on the platform, and he is running towards me. I am stepping into the carriage, so I drop my bags on the floor and come out the train again. He stops right in front of me, breathless. We stare at each other. I hug him tightly and he hugs me tightly. I bury my head into his arms. I see

手持柏林的車票，我半點想去的念頭都沒有。柏林無人可以和我會晤，我對德國了無所悉。我一心只想回到倫敦，回到我愛人身邊。

　　家包含了一切。家不只是性愛，不只是美味的三餐，不只是明亮的臥室，不只是寒冬的熱水澡，家包含這些，以及更多。

　　月台的擴音器大聲宣告時間已到。二十點十一分。火車四分鐘內開動。我環顧周遭，準備上車。驀然間，有人向我的方向跑過來。是他。那個門階上請我喝咖啡的男人。他在月台上奔跑，直直向我奔來。我已經踏上車廂，趕緊行李地板一扔，退出車外。他在我面前收步，氣喘噓噓。我們彼此對望，我緊摟住他，他也緊緊摟住我。我的頭直往他懷裡鑽。我看見自己的淚水沾溼他的黑色皮夾克。那皮夾克的氣味很怪，卻又如此熟悉。

　　我哭了：「我不想去……我覺得好孤單。」

　　他將我摟得更緊。

　　「不想去就別去。」

　　「可是我必須要去，」我說。

　　鈴聲響起。火車終於開動。當他的背影於月台消失，我擦乾眼淚。感覺很怪。我不明白自己身上發生了什麼，但的確有事情發生。如今結束了。結束。我正離開阿姆斯特丹，沒辦法回頭。我知道這趟旅程我得撿拾磚塊，搭建自己的人生。我得變得堅強牢固，別再哭哭啼啼。我拉下車窗，坐上自己的位子。

my tears wet his black leather jacket. The smell of the leather jacket is strange, but somehow so familiar.

I am crying: "I don't want to go . . . I feel so lonely."

He hugs me, even tighter.

"You don't have to go."

"But I have to go," I say.

The bell rings. The train starts to move. When his back disappears off the platform, I dry my tears. It is so strange. I don't know what has been happened on me, but something has happened. Now it is over. It is over. I am leaving Amsterdam. There is no way to return. I know I am on a journey to collect the bricks to build my life. I just need to be strong. No crying baby anymore. I pull down the windows, and sit down on my seat.

Berlin

Berlin is the capital and largest city of Germany in the northeast part of the country; formerly divided into East Berlin and West Berlin, the city was reuni-fied in 1990.

"The size of China is almost the size of the whole Europe," my geography teacher told us in middle school. He drawed a map of China on blackboard, a rooster, with two foot, one foot is Taiwan, another foot is Hainan. Then he drawed a map of Soviet on top of China. He said: "This is Soviet. Only Soviet and America are bigger than China. But China has the biggest population in the world."

I often think of what he said, and think of how at school we were so proud of being Chinese.

It seems that I can't stop to keep meeting new people. When I was in London, I only know you, and only talk to you. After left London to Paris, I was still in old habit and didn't even talk to a dog in Paris. English told that French are arrogant they don't like speak English. So I didn't try talk to anybody in France. But that's good for me. I don't even need to remember how to speak Chinese there. After Paris, I tired of museums. No more dead people.

Opposite my seat a young man in his black coat and red scarf is reading newspaper. It is of course foreign language newspaper. And I don't know the writing of that language at all.

【柏林】

德國首府及第一大城，位於東北部；從前分割爲東柏林和西柏林，一九九○年統一。

「中國的疆域幾乎等於全歐洲的加總，」中學時我的地理老師這樣告訴我們。他在黑板上畫出中國地圖，一隻公雞，兩隻腳，一腳代表台灣，另隻腳代表海南島。接著，他在中國上頭畫出蘇聯的地圖。他說：「這是蘇維埃。只有蘇維埃和美國的領土大過中國。但中國的人口數世界第一。」

我常想起他這番話，那時候在學校我們身爲中國人是何等驕傲。

看起來，我似乎沒辦法停留在一個地方多認識幾個人。在倫敦的時候，我只認識你，只有你可以說話。離開倫敦到了巴黎，我德性未改，甚至連狗都懶得搭理。英國人總說法國人眼高於頂，不屑講英語。所以在法國我根本沒開口的打算。其實這樣也好，我連費心揣摩中國話怎麼講都省了。去過巴黎之後，博物館都看膩了，別再給我一堆已故人士。

對面坐了個年輕人，黑大衣紅圍巾，正在讀報紙。那當然是外國語言的報紙，我大字不識一個。

穿黑大衣紅圍巾的年輕人暫停讀報，對我的現身投以一瞥，又回到他的報紙。但很快地，他放下報紙，瀏覽窗外的景色。我同樣面朝窗外，什麼風景也看不到，有的只是暗沉的夜

Young man in black coat with red scarf stops reading the paper, and gives my presence a glance then back to his paper. But very soon he stops his reading and looks at the views outside of the window. I look at the window as well. There are no any views. Only the dark night, the night on no name fields. The window reflects my face, and my face observes his face.

Only him and me in this small carriage.

"Berlin?" He asks.

"Yes, Berlin," I say.

We start to talk, slowly, bits by bits, here and there. His English speaking accent not easy understand.

"My name is Klaus."

"OK. Klaus," I say.

He waits, then he asks: "What is your name?"

"It is difficult to pronounce."

"OK." He looks at me, seriously.

"I am from China, originally," I say. I think I should explain before he asks.

"Originally?" he repeats.

"OK, I have lived in London for several months."

"I see. I am from East Germany." He stops. Then he says, "Your English is very good."

Very good. Is that true? If it is, he doesn't know how mad I have studied English every day, and even now, on the trip.

So, on this train, this new person, Klaus. He is a stranger to me. Train is really a place for films and books to set up the story. And I can feel me and this man we both want to talk, to talk about whatever.

He says he was born in Berlin, east of Berlin. He says he

159

色，無名野地的夜色。車窗映照我的面龐，我的臉觀察他的容貌。

狹小的客廂裡只有他和我。

「柏林？」他開口。

「對，柏林，」我說。

我們打破沉默，慢慢的，一點一點，這裡那裡，隨意開口。他的英語口音不容易聽懂。

「我的名字叫克勞斯。」

「好的。克勞斯，」我說。

他稍等一會，然後問道：「妳叫什麼名字？」

「我的名字很難發音。」

「好的。」他看著我，一本正經。

「我從中國來的，原本的時候，」我說。趁他問之前先解釋算了。

「原本的時候？」他重複。

「是的，我已經在倫敦住了好幾個月。」

「了解。我從東德來的。」他停頓。接著說，「妳的英語講得很棒。」

很棒？此話當真？果真如此的話，他可不曉得，我每天英語學到瘋狂的地步，即便是當下，旅行的途中。

所以，這班列車，這位新認識的先生，克勞斯。對我而言，他算陌生人。火車真是個好地方，多少電影或小說把故事場景設定在這兒。我感覺自己和這位先生兩人都有話想講，隨便什麼話都好。

他說他在柏林出生，東邊的柏林。他說他對東柏林瞭若指掌，大街小巷，每個角落。幸運的傢伙，這班車開往他的老

knows everything about East Berlin, every corner, every street. How lucky, this train is leading to his home, his love.

The night train is moving slowly. It is certainly not a fast train. Only non-important passengers would take this train, or holiday maker.

We lie down opposite each other on the couches in the tiny carriage of the train. A strange position, lying there, he and me. We talk more about Berlin.

He says that he is training in Diplomatic Department in Berlin. Before that he was a lawyer. He wanted to change his career and to live in abroad. He says he used to have for eight years a girlfriend who lives in B-a-v-a-r-i-a (B-a-v-a-r-i-a, he spells slowly to me). He explains it is in the south of Germany, but of course I don't have any idea where is this B-a-v-a-r-i-a. He tells me his girlfriend one day came to Berlin and knocked his door. She told him she wanted to finish this relationship. So he finished it in pain, as she decided. And he decided to change his life and go to work in other countries. I understand Klaus's story, I understand that feeling want to be far away from the past. I tell him I understand him.

Also I tell him about you, the man who I love so much, and the man who makes sculptures in London. I tell him my feeling about you—and how you tell me I have to travel alone.

We talk, then sometimes no words, and just listen.

Eventually the sun comes outside of the window.

"We are getting there," Klaus says.

Berlin has a heavy colour, big square buildings. Like Beijing.

家，他心愛的所在。

夜行列車速度緩慢，顯然非屬快車班次。僅有無要務在身的旅客才會搭乘，或者是不趕行程的遊客。

我們各自躺下，躺在彼此對面，狹小的客車廂長椅上。生疏的姿勢，躺在那兒，他和我。我們聊起柏林更多點滴。他說他在柏林的外交部門受訓，更早之前從事律師工作。他想轉換跑道，到海外生活。他說之前有個交往八年的女朋友住在巴—伐—利—亞（巴—伐—利—亞，他慢慢拼給我聽）。他解釋說那裡位於德國南部，不過當然我沒概念這巴—伐—利—亞在哪兒。他告訴我，一天他女朋友來到柏林敲他的門，告訴他，她想要結束這段感情。反正女的已經下定決心，他只得忍痛分手。於是他決定改變生活，想辦法到外國工作。我能理解克勞斯的故事，我理解那種想要遠離往事的心情。我跟他說我懂。

我還告訴他你的事情，我深愛的男人，在倫敦創作雕塑的男人。我提起自己對你的感情——以及你如何說我必須單獨遠行。

我們天南地北，有時找不到話語，光是聆聽。

終於，窗外太陽升起。

「我們快到了，」克勞斯說。

柏林的建築顏色沉重、廣場寬闊，像北京。

「妳柏林打算住在哪兒？」他問。

「還不曉得。或許會住 YMCA 的青年旅社，我有歐洲火車通卡可以打折。」我亮出通卡給他看。

「我住的地方附近有一家 YMCA，願意的話我可以帶妳去。」

"So where you will stay in Berlin?" he asks.

"Don't know. Maybe YMCA youth hotel, because I can have discount from my Europe train pass." I show him my pass.

"I can take you to a YMCA near my flat, if you want."

"That's very kind of you. Please. I don't know anywhere."

"No problem," he says, and pulls down his luggages from on our head.

I take my rocksack and follow him, just like a blind person.

The early morning air feels cold, like autumn coming. Occasionally, one or two old mans in a long coats walk aimlessly in the street, with the cigarettes in their lips. Under the highway there is bridge. By the bridge there is a sausage shop, lots of large mans queue there to get hot sausages. Gosh, they eat purely sausage in the morning! Even worse than English Breakfast. The morning wind is washing my brain, and my small body. This is a city with something really heavy and serious in its soul. This is a city which had big wars in the history. And, I feel, this is a city made for mans, and politics, and disciplines. Like Beijing.

Then I see the flag, drifting on top of a massive building on a big square. Three bars: black, red, and yellow.

I ask Klaus: "Is that your country's flag?"

He is surprised: "You know nothing about politics?"

I admit: "Yes, I am sorry. I never know it. So many different flags, they confuse me."

He laughs: "But you"re from China. Everything in China is about politics."

Maybe he is right. This is a man must know this world very

161

「那真是太好了,麻煩你。我任何地方都不認識。」

「沒問題,」他說,從我們頭頂上取下行李。

我提起背包跟在後頭,活像個盲人。

清晨的寒氣逼人,秋天已至。時不時出現一兩位老人家,身裹長大衣,漫無目的走在街上,唇間叼根香菸。公路下方有橋,橋邊有家香腸小鋪,不少大男人排隊買熱騰騰的香腸。他們一大清早只吃香腸!還比不上英國的早餐嘛。晨風灌洗我的腦門,我的薄軀。這座城市的靈魂裡有種無可閃躲的沉重與嚴肅。這是掀起過歷史大戰的城市。而且,我覺得,這座城市屬於男人,政治,以及紀律。像北京。

接著旗幟映入我眼簾,寬闊廣場上巨大建物頂端飄盪的旗幟。三色橫條:黑,紅,黃。

我問克勞斯:「那是你們的國旗?」

他很驚訝:「妳真的完全不懂政治的事?」

我承認:「是的,對不起。我一竅不通。國旗太多了,我根本搞不清。」

他笑了:「可是妳來自中國。中國有哪件事和政治無關。」

或許他說的沒錯。這位先生想必是個世界通。

「所以那是德國國旗?」我猜測。

「對,沒錯。」

我盯著那面國旗,盯著黑紅黃的橫條。

「為什麼國旗最上面是黑色條紋?」我問。「看起來好危險!」

他又笑了,隨即收斂,同樣抬起頭凝望那面旗幟。或許他覺得我並沒有那麼呆。

國旗的黑條在頂端飄動,威武,沉重,讓人有點畏懼。按

well.

"So it is the German flag?" I guess.

"Yes. It is."

I stare at the flag, stare at this black red yellow bars.

"Why the black bar on top of the flag?" I ask. "It looks so dangerous!"

He laughs again, but then stop. He raises his head and looks up the flag as well. Maybe he thinks I am not so stupid.

Black bar of flag is powerful and heavy blowing on top, and I feel a little bit scared. In a reasonable designing, the black bar should be at the bottom, other wise . . . it might cause bad luck. It might cause the whole country's unfortunate.

As I remember, there is another country also has black bar on national flag, which is Afghanistan. But even Afghanistan put the black bar on the bottom instead of top.

I look up the sun through the flag, and the flag seems like a dark spot of the sun.

Through Alexanderplatz station, we are heading to east Berlin. I follow him, like a blind man following a stick. It is seven in the morning. We stand in front the YMCA Hotel. The door is not opened yet. We ring the bell. A man comes opening the door with his sleepy eyes, and he tells us that there is no vacancy until this afternoon.

So we leave YMCA, with our luggages. Standing in the middle of the street, Klaus says I could come to his flat if I want. Is very close to here.

"OK," I say.

Klaus flat is very tidy. White plain wall, double bed with blue colour bedding, bare wooden floor without carpet, white-

設計的道理來看，黑條應該放在最底下，否則⋯⋯它可能招來厄運，搞得整個國家流年不利。

就記憶所及，另外還有一個國家的國旗上面也有黑條紋，阿富汗。但阿富汗也曉得要把黑條放在底下，而非頂端。

我仰望旗幟後面的太陽，那面國旗有如黏著太陽的黑點一般。

經由亞歷山大廣場站，我們前往東柏林。我亦步亦趨，像盲人依循拐杖。時間是清晨七點。我們來到青年旅社門前。大門尚未開啟，我們只好按門鈴。一個男的睡眼惺忪應門，他告訴我們要到下午才有空床位。

我們只好提起行李，離開 YMCA。站在馬路中央，克勞斯說不介意的話，我可以先到他的公寓。離這兒很近。

「好啊，」我說。

克勞斯的公寓滿整潔的。白色素牆，雙人床鋪著藍色床單，光潔的原木地板，沒有地毯，白磁鋪面的浴室，廚房雖小，但設備齊全，一張書桌配上皮椅，木質衣櫥和一個書架。就這些。

浴室裡沒有女用化妝品或香水，沒有任何女人的標記。

他到小廚房煮了一壺咖啡。牛奶沒了，他打開冰箱之後說。我們喝咖啡，他加了點糖，我則敬謝不敏。我看見了，他的冰箱裡只有一條可悲的奶油，和兩顆乏味的雞蛋。他提到明年將會離開柏林，展開他的外交生涯。他抓了枝筆，寫下公寓地址和鄰近的地鐵站，然後交給我。別走丟了，他說。

接著，他打開衣櫥，換掉上衣。裡面起碼掛了二十件各色襯衫和十條領帶。看起來有人將它們妥當地燙過。誰幫他燙的衣服？他穿上一套鐵灰色西裝，打了暗紅領帶。

tile-pasted bathroom, small tidy kitchen with everything there, writing table with a leather chair, wooden wardrobe and a book shelf. That's all.

No woman's make up or perfumes in the bathroom. No any sign of woman anyway.

He makes a pot of coffee in his small kitchen. No milk, he opens the fridge and says. We drink the coffee, and he puts some sugar in. I don't want any sugar. I can see there are only a piece of sad butter and two boring eggs in his fridge. He says he will leave Berlin next year, then start his diplomatic job. He grabs a pen and writes down address of flat and nearby tube station. And he gives it to me. Don't get lost he says.

Then he opens the wardrobe and changes his tops. There are at least twenty different colour's shirt and ten different ties hanging inside. And it seems they are all being ironed by someone properly. Who ironed his clothes? He puts on a grey-silver-colour-suit, and a dark-red-tie.

"You can leave your bags here, so you can walk around in Berlin. I'll be back this evening from work."

So I say yes, yes, yes to him, to Klaus. He seems nice man, no harm, only warmth. I can trust him. We walk to bus stop where goes to his office. Several office man and woman in suits and with black leather bags also waiting. Then the bus immediately coming. He kisses on my cheek and says see you tonight at home. It is so naturally, just like in a Western TV, a husband says goodbye to his wife every morning when he leaves to work. I see him disappear with the bus. And I have a strange feeling towards him.

Now I am alone, wandering around in the city of Berlin. I

「妳可以把背包放在這兒，走路到處逛逛。我晚上下班就回來。」

我只有對他說好，好，好，對克勞斯。他似乎人很好，無害而溫暖，可以信賴。我們走到他要去上班的公車站。已經有好幾個身著套裝的男女上班族提著黑色皮包等候公車。車說來就來。他親親我臉頰，說晚上家裡見。如此自然，就像西方電視節目演的，每天上班前先生對太太道別。我看著他隨公車離去，心裡滋生一股異樣的感覺。

又剩下自己一個，柏林四處走馬看花，感覺自己渾身無所遮掩。這座城市我了無牽掛，對此地我沒有愛意，我沒有恨意。

德國有什麼東西值得我認識？柏林圍牆？社會主義？還是二次世界大戰？法西斯分子？他們幹嘛憎恨猶太人？奧斯威辛怎麼沒有設置在他們自己的國家裡？中國的歷史教科書有提到一些德國的東西，但讀了平添更多的疑惑。

我只曉得他們有香腸，橋底下販賣各種口味的香腸。人們手拿木籤當街吃起香腸。記得今天早上，一位儀表堂堂的先生站在小鋪前，大嚼擠滿番茄醬的香腸，胳膊還夾著公事文件。我對柏林的了解僅止於此。

這一切格外令我想起北京。四四方方的格局，直通通的大道，切右，切左，沒有彎彎曲曲。還有好幾處更巨大的廣場街區。非得像毛主席這樣話說了算的領導才能打造如此規矩的城市。不過，這裡當然比北京古老許多。北京大規模的建物都在最近十五年以內落成──或者毋寧說：最近十五天以內。大部分街道上的路樹都是新栽的，時間不會超過五年。歷史的北京已經不再，徒留空洞的紫禁城供觀光客拍照留念。

feel really naked. I care about nothing of this city. I have no love or hate whatsoever towards this city.

What I should know about Germany? The Wall? The Socialism? Or the Second World War? The Fascist? Why they hated Jews? Why Auschwitz is not set in their own country? The history text book in China told us a little about Germany, but very confusing.

I only know they have sausages, different taste sausages sold under the bridge. And people eat the sausage with a wooden stick in the street. I remember this morning a very noble-looking man in front of sausage shop, and was eating tomato-sauce-covered-sausage with his office files under his arm. That's my understanding of Berlin.

It remind me so much of Beijing. The city is in square shape. Straight long street, right, left, no wandering. And some more bigly square building blocks. It must need a dictator like Chairman Mao to make a city like this. But of course this city look much more older than Beijing. Big buildings in Beijing came out from last fifteen years—or I would rather say: last fifteen days. Most of trees standing in Beijing streets are new trees, which being planted maybe no more than five years. History in Beijing doesn't exist anymore, only empty Forbidden City for tourists taking photos.

I pass by that sausage shop under bridge again. The steams come out from the food. It smells good. It seduces me to want have some sausages too. I give three euros to the man in the shop, and he kindly gives me a big pack of hot sausage, with green mustard and red sauce by the side. It look exactly like a lump of shit. But it tastes good.

我再度經過橋下的香腸鋪。食物冒著熱騰騰的蒸汽，味道無以抵擋，聞了教人食指大動。我付給店家三歐元，他慷慨遞來一大包熱香腸，旁邊附上綠芥末和紅沾醬，模樣挺像一坨大便，不過味道很正。

　　我人身在柏林，然而心繫倫敦，為你留駐。我魂不守舍，只想找處網咖好發伊媚兒。我對你萬分思念。

　　你今早在倫敦寫信給我，或者寫於昨天晚上：

　　「雖然我們身體分隔兩地，但感覺妳依然在我身邊。」

　　我看完馬上回覆。我說自己一個人上路真的好孤單，半點意思也無。

　　然而你回答我：

　　「我們西方人早已習慣孤單。我認為體驗孤單對妳有益，妳可以自我探索那種感受。要不了多久，妳會開始咀嚼孤獨之樂。到時候自然不會再那樣害怕了。」

　　我在網咖裡翻來覆去讀這封伊媚兒，不明白你究竟用意為何。

　　我走到大街旁的咖啡館，坐下來讀了幾頁《親密關係》，想說看能否拉近我倆的感受。我點的起司蛋糕不小心沾到書皮。這本書令人沮喪，你怎麼教我看這種東西。書裡寫一個中年男子，拋妻棄子，斷絕家庭生活。你跟我一起生活便是這種心情？你就是這樣才送走我遊歷歐陸，要我探索孤獨？我氣壞了，放下書本，環顧室內。

　　咖啡館蠻摩登的，紅黑交錯的桌椅排成幾何圖陣。過度刻意的設計，反倒令人不太舒服。我要你馬上在我面前現身，剝光我的衣服，揉捏我的肌膚，再用力緊抱我。噢，我想跟你做愛，現在就要，當下此地。唯有做愛方能趕走這種孤單。唯有

My body is in Berlin, but my heart is left in London, left for you. I don't feel myself together. All I want do is find some internet cafe write emails. I cannot stop thinking of you.

You wrote me from London this morning, or maybe you wrote from last night:

"Although our bodies are separated, I still feel as if I am with you."

I write to you back immediately. I say it is too lonely on the road on my own. I don't see the point.

But you write me back:

"In the West we are used to loneliness. I think it's good for you to experience loneliness, to explore what it feels like to be on your own. After a while, you will start to enjoy solitude. You won't be so scared of it anymore."

I read this email again and again in internet café not knowing your exactly meaning.

In café by big street I go and sit read some pages of Intimacy hoping it make me feel close to you. The cheese cake I just had is sticking on the cover of the book. It is very depressed book, I don't understand why you want me to read. It is about a middle-aged man leave his wife and children, to abandon his family life. Is that how you feel living with me? Is that the reason you sent me off to travel the Continent explore my solitude? I feel angry. I put down book, looking around the room.

Is a modern café, the red and black colour chairs and tables are all in geometry shape. So much designing here, it almost feels uncomfortable. I want you suddenly turn up in front of me, and take off my clothes and squeeze my body and hold

做愛能夠撫慰靈魂。我要你緊抱我直到發疼，你的揉捏令我體膚痛楚，同時陶醉。好怪，這麼疼痛的歡愉。

我漫遊了一整天，在超大的購物廣場看人，在蕭索的公園看人，在肉品市場看人。人們穿的戴的好多好多皮製品。即便是星巴克裡擺的也是皮革沙發。這國家怎有辦法做出數不清的皮革？無所逃於皮革間的一天。這裡坐坐，那裡走走，胡思亂想，終於等到夜晚降臨。我走回克勞斯的寓所。還好，沒出差錯，街道正確，大門正確，門牌號碼正確。因為這張柏林地圖來自倫敦，你給的。我不禁猜想，你何時造訪此地，待過哪些場所。領先我二十載的往昔人生，難怪你有一籮筐的故事，還有祕密。

我按下門鈴，沒有回應。按了又按，門後來才開。克勞斯一副駭人的模樣，身體倚著門框，膝蓋幾乎落地。他在我面前倒下。

他發高燒，頻頻嘔吐。他拉肚子，剛從浴室出來馬上又吐，顯然病得不輕，甚至來不及衝到廁所便吐在床上。

我嚇壞了。怎麼回事？他吃壞什麼東西？他會掛掉嗎？雖然僅僅和這個男人在夜車上共處九個鐘頭，如今我得對他的生死扛起微小的責任。但我該如何應變？

我坐在床邊遞給他一杯水，他一喝馬上衝進浴室吐掉。他躺回床上，對我說抱歉。我將他的手握住，在一旁躺下，感覺他的身體發燙。沒一會他又往廁所跑。吐啊吐的，直到胃裡再無任何餘物可吐。

「麻煩拿張紙給我，還有筆，」他說。

我從桌上找來紙和筆。

「拜託，出門幫我買一下這種水，標籤上有紅星和獅子。」

tightly. Oh, I want to make love with you, make love with you right now, right here. Only making love can wipe out this loneliness. Only making love can touch the soul. I want you hold my body painfully tight. I feel hurting when you squeeze my body like that, but at the same time I feel contented. It's strange. Pleasure could be so painful.

I wander around for whole day. In the big shopping mall watching people. In the stagnant park watching people. In the meat market watching people. Lots leather here on people's clothes. Even in the Starbucks, the sofas are leather sofas. How come so much leathers being produced in this country? A long day of leatherness. Sit and walk and dream. Eventually it comes to the evening. I walk back to Klaus flat. Yes, no mistakes, the exactly right street, and the exactly right gate, and the exactly right door number. Because I got this Berlin map from London, from you. I wonder when you have been to Berlin and where you stayed. Your life before is twenty years ahead of me. No wonder you have so many stories, so many secrets.

I press the doorbell, nobody comes. Again, and again, I press it. Then the door opens. Klaus looks terrible. His body leaning against the door and his knees almost reaching the floor. He falls in front of me.

He is in high fever. He vomit often. He has diarrhoea. He spits out when he comes back from bathroom. He is terribly ill. He even vomit up on bed before he rushes to toilet.

I am so scared. What happened? Did he eat something bad? Will he die? Although I only know this man nine hours on night train, I have small responsibility to his life now. But what

他寫下那種水的品名：Gerolsteiner Stille Quelle（杰羅斯特內爾寧靜泉）。

我一時傻眼。德國人好樣的！光水的名稱能搞到這麼複雜！

我買回四大罐塑膠瓶裝水。他喝下去了，Gerolsteiner Stille Quelle，一口一口慢慢地，然後躺了回去，陷入半睡狀態。我到浴室擰了一條溼毛巾，折好敷在他額頭。

時間好晚了，飢腸轆轆。那傢伙躺在床上勉勉強強呼吸。我打開冰箱，決定將那兩顆孤零零的蛋煮來吃。鍋子找到，注好水，點了瓦斯，蛋放下……瞧，這德國人的廚房我還是變得出花樣，雖然在陌生的地方煮東西有點怪怪的。那兒還有茶包，順便泡點來喝。這回有加糖，可餓壞了我。

吃下兩顆水煮蛋沾鹽巴，回到床上。感覺上他的體溫依舊居高不退，我起身找到電話，可究竟該撥哪個號碼，999？911？221？123？柏林的系統像倫敦或是中國？我放棄電話回到他身邊，取下他額頭汗溼的毛巾，再用冷水擰過。前一刻，我心想，他人還和他的單身公寓一般光潔，怎麼這會兒如此凄慘落魄。真搞不懂德國人。我把燈關了，挨著這男的身邊躺下。

柏林逛一整天疲累不堪，我拉過來一點他的絨被蓋住身體，很快沉入夢鄉。

我被他的體溫碰醒，燒得很。他渾身汗，整張床搞得溼溼黏黏，嘴裡不知嘟嚷什麼：

「可以給我點水……？」

他的呼吸濁重困難，好似馬拉松跑到最後階段。

然後他說：「我好冷好冷。」

I am going do?

I sit on his bed and give him a glass of tap water. He drinks but straight goes to bathroom to spit out. He lies down on bed again, and says sorry to me. I hold his hand. I lie down beside him and feel his body is like burning. Then he rushes to toilet again. Vomit, till nothing can be taken out from his stomach anymore.

"Give me a piece of paper, and a pen," he says.

I find pen and paper on his table.

"Please, go out and buy me this kind of water, with a red star and a lion on the label." He writes down the name of the water: *Gerolsteiner Stille Quelle.*

I can't believe what he wrote! What a German! Water can have such a complicated name!

I come back with four big plastic bottle of water. He drinks. *Gerolsteiner Stille Quelle.* Slowly. Then he lies back to the bed, half sleep. I return to bathroom to fetch a wet towel, and fold it to put on his head.

It is very late, and I am hungry. The man lying on the bed is breathing difficultly. I open fridge and decide boil the only two eggs. Finding the pot, filling the water, switch on the gas, putting in the eggs . . . Look, I can make something in this German kitchen, though it's uncomfortable to cook in some stranger's home. There are some tea bags there, so I make tea. I add some sugar this time, as I am too hungry.

After eating two eggs with salt, I come back his bed. I feel his temperature is still rising. I get up to find his telephone. But I don't know which number I should dial. 999? 911? 221? 123? Is Berlin system like London or China? I give up the tele-

我在衣櫥找來另一件絨被。但兩件蓋上我就太熱了。我把衣服脫光，只剩一件內褲，鑽進被窩。兩層羽絨被底下，他抱住我還在發抖。我任由他抱著。看著我的豹紋胸罩躺在地板上，心裡有股異樣感覺。

　　他的臉轉過來，對著我低語，模模糊糊：

　　「別離開我……」

　　我聽他講，再也睡不下。他偎著我，身體發燒。我抱他，他擁緊我光溜溜的身體。

　　我們像這樣睡，如此親密，直到隔晨……

　　第二天，他好多了，但還是虛弱，沒辦法出門。我收拾浴室，沖洗廁所，清理床邊的衛生紙。他從昨晚喝掉三大瓶水，現在只剩一瓶。我泡了茶，幫他杯裡加點糖。我的背包還扔在地上，根本沒打開過。

　　「你曉得昨天晚上對我講了什麼？」我想提醒他，看他到底怎麼說的。

　　「恐怕昨天晚上的事我記不清楚。我人腦袋裂開，一定像團狗屎，」他說，有點難為情。

　　「所以你半點都不記得昨晚的事？」我略感失望。

　　「我記得麻煩妳去買水。還有妳照顧我。太感謝了，我以為自己會掛掉。」

　　「沒什麼。其實我也有點害怕。」

　　他喝茶，動作放慢。我不知道接下來怎麼辦。我該離開？還是留下？我感覺自己比較想留下來陪他。

　　「你想我是不是該在柏林多待幾天？」我問。好希望自己別這樣問。真討厭。

phone and come back to him. I take out the sweat-soaked towel on his forehead and cool it again in the cold water. I am thinking one moment he was so tidy like his bachelor's flat, but another moment he is so messed and fucked up. I don't understand Germans. I switch off the light and lie down beside this man.

I feel so tired by walking around in Berlin whole day. I pull over bits of his duvet to cover my body. Quickly I fall into my dreams.

I am waking up by his heat. It is so hot. He is sweaty and everything on the bed is wet and sticky. He says something not clear:

"Can I have some water . . . ?"

His breathe is heavy and difficult, like he is running at the end of a marathon.

Then he says: "I feel very very cold."

I find another duvet in his wardrobe. But now I am too hot under both these duvets. I take off all my clothes, only have my pants left. And I get into the bed again. Underneath two covers of duvet, he hugs me, but still shivering. I let him hug me. I see my leopard-pattern bra lying on the floor, and I feel a bit strange.

His face turns to me, and murmurs, very unclear:

"Stay with me . . ."

I hear him. And I am not sleepy anymore. He lies beside me, with the fever. I hug him. He holds my naked body.

We sleep like this, so close, until next morning. . . .

The second day, he is feeling better, but is too weak go out. I

「唔，我不曉得。看妳怎麼決定。嘿，非常感謝妳幫我這麼多，特別是我們根本不算認識。現在的狀況是，我下午得進辦公室……」

他看起來和我昨天晚上距離好遠。

「你覺得以後有可能到倫敦來嗎？」我問，又一次討厭自己。

「我不曉得，」他含糊地說。

「那中國呢？」

「我想不太可能……」他笑了。

沒有任何理由在人家的單身公寓賴著不走，連柏林都不能再待。我現在便想離開柏林，越快越好。

我給你寄了張明信片：

最親愛的，

我正要離開柏林。說真的，接下來想去比較暖和的地方。我不清楚自己是否喜歡獨自旅行，看人家火車上都是情侶或一家老小結伴出遊度假。對我這不算度假，這是你派給我的家庭作業。祝你快樂。

摯愛
你的Z

明信片上頭的圖片是柏林圍牆。牆身到處亂塗亂抹，醜斃了。

開往車站的公車上，我聞到身體猶有昨夜克勞斯高燒的汗

tidy the bathroom, flush the toilet, and clean the tissues by the bedside. He drank three bottle of water since last night, now only one bottle left. I make some tea, and add some sugar in his cup. My rocksack is still on the floor, without opening it yet.

"Do you know last night you said something to me?" I want to remind him, to find out.

"I'm afraid I can't remember much about last night. My mind was blown up. I must look like shit," he says, a little embarrassed.

"So you don't remember anything about last night?" I am bit disappointed.

"I remember I asked you to buy some water. And you looked after me. Thank you so much. I thought I was going to die."

"That's OK. I was a bit scared, actually."

He drinks his tea, slowly. I don't know what do next. Should I leave? Should I stay? I feel like want to stay with this man.

"Do you think maybe I should spend more time in Berlin?" I ask. Gosh, I wish I didn't ask like that. I hate myself.

"Well, I don't know. It is your decision. Look, thank you so much for everything you did, especially considering you don't even know me. The thing is, I have to go to the office this afternoon . . ."

He looks distant to me from last night.

"Do you think you might come to London one day?" I ask, keep hating myself.

"I don't know," he says vaguely.

"What about China?"

味，我問自己：我愛上他了嗎？我不認識克勞斯，這東柏林的
傢伙，但我覺得和他很親。瞧，如今我擁有自己的隱私，且看
到時候回倫敦我是否會向你坦白。

"I think that's very unlikely . . ." He laughs.

There is no reason for me to stay here in this bachelor's flat anymore, not even stay in the city of Berlin. I will leave Berlin right now, immediately.

I send you a postcard:

My dearest,

I am leaving Berlin. I really want to go down to somewhere more warm. I don't know if I like to travel on my own. I see all the lovers and families on the train they travel together on their holiday. For me it is not a holiday, it is something like homework from you to me. I wish you are happy.

Love,
your Z

It is a postcard with the picture of Berlin Wall. Messy drawing everywhere on the wall. It is ugly.

Sitting on bus to station, I can still smell my body having sweat from Klaus fever last night, and I ask myself: Did I fall in love with him? I don't know Klaus, the man in east Berlin, but I feel close to him. Look, now I have my own privacy, and I don't know if I would tell you when I come back to London.

Venice

Venice is the capital of the northeast Italian region of Veneto; built on 118 alluvial islets.

I arrive in Venice after hours and hours sleeping on train. Walk out from station, there are waters everywhere, or say, river, or should say canals. I don't know if these waters are part of sea. But it is midnight, and very dark. Bad time. It mean I have to pay a hotel for over night staying, and I don't know where am I now. I hope I can search twenty-four-hour cafe to kill the night before the morning starts, then I can find hotel for tomorrow more easy.

On the wall of St Lucia train station, there are some posters hanging there, both in Italian and English, and also in characters like India language. The English says: "Venice Asian Art and Culture Festival". I notice it is during this week. That a good thing for me. There are several people also just coming out from station, and looking in map. They argue something on the map, probably argue in Italian, or maybe French, or maybe some other Europe language I not understand.

A man in that group comes to me: "Parla Italiano?"

I shake my head.

"English?"

"Yes," I answer.

"Do you know where is the party?" He looks friendly.

"What party?" I say.

【威尼斯】

義大利北部維內托地區第一大城;建於 118 座沖積小島之上。

火車上一個鐘頭睡過一個鐘頭,終於抵達威尼斯。出了火車站,舉目可見水色,或者說,河流,或者應該說運河。不曉得這些流水是否屬於海洋的一部分。時近午夜,暗朦朦的,真會選時間。這表示住進旅館還得多花一天過夜的錢,但我根本不曉得人在哪兒。但願找到一家二十四小時不打烊的咖啡館,將天亮前的黑夜打發過去,這樣明天再找地方住也比較輕鬆。

聖路西亞車站的牆上,貼著幾張海報,同時印有義大利文和英文,還有看似印度語的字母。英文寫著:「威尼斯亞洲藝術文化節」。我注意到時間恰好是這禮拜,對我來說這消息還不賴。有一群人也剛從車站出來,忙著看地圖。他們七嘴八舌,講的大概是義大利話,或者法語,或者其他我不懂的歐洲語言。

那伙人裡面有位先生向我走來:「講義大利話嗎?」

我搖搖頭。

「英語?」

「是的,」我回答。

「妳曉得派對地點在哪兒?」他很友善的樣子。

「什麼派對?」我說。

「妳不是來這兒參加亞洲藝術節的?今天晚上有辦派對。

"You are not here for this Asian festival? There is party tonight. We are going there now. I hope it's not too late."

The man speaks very unclear English, but he seems very keen on Asian.

"No, it won't be too late. It will be too early," one of his friends says.

"Come along with us if you want," the man says. "We can get you in."

I am hesitating. Should I go? If I can't find that twenty-four-hour cafe it could be a solution.

"Maybe I come later?" I say, putting on my heavy rocksack.

"OK," says the man. "If you decide to come just tell them you know Andrea Palmio and they will let you in." His friends are waiting behind for him to go. "By the way, the place is called Pachuka, and you need to take the boat to Lido . . ."

He pass me piece of paper with the Pachuka name on. Then they disappear with his sincere voice.

Lido? I know *Lido Holiday Inn Hotel*. It is the very expensive hotel in Beijing and Shanghai. Only foreigners live there, and Starbucks inside of those hotels in China. But, here, is the party also in *Lido*? Is it posh hotel too? Why I need take the boat to get there? Confused by all these thoughts, I walk alone to the waterbank, indecisive. Maybe I should go and pretend I am one of the famous Asian artists in the party. Westerners can't tell the difference of a group of Chinese. In their eyes, we all look the same. I decide ask someone the way to this *Lido*.

Taking the night boat, I am heading to the other side of Venice. I feel like living in the old time of south China, that

我們現在要趕過去，希望時間不會太晚了。」

這位先生英語講得不清不楚，不過似乎對亞洲人很熱心。

「不對，哪會太晚。應該是太早才對，」他一位同伴如此說道。

「願意的話可以跟我們一起去，」那先生說。「我們可以帶妳進去。」

我心下躊躇。去還是不去？如果找不到二十四小時的咖啡館，這倒也是個解決辦法。

「我可能晚點過去？」我說，背起沉甸甸的行囊。

「好的，」他說。「你果妳來的話，就說妳認識安德烈‧帕密歐，他們會讓妳進去。」他的朋友在後頭等著要走。「還有，那地方叫帕丘卡，你先搭船到麗都……」

他給我一張卡片，上面印有帕丘卡的店名。一行人隨他真摯的聲音消失。

麗都？我知道麗都假日飯店。非常高檔的飯店，北京上海都有，住的都是外國人，星巴克在中國便是開在裡面。不過，這裡，派對也在麗都舉辦？一樣奢侈的大飯店？為什麼去那兒還得搭船？滿腹疑惑，我舉步獨自走到水岸，舉棋不定。或許該去派對那兒，假裝我也是有名的亞洲藝術家。西方人碰上中國人在一起很難分辨。在他們眼中，我們都是一個樣。我決定找人問路到麗都去。

登上夜船，往威尼斯另一端前進，我自覺有如回到昔日中國的江南，人們上哪兒都得坐船。我盯著水面，這是海嗎？真正的海？黑暗中甚至水的顏色也瞧不分明。和照片或電影裡的海比起來根本是兩碼事，和你描述給我聽的也大不相同。這種

people have to take boat to get to other places. I am staring at the water. Is this the sea? A real sea? I can't even see colour of water in the dark. It is very different the sea on pictures or in the film. It is also very different what you described me. I don't think anyone want swim in this water. Also, the sea is being stopped again and again by the city. How could be possible a city still stands here without sinking? I thought a sea is boundless. I am disappointed. I want tell you immediately how I'm feeling now. Chinese always say West culture is a blue culture, Chinese culture is yellow culture. This because West from the sea, and China comes from the yellow sand.

I don't understand the sea.

One hour later, I stand in front of "Pachuka". From the outside it looks like a large restaurant or a night club. Neon lights everywhere. There are two very big men in the black suits, stopping everybody in front of the door. Some fashionable looking Italian mans and high-heel womans get in, with the invitation tickets holding in their hands. There are several India womans dressed up like queens or princess, also get into the door. It must be a really posh place, I wonder. I am glad I come here. But right now I can't remember that man's name. Gosh, why Western names are so difficult remember? So I wander around the door with my rocksack on shoulders and try to recall that name back. Antonia? Anthony? Andrew? Alexander? Antonioni? Which one sounds more closer?

Encouraging myself enormously, I walk to the door man: "My friend asked me come here. He is inside."

The door man answers in very rude and bad English: "Sorry. It is a private party."

173

水不會有人想跳下去游泳。而且，海水一再被城市阻斷，這地方怎麼可能仍舊屹立不沉？本來以為大海遼闊無邊的，好失望。真想對你傾訴此刻的感受。中國人老說西方文化是藍色文化，中國文化則是黃色文化。因為西方文明源自海洋，中國文明源自黃土。

經過一個鐘頭，我來到「帕丘卡」。外觀看起來，它像一間大餐館或是夜店。霓虹四處閃動。兩個大塊頭一身黑西裝，守住大門擋人。幾個時髦裝扮的義大利佬和高跟鞋女郎進去了，手上晃著邀請卡。還有幾個印度小姐，皇后或公主般的衣裝，也登堂入室。這地方鐵定超高檔的，我猜。很高興我來對了。但這會兒卻記不起那位先生的名字。西方人的姓名怎會如此難記？我肩掛背包，門前徘徊，努力回想那名字。安托尼？安東尼？安德魯？亞歷山大？安東尼奧尼？哪個聽起來比較像？

鼓足勇氣，走近門口把關的先生：「我有朋友叫我到這裡來，他人在裡面。」

守門的用彆腳的英語粗魯地打發我：「抱歉，私人聚會。」

「對，我知道，可是有朋友邀請我來，他現在就在派對裡面，」我堅持。

「妳朋友什麼名字？」

「安托尼，安東尼，不，安德魯。還是安東尼奧尼……你曉得我是中國人，你們國家的名字我不會發音。」我真是丟臉到家。

「妳朋友幹嘛的？」

「他是……他是藝術家的經紀人。」我只開過幾次口，半

"Yes, I know. But my friend invites me to come, and he is just inside the party," I insist.

"What's your friend's name?"

"Antonia, Anthony, no, Andrew. Maybe Antonioni . . . You know I am a Chinese and I can't pronounce your country's name." I am embarrassed myself.

"What does your friend do?"

"He is . . . he is the manager of the artists." I just open my mouth randomly. I don't know him at all, and I don't think he is a manager of the artists.

One of the doormans takes it a little serious and goes in side to ask somebody. One minute later he comes out:

"Sorry, we can't let you in."

"But he invites me here. I should get inside!" I am pissed off.

"Sorry *Signorina*," the door man says emotionlessly. "No invitation, no entry. *Basta*."

A posh car arrives, and three people come out with strange costumes and shining shoes. The bounce men say Signori to them, and they walk straight into the door. The music is loudly coming out from the party, and laughings. Nobody wants to take me in or even look at me a second. Why I don't look like one of the Asian artists? I wish I wear skirt, or some old-fashioned stupid traditional Chinese costumes.

I wander outside of the Pachuka like a wild night dog, no where to return. Then I see a very big and very long car arrives abruptly. Shit, it's a Cadillac! Comes out eight. Yes, one, two, three, four, five, six, seven, eight young womans. All blonde, with shining long golden hair. They wear the same miniskirt,

點也不認識他，我也不覺得他像藝術經紀人。

其中一個守門的考慮了一下，進去裡面請示。一分鐘後他現身：

「抱歉，我們不能讓妳進去。」

「但他邀請我來的。我得進去才行！」我冒火了。

「抱歉了小姐，」守門的板著聲音說。「非請莫入。就這樣。」

一輛豪華轎車停下，出來三個怪異裝束，鞋面閃亮的傢伙，兩個大塊頭稱呼先生後，他們長驅直入。派對播放的音樂震耳傳出，還有笑聲。沒有人願意帶我進去，甚至連一眼都懶得瞧我。怎麼我看起來就是不像一位亞洲藝術家？要是穿上裙子就好了，或是那種蠢兮兮的中國傳統服飾。

我在帕丘卡外頭胡亂徘徊，有如喪家之犬，無計可施。突然間有輛加長型大轎車停靠，媽的，凱迪拉克！出來八個。沒錯，一，二，三，四，五，六，七，八個年輕小姐。全部是金髮妞，惹眼的金色長髮，同一款迷你裙，同一款胸罩般的銀色緊身上衣。銀色迷你裙短到半截屁股露出來跟人打招呼。她們苗條得要命，玲瓏有緻，全員足登白色高跟長靴，看起來像是同一位長頸鹿媽媽生出來的長頸鹿。這些性感尤物，由一位女經理領軍，鞋跟敲在沙沙的地面：恰，恰，恰……她們列隊昂首跨過大門。兩個守門的眼珠死盯小姐身上，結冰一般，動彈不得。這些性感尤物來這「私人宴會」幹嘛？跳豔舞？她們裡面可沒有一個亞洲人。或者她們只是來這兒陪尊客喝喝香檳而已。

我在門前少說站了一個鐘頭，打量這些魅力十足的嬌客。然後有輛計程車駛近，車上下來一個男的。是他，兩個鐘頭前

and the same tight silver tops look just like bras. The silver miniskirts are so short people can see half of their bottoms. They are extremely slim, shapey, and all wear white high-heel long boots. They look like giraffes from the same giraffe mother. These sexy machines, leaded by a woman manager, their high-heels click the sandy ground: cha, cha, cha . . . They line up and one by one walking into the door. Two door mans fix their eyes on these girls body, like being deep frozen, can't move. What are these sex machines doing in this "private party"? Lap dancing? None of them are Asians. Or they will just drink champagne with posh mans guests?

I must have stayed in front of door nearly an hour watching all those fascinating guests. Then I see a taxi coming. And a man comes out from the taxi. That is him, the man I met two hours ago! Why did he arrive so late? Are Italian mans all like that?

"Antonia!" I shout.

Perhaps right name because he doesn't correct me, or maybe he didn't understand I am actually shouting his name.

He walks to me and apologise:

"I am very sorry about this. My friends changed their mind. They wanted to go somewhere else instead. In fact, it was better than this party. Let me take you to the other place." His English accent is almost inunderstandable.

"All right."

I don't want to tell him I wait here for so long. It would be not cool to let him know. So I follow him and get into his taxi.

Inside of taxi, so close, I can see his face clearly. He looks bit formal in his plain suit and black leather Made-in-Italy

遇到的那位先生！怎會這麼晚才到？莫非義大利男人都像這樣？

「安托尼！」我叫道。

或許名字無誤，因為他沒有更正我，或許他不曉得我嘴裡嚷嚷的是他的名字。

他邊走過來邊道歉：

「真是對不起，我朋友他們臨時改變主意，跑去別的地方。其實，那兒比這裡的派對還棒。我現在就帶妳過去。」他的英語口音幾乎沒法聽懂。

「好的。」

我不想告訴他我已經在這兒苦熬一個鐘頭。讓他知道的話太遜了。我隨他坐上那輛計程車。

計程車裡，兩人靠得很近，可以清楚看見他的臉。素色西裝配上黑色義大利製皮鞋，略顯拘謹，頭頂中央部位髮絲稀疏。他似乎人蠻好的，不過有點沉悶，如果要我評斷的話。

「你是幹哪行的？」我問。

「我是個酪梨，」他回答。（編按：義大利文的律師avvocato與酪梨avocado的發音相似）

「酪梨？」我聽了大感訝異，水果也算一種職業？「請幫我解釋解釋，」我請求。

「如果妳要被關進牢裡，可以僱我幫妳打官司，」他說。

「呃⋯⋯像律師那樣？」

「沒錯！沒錯！酪梨就是律師。」他很高興我能聽懂。

「那妳呢？」他問。

「我⋯⋯我只是來玩的。其實我正在學英語。」

「在威尼斯？」他的興致來了。

shoes. His hair is very few in the middle of his head. He seems sincerely but a little boring, if I can judge like that.

"So what you do?" I ask.

"I am an avocado," he replies.

"Avocado?" I am surprised to hear. Is a fruit also a job?

"Please explain me," I ask.

"If you are going to be put into prison, you can hire me to help you in the court," he says.

"Ah . . . is like a lawyer?"

"Yes! Yes! Avocado is lawyer." He is pleased that I understand.

"What about you?" he asks.

"I am . . . just a tourist. Actually I am studying English."

"In Venice?" His interests are aroused.

"No. No. Studying English in England," I say.

"Oh, your English is good."

"Thank you. But why you are to do with this Asian culture festival?"

"Because of my friend, he is an avocado too. He gives legal advice to this organisation so he said, "Andrea, come along too'."

"I see."

Gosh, not another avocado. At least now I know his correct name.

The taxi stops in front of a disco. Behind the disco is really the open sea. Is like a big pond full of black ink. I feel dangerous, as I think it's very easy to fall into that black pond.

It is a public disco, not "private party". It is already 2:30, the endless night. The music is so loud. American disco, it is too

「不，不，學英語是在英國，」我說。

「噢，妳的英語很棒。」

「謝謝。可是你跟這裡的亞洲文化節有什麼關係？」

「都是因為我朋友。他幫主辦單位做法律顧問於是就說，『你也要一起來』。」

「我懂了。」

不是那個酪梨！

計程車開到一家迪斯可前面，舞廳後頭便是空曠的海面，像個大池塘注滿了黑墨汁。我覺得恐怖，不小心的話很容易跌入那黑池塘。

這是誰都能進來的迪斯可，非屬「私人宴會」。已經兩點半了，夜無止境。音樂震天價響，美式迪斯可，我可無福消受。好多青少年在裡面瘋，我只想趕緊閃人。但安托尼一把將我拉進舞池，他那伙朋友全在裡面扭肩晃腦。我們在舞池中央跳啊扭呀，我的背包不時拐到別人，癲狂的樂音不斷重重敲擊我的腦門。噢，跳這種舞真是要命，我的文化讓人放不開。我的動作準是醜到不行，猛爆的音樂對決我僵硬的骨架。至於安托尼，他看起來不錯，一副很享受音樂的樣子。他的舞步有些古板，但總比我強上許多。

我快受不了，人群當中無聊透頂，在那兒像匹馬光站著都能睡著。

「妳還好嗎？」安托尼舞近我，姿勢近乎漫步。

「我有點疲倦。其實我想走了，」我說。

「真的？妳要住哪兒？」

「我還沒找到住的地方。」

「還沒找到？那妳現在打算去哪兒？」音樂吵成這樣，安

much for me. Lots of teenagers dancing inside. I want to leave immediately. But Andrea pull my arm into the dancing floor, and I see his friends are all there shaking their shoulders and tingling their heads. So we are dancing right in the middle of the floor, everyone tripping over my rocksack, and my head being hit heavily every single second by the crazy music. Oh, gosh, I can't dance like that, this is not my culture. My movements must be really ugly. It is a battle between the violent music and my boney body. And Andrea, he looks OK. He seems enjoying the music. His dancing style is a bit serious, but I am sure it better than mine.

I am getting so bored. So bored in the crowds. I can just stand there and fall in sleep like a horse.

"Are you OK?" Andrea dances towards me. His dancing almost like a slow walking.

"I am bit tired. Actually I want to go." I say.

"Really? Where you stay?"

"I don't have a place to stay yet."

"You don't? So where you are going to go now?" Andrea is talkative in the extremely loud music.

"I don't know."

"Well, if you want, you can stay in my hotel. My room has two beds."

"Really?"

"Yes, no problem."

The taxi puts us in the middle of nowhere. Suburb, definitely suburb. There is a very simply looking hotel in front of us.

"Look, the sea is just over there."

托尼倒是口齒伶俐。

「不曉得。」

「唔,不介意的話,妳可以住在我的旅館。我房間有兩張床。」

「真的。」

「真的,沒問題。」

計程車把我們載到不知名的所在。郊區,絕對是郊區。我們前面有家不怎麼起眼的旅館。

「瞧,海就在那兒。」

我看向安托尼手指的地方,只見一片漆黑。

「看見沒有?」他問。

「好像有,」我說。

他按下門鈴,我覺得很難為情。已經四點半了,讓旅館的人看見他帶一位中國女孩子回來,不知作何感想。

他又按了按門鈴。

「妳知道裡面那男的,耳朵不太靈光,」他解釋。

「沒關係,」我安慰他。

終於,來了個老先生把門打開,眼皮懶得睜開多看一眼,道了聲「晚安」便直接回房睡覺。

安托尼的房間就在一樓旅館大門旁邊,明兒一早櫃檯馬上會發現我,真糗。

他打開房門,把燈點亮,然後嘴裡嚷嚷好像罵著義大利髒話,一副驚嚇的樣子。

「怎麼了?」我問。

「這裡有小動物,」他叫嚷。

I look to where Andrea is pointing but there is only inky darkness.

"Do you see it?" he asks.

"Kind of," I say.

He presses the door bell. Gosh, I feel embarrassed. It is already half past four and if the hotel people know he brings a Chinese girl back, what they will think?

He presses the bell again.

"You know the man inside, his ears are not very good." he explains.

"OK," I comfort him.

Eventually there is a very old man opens the door. He even doesn't bother to raise his eyes to look. He says, "*Buona sera*" and then straight back to his room to sleep.

Andrea's room is in ground floor, just by main door of hotel. I am thinking tomorrow morning the reception will discover me easily and shame me.

He opens the room, and switches on the light. Then he shouts something like swear in Italian. He is scared.

"What is it?" I ask.

"There are some little animals here," he shouts.

"Where?" I can't see anything.

"Here! Look the floor!" He points. There are some ants, big ants. They are moving around.

"Oh, just some ants." I comfort him again and start put my feets on the ants, crush them with my shoes.

Andrea looks disturbed deeply. He runs into bathroom and pulls some toilet paper out. He kills rest of ants with paper, and flushes the paper into toilet.

「在哪兒？」我沒看見東西。

「這裡！妳看地上！」他用手指著。原來是螞蟻，大隻的螞蟻，地上爬來爬去。

「噢，只是幾隻螞蟻。」我又出言安慰他，舉腳踩去，螞蟻葬身鞋底。

安托尼異常驚恐，跑進浴室拉出長串衛生紙。他用紙壓死剩下的螞蟻，再扔進馬桶沖掉。

房裡有兩張單人床，他倒是沒有騙我。我除去全身衣物，只剩內衣褲。我的睡衣壓在背包底層，懶得解開。他進浴室梳洗時，我已經上下嚴實蓋緊。兩分鐘後他出來，左右打量了幾秒。他一定很驚訝我怎麼沒兩下便鑽進被窩。接著他問：

「燈要關嗎？」

「對。明天見。」我說。

黑暗中，他很快便傳出鼾聲。老實的鼾聲，我自忖，他人心地很好，然而就是不夠吸引人。或許這樣才算正常。數一下距離清晨的時間，再過兩個鐘頭便是破曉，到時候就能離開這該死的麗都島前往威尼斯……

我差不多睡著了。性的念頭，不對，我夢見性的事情。蕾絲邊的春情，我和一個臉認不出來的女人。她好像在親吻或撫摸我的胸部。接著我突然清醒，有人把嘴壓在我唇上。睜開眼睛，安托尼正親著我。幽暗中他看起來真夠蠢的。

「不要。去睡覺，安托尼，」我說，有點噁心。

「安托尼！我的名字叫安德烈，」他說，然後乖乖聽話，回到他的床上。他樣子好滑稽，一條短褲頭，還披著白襯衫，兩條光腿沒幾兩肉，毛茸茸的。

我不想再睡。永無止境的國際鐵路列車上有的是睡眠時

There are two single beds. He didn't cheat me at all. I remove all my clothes, only left underwear. My pyjamas bottom of rocksack and don't want unpack. I cover myself tightly while he is in toilet brushing and flushing. Two minutes later he comes out and looks around for several seconds. He must be surprised to see how quick I am inside of the duvet. Then he asks:

"Should I turn off the light?"

"Yes. See you tomorrow," I say.

In the darkness, I hear his snoring quickly comes. Honest snoring. I can tell. I am thinking he is quite a nice-heart man, but somehow he is not very interesting. Or maybe he is just normal. I count the hours to the morning. Two hours later it will be a sunny morning, and I will leave this damn island Lido and go to Venice. . .

I am almost fall sleep. Thinking of sex, no, I am having a dream about sex. Lesbian sex, me and a woman who has an unrecognisable face. Maybe she kisses me or touches my breast. Then I am suddenly awake. I feel somebody's lips press my lips. I open my eyes. Andrea is kissing me. He looks very stupid in the dim light.

"No. Go back to sleep," I say. I feel a little disgust.

"Antonia! My name is Andrea," he says, then obediently, he goes back to bed. He looks funny. Wears a shorts but still with his white shirt. His two naked legs are a bit skinny and hairy.

I give up sleeping. I can sleep anytime in my forever Unlimited Inter-Rail train, so why waste time here in Lido? I get up and dress up. I brush my teeth and take all my belongs. Very quietly I close the door behind me.

間，幹嘛在麗都這兒浪費生命？我起身穿好衣服，將牙刷過，撿起全部家當，旋風般關上身後的門。

　　晨光從未如此明亮清新。和風拂過我的黃色體膚，無拘無束，感覺自己的身體全然自由舒暢。我走向海邊，海面浮游幾艘輕舟。真實的藍色海水，純粹如夢。那海水強大的磁力令我不由自主舉步靠近。你說的沒錯，海好美。

　　「我覺得活得好難受，」一次你對我說。

　　「怎麼會？」

　　「覺得人生只有無盡的空虛。」

　　「那你打算怎麼辦？」

　　「我想找到幸福。」

　　「你不可能永遠幸福，人總是會有難過的時候。不是嗎？」

　　「可是我的人生毫無幸福可言？」

　　「那有什麼能夠讓你最接近幸福？」

　　「……海。」

　　有一天我們這樣對話，在倫敦我們家裡。此刻有如重播一般，迴響於浪波之上。

The morning is never been so bright and fresh to me. The wind is blowing my yellow skin. I feel free. I feel my body is entirely free. I walk to the seashore. There are some little boats are swinging on the sea. The sea is truly blue. Pure blue like a dream. The water is like a magnet, attracting my body towards it. I agree with you, sea is beautiful.

"I feel sad about my life," you once said to me.

"Why?"

"Everything feels empty and endless."

"What you want then?"

"I want to find happiness."

"You can't have happiness at all times. Sometimes you will be sad. Don't you think?"

"But I don't see any happiness in my life."

"Then what's your most near happiness?"

". . . The sea."

That was our conversation one day, in our home in London. Now it is like a replay. It echoes above the waves.

Tavira

Tavira is situated in the southeast corner of portugal; it is considered to be one of the most picturesque town of the Algarve region.

A very slow and old train, clink, clink, clink . . . it is so slow that it's like I am sitting on a real time machine. I can feel the time moving in the space physically. It is much more interesting than watching clock.

The train moves along the south coast of Portugal. I didn't stay in Madrid or anywhere in Spain because I lost eighty euros when train stopped in Madrid. Maybe they are being stolen. I didn't feel like to stay in the big city anymore. It is always aggressive in the city. Here, the train patiently takes me to Tavira, a little town close to Atlantic Ocean, yellow sand everywhere.

Out of the station I find blocks of old residential houses, decayed in the hot sun. I walk to a corner cafe between two streets, white plastic tables and white chairs outside. I sit down, breathe out, get rid of the stale and take in the fresh. Suddenly I feel everything slow down and stop. In the shade of sun, two old local mans with very dark skin sit on the chair. They are smoking, quiet, in the morning. Two little tiny coffee cups are left empty in front of them. Everything is brewing very thick in the early morning here, like the sun, with passionate beams. They got a real sun here in their sky, not like in England. English sun is a fake sun, a literature sun.

【塔維拉】

位於葡萄牙東南角；公認乃葡國阿爾加維省最風光明媚的城鎮之一。

　　慢吞吞的老火車，可登，可登，可登……速度慢到有如坐上真正的時光機器，我可以感覺分分秒秒在空間具體的移動。這比看時鐘要有趣多了。

　　火車沿著葡萄牙南部海岸線跑。我沒有在馬德里或西班牙任何地方逗留，因為火車一停靠馬德里我八十歐元就不見了。或許是被人偷走的。我沒有興致再去造訪任何大城，那種地方老是全副武裝。這會兒，老火車不慌不忙載我奔赴塔維拉，鄰近大西洋的一個小城鎮，隨處可見黃色的沙灘景致。

　　一出車站，映入眼簾的老舊街區住宅，烈日下呈現斑駁姿色。走到街角一處咖啡館，外頭擺了幾張白色塑膠桌和白色椅子。我歇腿坐下，吐氣，將穢氣趕走，新鮮的吸進肺裡，頓時感覺天地萬物放慢，靜止不動。陽光遮蔭底下，兩位本地老先生膚色黧黑，坐在椅上。晨光當中，他們抽著菸，安安靜靜，兩只小小的咖啡杯空在面前。此地清晨所有的景物幾經熟成，風味醇厚，瞧那陽光，熱切迎人的鋒芒。人家天空裡的太陽可是貨真價實，哪像英國，英國的太陽是捏造的，出自文人手筆。

　　咖啡館另一頭是雜貨鋪，擺了好些蔬菜水果。店外站了個年輕的女士，看起來好像瘋了，我是說，真的瘋了。她不知對

The other side of the cafe is a grocery shop. Some vegetables and fruits are being sold. A young woman standing outside, she seems mad, I mean, real mad. She keeps talking to nobody, and there is no anybody there at all, not even a wild dog. She wears fleshly red lipsticks like she just drank a glass of blood. Sometimes a car passes by and she talks to the car. Strange, somehow there is always a mad woman in any little town in the world.

A young girl, looks like a backpacker, a tourist, wanders in the street. She wears a tight lemon-colour T-shirt. Her young lively breasts drag those old local man's eyes. As she disappears into the end of the street, two old mans withdraw back their eyes, and both exhale the smoke from their mouths. It must be a pleasure for them, in the morning street, seeing a young active breast under the lemon T-shirt.

The sunlight is like a knife cutting off the earth, half of the world is in the shadow, and the other half is bright. It is like a black and white movie, and everything is in slow motion. The sky is deadly blue, blue and blue. In alley ways, the old houses are silent, with rusty iron balcony and wooden window. They are sucking people's soul. I understand why some foreigners travelled to a strange town for a short stay, but one month passed by, and then three months passed by, still there, and eventually ended up to live there for the rest of their life. That strange power, forces a person settle down a foreign land, whatever how wild he was. I can feel that strange power. It is something opposite of adventure, something comes from the living habits, and acceptance of monotonous, the monotonous of everyday's life.

誰一直講話，但那兒根本沒站人，連隻野狗的影子也沒有。她塗著肉汪汪的紅色唇膏，好像剛剛喝下一杯血。偶爾汽車駛過，她便對人家的車子念念有詞。這可奇了，怎麼普天下的小鎮都少不了那麼一位瘋女士。

有個年輕女孩，看起來像背包客，天涯游子，街道上閒晃。她穿一件緊身檸檬黃T恤，青春朝氣的胸脯一路緊勾兩位本地老先生的眼珠。直到她的身影消逝於街道盡頭，他們才依依不捨收回視線，大口吐出菸霧。何等的賞心樂事，清晨街道上，看一對青春的咪咪於檸檬黃恤衫下蠕動。

鋒利的陽光切開地表，半個世界陷入陰影裡頭，半個世界明亮，恍如黑白影片，慢動作播放一切。天空藍到不行，藍之又藍。小巷弄裡的老房子不露聲色，鏽蝕的鑄鐵陽台和舊木窗，吞食人的魂魄。這下我懂了，外國人行至一處陌生小鎮，盤桓數日，一個月過去，三個月過去，人還不走，結果竟至終老於當地。奇特的力量，迫人在異國的土地落腳生根，管他原本如何浪蕩不羈。我能感受那股奇特的力量。它和冒險犯難相對立，扎根於生活的習癖，接納一成不變，日常生活的一成不變。

和老先生一起坐在街角的咖啡座，烈日下昏昏欲融。我的身軀解體，飄散虛空。那股奇特的力量將我全部的存在吞噬。我怕。

我在米娜民宿，一間便宜旅店的頂樓找到房間。房間雖小，收拾得還算乾淨。美麗的晴空照耀下，令人格外舒坦。我喜愛這種地中海風格的小旅店。陽台望出去，可以見到河流蜿蜒入海。暗黃的沙灘，色彩繽紛的屋宇。三兩位老人家坐在河

Sitting in this corner cafe with old mans, I am melted under the hot sun. My body is losing its shape, and floating in the air. My entirely existence is being sucked by a strange power. It scares me.

I find room on top floor of Residencia Mina. A budget hotel. The room is narrow but clean. With the beautiful sky light it feels light hearted. I love this small Mediterranean-style hotel. Standing on balcony I can see the river wriggle and connect to the sea. The sand is dark yellow, and the houses are colourful. Two or three old mans sit on the bridge above the river, smoking, chatting. The old streets, the green bushes, the sea birds . . . All these are exposed under the sun. I feel very close to the nature, the happy side of the nature.

I climb the steps up to roof of hotel. It is like a tropical garden, full of pot-planted palm trees and flowers. The sea not far away, shining in the distance. There are several ferries carry people to the outskirt part of beach. It is high noon, and the late summer sun is really hot. I take off my shirt, letting my body naked. It feel so good I take off the rest of my clothes. My soul is dancing. If happiness is a brief matter, then I am in this brief moment. I wonder whether the sadness inside a human sometimes is just because of lack of sunlight.

I think of you, while I am naked lying on the roof garden. We used to make love so often in your garden, by the fig tree. I remember all those details of when we were making love. I remember that you would take out my earrings before we make love. I remember that they were always entwined in my hair, very difficult to come out, but you would try hard to

邊橋上，或抽菸，或閒聊。老街弄，綠灌叢，海鳥飛起飛落……所有景物袒露於陽光底下。感覺和自然格外親近，自然喜樂的那一面。

我拾階爬上旅店天台，宛如來到熱帶園林，好多盆栽的棕櫚和花木。海很近，舉目可見閃亮的海面。幾艘渡船方便人們深入海濱遠端。時近正午，夏末的陽光依舊炙熱。我除去衣衫，讓身體赤裸，感覺無比暢快，我將剩下的衣物剝個精光，靈魂躍然起舞。如果幸福是短暫的，我便置身這短暫的時刻當中。不禁要懷疑，是否人的悲傷有時候僅僅只是因為缺少陽光。

光溜溜躺臥屋頂花園，我想到你，以前老是和你在庭院裡做愛，無花果樹旁邊。全部的做愛細節都在我腦海裡。記得做愛前你都會先幫我把耳環拿掉，每次老是被頭髮糾纏，難以取下，你得費一番手腳才能達成任務。這個情節想到你的時候永遠記得。

下意識想摸我的耳環，但東西不在那兒。我焦躁難耐。我的乳頭硬了起來。火辣的豔陽下，只想袒露自己，任人撫摸。我想起車站無聊等候時買的一本書：

樂為女人或如何
隨心所欲享受高潮

問題：「如何增進技巧？」

有兩種方法可以幫妳增進自慰技巧：

remove. That is you. That is one of the details I will always remember about you.

Unconsciously, I touch my earings, but they are not there now. I am getting restless. I feel my nipples getting hard. I want to be exposed and touched in the hot sunlight. I think of book I bought in the train station while I was bored waiting:

Women's Pleasure or How To Have An Orgasm As Often As You Want

Question: "How do I build up my skills?"

There are two ways in which you build up your masturbation skills:

1. By doing it more frequently.
2. By doing it in a variety of different situations. This creates the sexual versatility that is so important to your progress.

Below are fifteen different ways of masturbating that you can practise. These fifteen methods are divided into four lessons.

Lesson 1: Masturbation in private
Lesson 2: Masturbation in semi-public
Lesson 3: Masturbation in public
Lesson 4: Improving your timing

Masturbating, I never tried it before. Nobody Western would believe that I never try to masturbate as a twenty-four-year-old woman. Or maybe I did but I didn't know what I was doing. Sex in my understanding means something to do with a man,

1. 多加練習。

2. 多嘗試不同的情境。創造多變化的性事特別有助於妳的進步。

　　以下列出十五種自慰練習法。這十五種方法又可區分成四項課程。

課程一：於私密處自慰

課程二：於半隱密處自慰

課程三：於公共場所自慰

課程四：延長自慰時間

　　自慰，我未曾嘗試過。西方人打死不相信我這個二十四歲的女人還沒有自慰經驗。或許我試過，但不清楚自己在幹嘛。我的觀念裡，性是和男人做的，不是自己來的東西。自己搞就好像自言自語一樣：有點不對勁。那一次看過蘇活區的偷窺秀，壓根沒想到自己可以這樣玩。我還是相信沒有愛就沒有性，性是愛的表達。但如今這種想法不知怎地變了，我被體內的情慾折磨，強烈要求滿足的慾念。

　　「妳應該學習愛撫自己的陰蒂。」有次在床上你這麼對我說。我們裸著身體，剛剛做完愛。

　　你的手撫摸我的身體。「想達到高潮的話，可以自己摸這個地方。」

　　我記得這番話，但從未自己做過，有你在一起，我何必自己來？

　　米娜民宿的天台上，越過花花草草，陽光穿透我的肌膚。微風中枝葉款擺作響，我開始撫摸自己。

but not to do with myself. Having sex with oneself is like talking to oneself: bit mad. When I saw that Soho peepshop, I never thought to do with me. I also believed no love then no sex. Sex is an expression of love. But somehow this idea is changing. Now I feel tortured by the desire inside my body, and I feel strongly how much this desire wanting to be fulfilled.

"You should learn to play with your own clitoris." Once you told me this on the bed. We were naked, and we had just made love.

Your hand touched my body. "If you want to have an orgasm, you should touch yourself here."

I remember this conversation. But I never did it with myself, because I was always with you. Why do I have to?

On the roof of Residencia Mina, through the trees, the sun penetrates my skin. The leaves rustle in the mild wind. I start to touch myself.

The juice flows from my cave, and my fingers touch my hidden lips. Up and down. A great urge coming over me like a high tide flooding my body. The only thing I can see is the blue sky. The deep blue, like a boundless sea. The dry leaves under my skin are wet from my desire.

My body starts to shake. My breath gets difficult. My cave wants to devour something. I want to shout. It is almost painful, I feel like crying.

And I scream.

On my own. With myself. I did it. It is like dream.

For the first time in my entire life, I came by myself.

I can be on my own. I can. I can rely on myself, without depending on a man.

洞穴分泌汁液，我的指尖輕撫密唇，上上下下。迫切的衝動潮浪般沖刷，淹沒我的肉身。眼中唯一可見的只有藍天。碧藍遼闊，宛如汪洋無際。我肌膚底下的乾葉隨慾望而溼潤。

　　我的身體開始顫抖，呼吸急促。我的洞穴渴望吞沒某物。我想吶喊，似痛非痛，幾乎想哭。

　　我叫出聲來。

　　一個人。靠自己。我做了。好像在作夢。

　　這輩子就這麼頭一回，我自己出來了。

　　我可以自己來。我行。我可以靠自己一個，不用仰賴男人。

Faro

Faro is the capital of the Algarve region and the southernmost town in Portgal; tourism now dominates the economy.

The train from Faro to Lisbon will depart at 1:30 in the afternoon. It's twelve o'clock now. I learned Faro is a *resort* town. From the dictionary the resort place must be a very nice place, but in reality it is the opposite. Faro is very concrete. Almost ugly. What should I do in little *resort* to kill one and half an hour?

I walk around the train station with my rocksack on my back. The sea is just by the train station. But this sea smells bad. Between the sea and the inner land is an industry space, no beach. The rocks nearby the shore are dirty, polluted. It smells pee or something unpleasant. But some seagulls still convolute there. I feel sorry for those seagulls. I walk back to the street nearby the train station. People sitting outside of cafés looks at me. I can feel their curiosity to me. I bet there is few Chinese people come to this town. What is like looking this Chinese girl through their eyes? Without a companion with her, lost herself in the street, doesn't know what to do about her life . . . Or maybe they just think of Chinese food when they see me.

12:30, still have one hour left to go to Lisbon. I sit outside of a cafe, having a small cup of bitter espresso. How many cups of espresso the Portuguese have in one day? What is like

【法洛】

阿爾加維省首府，葡萄牙南境邊城；以觀光為經濟命脈。

　　法洛開往里斯本的火車預定下午一點三十分發車。現在才十二點。我知道法洛是觀光勝地。根據辭典的說法，觀光勝地應該風景宜人，實則恰好相反。法洛的人工水泥太多了，真醜。這種小觀光勝地能找到什麼樂子打發一個半鐘頭？

　　肩掛背包火車站周圍晃悠，旁邊就是海。但這裡的海氣味欠佳。介於海和內陸之間夾雜一片工業區，看不到沙灘。臨岸的岩塊髒兮兮，汙染嚴重，還傳來陣陣尿騷味，或什麼令人皺眉的東西。儘管如此，還是有海鷗在那兒盤旋，真苦了那幾隻海鷗。我走回車站附近的街道。坐在咖啡館外頭的人直盯著我，顯然相當好奇。我敢打賭這地方沒見過幾個中國人。他們眼中如何看待這個中國女孩子呢？沒有同伴，迷路了，活著不知道幹嘛……搞不好人家看到我只會想起中國食物。

　　十二點三十，離開此地前往里斯本還有一個鐘頭。找了家咖啡館外面坐著，小小一杯苦味難當的濃縮咖啡。葡萄牙人一天之內要喝下多少杯濃縮咖啡？那是什麼光景，滿肚子咖啡因加糖加尼古丁加可口可樂？那可會導致激情過度？生命可會永不疲倦？

　　濃縮杯見底。我拿出小本簡明辭典讀起《寂寞星球里斯本指南》。隔壁桌的先生正喝起他的第二杯濃縮咖啡。我知道他

if one's body full of caffeine and sugar and nicotine and Coca Cola? Will it bring too much passion? Will the life be more energetic?

The espresso cup is dried up. I start to read Lonely Planet on Lisbon with my small Concise dictionary. The man in the nearby table is drinking the second cup of espresso. I am aware his watching on me. He is lighting a cigarettes now. He looks at the street, and then the blue sky, and me again. Now he stands and comes to me, and he sits on the chair very near to me.

He says: "Can you understand it?"

"Understand what?"

I close my guide book and look at him. He seems a very physical person, maybe he does low jobs. But he can speak good English. He is short, dark, energetic, solid strong body, broad chest, impressive face, intensive brown eyes.

"Understand the language. Because you are checking the dictionary all the time."

Inside of his mouth, something strange. Some teeth missing there.

"Well, you know, I am a foreigner." I am a little embarrassed.

"Don't read the book. Look at the view. You should see it, not read the guide book." He surveys my books. There is Fernando Pessoa's *Book of Disquiet lies on top.*

"OK," I say. He is definitely from local. I wonder if he reads Fernando Pessoa. He looks like a person doesn't read any book at all.

"How many days you are going to stay in Faro?" he asks.

"Not anymore. I just came here for taking train to Lisbon, in

在打量我。他又點起香菸，看看街頭，望望藍天，眼睛又轉回我身上。然後他起身過來，一屁股坐上我身邊的椅子。

他說：「看得懂嗎？」

「什麼看得懂？」

我闔上指南，眼睛看著他。他壯壯的，或許做慣了粗活，不過英語講得很好。他個子不高，黝黑，精力旺盛，體格壯碩，胸膛厚實，很性格的臉，棕色眼珠異常分明。

「看得懂那語言，因為妳一直在查字典。」

他嘴裡有點異樣，缺了幾顆牙齒。

「噢，你曉得，我是外國人。」我有點窘。

「別悶頭看書，看看周遭的景觀。妳應該用眼睛感受，別管旅遊指南怎麼說。」他審視我的書本，最上頭是費爾南多·佩索亞的《惶然錄》。

「好啦，」我說。他鐵定是本地人。我懷疑他讀過費爾南多·佩索亞，他看起來什麼書都不屑一顧。

「妳打算在法洛待幾天？」他問。

「沒有。我只是來這裡搭火車到里斯本，還有一個小時就走。」

聽了這話，他沒做任何表示。人家沒必要跟我多攀關係，我猜。

「你知道法洛的舊城區在哪裡？你覺得一個小時夠我走到那地方再回來嗎？」我問。

「不會太遠。要的話我現在可以帶妳去。」

「你沒有其他事情要忙？」

「今天沒關係。跟我來就對了。」他站起來過去把帳付了。我連忙起身，將書本收進包包裡。

one hour."

By hearing this, he has no comments. There are no needs to develop more connection from his side, I guess.

"Do you know where is the old town of Faro? Do you think I can have time to walk there in one hour and come back?" I ask.

"Not very far. If you want I can take you to there."

"Don't you have anything to do?"

"Not today. Come with me." He stands up and goes to pay the bill. I stand up as well, put my books in my bag.

As I follow him, I look his back. A very physical manly back. A little short. A very earthy person. I wonder if he works in a local restaurant, or works on a wine factory, or maybe he is a sailor, a carpenter, a trolley driver. . . .

The old town of Faro is nothing very special, except for the old slipperly cobblestone ground. I like these cobblestones, they were being grind so smooth by thousands of millions people's foot through centuries. They got stories in them. Then we walk into an old square. This man wants to show me the church. But the old church is closed today, so does the museum. Do people not working here in the afternoon time? Only a small souvenir shop opened, selling some postcards about Faro in the nineteenth century. The middle-day sunlight is strong. We want buy ice cokes from that souvenir shop. He only pays his coke, I notice. Of course, it is fair for him.

We drink ice coke, wander on the empty cobblestone square.

"I'll take you to the seaside, then you can go back to the train station." He walks beside me.

"I already went there. It is not very beautiful." I want to be

一路跟隨，我觀察他的後背。非常壯碩的男性脊樑，有點五短身材，土味十足的男人。我猜想他可能在本地餐館幹活，或者是酒廠工人，也可能是船員，木匠，電車司機……

　　法洛的舊城區沒什麼看頭，除了地上滑順的老圓石鋪面。我喜歡這種圓石，幾個世紀下來，它們被數不清的腳步踩踏得如此光滑。它們飽經人間冷暖。我們來到一處老廣場，這男的想帶我去看教堂，可巧老教堂今天休息，博物館也沒開。難道這裡的百姓到了下午就不用工作？只有一間小禮品店營業，販售一些關於法洛十九世紀時期的明信片。中午的陽光強烈，我們想在禮品店買可樂喝。他只付了自己可樂的錢，我有注意。當然，這樣沒什麼不對。

　　我們喝著可樂，走過空蕩蕩的圓石廣場。

　　「我帶妳去海邊好了，到時候妳可以自己走回火車站去。」他和我並肩。

　　「那裡我去過了，風景不怎麼樣。」我不想講假話。

　　「不會，相信我好了。我會帶妳去很棒的地方。」

　　「好。」

　　他接過我沉重的背包，掛在肩上。

　　我們沿著鐵道旁邊的海岸走過去。前面遇上一窪溼地，泥濘渾濁，髒死了。那塊溼地映射正午的強光，看起來詭異，危險。他和我之間有種異樣的氣氛。他的人太過親切，太過隨興，日常生活看不出到底目標何在，不過同時顯得非常性感。我不清楚這種性感從何而來，或許來自他精壯的體貌。或許這種感覺純粹來自我自己，來自我的寂寞孤單。我的身體在期待，強烈的陽光底下有某些東西再也藏不住。

　　他牽起我的手，我完全沒有抗拒之意，連自己也不懂為什

honest.

"No, believe me. I'll take you to a nice place."

"OK."

He takes my heavy rocksack, and puts it on his back.

We walk along the seashore beside the railway. A marsh is just in front of us. It is muddy, and dirty. The marsh reflects the high noon's sunlight. It looks bizarre and dangerous. There is something very strange between him and me. He is almost too kind, too random, without any goal in his daily life. At the same time he is also very sexual. I don't know where this sexual feeling exactly from, maybe from his very physical looking. Or maybe this sexual feeling from myself, from my aloneness. My body is waiting for something, and something has to come out under the intensive sun.

He takes my hand, and I don't refuse at all. I don't know why. He holds my hand into his hand so tight that in one minute our palms are sweaty. I could feel there is something strong inside of his body. But I am not sure if I enjoy this intimacy. I am a bit confused. We walk side by side like two longterm friends. I know I don't love him at all, and maybe I even don't like him, but somehow I desire him. It is strange.

Maybe the more people live close to the south, the more they are talkative. They have to take out the extra energy inside of their bodies from the sun. Now he is doing a monologue:

"I don't like Faro, you know. It is not as nice as other places in Portugal. It is full of English people. Food is expensive, and everything is for tourists. But why I am here? Why I am sitting here doing nothing? Because I lost my four teeth, six years ago. Four! Can you see here? A motorbike accident. A big

麼。他把我的手牢牢握住，沒一分鐘我們掌心便溼了。我的體內有股強烈的感受，但不確定是否樂於和他如此親密。我七上八下。我們並肩而行有如兩位老友。我清楚自己對他毫無愛意，甚至連喜歡都談不上，然而就是有那種慾望。頂怪的。

或許人住得離南方越近，就越喜歡講話。他們必須發洩體內陽光孕育的多餘精力。此刻他正發表長篇獨白：

「我不喜歡法洛，這裡沒有葡萄牙其他地方好。到處一堆講英語的傢伙，吃的東西又貴，全靠觀光客做生意。那我怎麼還在這裡？一直窩著閒閒沒事可幹？因為我掉了四顆牙齒，六年前發生的事。四顆耶！這裡看到沒？一場摩托車意外，嚴重的意外。之前我有三台摩托車，你曉得。但現在沒有半台，那次以後全賣掉。我再也不敢碰摩托車，再騎的話我會死翹翹。六年來我一直在等醫療保險下來整修我的牙齒。六年了！妳相信有這種鳥事？王八蛋！這國家辦事比烏龜還慢！文件來文件去，最後終於搞定了。所以這次才會回來，準備把牙齒弄好。我之前在德國工作。看上面這裡，你看到沒？就這兩顆牙齒？他們要把上面這兩顆先拔掉，到時候我就有新的了，六顆新牙齒。」

帶著嶄新目光，我再度審視他的牙齒，真是印象深刻。人的嘴巴怎能任它一直空著?! 他的舌頭不會著涼嗎？

「你之前怎會跑到德國？」

「我到德國工作，在科隆。我當廚師，廚師妳知道吧？我煮東西給人家吃。科隆是個好地方，真的，那裡的人很友善。我在科隆賺不少錢。妳曉得，這地方的經濟狀況不怎麼樣，只有天氣不錯……」

我們的手一直牽著沒放，來到一棵棕櫚樹下。好幾個空可

accident. I had three motorbikes before, you know. But not anymore, since I sold them all. I am not going to touch motorbikes anymore. I would die if I ride motorbike again. I have been waiting for the medical insurance to fix my teeth for six years. Six years! Can you believe it? Bastards! Things are so slow in this country! Papers and papers. Finally it is arranged. That's why I came back here, to get my teeth done. I worked in Germany. Look up here, can you see here? These two teeth? They'll take out these two from the upper jaw, and I am going to have my new teeth, six new teeth."

I look at his teeth again, with my new eyes. It is really impressive. How a person left the mouth so empty?! Does his tongue feel cold?

"But why you were in Germany?" I ask.

"I worked in Germany, you know, in Cologne. I was a chef. You know what a chef is, don't you? I cooked for people. Cologne is a good place, yes, the people are friendly there. I earned good money in Cologne. You know, the economy is no good in this country, only the weather is good here . . ."

Our hands still hold together. We stop under a palm tree. Some empty coke tins, empty crisps bags spread around the tree. There are rocks by our feet, but covered by the dead small fish and dry weeds. So much polluted, it smells horrible. He leads me against the tree, and hugs me, and kisses my neck. Then kisses my ears. His lips are hot. And his tongue is strong, almost violent. I don't refuse him. Maybe I also want it. Then he touches my breasts. He presses his palm on my lower body. His breathing becomes strong and heavy. I hug him too. And I can feel his heart beating fast. The sun, the sweat, the salty

樂罐，脆薯片空袋四下亂扔。我們腳邊的岩塊布滿死掉的小魚和乾雜草。好多汙染，可怕的氣味。他讓我倚著樹，擁抱我，親吻我脖子，然後親耳朵。他雙唇火燙，舌頭使勁，近乎蠻橫。我沒有抗拒，或許自己同樣需要。接著他摸我胸部，手掌按壓我下身。他的呼吸變得又沉又重。我也抱住他，可以感覺他的心跳加速。陽光，汗水，鹹鹹的海風，汙濁空氣，樣樣刺激我們的慾望。

我說：「我覺得我想要你。」

這男的巴不得有這句。事情來得又快又自然。找了塊平坦的岩地，我解下牛仔褲，坐上燙人的石塊，胯下全裸。他跪下，埋首於我的大腿之間。溼答答，全部溼得一塌糊塗，我的胯下，他的舌頭，汗涔涔的皮膚，我的豹紋內褲。浪濤洶湧，浪濤將人從沙灘捲走。他手伸向自己的牛仔褲，隨即解開鈕釦。

「別插進去，拜託。」我不知如何表達，突然間對當下的行為感到恐懼：「不要，我不想那樣。幫我舔就好了。拜託，拜託，」我央求他。

當下明白我不想讓他進入我的身體。不要，那實在太噁心了。

但他已經無力克制。他從牛仔褲掏出老二，插進我體內，動作粗魯，近乎粗暴。

我抵住岩塊，混雜著性慾和噁心的感受。陽光令我的腦袋發疼。我無法呼吸。不知怎的，我憎惡他的行為。然後他來了，出來了像頭蠻牛。他拔出，精液滴落熱燙的石頭，整張臉火紅。

我再也不會相信這傢伙，我對自己說。他跟我之間不會再

wind, the stinking air, everything is stimulating our desires.

I say: "I think I want to have sex with you."

This man takes what I said. And everything comes rapidly and naturally. Finding a piece of flat rock, I unzip my jeans, and I sit on top of that piece of hot rock, with my naked crotch. He kneels down and he buries himself between my legs. It is so wet, everything is so wet, my crotch, his tongue, his sweaty skin, and my striped underwear. It is like the tide, a strong tide comes taking people away from the beach. His hands reach his jeans, and untie the button at the same time.

"But no plugging in. Please." I don't know how to say that. And I am suddenly scared by what we are doing: "No. I don't want that. Just using sucking me. Please, please," I beg him.

I just realise I don't want he enter into my body. No. It would disgust me so much.

But he couldn't control himself anymore. He takes out his penis from his jeans and pushes it into my body, rough, almost violent.

I am leaning on the rock. I feel sexy but I also feel disgusting at the same time. The sunlight makes me headache. I can't breathe. Somehow I despise him doing that. Then he comes. He comes like a bull. He pulls out, the sperm dripping on the burning rocks. His face is completely red.

I will never trust this man again I tell myself. Nothing will be between him and me anymore. Not anymore, I swear to myself. I feel a strong guilt, and danger. I despise myself.

We put on clothes, and the dirty feeling of my body is overwhelming. It sticks on my skin, my underwears, my jeans, and my white T-shirt. It is under my skin. And the sea seems even

有任何瓜葛。不會再有，我對自己發誓。我有強烈的罪惡感，危險感。我鄙夷自己。

我們將衣服穿上，我感到渾身污穢。我的皮膚，我的內褲，我的牛仔褲，我的白T恤全部發臭，皮膚底下也是。連海看起來也比之前更髒，更多污染。空塑膠瓶半截露出沙地，黑塑膠袋漂浮在白沫的海面。我只想趕緊離開這地方，離開他，越快越好。

火車快開了。車站咖啡吧裡，他站在我身後。我想買點水，想找個地方像是廁所可以清理自己。我受不了皮膚上的塵土，受不了來自他身體的怪味。他衣服的香水味好濃，我一秒鐘都沒辦法再忍耐。它讓我想吐。火車進入視線距離時，突然他說：

「發生一件事很糟糕。」

「什麼？」

「看這兒。」他轉過身來，讓我看他牛仔褲後面的口袋。口袋底下有個破洞。

「我剛才掉了五十歐元，」他說，憂心忡忡的語調。

我看著他，那張臉滿是空洞和茫然。我想了想他剛說的話。他本來好酷的，或者說半個鐘頭以前。這會兒變得如此脆弱不堪，轉眼之間。遇見他的時候，我以為他不過是個在咖啡館享用濃縮咖啡的普通本地人。我以為他單純快樂一如葡萄牙的天氣。而如今我不知道該做何感想了。

「這下我連坐公車回家的錢都沒了，」他說，手還插在破洞的褲袋裡。

火車到站，車門開啟。

dirtier and even more polluted than before. Empty plastic bottles half buried in the sand. Black plastic bags floating on the foaming sea water. I just want to leave this place, leave him, as quick as possible.

The train is ready to leave. He is standing behind me in the train station cafe. I want to buy some water, and I want to find a place like a toilet can wash myself. I can't stand the dirt on my skin, and I can't stand the strange smell from his body. His clothes smells of strong perfume. I can't stand it for one more second. It makes me vomit. But as the train approaches into the sight in the distance, he suddenly says:

"Something very bad happened."

"What?"

"Look here." He turns around and shows me the back pocket of his jeans. There is a hole underneath the pocket.

"I just lost fifty euros," he says, with a worried tone.

I look at him. His face is covered by emptiness and vagueness. I think of what he just said. He was quite cool before, or say half an hour ago. Now he becomes very weak, suddenly. When I met him, I thought he was just a normal local man having espresso in a cafe. I thought he was just as simple and happy as the weather in Portugal. But now I don't know what to feel anymore.

"Now I can't even buy a bus ticket to go back home," he says. His hand is still on his pocket with a hole.

The train arrives and the door is opened.

What should I say about that hole? What should I do about this strange fifty euros? No, don't start to think. Don't start to

關於那個破洞我該說點什麼？對這蹊蹺的五十歐元我該做何反應？不，想都不要去想。什麼也別開口。放下這道題目，別問，什麼都不要再說。我從他肩上接過我的背包，毫不遲疑走向月台。

「拜，」我說，擠出冰冷笑臉。

我跨上列車，沒有回頭。別回頭現在。車門在我身後闔上，感謝老天爺。結束了。

我直接走向車上的洗手間，卸下包包扔在廁所地上。我脫掉衣服，牛仔褲，內褲，轉開水龍頭，將自己全部徹底洗過。

talk about it. Just leave this topic. Don't ask, don't say anything more. I take my rocksack from his shoulders, and I walk to the platform without hesitation.

"Bye," I say, with a cold smile.

I step on the train. Don't look back. Don't look back now. The door is closed behind me, thanks God. And that's it.

I walk straight to the toilet on the train. I unload my bags on the floor of toilet. I remove my clothes, my jeans, my pants. And I turn on the tap. I wash myself completely.

Dublin

Dublin is the capital and largest city of the Republic of Ireland in the east-central part of the country on the Irish Sea.

Dublin, my last stop. I flew Dublin. I am not in Continent anymore.

This is the most western place I ever been in my life. I never been to States, and anway I don't know if States is more west than Europe since the earth is round. When I was in China, I thought Dublin is in the middle of Berlin, because that's how Chinese translated the word "Dublin". Also I thought London in the middle of the whole Europe, because Britain sounds so big: "the empire on which the sun will never set". So London must be in the centre Europe just like Chinese character for China, "中國", it means a country in the centre of the world.

I have some difficulties from the start—I am being stopped at the customs in the Dublin airport.

"Do you have a visa?" the immigration officer sitting in the glass box asks me seriously.

Is he blind or something? Can he not see those important stamps on my passport? I stare at him, with big confidence: "Of course I have visa."

"Where is it?" He throws my passport on the table.

I am a bit annoyed by this Westerner. I grab my passport back and open page where I got Schengen Visa stamp.

"Here it is!" I point the visa to the blind man. "Can't you see

【都柏林】

愛爾蘭首府，第一大城，位於東部中央位置，臨愛爾蘭海。

　　都柏林，我的最後一站。我坐飛機到都柏林，揮別歐陸。

　　這是畢生所至最靠西邊的地方。還沒去過美國，不過反正我也不清楚美國是否比歐洲更靠近西邊，因為地球是圓的。從前在中國，以為都柏林位於柏林的中央位置，因為「Dublin」這個字的中譯便有此意。同樣我以為倫敦位居整個歐洲的核心，因為不列顛聽起來如此氣派：「日不落帝國」。所以倫敦應該位於歐洲中央，就像「中國」這個字代表全世界最核心的國家。

　　一開始就有麻煩──我被都柏林機場的海關攔住。

　　「妳有簽證嗎？」坐在玻璃箱裡的移民官嚴肅地問我。

　　眼睛瞎了不成？我護照上那些重要的戳記他都看不見？我瞪著他，氣勢十足：「我當然有簽證。」

　　「在哪兒？」他將我的護照扔到桌面。

　　這西方佬有點惹惱我。我一把抓回護照翻到蓋有申根簽證那頁。

　　「這裡！」我指給這不長眼的傢伙看。「你沒看到這裡有申根簽證？」

　　「可是我們不屬於申根國家，」那先生語調十分冷靜。

　　我糊塗了：「可是人家說你們愛爾蘭通用歐元，就像法國

it is a Schengen visa?"

"But we are not in a Schengen country," says the man in very sober voice.

I am confused: "But I was told that your Irish use euros, just like in France, or Germany!"

"That doesn't mean we are a Schengen country. You need a visa to come into this country."

For one moment I really scared. Then I remember my UK visa. Quickly I find page where I have my student visa stamp from UK Embassy. I am so clever.

The man looks at the visa one second only and says, "We are not part of the British Empire either."

He throws my passport on the table again.

I stare at that officer and don't know what to do. Will they send me back to the UK? Or will they send me back to China, straight away? I don't have return ticket. If now they send me back, will I need to pay the air tickets? Or will they pay the fee?

I am standing in the corner of the Customs, all the passengers passed by, and new passengers from some other strange countries all left too. I am remained alone. After a while, I see the officer gives my passport to a new officer, then he leaves. This new officer is a very kind man, probably he is from less-west-country. He lets me fill a form, then he checks through the form. And then he lets me stand in front of the camera. Gosh, I never notice there is a camera underneath the glass box of the customs! I stand there and try to smile and being innocent. The nice man says OK, and he stamps on my passport.

"What is that stamp?" I am so worried that he stamps some-

一樣，或是德國！」

「那不代表我們屬於申根國家。妳需要簽證才能入境本國。」

這下我眞的慌了，然後想起我有英國簽證，趕緊翻到英國大使館幫我蓋上學生簽證那一頁。眞是太聰明了。

那先生只瞄了簽證一眼便說：「我們也不是大英帝國的成員。」

再一次將我的護照扔到桌面。

我瞪著那官員，不曉得如何是好。這下子他們會把我送回英國？還是直接送回去中國？我沒有回程的機票。如果他們現在遣送我，機票錢要我自己出嗎？還是費用由他們負責。

我呆立在海關的角落，全部旅客通關完畢，來自另一個陌生國家的旅客也都走得乾乾淨淨。就剩下我一個還在這兒。過了半晌，那個官員將我的護照交給另一個接班的官員，然後離開。這個新的官員人很客氣，或許來自比較不那麼西方的國家。他讓我填了一張表格，檢查過後，讓我站在一架相機前面。我沒料到海關玻璃箱底下還放了這麼一架相機！我站在那裡努力擠出笑臉，一副無辜模樣。這客氣的先生說可以了，在我護照蓋上戳記。

「那是什麼的蓋印？」我很擔心他蓋了什麼糟糕的戳記，未來會有麻煩。

「它表示下一次，如果妳沒有簽證跑到愛爾蘭來，就算違法了。」他把護照還我，上頭有個黑印准我短期入境，不准打工。

「妳瞭解嗎？」那官員問。

「是的，是的，謝謝你。」

thing terrible, terrible for my future.

"It means next time, if you come to Ireland without a visa, you will be illegal." He gives me back the passport with a black stamp allowing me short-period stay provided no working.

"Do you understand?" the officer asks.

"Yes. Yes. Thanks you."

I hold the passport like holding rest of my life.

Walking around Dublin I lost myself again. I am wandering in a park—St Stephen's Green. There is a lake in the park, and some swans live there. There are also some weird birds with green neck swimming on the water. The rain arrives, it is like rain curtain. It rains intensely. Nobody, no any plants, no any single leafs, can avoid the madness of the rain. I run out of the park. By the park, there is a hotel called The Shelbourne Hotel. I walk in.

The hotel is marvellous. Somebody plays piano in the lobby. There is a fireplace, or no, two in the ground lobby. The fire is burning. I stare at the fire. I love watching fire, better than TV —the way it changes the shape all the time. The burning things inside are not like coal, or charcoal, or wood. It is a kind of black, long square piece of bar. I never see that before. I sit down on the old-soft-posh-arm-chaired sofa and feel the fire sucks my wetness from the rain.

"Excuse me, do you know what is this stuff burning in the fire?" I ask an old gentleman on next sofa. He is in black bowler hat and dark coat, with his tall black umbrella. He is like from Sherlock Holmes story, an old detective.

我手捧護照，有如捧著往後的餘生。

　　都柏林走著走著，我又迷路了。逛到一處公園——聖史蒂芬綠園。公園裡有座湖，住了幾隻天鵝，還有一些綠脖子的怪鳥湖面優游。雨開始下，有如水幕，又密又急。沒有人，沒有植物，沒有任何一片葉子有辦法躲過雨水的潑辣。我跑出公園，旁邊有家旅館叫薛爾邦飯店，我走了進去。

　　這家飯店真不可思議。大廳有人演奏鋼琴，還有一座壁爐，哦不，有兩座在一樓大廳。爐火燒得正旺。我盯著火焰。我喜歡看火燃燒，比電視好看——火的形狀沒有一刻固定。裡頭燒得似乎不像煤炭，也不是木炭或木材。那東西黑黑的，長條狀，以前沒有看過。找了張舒適氣派的老扶手沙發坐下，感覺火光將我身上的溼雨吸走。

　　「不好意思，請問您知道火裡面燒的東西是什麼嗎？」我請教隔壁沙發的年長紳士。他頭戴圓頂黑禮帽，深色大衣，長長一把黑傘，有如福爾摩斯故事的人物，一位老偵探。

　　「抱歉？」老先生說。

　　「你曉得這東西，用來燒的東西，你們都怎麼叫的？」我指向壁爐。

　　「喔，那是煤磚，親愛的，」老先生得意回答。

　　「煤磚？聽起來怎麼像是法國麵包？」

　　「我們還叫它泥炭塊，親愛的，」老先生加上一句，「或是泥炭。」

　　老先生望著我大惑不解的神情。他站起來表演，讓我容易明白：「從前我們愛爾蘭人拿鐵鍬挖出泥炭，再把它弄乾。」他做出又挖又劈的姿勢。

"I beg your pardon?" the old man says.

"You know this stuff, the stuff is burning, what do you call that?" I point to the fireplace.

"Ah, those are *briquettes*, my dear," the old man answers proudly.

"Briquettes?" Why it sounds like a French bread?

"We also call it peat, my dear," the old man adds, "or turf."

The old man look at my deeply confused face. He gets up to perform for me, to help me to understand: "In the old times we in Ireland used spades to cut the turf. Then we'd dry it." He is doing the gesture of digging and chopping.

The old man has very strong accent, and my English listening comprehension becomes hopeless.

"Turf" Or "Tofu"? I don't understand this word. Gosh, why they don't simply call it "black burning stuffs"?

A young handsome waiter comes with a menu.

"Would you like to order something?" the waiter asks politely.

"Yes, sure." Of course, I have to pretend somebody posh from Japan or Singapore. I shall leave here as soon as my clothes are dried up.

The waiter gives me a big book of menu.

The old man pays the bill. He takes his tall-huge-old umbrella and salute with his black bowler hat to me: "Good bye, young lady."

Five days in Ireland, I am lying on bed inside of youth hostel just reading *Intimacy*. Sometimes I look up in the dictionary, but the more I read, the less I care the new words like

老先生的口音很重，我的英語聽力沒得指望。

「特福」（turf）還是「豆腐」（tofu）？我搞不清楚這個字。怎不直接叫「黑色燒火的東西」就好？

一位年輕帥氣的服務生拿了菜單過來。

「請問您想點東西嗎？」服務生禮貌地問。

「對，好。」當然，我得裝成來自日本或新加坡的上流人士。等衣服乾了趕緊閃人。

服務生遞給我菜單好大一本。

老先生把帳付了，拿起他誇張的舊雨傘，用圓頂黑禮帽對我致了個意：「再會了，小姐。」

愛爾蘭五天的時間，我全耗在青年旅社被窩讀那本《親密關係》。偶爾翻個辭典，不過一路讀下來，我越來越不在乎那些生字，比如柴契爾夫人迷，以及特普西柯拉（舞蹈繆思）。我不在乎它們的意義。反正不靠辭典我也能夠完全理解整個故事。書裡面，男主角想從妻子那兒得到的便是親密感，可是太太沒辦法給，所以他離開尋求新的愛人，尋求新的，熱情的人生。難道你不曉得我要的也是能夠和你親親蜜蜜。

在都柏林，那天早上把書的最後一頁讀完，我決定儘快回到倫敦。我已厭倦到處跑來跑去，我渴望見到你。

青年旅社裡三兩下收好行李，我走出這擠滿聒噪大學生和嬉皮的地方。或許這些人不需要親密關係，大概現有的已經夠了，還是當他們耳戴 i-pod，夜店整晚狂舞不休時，親密關係又能算什麼。

Thatcherites and *Terpsichorean*. I don't care what they mean. I understand the whole story completely anyway without dictionary. In that book, what the man wants from his wife is the intimacy, but his wife doesn't give it to him. So he leaves for a new lover, for a new, passionate life. Don't you know that all I want is be intimate with you?

In Dublin, that morning I finish reading the last page of the book, I decide go back London as quickly as possible. I am tired of travel. I am longing to see you.

I quickly pack my bag in the youth hostel and I walk out of this place where full of loud university students and hippies. Perhaps these people don't need intimacy, or they have got it enough, or it worth nothing to them while they listen i-pod and dance in the clubs all night long.

October

self

n. **1.** distinct individuality or identity of a person or thing; **2.** one's basic nature; **3.** one's own welfare or interests.

The plane touches down at London Stansted airport. It is afternoon. Outside is raining, dim as usual. I am standing by the luggage belt, waiting for my rocksack. Has it gone to Los Angeles or Delhi or something? Everybody took their luggages but mine doesn't come. Almost an hour later, last person took his suitcase from the belt.

I go to the "Lost Luggage" counter to report. A man apologises to me and says he will find out and contact me. Luckily, I have my passport with me.

You are not waiting meet me so I take train to home. I have nothing to bring back from my travel. I lost my *Dubliners*, lost my Fernando Pessoa, lost *Intimacy*. I also lost all the maps you gave to me. And I lost my toothbrush, lost my clothes and lost my address book. I only have the stories that happened in an East Berlin flat, in Amsterdam under the wisteria tree, on the Lido in Venice, in Faro . . . They stay in my heart and my skin.

London evening: everything comes back to me quickly. The slow and noisy tube, the oily fish and chip shop, the dim and crowded pubs, the raining streets with people waiting for their never-coming bus. London is such a desolate place.

The house is empty. But everywhere smells of you. And there is much mess. All your tools are on the floor. And your

199

【自我】

〈名詞〉**1.** 人或物的顯著個性或特質；**2.** 個人基本特質；**3.** 個人利益得失。

　　飛機降落倫敦史丹斯德機場。時間是下午，外頭下著雨，陰暗如常。站在行李輸送帶前等候我的背包，它跑去洛杉磯或新德里哪兒不成？每個人陸續領走行李，只剩我的還沒出現。約莫一個小時之後，最後一位仁兄從輸送帶領走他的皮箱。

　　我走到「行李遺失」櫃檯去報告。一位先生向我致歉，說他找到以後會跟我聯絡。幸運的是，護照在我身上。

　　你沒來接機，我得自己搭車回家。這趟出門兩手空空回來，我的《都柏林人》丟了，我的費爾南多·佩索亞丟了，《親密關係》丟了，你給的地圖也丟了，還有我的牙刷，衣服，聯絡簿全部丟光。我只剩那些故事，發生在東柏林一間公寓的故事，還有阿姆斯特丹紫藤底下，威尼斯麗都，法洛……它們留在我的心和皮膚裡面。

　　倫敦的夜晚：所有東西一轉眼都回來了。慢吞吞的嘈雜地鐵，油膩的炸魚薯條小攤，昏暗熙攘的酒吧，落雨街頭始終等不到公車的民眾。倫敦真是悽涼。

　　家裡空的，不過處處有你的氣味，亂到極點。你的工具全扔在地上，一袋袋黏土和石膏堆在客廳，廚房桌上整排骯髒的茶杯，還有個澡盆雕塑，塑膠做的，躺在地板中央，彷彿有意捉弄我。唯獨院子裡的植物自管自活著。沒有花的果樹挺立在

bags of clay and plaster are piled up in the living room. In the kitchen I find a line of dirty tea cups on the table and there is a sculputure of a bath, made from plastic, lying in the middle of the floor. It is making joke of me. Only the plants are living quietly in the garden. The fruit tree without flower stands there, still holding the peace of the garden. There are yellow leafs everywhere covering your sculptures. I pick up one fig. It is almost rotten and the juice immediately comes out. I taste it, very sweet. The seeds are sandy in my mouth. In these five weeks I am absent, nature changed so much. Every plant has a different shape. And you? In these five weeks, has anything changed on you?

I turn on the radio. Weather report, as important as yesterday and tomorrow. A man talks with a very low tone like he just knew England lost football match:

"The rest of today will be overcast, with rain predicted for much of the weekend. There's a small chance of occasional sunshine so let's keep our fingers crossed. . . ."

Yes. Let's keep our fingers crossed.

I wash all the tea cups, and all the dirty plates. I sweepthe floor, and I let your sculptures lean against the wall. I put all your socks and smelly shirts into the washing machine. I tidy your table. Then I sit and I wait.

When the last beam of light in the sky has disappeared, you come back home with a bunch of your friends. You hug me, say hello to me, just like you would hug and hello another friend. Then everybody sits down, smoking cigarettes, having tea, talking English jokes, and laughing loudly. I never could understand jokes. And I know you hate smokers, but now you

那兒，依舊守護庭院的寧靜。你的雕塑落滿黃葉。我撿起一枚無花果，快爛了，汁液說流便流，試了一口，好甜，感覺嘴裡細籽沙沙的。幾個禮拜不在，自然變化如此之大，植物樣樣改了面貌。那你呢？這五個禮拜你可有任何改變？

收音機轉開，氣象報告，重要性一如昨天或明天。播報的先生語調低沉，有如方才得悉英格蘭輸掉足球賽事：

「今日天氣多雲，整個週末應該都是雨天，仍有一絲機會偶見陽光，讓我們祈求好運……」

沒錯，讓我們祈求好運。

我將所有茶杯洗了，還有全部的髒盤子；地板掃過，你的雕塑挪靠牆邊；襪子和難聞的襯衣扔進洗衣機，桌面收一收，然後坐下開始等待。

等到天空最後一抹微光消逝，你終於返家，還帶回一票朋友。你抱我一抱，說聲哈囉，就像你也會抱其他朋友說哈囉的樣子。然後人人找位子坐下，開始吞雲吐霧，喝茶，講英國笑料，高聲亂笑一通。那種笑話我從來不懂，而且你本來討厭人家抽菸，這下他們家裡到處愛怎麼抽就怎麼抽。友誼，好高尚的字眼。

我努力融入談話，卻處處碰壁。

你的朋友討論起變性手術，將人從男性變成女性。有個女生濃妝豔抹，大波浪金髮。不過有點不對勁，怎麼看她都像個男的。或許人家曾經當過男人，我怎麼曉得。

她是箇中專家：

「他確定要做？跟你講好了，達令，如果真有下定決心，那應該到美國去做比較好。我可以把全部資料給他，包括費用的明細。」

let your friends smoke everywhere in the house. *Friendship*. A respectful term.

I try to join in the conversation, but it is frustrating.

Your friends are talking about transsexual surgery, turning a person from male to female. One woman has very heavy make-up and long blonde curly hair. But there's something strange about her, she somehow looks very manly. Probably she was a man before. Gosh, how do I know.

She is an expert:

"Is he sure about it? I tell you, darling, if he really wants to do it, then he should get it done in the States. I can give him all the contacts, and a breakdown of the costs."

"So, how much does it work out at?" one of your friends is eager to know.

"Well, Dr Brownstein's fee is about $7,750, and the Surgical Facility fee is around $3,000 . . . but then there's a whole list of other shit—the Anaesthesia costs $700 . . ."

"Bloody hell!" the eager one says.

"So, tell us a bit more about the surgery," another asks.

"Well, it's a pretty complicated process. The doctor has to create a vagina, and work out the maximal clitoral and vaginal sensation, but minimising scars . . ."

I am chopping some carrots and try to follow the conversation. The carrots are so hard.

I listen, and listen, and listen carefully, I even stop chopping carrots. But in the end I am lost. I am an outsider. And nobody can deny this. I am just somebody's peasant wife. I feel lonely. I just want to talk to you, without the others here. I feel like all the expectation I collected on the journey is going to nowhere.

「到底全部要多少錢？」你一位朋友很想知道。

「唔，布朗斯登醫生的費用大概是美金七千七百五，手術材料費三千左右……可是還要加上其他一些有的沒的——麻醉就要七百……」

「我的媽呀！」好奇的傢伙說。

「那手術本身要怎麼進行？」有人提問。

「哼，過程可複雜了。醫生得整出一條陰道，盡可能讓陰蒂和陰道像真的一樣有感覺，可是疤痕要小到……」

我邊切胡蘿蔔邊努力跟上對話，偏偏胡蘿蔔又好硬。

我聽了又聽，努力豎起耳尖，甚至胡蘿蔔也放下不管了。可是到後來我還是懵懵懂懂。我是個局外人，不承認還不行，我只是某某人的鄉下老婆。好寂寞，我只想和你講講話，不要有別人在場。感覺好像旅途一路積累的期待消失無蹤，只剩氣苦，我懷疑自己這五個禮拜不在家對你可有任何差別。

他們繼續熱烈討論變性話題，我偷空告訴你我丟了背包，而且你的地圖也全部弄丟。你說沒關係，那些地圖已經不需要了。

有個朋友聽到我剛從歐洲回來。

「那妳有去都柏林？」

「有。」

「如何？」

「還不錯。」

另外有人問：

「巴黎怎麼樣？」

「巴黎不錯，」我回答。

第三個問：

I am getting bitter. I doubt if my absence of five weeks in this house affect you at all.

While they carry on their intense conversation about transsexual, I tell you that I lost my rocksack. And I lost all your maps. You say never mind, you don't need those maps anymore.

One of your friends heard I just came back from Europe.

"So you went to Dublin?"

"Yes."

"How was it?"

"It was good."

Another person says:

"How was Paris?"

"Paris was good," I answer.

The third person asks:

"Did you like Venice?"

"Yes, I did."

"That's good," she replies.

Is that how English people speak? If so, then I must be a bit English now.

Eventually all your friends leave. Only the trails of smoke drift around the ceiling, and empty glasses stay on the table. Here we are, face to face, only two of us.

You put the kettle on, and sit down towards me.

"So, how are you my darling? Do you want a cup of tea?"

"No."

"Are you sure?"

"Yes. If you want some then you have some. I don't want any."

「妳喜歡威尼斯嗎？」

「喜歡啊。」

「那很好。」她答。

英國人講話的方式就這樣？如果是的話，那我現在鐵定有英國人的樣子了。

最後你的朋友終於走了，只剩煙霧尾巴飄在天花板打轉，以及桌上一堆空杯。好了，臉對臉，只有我們兩個。

你擺上茶壺，坐下來向著我。

「噢，還好嗎，我的達令？來杯茶好不好？」

「不好。」

「妳確定？」

「對，想喝的話你自己喝，我不要就對了。」

「好罷。」你看著我，觀察我臉上的情緒。

「你愛那麼多人，可是我只愛你一個。」我出聲，非常痛苦。我想直接把主題推上火線。

「這下又怎麼了？妳認為我不愛妳？」

「我感受不到以前和你的那種親密。」

「怎麼會這樣？」

「我不知道。感覺好像你現在沒有真正需要我，而且你從來就沒有真正需要我過。真不曉得我回來這裡要幹嘛。」

「怎麼這樣說？哪有什麼東西改變，我還是跟以前一樣。」

「可是你感覺好冷淡。我們這麼久沒做愛，你進門的時候連親都不親我一下。我這麼想你，每天一有空就寫伊媚兒給你，可是數數看過去這整個月你一共寫給我幾封伊媚兒？才五封！你明明曉得我今天晚上回來，還把一堆朋友帶來家裡。難道你都不想和你的愛人私下獨處？你的朋友是不是比愛人重

"OK." You look at me, and observe the mood on my face.

"You love lots of people, but I only love you." I speak, painfully. I just want to push the subject right to the front line.

"What's the problem now? Don't you think I love you?"

"I don't feel that intimacy with you like before."

"Why not?"

"I don't know. It feels like you don't really need me, and you never really needed me. I don't know why I came back here."

"What do you mean? Nothing has changed. I'm the same person as before."

"But I feel you are cold. We haven't made love for such a long time but you didn't even kiss me when you walked through the door. I missed you so much, I wrote you emails everyday as possible as I can, but how many emails did you write to me in the last whole month? Only five! You knew I would be back tonight but you still brought your friends. Didn't you want to be with your lover *privately*? Are your friends more important than your lover?"

I am so angry. I can see my anger everywhere in the house.

"Of course I love you. But that doesn't mean I have to abandon my friends. I think you are being a bit selfish," you say.

"Thank you! Yes, I am a very *selfish* person. I am so selfish that I want to have a quiet night with my lover after five weeks travel!"

I try hold my anger back. I don't know what I can say. I know you didn't have sex with anybody when I was away, and I am the one did all these messy things. How can I blame you? But at the same time I feel so disappointed about you.

要？」

我怒火中燒，怒焰波及整間屋子上下。

「我愛的當然是妳，但不能因為這樣叫我不顧朋友。我覺得妳這樣有點自私，」你說。

「謝啦！沒錯，我這個人非常自私。我自私到旅行五個禮拜回來只想和我的愛人安安靜靜共度一晚！」

我試圖控制怒火，不曉得話怎麼說比較好。我知道這段期間你沒和別人怎麼樣，搞出亂七八糟事情的人是我，怎有資格怪東怪西？不過我就是對你感到失望。

「我覺得你已經不把我當一回事了，」我吼道。

我走進浴室，打開熱水，脫掉衣服，將全身的塵埃洗淨。

那一晚我們挨著身體躺下的時候，我感覺被剝離。我們再也不是一體。這是第一次浮現這種感受。有個巨大執迷的「自我」從我的身體脫離，冷眼看著你的身體，即使當我們做愛，當你的身體深深進入我的身體……

我們中國人不鼓勵使用「自我」這個詞。工作單位的老同志會說，你們怎麼可以光想到「自己」卻不顧慮其他人和社會整體？

「自我」站在「團體」和「集體主義」的對立面。「自我」乃共產黨之大敵。中學裡人家教我們「最可敬者」應該忘掉他自己，不該滿足自己的私慾。

我記得中學時，全班每個禮拜五下午都會到養老院。那個地方很大，收容無依的老人，不過棄嬰也有收養。那些嬰兒都是女的，從垃圾堆或街頭撿來的女嬰。記得有個房間睡滿了小嬰兒。我們從家裡帶來肥皂臉盆，幫忙洗尿布和衣物。記得有

"I don't think I am a special one to you at all," I shout.

I walk into the bathroom. I turn on the bath. I take off my clothes. And I clean myself away from all those dusts.

The night when our bodies lie down side by side, I feel I am detached. We are not one body anymore. This is the first time I feel this. There is a big obsessed "self" separating itself from my body and looking at your body. Even when we make love, even when your body is deeply in my body . . .

We Chinese are not encouraged to use the word "self" so often. The old comrades in the work unit would say, how can you think of "self" most of the time but not about others and the whole society?

The "self" is against "group" and "collectivism". The "self" is the enemy of the Communist party. In middle school we were taught "the most admirable person" should forget about himself, shouldn't satisfy his own needs.

I remember in my middle school whole class went to the Old People's House every Friday afternoon. It was a big place for old lonely people to stay, but also abandoned babies were being raised there. The babies were always girls, girls who had been found in the rubbish bin or in the street. I remember there were lots of tiny babies sleeping in one room. We brought our soaps and basins from home, to wash the nappies and clothes. I remember several baby girls have strange white spotted skin and white hair. We were frightened to see that. We were told these babies had a special skin disease. We were scared to touch them in case our body turned to white too. And I remember two babies with strange shapes of the body. Their fingers

幾個女嬰長著奇怪白點的皮膚和白髮絲。我們害怕不敢多瞧。據說她們得了特殊的皮膚怪病，我們好怕碰到的話身體也會變成白色。還記得有兩個小嬰兒身體畸形，她們手指連在一塊，一邊的腳糾結如藤蔓。我怕得要命。不過這讓我們體會到其他人類的不幸和苦難；讓我們明白和這些無望的人相比自己是何等幸運。

然而此地，這雨下不停的老牌資本主義國度，「自我」代表一切，「自我」乃萬事萬物的創造來源。舉凡藝術，商業交易，時尚，社會體系，無不根植於此一「自我」。世界和「自我」的聯結如此強大。「自我」威力無窮，誰曰不宜。

were bound together, one of the legs twisted like vines. I was horrified. But it taught us to understand other mankind's miseries and sufferings; to understand how lucky we are compare with these hopeless people.

But here, in this rainy old capitalism country, "self" means everything, "self" is the original creativity for everything. Art, business, fashion, society system, all deeply depend on this "self". The connection between the world and "self" is so strong. "Self" works incredibly well.

abortion

n. **1.** operation to end a pregnancy; **2.** *Informal* something grotesque.

My period still didn't come. I wait one week. Then two. Not a single drop of blood. In a vague afternoon, I decide to go to the pharmacy buy a pregnancy test box. I come back home and you are not here. I shall find out on my own. The blue symbol shows a cross: positive.

Holding the pregnant test sample in my hand, I don't know if this baby is from you. I really don't know. I look at that cross again and my body feels so dirty. I want to wash myself.

I wait the whole day for you to come back home. When you come back in the evening, I tell you. I say I need to go to hospital and have an abortion. As quick as possible. Surprisingly, you don't say anything. You don't even ask when it happened, and you don't even ask if it is from you. You just look at me with sad face and I start to cry. You put your arms around me and hold me tight.

Five days later you drive me to a clinic in Richmond, with your broken white van. We stop in a petrol station. Is it very far away? I ask. Not very far, you answer, we will get there soon. Your van is old but it is never really totally broken down. Highway. So many cars. So many traffic lights. I feel dizzy. Everything goes fuzzy. I don't know what you are thinking about this baby might be yours. All I know is you hold my

【墮胎】

〈名詞〉**1.** 流產手術；**2.** 畸形。

　　我的月經還是沒來。等了一個禮拜，兩個禮拜，半滴血也沒有。一個雨霧濛濛的下午，我決定去藥局買驗孕棒。回來時你人不在，正好可以自己弄個明白。藍色標記顯示叉叉：中獎了。

　　手裡捏著驗孕棒，不曉得這孩子是否由你而來。我真的不知道。又看了一次叉叉，身體覺得好髒，我得清洗自己。

　　一整天等你回家。等到晚上你回來，我把事情說了。我說我必須上醫院把小孩拿掉，越快越好。驚訝的是，你不置一詞，甚至沒問何時發生的，也沒問那是不是你的小孩。你只是難受地看著我，我哭了起來。你手圍住緊緊摟著我。

　　五天後，你開著破爛的白色小貨車載我去瑞奇蒙一間診所。我們在加油站停車。地方很遠嗎？我問。不會很遠，你答，很快就到了。你的貨車雖老，倒還沒真的掛掉過。公路上，車水馬龍，紅綠燈一個接一個。我感到頭暈，景象模糊難辨。不曉得你心裡究竟怎麼想的，這孩子有可能是你的啊。一路你只是將我的手緊握，只有換檔時才鬆開。我感覺你是我唯一的依靠，你是我的救星。

　　醒來時我人躺在推床，沒感覺任何異狀。護士送來柳橙和

hand very tight, only let go change gear. I feel you are only stable thing to me. You are my life.

I wake up on a wheel bed, without feeling anything unusual.
I eat the orange and biscuits the nurse gives to me. I put on my coat and find my shoes back. No more fear anymore, only the sorrow of emptiness. I walk slowly back to the resting room. I see you. You stand up from piles of newspaper, walk towards me.

餅乾讓我填肚子。我把外套穿上，找回鞋子。恐懼已經過去，只剩空洞的悔恨。緩步走回休息室，你在那兒。你從報紙堆裡起身，向我迎來。

nostalgia

n. sentimental longing for the past.

"You need nourishment," you say to me.

So you buy lots of food for me from Tescos. The baby is gone so I shall eat a lot to fill the emptiness. Salad, shrimp, fried chickens . . . Everything on the back of the package is "*Produced for Tesco Stores Ltd*". In my hometown, when a woman has abortion, her mother cooks eel ginger soup, or a soup made from dates and lotus seeds. But not here. Here, Tesco packages look after you.

You are cooking some obscure pie for me. It is called q-u-i-c-h-e. I have never seen it before. On the bag it says:

Even Real Men Eat Quiche!

Quiche, q-u-i-c-h-e. I can't believe it when I am swallowing this piece of shapeless hot stuff. Such an ambiguous piece of food. Totally formless. I wonder about what my parents would say if one day they come to this country, and they eat this. My mother probably will say: "It is like eating something from other people's mouth." And my father will say: "It must be left from earlier meal so they recook it but inside are already messed up."

I will agree with my father: it is a piece of big mess indeed.

【懷舊】

〈名詞〉懷舊之情。

「妳需要補充營養，」你對我這樣說。

你跑去特易購幫我買了一堆食品。小孩離開了我，我得多吃東西把空位填滿。沙拉，蝦，炸雞……每樣東西包裝背面都印有「特易購公司出品」。在我老家，女人流産的時候，她母親會燉薑片鱔魚湯，或是紅棗蓮子湯。不過這裡不來這一套。這地方，自有特易購的包裝食品照料妳。

你忙著幫我料理怪裡怪氣的餡餅，它叫法—式—鹹—派。我長眼睛還沒見過這種東西。袋子上寫說：

男子漢也愛法式鹹派！

法式鹹派，法—式—鹹—派。不敢相信嘴裡吞下這片不成形狀的熱玩意，什麼鬼醬糊的食物嘛，完全嚼不出什麼東西。哪天讓我爸媽來到這國家，吃到這種東西，看他們會講出什麼好話。我母親大概會說：「好像別人嘴裡塞過的東西再拿來吃」。我父親則會說：「這應該是上一頓吃剩的再拿來煮過，裡面早爛了」。

我傾向同意父親說的：一整片裡面都是爛糊。你告訴我實際上這是法國食品。我才不相信，英國人準是羞於承認自己搞

You tell me it is actually from France. I don't believe you. I think the English are too ashamed to acknowledge it is their food. So they say it is French to defend themself.

But, in the evening, you cook a fish for me. Not cod, not seabass, not any typical English fish. It is a silver carp. It is like my hometown's fish. It smells of the river nearby our house. I remember I studied a word before, and I remember how to pronounce this word. No-stal-gia. Eating carp causes my *nostalgia*.

出這種玩意，於是宣稱它是法國食品好為自己辯解。

　　不過，到了晚上，你燒魚給我吃。不是鱈魚，不是海鱸，不是任何常見的英國魚類。是鰱魚，和老家的魚好像，聞起來有我們家附近那條河的味道。教人想起以前學過的一個字，我還記得如何發音：「哠—是它了—寂」。嘴裡的鰱魚勾起我無限懷舊之情。

age

n. **1.** the length of time a person or thing has existed; **2.** the time of life; **3.** the latter part of human life; **4.** a period of history; **5.** a long time.

Today when you unload some box from your van, you become extremely tired. You become really old. We used to look like five years difference in other people's eye, but now obvious twenty years gap between us. This makes me feel a little sad about you. You look at me, a small smile. There is a shadow underneath your eyes. Maybe it is me made you old. I not go out earn live. And I always demand love from you. I demand love by showing my vulnerability, again and again. I remember at the beginning of us, you have a perfect hair. But now, there is a bit grey hidden behind your ears. And your wrinkles, they are at the corner of your eyes. Sometimes I wonder if you saw these wrinkles, if you saw your grey hair hidden behind your ears.

You used to believe in totally individual life, no family, no marriage. You used to think that a personality could never be change. But recently you said, "People do change, they always change." Look at now. You are forced by my vulnerable to show a solid love to me, to show a practical love to me. Since abortion you try hard to keep a family with me, by doing the practical things. You are tired, physically, and maybe spiritually as well.

Is this the love I want from you? Maybe I always want you

【年紀】

〈名詞〉**1.** 人或物的存活年限；**2.** 人生某一時期；**3.** 老年；**4.** 歷史年代；**5.** 長久時間。

　　今天你從貨車卸了好幾箱貨，人累到不行。你眞的老了。之前別人看我們好像只差五歲，此刻二十歲的差距明顯擺在眼前。我覺得對你有些難過。你看看我，一抹微笑，眼窩下掩不住陰影。可能就是我害你變老的。我沒出去外面幫忙賺錢，又不停向你索愛。我利用自己的脆弱向你索愛，一次又一次。記得我倆初認識的時候，你有一頭豐美的頭髮。而如今，你耳後藏了幾許飛白，眼角的皺紋日益明顯。有時想說不知你是否看見這些皺紋，是否看見耳後躲藏的灰髮。

　　以前你相信個人全然獨立的生活，不要家庭，不要婚姻。以前你認爲人的個性可以堅守不變。但近來你說：「人會改變，怎麼樣都會改變。」看看現在，你被迫屈服於我的脆弱，對我展現愛的牢固，展現愛的實際。墮胎之後你努力和我維持家庭，擔負實際的工作。你疲累不堪，肉體如此，或許心靈亦復如此。

　　我所寄望於你的便是這樣的愛嗎？或許我眞的一直希望你變老，希望你在別人面前的魅力消失無蹤。等你變成弱者，我們之間才能平等。

　　我走到小貨車旁邊，幫忙你搬那些箱子，裡頭滿滿的酒瓶。這些酒箱兩天內要送到幾家店去。箱子非常重。你不敢留

become old, always want your charm in front of others disappear. So you would be weaker. Then we could be *equal*.

I walk towards to your van, and I help you to move the boxes which are full of bottles of wines. These boxes will be delivered to some shops in two days. The box is heavy. You will not leave in the van, because gangs in Hackney smashed your van and tried to steal whatever they could steal. You can't trust people here, you said. We carry the box into kitchen, and put on ground, carefully and slowly.

"Why you have to do this kind of job? Why don't you try hard sell your sculptures?" I ask. "Why you need always more money? You own your house. Is that not enough?" I continue. "If big problem, we can just move to China where your West money make you rich."

"Listen, why can't you just shut up for once and let me do my own thing," you say.

I hate myself being so needy. The way I want of love, is like a hard toothbrush try to brush bad teeth, then it ends up bleeding. The harder I try, more blood comes out. But I believe love can cure everything, and eventually the teeth will not bleeding anymore. I still think love is the hope, of everything.

"*Just the two of us, we can make it if we try. Just the two of us, building castles in the sky. Just the two of us, you and I . . .*"

The music is very loud comes out from neighbour's window.

在車上，因為哈克尼的混混會砸破貨車，偷走裡面所有東西。這裡的人不能相信，你說。我們合力搬進廚房，放在地上，謹慎地，動作緩慢。

「你怎麼都要選這種粗活來幹？怎不多花心思推銷你的雕塑？」我問。「你怎麼老是怕錢賺得不夠？你自己明明已經有房子，還擔心什麼？」我繼續。「如果到時候真的不行，我們可以搬到中國，你西方的錢已經足夠在那兒過舒服日子了。」

「聽好，妳就不能把嘴巴閉上一次讓我好做事，」你說。

我好恨自己如此貧乏。我對待愛的方式，就像拿硬邦邦的牙刷去刷壞掉的牙齒，結果只有流血而已。我越用力，血流得越多。但我相信愛終能療癒一切，牙齒終有停止流血的時候。我依然相信愛代表希望，一切東西的希望。

「就只有我倆，只要努力就能實現。就只有我倆，空中也能築起城堡。就只有我倆，你和我……」

從隔壁人家窗口傳來的音樂開得很大聲。

lighthouse

n. a tower with a light to guide ships.

The train takes us to Wales. It is our first holiday together. It feels fresh. We should have done this long ago, we should have done this before we started fighting, before everything fell apart. Now I know why there are so many holidays in the West.

It was your idea to come to this place. You want to leave city, you want your lungs to inhale the air from the mountains and the sea. And I agree. I agree because I think travelling together may help us, may remove the illness in our relationship.

In the windy afternoon, we arrive at west Wales. Coming out from the train, I breathe out the filth from London. The Irish Sea is underneath the mountain. The sky is high, and the trees are dark green. People in Wales walk slower than in London. They move slowly, drive slowly, laugh slowly, they spend time slowly. You said to me, ancient people believed humans would lose their soul if they walked too fast. So people here must have strong soul.

The mountain climbs up from some huge rocks. Piles and piles of black rocks tumble down to the sea. We walk from the valley to the mountain. The mountain is enormous. It is continually connected to another mountain, and another mountain

【燈塔】

〈名詞〉指引船隻的燈塔。

　　火車載我們來到威爾斯。這是你我首次一起出遊度假，感覺好新鮮。我們早就應該這麼做了，早在兩人開始吵架，沒有一件事順遂之前。這下總算明白何以西方人需要如此多的假期。

　　選擇此地是你的主意。你想遠離都市塵囂，讓肺葉盡情吞吐山巔海湄的空氣。而我也同意，因為我想一起出門旅遊或許有助於我倆，或可滌淨你我之間的陰霾。

　　午後陣陣強風中，我們抵達西威爾斯。下了火車，我使勁吐出倫敦的穢垢。山腳下便是愛爾蘭海，天空開闊，樹林濃綠。在威爾斯，人們腳步比倫敦慢多了。他們走路慢，開車慢，笑起來慢，凡事皆慢。你告訴我，古時候人們相信，走路速度太快的話，會把靈魂給走丟了。如此說來，這地方的百姓想必靈魂勇健過人。

　　山勢順著巨巖拔高，纍纍岩塊隨時可能墜海的樣子。我們從村落步行往山區邁進。群峰層層，一山接過一山，還有一山，高不可攀，幾乎要碰觸到天堂。峭壁直劈而下，不見寸草。或許風勢太過強勁，不利植物生長。如此嚴峻的景致，容不下一絲猶豫，含糊。山裡一路往上走，舉目所見的草都長得粗短牢固，根部扎入土壤有如鐵釘。腳下的土地同樣堅硬異

behind. So high, it is close to the heaven. The cliffs are steep, without any plants. Perhaps the wind too strong for plants growing. Such a bleak landscape, there seems no hesitation, no confusion. When we walk on the mountain, we see the grass grows short and hard, rooted into the soil like needles. And the soil underneath my feet is very hard too. Climbing, climbing, I can hear my breath and yours, heavy and strong.

We walk into the bushes, the yin side of the mountain. It is dark and muddy. Roots are everywhere underneath my feet. We walk into the forest. The forest is decaying, wet and lush. The world becomes even quieter. You are loving it. Your body becomes lively, and you look like a man in his twenties. The birds are singing on branches, and leafs brush against each other in the wind. We sit down, inhaling and exhaling. You pick up chestnut case beside you. Green case is old, brown and sad. But when you open it, inside is silky and smooth and gentle. It smells of spring.

I see your love towards that chestnut, and I can feel my love to you.

The dark clouds quickly cover the sky, and the early evening of the winter arrives. There is something unknown hidden in the forest. There is something sucking the human soul. And I feel like soon we will be swallowed by the nature. I find the beauty of the nature can be a terror, but I don't know if you feel the same way.

We stay in a B&B, a very old stone house. It is a village in Pembrokeshire, a village on the mountain, a village buried in green weeds, a village hidden in the night fogs, a village which have the sky holds the stars and the moon.

常。爬呀，爬呀，你和我重重的喘息聲清晰可聞。

我們進入灌叢，山的陰面。光線暗，處處泥濘。每一步都會踩到雜根。我們步入林中。林木蛀蝕，潮溼，蒼翠。世界變得更加靜默。你愛這種地方，你的四肢五骸注滿活力，看起來有如回到二十來歲。鳥兒枝頭啼鳴，繁葉風中婆娑。我們坐了下來，深深吸吐。你隨手撿起一枚栗子，青殼已老，泛褐，黯淡。不過一剝開栗殼，裡頭光潔，平滑，柔嫩。味如春天。

我見識到你對那枚栗子的愛意，同時感受到我對你的愛意。

暗雲迅速占領天空，冬夜提早降臨。林中藏有某些未知之物，伺機吸人精魄。我感覺一不小心大自然會將我們兩個一口吞了。我察覺自然之美蘊藏驚怖，不曉得你是否也有同樣感受。

我們找到一家 B&B，非常老舊的石屋。這是彭布魯克郡的一個村子，山地村落，埋在蒼茫野草裡，隱身夜霧當中，天空守護著星星和月亮的小村。

夜裡我失眠。雨落不止。抵達此地之後沒一秒鐘闔過眼。想必是因為無法習慣這裡的寧靜。這寧靜太過強烈，近乎震耳欲聾。隨處靜到各種聲響傳入耳中，甚至能夠聽見地衣默默生長。

和你一起躺在床上，躺在這間陌生的石屋裡，我知道雨水覆蓋著森林，海面翻滾，不眠不休，距離我倆不遠之處。月亮引誘浪波，潮水激情湧盪。雨水滴落在我們眠床上頭的頂蓋，雨水滴落石屋旁邊的池塘，滴落窗邊的咬人貓。整個世界都在下雨，全世界溼漉漉的，沒有一個地方能夠保持乾燥，沒有方寸能夠倖免。

I lose sleep during the night. It is raining all the time. Since we arrived here I haven't slept for one second. I think it is because I can't get used to the quietness here. The quietness is so strong that it is almost unbearable noisy. It is so quiet everywhere that I hear all kinds of noises. I even can hear moss growing.

While I am lying on the bed with you, in this strange stone house at night, I know the rain is covering the woods, and the sea is tossing, ceaseless, in a not very far distance. The moon seduces the wave and the tide is moving like crazy. The rain drops on the ceiling above our bed, on the pond outside of the house, on the stinging nettles by the window. The whole world is raining. The whole world is drowning. There is no single place can remain dry, not even an inch.

The next morning, the rain becomes lighter, and the wind is less strong. We come down to the sitting room, having hot coffees with breakfast by the fire. It is safe and warm inside. Outside is *gloomy*. That is the word. But you don't agree. I say I don't want to go out anymore. I swear. You laugh at me. You say you love this kind of weather. You say that is what you love about the nature. Nature is powerful, and this power is beautiful.

"Shall we go to the lighthouse?" you ask.

"Lighthouse? Virginia Woolf's lighthouse?" I remember the book you gave to me.

"No, this one is more beautiful."

"Where is it?"

"Come with me." You stand up.

We borrow an umbrella from the old lady who owns B&B,

第二天清早，雨水稍歇，風勢減弱。我們下樓，在起居室的壁爐邊享用熱騰騰的咖啡和早點。屋子裡舒適溫暖，外頭只有陰沉可言。但你的看法不同。我說死都不想再出門了，我發誓。你取笑我，你說這種天氣才有意思，大自然迷人的地方就在這裡。自然變幻莫測的威力正是絕美所在。

　　「我們去燈塔那邊好不好？」你問。

　　「燈塔？維吉妮亞·吳爾芙的燈塔？」我想起你送的那本書。

　　「不是，這一座比那美多了。」

　　「在哪兒？」

　　「跟我來就對了。」你站了起來。

　　我們跟老闆娘借了把傘，離開壁爐，再度往自然出發。我皮靴昨日踩踏的泥濘未乾，這雙都會鞋形狀都變了，顯然和此地八字不合。早知道應該買雙膠靴，雨衣也要。

　　路好遠，兩腿跋涉森林和農場。約莫一個半鐘頭之後，燈塔出現了。它聳立在丘陵底端，面朝大海。塔身周遭別無他物，連羊都不見半隻，感覺有如築在世界的盡頭。我們朝它走去，塔身越來越近，越來越大。高聳，細瘦，挺拔，像年輕男子的陽物。它全然孤獨。

　　我們在燈塔旁邊坐下。鷗鳥俯衝水面，波浪呈深綠色。我想像入夜時分，黑暗當中，塔燈轉動，一一掃過山崗，草原，小徑，沙灘，海。我想像塔燈搜尋不懈，或許什麼也搜尋不到。

　　「會有船開往海的另一邊嗎？」我問。

　　「有，但不是今天，不是每天都有，」你說。

　　「我們去打聽看看什麼時候有船好不好？有的話就可以坐

leaving the fireplace and head to the nature again. My boots are still wet from yesterday's mud. It is a pair of city boots, losing shape here. They don't belong to this place. I should buy a pair of rubber boots, and a raincoat.

It is a long walk, through the woods and farms. After about one and half hours, we see the lighthouse. It is standing at the bottom of the hill. It faces to the sea. There is nothing else around it, not even a sheep. It feels like is built at the end of the world. We walk towards it. The lighthouse becomes closer and bigger. It is tall, thin, erect, like a young man's penis. It is totally alone, and solitude.

We sit down by the lighthouse. The seagulls are diving in the water. The waves are deep green. I imagine during the night, in the darkness, the light turns around, wiping off the mountain, the grassland, the path, the beach, the sea. I imagine the light searching, but maybe searching for nothing.

"Is any boat going to the other side of the sea?" I ask.

"Yes, but not today. Not everyday," you say.

"Shall we ask around when there will be a boat here? So we can take the boat to see the other side."

"You go if you want. I'd like to stay here," you answer.

"But there is nothing here," I say.

The current is quiet. The lighthouse is keeping something secret, a secret which I don't understand.

The city weakens your energy. But you become alive again in this place. Finding a snake or an earthworm under the grass, is more surprising than making art; seeing a dolphin dancing in the sea is more interesting than making art; watching a beam of red flowers turned into a string of beans is more satisfying than

船到另一邊玩。」

「妳想去就去沒關係，我待在這裡就好，」你回答。

「可是這裡什麼東西都沒有，」我說。

海流無語。燈塔守護著某種祕密，我茫然無知的祕密。

大城市削弱你的能量，這地方卻令你重拾活力。草叢裡發現一條蛇或蚯蚓比藝術創作更令人驚奇；觀賞鯨魚戲水比藝術創作更富趣味；看那招展的紅花變身為一串豆莢比藝術創作更令人心滿意足；聆聽黃蜂啜吮花蕊的樂趣遠遠勝過藝術創作。我覺得你天生適合大自然，何不乾脆待在此地就好？幹嘛勉強返回倫敦？你應該留下來，不用再顧慮我。

再度把筆記本翻開，審視逐日辛勤累積的成果，不斷把更多的生字和語句寫入空白紙頁。我想多學幾個字彙有助於和別人溝通，最好能把整本辭典都搬進腦袋。不過，來到這偏遠地區，無人的仙境，辭典這一套又有什麼用？嘴裡說的是中文或英語無關緊要；人是啞巴或聾子也沒關係。語言已經不重要了。自然界有的只是單純物質性的存在。

making art; listening a bumble bee sucking a bud is more pleasant than making art. I think you are born for nature. Why not stay here? Why force yourself to return London? You should stay, without considering me.

I open my notebook again, looking at my everyday's study, my everyday's effort. I see myself trying hard to put more words and sentences into blank pages. I try to learn more vocabularies to be able to communicate. I try to put the whole dictionary in my brain. But in this remote countryside, in this nobody's wonderland, what's the point of this? It doesn't matter if one speaks Chinese or English here; it doesn't matter if one is mute or deaf. Language is not important anymore. Only the simple physical existence matters in the nature.

November

pathology

n. the scientific study of diseases.

You, my English patient, keep feeling ill. I used to lie beside you, whenever you suffered from headache or bodyache. I would just stop what I was doing and come to lie beside you. But after so long, so often you get ill, somehow I run out of patience.

"Honey, I know how to cure your depression: practice yoga every morning, ride your bike every afternoon, and go swimming every evening."

"Perhaps I just need to find the right medicine."

"No. I don't think you can solve it under the medication way. The problem is from your Qi, your energy."

You lie there, look at the ceiling vaguely: "Every morning I wake up and I feel tired before I'm even out of bed."

"That's because your illness is brought from your thoughts. You hate this society so much, and you feel so fed up with this place. You don't have any disease. You are just like your old van, old, too old, every part of the mechanic fell apart. Remember? Your white van and you, used to be so energetic."

"I just wish I knew what it was that was wrong with me."

"You Westerners always want to precisely name illness. But in China, we don't name all these kind of diseases. Because we think all the illness actually causes from very simple reason. If

【病理學】

〈名詞〉疾病之科學研究。

　　你，我的英倫情人，身體一直不舒服。每當你頭痛或身體哪裡疼痛，我便躺在一旁陪你。我會放下手頭的任何工作陪在你身邊。不過時間一久，你生病的次數又太過頻繁，弄到後來我也失去耐性。

　　「親愛的，我知道如何治好你的沮喪：每天早上練練瑜珈，下午騎自行車，晚上再去游泳。」

　　「或許我只要找到對症的藥物就會好了。」

　　「不，我不認爲你光靠吃藥就能解決問題。毛病出在你的氣，你的能量。」

　　你躺在那兒，兩眼無神盯著天花板：「我每天早上醒來，還沒下床就覺得好累。」

　　「那是因爲你的病都是胡思亂想引起的。你厭惡這個社會，對這地方忍無可忍。其實你不是生病，只是跟你的老貨車一樣，太過老舊，全部零件都要解體了。還記得嗎？你的白色貨車跟你，以前精力十足。」

　　「要是知道我的身體到底哪裡不對勁就好了。」

　　「你們西方人老是講究病名正確。可是在中國，我們不會操心所有疾病都要冠上名稱。因爲我們認爲所有病症的源頭都很單純。想把疾病治好，首先要能安定整個身體，光靠吞藥丸

you want to solve your illness then you must start to calm your whole body, not just taking pills every time."

"OK, tell me more." You rise your head from the bed.

"There are three general classes of the causes of illness in Chinese medication. Internal Pathogenic Qi, External Pathogenic Qi, and Trauma. Internal Pathogenic are organ disfunction, External Pathogenic are Qi from outside the body which enter the body, and Trauma is trauma."

"Trauma is Trauma?"

"I guess Trauma causes Qi and blood to leave the normal currents of flow. And it causes the stagnation of your inner energy. So parts of your body will be suffered from the lack of Qi. That's why you get tired everyday easily. And that's why you get headache regularly."

"How do you know all this?" You stare at me.

"Because I am a Chinese."

"You mean all Chinese people know about this?"

"I think so."

"Are you serious? Even the ones who work in the Chinese takeaway on Hackney Road?"

"You can ask them, next time when we pass by," I say.

"You know, you never tell me things like this." Now you get up from the bed. You must feel better.

"But you never really ask me. You never really pay attention to my culture. You English once took over Hong Kong, so you probably heard of that we Chinese have 5,000 years of the greatest human civilisation ever existed in the world . . . Our Chinese invented paper so your Shakespeare can write two thousand years later. Our Chinese invented gunpowder for you

是沒用的。」

「好，多講點來聽。」你從床上把頭抬起。

「依照中醫的講法，一般生病的原因可以分成三類。內症病氣，外症病氣，以及外傷。內症指器官功能失調，外症指外氣侵入人體，外傷就是傷口。」

「外傷就是傷口？」

「我猜傷口會導致氣血流動偏離正常管道，使得內部能量受到阻礙。身體有些地方氣虛，人就不舒服。你就是這樣每天才會疲倦，而且常常頭痛。」

「妳怎麼會懂得這些東西？」你盯著我瞧。

「因為我是中國人啊。」

「妳的意思是中國人都懂得這一套？」

「應該吧。」

「妳說真的？哈克尼路那家中國外賣餐館的店員也懂？」

「你可以問他看看，下次我們有經過的時候，」我說。

「妳看，妳從來沒有跟我講過這些東西。」你已經從床上爬起來，想必感覺好多了。

「那是你從來沒有認真問我過，你從來沒有真正關心我們的文化。你們英國人以前統治過香港，所以你可能曉得我們中國擁有五千年全世界最偉大的人類文明……我們中國發明紙張好讓兩千年後你們的莎士比亞可以寫出東西。我們中國發明火砲讓你們英國人和美國人轟炸伊拉克。還有我們中國發明指南針讓你們英國人飄洋過海去統治亞洲人和非洲。」

你瞪著我，啞口無言，接著離開床鋪，擺上茶壺。

「要不要喝茶？」你問。

English and Americans to bomb Iraq. And our Chinese invented compass for you English to sail and colonise the Asian and Africa."

You stare at me, no words. Then you leave the bed, and put the kettle on.

"Do you want some tea?" you ask.

pessimism/optimism

pessimism *n.* the tendency to expect the worst in all things. optimism *n.* the tendency to take the most hopeful view.

A petal is a pessimist. A petal will fade away.

An old man's body is a pessimist, things are rotten and falling apart.

A buddhist is a pessimist in his reality, but in the end when he faces his death he is an optimist, because he has prepared for whole life to welcome the peace of death.

A farmer is an optimist, because he believes the potatoes will come out underneath the soil.

A fishman is an optimist, because he knows whatever how far he fishes, he will come back with his boat full of fish.

A pesticide is an optimist. It means sustain the good life by killing bad life.

Everyone tries to be an optimist. But being an optimist is a bit boring and not honest. Losers are more interesting than winners.

It is a quarter to six, and I am cooking dinner for you. It is already inky dark outside. I look at the clock and go back to kitchen checking the food. 6:00, then 6:10, then 6:20, then 6:30. I turn on the radio, listen to whatever I can understand. Finally it is 7:00. Since then every single minute cannot bear anymore. Paranoia takes over the kitchen. 7:30 now. You told

【悲觀主義／樂觀主義】

悲觀主義〈名詞〉凡事習慣往壞處想。樂觀主義〈名詞〉凡事習慣往好處想。

花瓣是悲觀主義者。花瓣終歸凋零。

老人的身體是悲觀主義者，零件腐朽，鬆動。

佛教徒現實上悲觀，但臨終面對死亡時又成了樂觀主義者，因為他全部的生命已經做好準備迎接死的平靜。

農民，樂觀主義者，他相信土裡可以冒出番茄。

漁夫，樂觀主義者，他知道不論漁船跑得多遠，終能滿載而歸。

殺蟲劑，樂觀主義者，幹掉壞的生命，讓好的生命繼續維持。

人人想要樂觀，不過當個樂觀主義者著實有點無聊，而且還得時常欺騙自己。輸家的樂趣往往勝過贏家。

六點差一刻，我正為你料理晚餐。外頭天色完全暗了。我看一下時鐘，回到廚房巡視食物。六點整，六點十分，六點二十，六點半了。我轉開收音機，隨便聽看哪個節目容易入耳。終於挨到七點。從這一刻開始每分鐘都很要命。妄想症接管廚房。七點三十了現在。你有跟我說六點之前會到家，怎麼就不能準時一次？你忙著跟別人打情罵俏對不對？或者可能更糟……

me that you would be back home before six. Why you never on time? Are you flirting with somebody right now? Or maybe things much worse . . .

Trying to stop this painful visual imagination, I turn up the volume of the radio. Today's top news: "*A woman murdered her husband's pregnant lover after she discovered the love affair . . . She was found guilty in court this afternoon.*"

The soup is still bubbling on the fire but is nearly burnt. Murder . . . The whole world is crashed. The paranoia penetrates my body through my mind. My muscles are shaking badly, and my stomach starts aching. I am in the big nerve and I might do anything to destroy the furniture in this house, the symbols of our life together.

Love can be so pessimistic, and love can be so destructive. Love can lead a woman being lost, and in that lost world perhaps the only thing to do is leave to build a new world.

9:00, you come back home. I pour all the food into the rubbish bin. You are a bit scared seeing what I am doing. I say loudly, to myself, and to the whole house:

"Never cook food before the man comes back home!"

爲了克制歷歷在目的痛苦想像，我將收音機聲音調高。今天的頭條新聞：「一名婦女發現先生出軌後將他已有身孕的情婦謀殺……她今天下午於法庭被判有罪。」

　　爐火上的湯還在滾，快燒焦了。

　　謀殺……世界垮了。妄想穿刺我的身體，撕扯心神。我的肌肉顫抖，胃開始絞痛。我快發神經了，好想砸爛屋裡的傢俱，我們共同生活的象徵。

　　愛情原來可以如此悲觀，破壞力十足。愛情將女人帶往失落，那種失落的世界當中或許唯一的出路只有離開，重建新的天地。

　　九點整，你回來了。我把全部晚餐倒進垃圾桶。你有點害怕地看著我的動作。我對自己，和整間房屋高聲說道：

　　「男人沒到家之前千萬不要下鍋！」

electric

adj. **1.** produced by, transmitting, or powered by electricity; **2.** exciting
or tense.

Hair, bosom, hips, bend of legs, negligent falling hands all diffused . . .
    mine too diffused,
Ebb stung by the flow and flow stung by the ebb . . . love-flesh swelling
    and deliciously aching
Limitless limpid jets of love hot and enormous . . . quivering jelly of love . . .
    white-blow and delirious juice,
Bridegroom-night of love working surely and softly into the prostrate
    dawn,
Undulating into the willing and yielding day,
Lost in the cleave of the clasping and sweet-flesh'd day.

This is in a book from Walt Whitman, which sits on your
bookshelf covered by the thick dust. But during the last two
weeks it becomes my bible. I read it every day and I think I
understand it.

Jelly of love. I think of you. You are like the man in Walt
Whiteman's poem. I imagine you are naked by the sea, a wild
landscape behind you. You are a young man with a healthy
body and a free spirit. You are a simple farmer, with a natural
passion. You have beautiful hips and legs and hands, and you
have a strong love and sensibility to the nature. You are friends
with the seagulls, the bees, the dragonflies. And you know that
dolphin in the distance dancing on the sea. You walk through

【帶電】

〈形容詞〉**1.** 發電，導電，或使用電力的；**2.** 震驚的，強烈的。

頭髮，乳房，臀部，腿的彎曲，不經意低垂的手全都
　　四處散布……我的也四處散布，
漲潮驅動落潮且落潮驅動漲潮……愛的血肉
　　膨脹而又愉悅地疼痛
無限清澄的愛噴發火燙且龐然……愛的凝膠
　　震顫……白色喘息且狂喜的汁液，
愛的新郎之夜穩當且溫柔地幹活直到
　　破曉力竭，
起伏進入甘心柔順的白晝，
消失於交纏甜蜜血肉的白晝裂隙當中。

　　這是瓦特‧惠特曼書裡的詩句，在你的書架上蒙塵已久。不過兩個禮拜以來，這本書成為我的聖經。每天讀了又讀，自認心有所感。
　　愛的凝膠。我想到你。你就像瓦特‧惠特曼詩裡的人物。我想像你在海邊身體赤裸，背對一片荒涼的景色。你年輕，擁有強健的體魄和不羈的心靈。你是單純的莊稼漢，天生熱情。你有美麗的臀部和腿和手，你對自然懷抱強烈的愛意和敏感。你是海鷗，蜜蜂，蜻蜓的好友。你知道海面不遠處有海豚騰躍

the fields of apple trees, and pass by the farm houses, and then down to the sea. You body carries the smell of grass and the warmth of earth to the sea water . . . I look at your reality here. How could these things being taken away from you totally? You will die. You will die. You will die like a fish without water.

The life in the past and the life at the present are very different. When I first met you, I remember you always talked and smiled. You talked about interesting things in an interesting way, and you had a charming language. You used beautiful words, funny words, sexy words, *electric* words, *noble* words. Your language was as attractive as you. But what happened? It has changed. After all these fightings, all these miseries, you don't talk as the way you did before. You just listen; listen to my words; then stop listening and think of your own world. But I can't stop talking. I talk and talk, more and more. I steal your words. I steal all your beautiful words. I speak your language. You have given up your words, just like you gave up listening. All you do is sleep, more and more sleep.

起舞。你穿越蘋果園，走過農舍，一路往下來到海濱。你的肉體將青草的氣味和泥土的溫暖送入海水⋯⋯我看著眼下現實當中的你。怎麼可以讓人把這些東西從你身上奪走？你會消亡。你會死去。你會像離水的魚那樣涸竭而死。

過往的日子和現在天差地遠。初認識的時候，記得你總是談笑風生。你講的東西有趣，講話的方式有趣，你嘴裡吐露的語言迷人之至。你使用漂亮的字眼，風趣的字眼，性感的字眼，帶電的字眼，高貴的字眼。你的語言跟本人一樣具有磁力。不過到底怎麼回事？一切都變了樣。經過這些奔波折磨之後，你的言談失去昔日丰采。現在的你只會聽；默默聽我說話；然後連聽都免了，你遁入自己的世界。不過我沒辦法停嘴，我說了又說，喋喋不休。我偷走你的辭彙，偷走你所有美麗的辭彙。我口說你的語言。你已經放棄那些詞彙，同時也放棄聆聽。你唯一的活動只有睡覺，沒日沒夜的睡覺。

bestseller

n. a book or other product that has sold in great numbers.

Last night I had a dream. I dreamed I was a cookery writer writing for housewifes who bored with their unimaginative life. I dreamed my book eventually exposed on the most visible and conspicuous shelfs in Waterstones. I become a bestseller who has the fame in England, Scotland, and even in Wales. My book was called *Getting To Grips With Noodles: 300 ways of Chinese cooking*. Actually, at the beginning of my dream, there were only ten recipes of cooking noodles, but in the dream I had the idea that a year has 365 days and I should write at least 300 different recipes. Rest of sixty-five days in a year people can have rice or bread or alternative food they like.

I remember the first dish in my book is called:

Dragon In the Clouds

The recipe is: thin rice noodles with fried tofu and bean sprouts in a chicken soup. So everything looks white and gentle like clouds.

And other noodles dishes in my dream are:

Red River
Mussels with spring onions in chilli noodles soup

Double Happiness
Roast duck and pork with fried noodles

【暢銷書】

〈名詞〉暢銷書或其他暢銷商品。

　　昨晚我做了個夢。我夢見自己是烹飪作家，專爲厭倦單調生活的家庭主婦寫文章。我的書最終登上華特史東連鎖書店最醒目的架位。我成爲暢銷書作者，名聲傳遍英格蘭，蘇格蘭，甚至威爾斯。我的書名叫《麵食高手：中式烹調300招》。其實，夢境開端，我的麵條食譜只有十種，後來靈機一動，一年三百六十五天，我至少得弄出三百種不同的食譜。剩下六十五天就讓大家換換口味，隨意選擇米飯，麵包，或其他任何食物。

　　記得書裡第一道菜叫：

　　　雲龍

　　食譜如下：細米粉，配上炸豆腐，豆芽菜，雞湯作底。整碗看起來鮮白柔和，有如雲朵。

　　夢裡其他的麵條食譜還有：

紅河
淡菜青蔥辣湯麵

雙喜
烤鴨豬肉炒麵

Dragon Palace
Sliced eel with rice noodles in ginger soup

It's also about two-way-cooking, meaning either it can be prepared as Chinese food or it can become Italian spaghetti. For example, one can just change ginger into basil, or replace chilli to rosemary with a bit cheese, then noodles will get totally *different identity*.

End of dream, there are a group of fat middle-aged English womans talking about my book in a countryside teahouse. They are all having their afternoon teas and carrot cakes with my book opened on the table, and discuss where is the nearest Chinese shop that they can buy all the ingredients.

I wake up and I don't know where is this idea from. I guess from my hunger for Chinese food. I am longing to eat hot dumplings with fennel and pork stuffing, and I am dying for roasted duck and spicy beef. Abroad, thinking of food is every-day's obsession.

There is an important thing in the dream: I am too ashamed to use my real name on the cover of the book because I know as soon as I get famous in West, Chinese will find out immediately and make a fuss. A writer who doesn't write history or serious novels, but write about cooking noodles for English people—that would be a scandal in China. So I choose "Anon" as my name, the person who has no name.

Getting up from the bed, I feel hungry. I have a great urge to taste those specially made noodles but, when I try remember how to cook the dream noodles, nothing comes in my head. I open the cupboard and take out a pack of instant noodles.

龍宮
薑絲鱔魚米粉湯

書裡還教人如何一麵兩吃，中國菜的食材略加變化就成了義大利麵。比如，你可以把薑絲改成羅勒，或者辣椒換成迷迭香，再加上些許起司，麵條的身分馬上改頭換面。

夢境結尾，幾個中年發福的英國婦女坐在鄉間一家茶館談論我寫的書。她們享用下午茶和胡蘿蔔蛋糕，我的書攤在桌面，話題已經進行到附近哪裡有中國雜貨店可以買到全部的食材。

我醒來，不曉得怎會作出這樣的夢。我猜大概是自己對中國菜饑渴過度。我好想吃熱騰騰的茴香豬肉水餃，還有要命的烤鴨和醬爆牛肉。人在異鄉，每天著魔般想念這些吃的。

夢裡還有件事很重要：我太丟臉了，書的封面不敢印上本名，我知道一旦在西方有了名氣，中國人一定馬上開始大驚小怪。好好一個作家，不寫些歷史或正經的小說，竟搞出教英國人煮麵這種名堂——在中國馬上會鬧出醜聞。所以我選了「阿儂」當作筆名，沒有名字的人。

從床上起來，肚子餓了。好想趕快嚐到那些特製麵食，然而，當我回想夢中的麵條食譜時，腦袋卻空空如也。我打開櫥櫃，拿了一包泡麵出來。

December

future tense

The Future Tense Sometimes when we talk about the future, we are just predicting. We are saying what we think will happen, without any reference to the present. At other times, we are really talking about the present and the future together. This happens, for example, when we talk about future actions which are already decided, or which we are deciding as we talk: making plans, promises, threats, offers, requests.

Mrs. Margaret say I am no good at verbs, particularly future tense. "Don't worry," she says. "It's an Asian thing. You'll get over it."

How is "time" so clear in the West? Is being defined by Science or by Buddha? Reincarnation, it is not past or future. Is endless loop. A circus, ending and starting is the same point.

At beginning I don't have concept of *tense* when I speak English. But now I think I understand more than before, after all our battles.

Sun Tzu, the Chinese master who lived 2500 years ago, says in the *Art of War for Executives*:

The ultimate warrior is one who wins the war by forcing the enemy to surrender without fighting any battles.

But neither of us wants to surrender to the other, and neither of us can win the battle. Neither of us is an ultimate warrior. So the battle carries on and on, as follows:

ME: "I want future with you. A home, a house in beautiful place with you, plant some bamboos, some lotus, some jasmines, some of your favourite snowdrops." (When I describe this, the image so strong that it must be a will from my Last

【未來式】

有時論及未來的時候，我們只是大概預測。我們說出自認以後將會發生的事情，並未指涉當下的狀況。別的時候，我們所談的東西實際上同時涵蓋了現在和未來。例如，我們談及目前已經決定未來將要採取的行動，或者談的同時做出決定日後將要採取的行動：預先計畫，承諾，威脅，提議，請求。

瑪格麗特小姐說我的動詞還不夠好，特別是未來式。「別擔心，」她老是這麼一句。「亞洲人都有這麻煩，妳會克服的。」

時態果真是亞洲人的罩門？「時間」在西方怎會如此分明？存在的界定要由科學或是佛陀來做主？依據輪迴，它不屬於過去或未來，而是無盡的迴圈。一個圓，終點與起點同一。

一開始學習英語時，我沒有時態的概念。如今多少略有體會，經過我倆的風風雨雨之後。

孫子，二千五百年前中國的思想家，他在《孫子兵法謀攻篇》說：

不戰而屈人之兵，善之善者也。

不過我們兩個沒有人願意投降，也沒有人能夠贏得勝利。兩個不善征戰的人碰在一塊，火線只能沒完沒了，比如：

我：「我和你要有未來。要有家，漂亮的環境和你有一間房子，種點竹子，蓮花，茉莉，和你最愛的雪花蓮。」（描述的時候，這番景象太過逼真，鐵定是上輩子便許下的心願。）

你：「妳不能現在就料定未來。那樣才叫未來。」

Life.)

YOU: "You can't have the future now. That's why it's the future."

ME: "I disagree. Future comes from your plan, your real action."

YOU: "No, that's not true. The future only comes when it comes. I don't believe in promises. How can you know the future now? You can only know the future when you get to the future."

ME: "Does that me4an you don't want future with me?" (I look in your eyes painfully.)

YOU: "You"re always worried about the future. How can we think about getting married when we keep fighting? You"re never happy with the way things are, you always want it to be different to how it is. We can't be together if you don't accept my lifestyle and realise you can't change me. You can't always want me to be different from how I am."

You are right, I know. I can't say anything.

Again I feel like I am the wisteria vine, and I can't climb and rely on my tree, because that tree is falling.

"Live in the moment!" You impose this idea on me, again.

"Live in the moment," I repeat. Why do I have to? "Live in the moment, or live *for* the moment? Maybe you only live *for* the moment. That is so hippy. I can"t do that as a humble foreigner," I fight back.

"Well, to live in or to live *for* the moment, that's the same kind of concept."

"No. It is different," I say, strongly and angrily. I recently

我：「我不同意。未來從你的計畫產生，靠你的實際行動。」

　　你：「不對，不是那樣。未來的事到時候才會知道。我不相信人能夠承諾什麼。妳現在怎麼知道未來會如何？妳只有到未來那個時候才能明白。」

　　我：「你的意思是說你沒打算未來跟我在一起？」（我痛苦地瞪著你的眼睛。）

　　你：「妳老是煩惱未來的事情，我們現再已經吵成這樣，要怎麼考慮一起結婚？現在的狀況妳沒有一樣滿意，老想改變這改變那。如果妳沒辦法接受我的生活習慣，還有了解妳不能改變我這個人的話，我們在一起只有痛苦而已。妳不能一直想要我違背本性變成不一樣的人。」

　　你說得對，我知道。我無話可說。

　　再一次感覺自己有如紫藤，我不能攀爬依附我的樹幹，因為那棵樹傾頹倒地。

　　「活在當下！」再一次，你灌輸我這個觀念。

　　「活在當下，」我複述。憑什麼我要這樣？「活在當下（live in the moment），還是只活當下（live for the moment）？或許你不過是只活當下，那樣感覺好嬉皮，我這個卑微的外國人哪配如此，」我火力回擊。

　　「唔，活在當下或是只活當下，觀念都是相同的。」

　　「不，相同才怪，」我說，高聲且憤怒。瑪格麗特小姐剛剛教過我們分辨 in 跟 for 的差異。那絕對是不一樣的觀念。

　　「愛，」這個英國字：和其他英國字一樣有時態變化。「愛過」或「將愛」或「已愛」，這些特定的時態說明愛有其時

learned what is the difference between in and for from Mrs Margaret. It is definitely a different concept.

"Love", this English word: like other English words it has tense. "Loved" or "will love" or "have loved". All these specific tenses mean Love is time-limited thing. Not infinite. It only exist in particular period of time. In Chinese, Love is "愛" (ai). It has no tense. No past and future. Love in Chinese means a being, a situation, a circumstance. Love is existence, holding past and future.

If our love existed in Chinese tense, then it will last for ever. It will be infinite.

間限制，並非無窮無盡。它只活在特定的期限當中。在中國，愛就是愛，它沒有時態，不必區分過去式和未來式。愛在中國意指一種存在，一種情境，一種際遇。愛就是存在，維繫著過去和未來。

如果我們的愛情存活於中國的時態，它便能長長久久，愛無止境。

possess

v. **1.** to have as one's property; **2.** (of a feeling, belief, etc) have complete control of, dominate.

You tell me my love to you is like a possession. But how could I possess you when your world is so big? Maybe it not about possession, it more about me trying to fit into your life. I am living in your life. I am living inside of your body, trying to understand every single movement from your command. Every night I inhale and outhale your breath. The smells from your hair and your skin cover my hair and my skin. I know nobody in my life is as close as you.

I just hope night carry on like this, go on for ever. Hope our bodies can be always close like this, and our souls always can be side by side. I don't want the sun comes, the day comes. I know the light of day takes you away from me. Then you live in your own world, the world that has a big gap between us.

In the daytime, you stay with your sculptures, with your clay, your sand, your wax. You are making many moulds of human bodies. All the materials they lie there, quiet, with vague and unclear statements.

The conversation on the bed after we make love:

"Why you are always so interested in the body?"

"Because you will never get bored with the body." You rub the sperms on my skin slowly, trying to dry it. "Eating, drinking, shitting . . . The body is key to everything."

【占有】

〈動詞〉**1.** 擁有，占有（有如個人財物般）；**2.**（情感，信仰等方面）控制，支配。

　　你說我對你的愛像是一種占有。不過你的天地如此廣闊，我哪有本事占有你？或許那不是占有，比較像我在設法融入你的生命。我要進入你的生命當中，活在你的身體裡面，揣摩你的旨意所下達的每一個動作。每晚，我吞吐你的呼吸。你的髮香和體味包覆我的頭髮和肌膚。我明白這輩子沒有人比你和我更親。

　　我唯有指望夜晚不斷延續，直到永遠。指望我倆身體持續依偎，靈魂緊靠。我不願太陽升起，白晝降臨。我知道白晝的光線會將你從我身邊奪走，你會回到自己的世界生活，那世界在你我之間劃開一道鴻溝。

　　白天的時候，你的伴侶換成那些雕塑，換成你的黏土，你的砂石，你的石蠟。你做出許多人體的模子。它們全躺在那兒，悶聲不響，曖昧模糊地表達著什麼。

　　做愛後我們床頭的對話：

　　「你怎麼一直對人體這麼有興趣？」

　　「因為人體讓人永不厭倦。」你輕柔地擦拭我皮膚上的精液，想弄乾它。「吃，喝，拉，撒……人體是一切的關鍵。」

　　「可是你的雕塑怎會又醜又苦？」

　　「我不覺得它們醜。它們很美。」

"But why your sculptures ugly and miserable?"

"I don't think they are ugly. They are beautiful."

"Maybe. Beautiful in ugly way. But they are always in pain."

"That's what life is like."

I can't agree, but I can't deny either.

"My body always feels miserable, except for when I am making love," you say.

Your voice becomes sleepy, and you close your eyes.

I turn off the light. I stare at the darkness. I have enough thoughts to talk to the long night, alone.

「或許吧。醜得很美。不過它們老是受罪的樣子。」

「生命就是如此。」

我不同意，但也無法反駁。

「我的身體一直感覺受苦，除了做愛的時候，」你說。

聲音睡意漸濃，你把眼睛闔上。

我關燈，凝視著黑暗。我有滿肚的心思和長夜暢談，一個人。

Christmas

n. **1.** an annual festival on Dec. 25 commemorating the birth of Christ; **2.** period around this time.

Tomorrow is Christmas. We wake up to noises from neighbours" kitchen. They are probably arranging tables or chairs for their guests. You tell me we will stay in London until lunch, and then you will take me to see your family in the afternoon. I am curious, but also worried. Meeting your family is a big thing for me. That is again something to do with the future.

What happened to Jesus Christ at Christmas Eve? Was he hung on the cross? Did he almost reborn? We were taught when we were little that only the phoenix can be reborn. A beautiful huge bird, with the neck of a snake, the back of a tortoise, and the tail of fish. She eats dewdrops. She lives for a thousand years and, once that time is over, she burns itself in her own funeral pyre, and is born again from the ashes. Jesus must be something like a bird, the symbol of high virtue.

Winter is such a long season in England. Hackney Road is dim, dark, wet and obscure. But there is something extra which makes you and me nervous about this time. Neither you nor me kind of person likes celebrating festivals, plus I don't have any family here. Outside, neon lights are twinkling, shining like the fragile happiness.

Almost a year has passed. In the beginning, we were so pas-

【聖誕節】

〈名詞〉**1.** 每年十二月二十五的耶穌誕生紀念日；**2.** 聖誕節假期。

　　明天就是聖誕節。我們一早被鄰居廚房的噪音吵醒，他們大概忙著布置招待客人的桌椅。你說等我們留在倫敦吃過午餐，下午就會帶我去探訪你的家人。我很好奇，但又不安。和你的家人碰面非同小可，又是一件攸關未來的事情。

　　聖誕夜耶穌基督如何度過？他還掛在十字架上？他重獲新生了嗎？小時候，人家告訴我們只有鳳凰才能重生。美麗的巨鳥，長著蛇頸，龜背，魚尾，靠露珠維生。她的壽命超過千年，一旦時間走到盡頭，她會點燃柴堆自焚，再從灰燼當中浴火重生。耶穌和鳳凰必有共通之處，非凡德性的象徵。

　　英國的嚴冬真是漫長。哈克尼路黯淡，幽黑，潮溼，朦朧。不過這時節還有其他的因素讓你我神經緊繃。我們兩個都不是那種喜歡佳節大肆慶祝的人，加上此地又沒有我的家人。外頭閃爍的霓虹，有如脆弱的幸福明滅。

　　一年幾乎過去了。一開始，我們彼此滿懷熱情，如今一切變得蒼老，蒙上塵埃。每日清早你到轉角小攤買報紙，小咖啡店裡坐著吃早餐讀報紙。你寧可外頭找個地方讀報，你嫌家裡沒辦法放鬆。我是否應該出門把家裡的空間還給你？

　　下午到了。我們坐進白色小貨車，往英格蘭西南境開，開往低尾農場，你的成長家園。沿途的鄉間道路十分靜謐，似乎

sionate about each other. Now everything grows older, and covered by the dust. Every morning you go to that corner shop to buy newspaper. You sit in a small cafe having a breakfast and reading. You would rather read the paper outside somewhere, because you say you can't relax at home. Should I leave the house and give the space back to you?

Afternoon. We are in your white van. We are driving to the southwest of England, to Lower End Farm, the place where you grew up. The road towards the countryside is so quiet. Like a road nobody knows, as if nobody has driven through it before. It is getting darker. It is grey. The houses beside the road are all lighted. Ah, others are all happy, with their family. I hate Christmas.

I start to cry.

You look at me one moment, then look at the road. You know why I am crying. You keep quiet. Only the noise from the engine carries on.

"It will be all right," you say.

But I don't know what all right even means.

I stop crying. I calm down a bit. It's only four in the afternoon, but the sky in countryside is already deep dark, and the rain comes with the chilly wind. The wind blows the pine trees, the grass, and the oaks in the fields. The leaves are shivering, and the branches are shaking. There must be too much wind in English's blood.

Dim and muddy, it is the road leading to your childhood. . . .

That evening, you show me around the farm with torch. It is a big farm, extended to the horizon. Some sheeps or maybe cows in the distance, mooing.

無人知曉，未曾有人駛過。天色漸暗，灰幕掩至。路旁的人家全都亮起燈火。噢，人人歡樂，家家團聚。可恨的聖誕節。

我開始哭泣。

你稍看我一下，然後回到路面。你明白我為何而哭。你沒出聲，唯獨引擎持續賣力作響。

「會沒事的，」你說。

可我連什麼叫沒事都不清楚。

我止住淚眼，稍稍平靜一些。時間才下午四點，鄉野的天空已經完全暗了，雨水寒風交加。風刮過田野的松樹，草地，和橡樹。樹葉瑟縮，枝條顫抖。英國脾氣就是冷風颼颼。

朦朧，泥濘，一路通往你的童年⋯⋯

那天晚上，你拿著手電筒引我參觀農場。好大一座農場，遼闊無邊。遠處有羊還是牛，哞哞叫著。

這房子住了四個老女人：你母親，姥姥，兩個姊妹。還有三隻貓也住在這棟老農舍裡面。我在想這些貓咪該不會全是母的罷？沒有一個男的。你兩個姊妹，一個四十二，一個四十八。你說她們都沒結過婚，或許早已經習慣老小姐的生活，根本不想，也不需要男人了。你父親已經過世多年，爺爺也是。但女人全都活著。

你家裡這幾個女人，她們投身農務，一副辛勤操勞的樣貌。她們的臉龐久經寒風，兩頰冽紅。她們單純，略帶強悍。個性非常直接，每件小事意見毫不含糊。問題像是：

「莊？怎麼會有這種名字？妳說怎麼拼？」

「妳有看電視嗎，Z？」

「Z，從中國飛到倫敦要好多鐘頭？」

「該死的！十億。你們國家人口真有這麼多？」

There are four old womans in this house: your mother, your grandmother, your two sisters. Three cats live in this old farm house too. I wonder if these cats are all females? No man. Your two sisters, one is 42, another is 48. You told me they never get married. Maybe they get used to this old-girl-life, so they don't need or want a man anymore. Your father died long time ago, and so did your grandfather. But all womans survive.

These womans, in your family, they are all farmers. They look like they have had a hard life. Their faces, reddish on the cheeks from the chilly wind. They are simple and a little tough. They are very straightforward, and have very strong impression towards every little thing. Their questions are like these:

"Zhuang? What kind of a name is that? How do you spell it?"

"Do you watch TV, Z?"

"Z, how many hours does it take to fly from China to England?"

"Bloody hell! One billion. Are there really so many people in your country?"

They talk loudly, and laugh loudly, and chop the meat loudly in the kitchen. They remind me of my family. They are very different from Londoners.

There are about twenty silver and golden badges on the wall of dining room. These badges are hung under the photos of sheep and cows, the winners of some farming competitions. Several local newspapers are pinned on the wall, with pictures of your sisters hugging her award-winning cow. And the cow has a big badge hung on its neck too. I don't understand this competition between cow and cow.

233

她們嗓門大，笑聲響亮，廚房剁起肉來聲勢驚人。她們令我想起家人。跟倫敦佬截然不同。

　　餐廳牆上起碼有二十面金銀獎章。這些獎章掛在牛羊的照片底下，從一些農牧競賽贏來的。還有幾張本地報紙釘在牆面，上頭有你姊妹摟著得獎牛隻的照片，連牛的脖子上也掛著大獎牌。這種牛跟牛的比賽我真是一竅不通。

　　電視間裡則有一張羊的大海報。每隻羊的名稱都不同，長的樣子也真的有差。左邊一隻叫牛津羊，像一隻大胖狗，不過長著焦黑的鼻子和耳朵。右邊那隻叫達特穆爾種羊，雜亂的捲毛有如女人在髮廊燙過的頭髮。底下那隻叫埃克斯穆爾種羊，羊角彎曲，身體肥短如雪球……看不到任何一張人物照片。像一間綿羊博物館。

　　來到廚房，你母親正準備聖誕夜大餐。我看見餐盤畫上羊的圖案，茶杯有牛的繪像，茶壺的形狀則是一隻小山羊。

　　房子裡每樣東西看起來歷史悠久，和你姥姥年紀一般大。她已經高齡九十七，住在樓上。你帶我去請安，她只剩一把骨頭，手腳都不靈便了，連講話都沒有聲音，似乎也沒辦法認出你來。

　　我嘗試分辨濃厚的口音，理解這四個女人。說不上她們究竟算頑固或親切。你妹妹剁起肉來那股狠勁令我有點畏縮。這可是原因之一，讓你離鄉背井跑到倫敦，害年輕時候的你對女人退避三舍？

　　用過晚餐，大家累了，各自回房休息。我們兩個睡在客廳的沙發床。時近午夜，外頭整座農場籠罩在大幅的寂靜當中。沒有鄰居，沒有酒吧，沒有店鋪，沒有汽車，沒有火車。這地方遠離文明塵煙，簡直比我中國老家還慘。安靜的程度有如來

In TV room is a huge poster about sheep. Every sheep has its different name, and they do look like very different. The one on the left is called Oxford Down, look like a big fat dog, but with burnt black nose and ears. The one on the right is called Dartmoor, with messy curly wool like a woman in hair salon having an electricity perm. The bottom one is called Exmoor Horn with curly horns and short body like a snow ball . . . There are no pictures of human beings. It is like a sheep museum.

I walk into the kitchen. Your mother is preparing Christmas Eve supper. I see the plates with drawing of sheep, and tea cups with the picture of cow, and the tea pot is the shape of a little goat.

Everything in the house looks aged, as old as your grandmother. Your grandmother is ninety-seven. She lives upstairs. You take me to say hello to her. She is skinny. She is too old to move around. Also she is too old to talk. She doesn't seem to recognise who you are.

I try to understand these four womans, with their strong accent. I can't tell if they are tough or friendly. There is a certain kind of brutal feel from your sister when she chops the meat that makes me timid. Is that one of the reasons you left your hometown, came to London, and didn't want to be with any womans when you were young?

After the supper, everybody is tired and goes to bed. We sleep on a sofabed in the living room. It is midnight. The whole farm outside is covered by a big piece of silence. No neighbours, no pub, no shop, no car, no train. It is a place far away from civilisation. It is even worse than my hometown in

到世界的邊緣。偶爾一兩枚煙火遠處鳴響，剩下的只有北冰洋般冰封的世界。

聖誕節早晨，雪開始飄。農場敷上一層薄妝。我企盼這特別的日子，農場以欣喜迎接雪花。用過豐盛的早午餐，我們觀賞電視播出的女王談話，然後向你的家人道別，踏上歸程。你的母親和姊姊妹妹都在房子前面揮手，從貨車裡看著她們，我一陣難過。或許我們應該多停留點時間，至少吃過人家準備良久的聖誕節火雞。都是你說沒辦法再多待下去，連半天都不行，你說。駛離低尾農場，那些泥巴，綿羊，和冬草在我們身後漸行漸遠。

我們一路直接開回倫敦。街上不見半個人影，連隻鬼都沒有。有夠超現實的，幾乎棒到難以置信。

羽毛般的雪花緩緩掩蓋倫敦的髒汙。落雪對自己的威力了然於胸，它熟知如何減輕城市的蕭索，增添氣質。

我們停在哈克尼路一家咖啡館前，或許是唯一營業的店家。咖啡館老闆是外國人，可能來自中東地區。我猜聖誕節他寧可選擇開門營業，好過在東倫敦租來的地下室孤零零窩一整天。每張桌面都擺放美麗的紅花，一種綠葉紅花。我吃魚，你吃炸薯條。朝外頭看去，雪花天空飄落。咖啡館老闆對我們倆說「聖誕快樂」，想必非常高興這寂寞的日子終於有兩位顧客光臨。

China. So quiet, like it's on the edge of the world. Occasionally, one or two fireworks blow in the distance. But rest of the world is as frozen as ice in the Arctic Ocean.

On Christmas morning, it starts snowing. The farm has a layer of light snow. I hope the farm is happy to receive the snow on a very special day. After a big brunch, we watch the Queen's speech on TV, then we say goodbye to your family, and hit the road again. Your mother and your two sisters are waving their hands in front of the house. When I look at them from the van I feel sad. Maybe we should stay more time here, eat the Christmas turkey they prepare all day. But you say you can't stay in there any longer. Not even one more afternoon, you say. We leave Lower End Farm behind. We leave the mud, the sheep, and the winter grass behind.

We drive all the way back to London. There is nobody in the street, not even a ghost. It is surreal. Almost too perfect.

The snow is like feathers gradually covers dirty London. The snow knows its own power. It understands how to make a city less bleak and more gentle.

We stop in a local café on Hackney Road, probably the only one open. The cafe owner is a foreigner, maybe from Middle East. I guess he prefers to work in cafe at Christmas rather than spend a lonely day on his own in his rented east London basement. There are beautiful red flowers on every table. It is a kind of green-leafs-turn-to-red-flowers. I am having fish and you are having chips. We look outside. The snow is falling from the sky. The cafe owner says "Merry Christmas" to us. He must be so happy to see eventually two customers visit him on such lonely day.

January

betray

v. **1.** to hand over or expose (one's nation, friend, etc) treacherously to an enemy; **2.** to disclose (a secret or confidence) treacherously; **3.** to reveal unintentionally.

I don't know if time takes us into its fast whirpool, or we suck time into our inner world. It feels like Christmas just yesterday, but now here comes New Year's day. Last night we made love like desperate people. And we made love again this morning. It feels everything so empty. Desperation. Or fear. We need make something unforgettable in our memory.

The only thing I love completely, without any doubt, is your body. I love it. Temperature. Softness. Forgiveness. Maybe I can let you go, but not your body.

Kissing. I hug your warmth. I think of other bodies I encountered, which I never really in love with. I start to talk.

"You know lots of things happened in that month."

"That month?"

"Yes, that month."

". . . When you went Inter-Railing?"

"Yes." I look into your eyes. I really want you to know. If we don't have much to talk anymore, maybe we can talk about that month, when you were absent with me.

"Are there things you didn't tell me?" You put out your hand touch my face.

"But you never ask me! It's like the newspaper is more interesting to you than reality. You would rather read the paper

【背叛】

〈動詞〉**1.** 叛國，出賣朋友；**2.** 洩漏機密或他人私密；**3.** 無意中透露。

不曉得究竟是時間將我們捲入漩渦，亦或我們自身將時間吞噬。感覺昨天還是聖誕節，一眨眼新年就已到來。昨夜我們做愛，不要命似的。今天一早又再做愛。感覺每件事好空洞。絕望。或者害怕。我們必須做點什麼填補記憶的空缺。

我唯一全心熱愛，絕無疑問的，便是你的身體。我愛極了。它的溫度，柔軟，寬宏大量。或許我可以放過你，但身體得留下。

親吻。緊擁你的體溫。想起其他照會過，沒有真正愛過的身體，我開口說話。

「你知道那個月裡面發生了多少事情？」

「那個月？」

「對，那個月。」

「……妳搭國際鐵路的時候？」

「對。」看著你的眼睛，我真的想讓你知道。如果我們已經無話可說，或許可以聊一下那個月的事情，你不在我身邊的日子。

「妳有事情沒有告訴我嗎？」你伸手摸摸我的臉。

「你自己就不會問我！好像報紙寫的東西比現實生活有意思。你每天光看報紙，都不跟我聊天。」

every day than talk to me."

"So, talk to me now," you say.

I'm annoyed again. Why everything has to be like this? Why I am always demanding? Why there is no curiosity inside your heart anymore?

"OK. I met some mans on the trip, you know."

"What do you mean you met some men?"

"Yes, one in Amsterdam, one in Berlin, one in Venice and one in Faro . . ." I suddenly can see all these faces. I can see that Portugal man with the missing teeth walking beside with me down to the dirty rocky beach under the highnoon's sun . . . And I can see Klaus standing in a street of Berlin waiting for the bus. Probably now he walks into a shop to buy a bottle of mineral water with red star brand.

"And?" You become serious.

"Nothing."

"Nothing?"

"Nothing serious. Just, I had sex with a man who I only met for half an hour."

You stare at me. Your face is frozen. There is only four centimetres between my face and yours.

"But I didn't like that experience, actually . . ." I am a little worried to carry on this story.

There is no specific impression on your face.

Suddenly I remember a sentence I read from the bible on your shelf recently: *Father forgive them for they know not what they do.*

"I thought I should let you know, even you don't ask me," I continue. "And in Berlin, I was very much attached to a man,

「這樣，那妳現在講嘛，」你說。

我再度火氣上升。幹嘛每次都是這樣？都要我來拜託？你心裡怎麼已經沒有半點好奇？

「好。我旅行的時候遇到幾個男的，你曉得。」

「妳說遇到幾個男的什麼意思？」

「對，一個在阿姆斯特丹，一個在柏林，一個在威尼斯，還有一個在法洛……」突然間這些面孔歷歷在目。我看見那個缺了牙的葡萄牙男人頂著正午的驕陽陪我走下髒汙的岩岸……我看見克勞斯站在柏林馬路旁邊等候公車。搞不好此刻他走進一家商店買了瓶紅星商標的礦泉水。

「還有呢？」你嚴肅起來。

「沒什麼。」

「沒什麼？」

「沒什麼大不了的。只是，我和一個只認識半小時的男的發生了關係。」

你瞪著我，臉僵住了，和我的臉僅隔四公分的距離。

「不過那次的經驗我並不喜歡，其實……」我有點心虛繼續這個故事。

你的臉沒做任何特別的表示。

突然間，我想起最近從你架上的聖經讀到一句話：「父啊！赦免他們，因為他們所做的，他們不曉得。」

「我想我應該讓你知道這件事，即便你沒問我，」我繼續。「還有在柏林，我和一個男的貼在一起，我們火車上認識的。那時候他生病……」

這時我心煩意亂，但又覺得解脫。

你從床上起身，走向廚房，光著身體。你拿水壺加了點

whom I met on the train. He was ill at that time . . ."

Now I'm upset, but at the same time I feel relieved.

You get out from the bed and walk to the kitchen, naked. You add some water into the kettle, without any words. You put some dry mint into the tea pot. Then you stand there and wait for the water to be boiled.

"So if you didn't like it, why did you do it?"

Finally, you are angry.

"Because . . . I don't like distance."

"So you have to have sex with a stranger?"

There is silence between us.

"Every time I thought you might be with another man," you say, "I thought we should leave each other."

"Why?"

"I mean I should let you go."

"Go where?"

"When I was your age, I was like you. I wanted to experience everything, and wanted to try all kinds of relationships, all kinds of sex. So I know what's going on inside you. If you stay with me, and I see you going with other men, I will be lost."

Those words, I don't want to hear. You are afraid of being lost, but I am the person in the relationship being lost first.

"But you wanted me to travel alone!" I am crying.

"Because you are young . . . too young to be so serious with me," you say. "When you were away I often imagined you with other men, but then I stopped thinking about it. Even when you told me you were pregnant, I didn't think about it."

You stand there, let the water boiling in the kettle, without

水，不發一語，又把乾薄荷放進茶壺，站在那裡等水燒開。

「如果妳不喜歡的話，為什麼要做這種事。」

終於，你生氣了。

「因為……我不喜歡跑那麼遠。」

「所以妳就要和陌生人發生關係？」

兩人沉默。

「每次想到妳可能和別的男人在一起，」你說，「我就覺得我們應該分開。」

「為什麼？」

「我的意思是，我應該放妳走。」

「走去哪兒？」

「我在妳這個年紀的時候，也跟妳一樣。我想要體驗一切，想要嘗試各式各樣的關係，各式各樣的性。所以我了解妳現在是什麼狀況。如果妳跟我在一起，又讓我看見妳有其他的男人，我會瘋掉。」

那些話，我聽都不想聽。你現在怕瘋掉，這段關係裡先瘋掉的人可是我哪。

「是你自己叫我一個人出門的！」我哭了。

「因為妳還年輕……老跟我在一起怕會悶壞，」你說。「妳不在的時候我常常想說妳會遇到別的男人，然後就不敢再想下去。即便那時候妳說懷孕了，我都不願多想。」

你站在那兒，聽任壺裡的水繼續滾沸，沒有動作。

我感覺你的寒意籠罩整間屋子。我怕。我怕你這種態度，全世界最冷的態度莫過於此。

你開始自顧喝茶。烤箱裡放了塊素食牧羊人派，我最討厭的英國食物。如此可悲的東西，徒然顯示生命何等無聊，嚼不

move.

I feel your coldness covering this house. I am afraid of you. I am afraid of this kind of manner. It is the coldest manner in the world.

You start drinking your tea. A vegeterian shepherd pie is in the oven, the kind of English food I hate. Such a sad food. A kind of food shows how boring the life is. A kind of food without any passion.

We don't talk rest of the day.

You are doing something with your sculptures. Pouring hot wax into the mould. The shape is obscure. I am watching a New Year's TV programme, an animation about a nightingale. Oscar Wilde again, but this time it is visual and vivid. The nightingale is bleeding and dying, and the red rose is abandoned by the young man. "Love is better than life," the nightingale says.

Love is better than life! Even love brings death. Is this our New Year's wish?

出一絲熱情滋味。

　　這一天我們沒再說半句話。

　　你忙著弄那些雕塑，將熱石蠟倒進澆模。難解的形狀。我觀看電視的新年特別節目，夜鶯的動畫片。又是王爾德，不過這次在眼前生動演出。夜鶯淌著血死去，鮮紅的玫瑰被年輕學生扔了。「愛情勝過生命，」那夜鶯說。

　　愛情勝過生命！即使愛情帶來死亡。這就是我們的新年希望？

infinity

n. an endless space, time or number.

When I was in the primary school, the mathematics teacher taught us to count until we were too tired to count anymore. The teacher said that the last number is "infinity" . It is a number but numberless. One can count and count until the numbers become uncountable.

Infinity, it is an uncountable future.

Here, in our kitchen and bedroom, our battle is an infinity.

"Listen," I shout. "This is serious. I need to know if I should give up my job in China to stay here with you, or if I should go back to my country." I look at my passort on the table.

"What is your job there?"

"Did you never know my job?"

"I never understood when you talked about a government work unit."

"Well, I worked in a welfare office."

"And what's that got to do with a government work unit?"

"Everybody in China has a work unit, and I don't want to lose that if I have to go back. It is a lifelong paid job. It is safe, you know. If I lose that, I have no choice except making shoes with my parents."

"OK, whatever. You can't make decisions about a relation-

【無窮】

〈名詞〉無窮盡的空間，時間，或數目。

　　唸小學的時候，數學老師要我們數數，一直數到大家沒有力氣再數下去為止。老師說最後的那個數字就是「無窮大」，它是個數字，但數不盡。人可以一直數，一直數，直到數字沒辦法再數。

　　無窮，不可數的未來。

　　這兒，廚房和臥室裡頭，我們的爭吵無窮無盡。

　　「聽好，」我吼道。「說正經的，我得弄明白到底應該放棄中國的工作和你留在這裡，還是應該回去我的國家。」我瞧著擱在桌上的護照。

　　「妳那兒做什麼工作？」

　　「你到現在還不曉得我做什麼？」

　　「妳講的政府工作單位我根本沒聽懂過。」

　　「哼，我在一家福利社上班。」

　　「那跟政府工作單位有什麼相干？」

　　「在中國人人都有工作單位，如果還要回去的話，我可不想丟掉工作。那可是我的終身飯碗，有保障的，你曉得。如果丟了工作，我只剩回家幫我爸媽做鞋子這條路了。」

　　「好啦，不管怎樣，妳不能因為自己不想失去工作就硬要拿我們兩個的關係做決定。」

ship just because you don't want to lose a job."

Indecision, that's the term belongs to you. Is that why you are unhappy with your life?

"Do you want live with me for ever?" I start again. I have to. I'm too worried.

"I cannot say that. Nothing is for ever."

"You don't believe in that concept?"

"No. Because I don't know the future, do I? I don't know what the future will be like."

"But don't you wish you will be with me in the future?"

You are in silence for three seconds. Three seconds is very long for this question. Then you answer: "The future will decide for you, not you for the future. You" re from a Buddhist country, I would have thought you would know that."

"OK. From now on we don't talk about future. All I know is: our Chinese live in the expectation. *Expectation*, is that the word close to *Future*? The farmers grow their rice in the spring, and they water it and expect it grow every day. The rice sprouts turn into green and the rice pole grow up taller. Then summer comes and the farmers look forward to grain growing bigger. Then the autumn harvest, and the grain becomes golden. Their expectation is nearly fulfilled, but not compelete. After the harvest they separate the straw and millet. The straw goes to the shepherd's pens or the pig's yard, and the millet goes to the market for sale. All this is so that a family can have better life in the winter and in the coming Spring Festival. In the winter they burn the roots and grass on the fields to nourish the soil for next year's re-plant. Everything is for the next step. So look this nature, life is about the expectation, but not about

優柔寡斷,這句就是在說你。你人生搞得如此不快莫非就這原因。

「你有想要永遠跟我在一起嗎?」我再度出擊。沒辦法,我太擔心了。

「我沒辦法那樣說。沒有東西能夠永遠。」

「你不相信那種概念?」

「不相信。因為我不知道未來,對吧?我不知道未來會變成怎樣?」

「可是難道你不希望未來還是跟我在一起?」

你停頓三秒鐘。三秒鐘對這問題而言實在太久了。接著你回答:「未來到時候自然會為妳決定,而不是妳替未來下決定。妳來自信仰佛教的國家,我會覺得妳應該能夠了解那個道理。」

「很好,從現在開始我們就不要再講未來。我所知道的是:我們中國人活在期望裡面。期望,這個字和未來的意思接近嗎?農民春天的時候播下稻種,引水灌溉,期望它每日成長。然後秧苗轉青,禾桿抽高。夏天到來,農民期待穀粒碩壯。秋天收成時節,稻穗黃澄澄的。他們的期望近乎達成,但尚未完全。稻子一割完,又忙著打穀脫粒,稻草送去羊欄或豬圈,穀粒運至市場買賣。這些辛苦只為一家人冬天能夠溫飽,過個好年。冬天時,他們焚燒田裡的殘根和雜芒來養地,留待來年重新播種。每個動作都在為下一步做準備。所以看這自然的過程,生活依據期望來努力,不是依據眼前,不是依據今天,或是今晚。所以你不能只活在今天,那樣只會把日子毀了。」

你已經把耳朵關上,忙著動手將熱蠟注入模子。三種不同

now, not about today, or tonight. So you can't only live in today, that will be the doom day."

You stop listening. You are busy pouring hot wax into a mould. There are three different moulds, one is like a brain, and another one look like an eyeball, the third one is a big nipple. After wax pouring, you are waiting for it is cooled down, so you can pull the mould away from the wax.

Your pencil drawing is on the kitchen table. A drawing, lots of human organs, lie inside of a bath. Human bone, a leg, ears, lips, eyeballs, arms, intestines . . . it is almost ugly. Actually, very ugly. But also very strong. Once you said to me you think youself are ugly, though I don't feel like that. You said you are always fascinated by ugliness, ugly people, ugly buildings, ruins, rubbish.

I raise my eyes, contemplating the plastic bath you made. It sits there, silent, holding something vague, holding something heavy.

的模子，一個像人腦，另一個像眼球，第三個像是大乳頭。灌完蠟之後，你放著等它冷卻，之後再來開模。

　　廚房餐桌上有你的鉛筆草圖。還有一張畫滿人體器官的草圖擱在澡盆裡。人的骨頭，一條腿，耳朵，嘴唇，眼球，手臂，腸子……都是醜八怪的東西。真的，非常醜怪，不過也非常有力。有一次，你說你認為自己很醜，雖然我不覺得。你說你老是被醜給迷住，醜的人，醜的房子，廢墟，垃圾堆。

　　我抬眼，凝視你做的那個塑膠澡盆。它端坐那兒，沉默，表情曖昧，沉重。

expel

v. **1.** to drive out with force; **2.** to dismiss from a school etc permanently.

Today, my government work unit calls me. Suddenly, I am dragged back to that society.

The officer in the phone say seriously, in the Communist way: "You have a contract with us. We have to warn you to come back before you do wrong things there. Don't break our rules. Return back in one month according to the rule in our work unit, otherwise you will be Kai Chu (expelled) from our organisation."

Kai Chu!

Expelled!

I am so angry that I want to throw my phone away. A year in this country, I had almost forgotten how stupid those Chinese rules are. An individual belongs to the government, but doesn't belongs to herself. Yes, I want to be expelled. Please expel me. Please. But I also know they just threaten me. They always threaten the little people, in the name of the whole nation. And you don't have a chance against it. It is like Mao's little red book, it is written in the *imperative* tone.

【開除】

〈動詞〉**1.** 驅逐，趕走；**2.** 被學校等機關開除，永久地。

　　今天，接到我的政府工作單位打來的電話。剎那間，我被拖回那個社會。

　　電話裡的長官一板一眼，標準的共產黨口氣：「妳跟我們有合約。我們必須提醒妳回來，趁妳還沒犯下錯誤之前。別破壞我們的規矩。根據我們工作單位的規定，妳得在一個月以內回來報到，否則妳將會被我們組織開除。」

　　開除！

　　趕走！

　　我氣壞了，真想把電話甩開。來這國家一年，我幾乎已經忘記那些中國規矩有多麼愚蠢。個人屬於政府所有，而非屬於她自己。沒錯，我就是想要被開除。請趕走我吧，拜託。不過，我也明白他們只是在威脅我。他們總是威脅小老百姓，打著國家整體的名義。對抗它你根本沒有機會。就像毛語錄裡面的話，它以命令的語氣寫就。

dilemma

n. a situation offering a choice between two equally undesirable alternatives.

I read this word so many times on the paper and never understand it. Now, when think about whether I should stay here or go back China, I understand this word totally.

It is a difficult word just like what it means. Dilemma. Knowing this word, I also learn these words: *paradox, contradictory, alternative.*

"If I leave this country, or say we split up, what you will do?" I ask.

"I don't want to be with another woman."

"Why?"

"I don't want to."

"Why you don't want another lover?"

"I just want to be on my own."

"Really? And you don't want to be with a man lover either?"

"No. I don't want anybody."

"Really?" I think I don't understand you.

"Really. Look, you need me, and your love is a need. But I don't need anything, and I don't need you. That's why I can be on my own."

You say: "I'd like to be a monk. I want to give up everything: the city, desire, sex. Then I can be free."

【兩難】

〈名詞〉必須在兩難中擇一的困境。

我在紙上讀過這個字許多次，老是不解其意。這下子想到究竟要留在這兒或回去中國的時候，這個字我完全懂了。

它是個困難的字彙，就跟它的意思一樣。進退兩難。認識這個字，我同時學到這幾個字彙：似非而是，矛盾，二擇一。

「如果我離開這個地方，或者說我們分開，你會怎麼辦？」我問。

「我不會想找其他的女人。」

「為什麼？」

「我不想要。」

「為什麼不想再找一個愛人？」

「我只想自己一個就好。」

「真的？你也不想跟一個男的愛人在一起？」

「不。我不想要任何人。」

「真的？」看來我還真不了解你。

「真的。妳看妳需要我，妳的愛就是一種需要。可是我什麼都不需要，而且我不需要妳。所以我才能夠自己一個。」

你說：「我想去當和尚，放棄一切東西：城市，慾望，性。那樣我就可以自由。」

「我們應該彼此放手，」你對我說。

"We should let each other go," you say to me.

"But we still love each other," I insist. How can two lovers just decide to separate while they still in love with each other?

"We should leave each other." You look at me, as it is said by a priest, a sober priest in the church.

Suddenly I feel that you have already made up your mind. And nothing can be changed. But I still remember that love song you sang to me before, under your fig trees in the garden. The lyrics and the melody are still wandering around in my ears:

It's the heart afraid of breaking
that never learns to dance

I think you only want the joyful part of love, and you dare not to face the difficult part of love. In China we say, "You can't expect both ends of a sugar cane are as sweet." Sometimes love can be ugly. But one still has to take it and swallow it.

I start to deal with my immigration papers. I have to apply for an extension of my visa. It is frustrating. I need to show my bank details to the Home Office that I have stable income to live here, but certainly I don't have any income. Everything is family supported. How much money I left in my bank? Two hundred pounds? Or one hundred and fifty pounds by tomorrow? Most importantly, I don't have any reason to stay here, except for you. And I feel confused. I want to stay but I don't know if it is the right decision. My parents" opinions now seems don't bother me very much like before. Plus, they know

「可是我們還愛著對方，」我不依。兩個人還相愛的時候怎能說分就分？

「我們應該離開對方。」你看著我，口氣有如神父，教堂中冷靜嚴肅的神父。

突然間我感覺你已經下定決心，不會再有改變。但我還記得以前你對我唱的那首情歌，就在院子裡的無花果樹下。歌詞和旋律依舊迴盪在我耳邊：

害怕破碎的心
始終學不好舞步

我覺得你只想要愛情喜悅的部分，你沒辦法面對愛情艱難的部分。我們中國人說：「你不能期望甘蔗兩頭甜。」愛情有時難免醜陋，但一個人還是應該勇於面對，承受。

開始著手處理我的移居文件，我必須申請延長簽證。處處挫折。我得拿銀行資料給內政部看，表示有穩定的收入可供這兒過活，不過當然我沒半點收入。所有東西都是家裡供給的。銀行戶頭還剩好多錢？兩百英鎊？還是到明天為止一百五十鎊？最重要的一點，我沒有任何理由再留下來，除了因為你。我好困惑。想要留下，又不曉得這個決定是否正確。爸媽的意見已經不像以前那樣左右我，況且，他們根本不清楚我在這兒的狀況。

本來以為你會給我的生命帶來一切，以為你是我的耶穌，你是我的神父，我的光。所以一直相信你是我這裡唯一的家。如此缺乏安全感只因我好怕失去你，所以才會一直想要控制你，把你綁在我的視線之內，切斷你和世界，和其他人的聯

nothing of my life here.

I thought that you would bring everything into my life. I thought you are my Jesus. You are my priest, my light. So I always believed you are my only home here. I feel so insecure because I am so scared of losing you. That's why I want to control you, I want you are in my view always and I want cut off your extension to the world and your extension to the others.

I think of those days when I travelled in Europe on my own. I met many people and finally I wasn't so afraid of being alone. Maybe I should let my life open, like a flower; maybe I should fly, like a lonely bird. I shouldn't be blocked by a tree, and I shouldn't be scared about losing one tree, instead of seeing a whole forest.

繫。

　　想起那段歐洲獨遊的日子，我和許多人相逢，最終不再那麼恐懼孤單。或許我應該敞開生命，像一朵花；或許我應該飛翔，像隻孤鳥。我不該被一棵樹綁住，不該因為害怕失去這棵樹，忘了還有整片森林等我去見識。

timing

n. **1.** the choice, judgement or control of when something should be done; **2.** a particular time when something happens.

Today I read about tense again. It is a sentence from Ibn Arabi, an old sage, a very wise man living in the early thirteenth century. He said:

The Universe continues to be in the present tense.

Does that mean English tense difference is just complicated for no reason? Does that mean tenses are not natural things at all? Does that mean love is a form that continues for ever and for ever, just like in my Chinese concept?

About *time*, what I really learned from studying English is: *time* is different with *timing*.

I understand the difference of these two words so well. I understand falling in love with the right person in the wrong timing could be the greatest sadness in a person's entire life.

You had all this of beautiful energy inside when I first met you in the cinema. But things have changed. All our fight, all your strugglings with London, all of that has made you look like a small dried fig fell from the tree.

In our garden, in the last several days, figs fall from the tree, the fruit tree without flowers. They didn't grow or ripen during the summer, but they can't go through winter either. They are

【時機】

〈名詞〉**1.** 選擇，判斷，或控制某件事進行的時機；**2.** 某件事發生的特定時刻。

今天又是研究時態。這句話是伊本・阿拉比講的，一位古代哲人，十三世紀初的智者。他說：

宇宙萬物持續活在現在式裡。

這意思是說英語複雜的時態變化其實毫無道理？時態根本不算自然現象？這是否意味愛情在形式上會一直不斷地延續，就像我的中國觀念那樣？

關於時間，我從英語課裡真正學到的是：時間和時機不一樣。

我已經完全能夠理解這兩個字的差別所在。我了解到在錯誤的時機愛上意中人會成為一輩子最大的悲哀。

最初在戲院相逢之時，你擁有無比動人的內在能量。然而事過境遷，我們的爭吵，你和倫敦的掙扎折騰，凡此總總，讓你看起來有如一枚落地許久的乾癟小無花果。

我們的庭院裡，就在過去幾天，無花果紛紛從樹上墜落，沒有花的果樹。夏天時它們並未長大或成熟，然而還是躲不過寒冬。它們小小顆的，發育不全，青綠，皺縮成一團，像個未曾有過青春歡樂的小老頭。那些無花果表皮布滿小皺紋，神色

tiny, immature, greenish, and shrinking like an old man without a happy youth. Those figs are full of small wrinkles on the skin. They look very sad. In the morning, you walk to the garden, pick up those figs from the soil, and your palms are full of dirt and pity.

I remember those days when we first met. Then, the figs grew lively. I remember you once opened a big soft fig to show me the seeds inside. It was pink and delicate inside, and you would let me suck those sweet juice . . . Now it is winter, the time of dying, our hard time.

You see those tiny figs drop from the tree to the dirt, and you pick up them one by one. You come back to the kitchen and put these tiny green round things on the table, the table which we use for chopping vegetables, the table you always read newspapers, and the table which I use to study English and do my homework every night.

One, two, three, four, five, six, seven, eight, nine, ten, eleven, twelve . . . There are seventeen tiny figs on the kitchen table now. They are quiet, obscure, plain, and anonymous. They want say something to me, but eventually they are tired. They are dried up by the seasons, just like you.

I see your beauty is being diminished, by me. Day by day. Night by night.

哀戚。一大早起來，你走進院子，撿起地上的落果，手裡捧著塵土和那些小可憐。

還記得初認識的日子，無花果一派生氣蓬勃。記得有次你剝開好大一枚軟熟的果子，讓我看裡面的細籽。果子內壁粉紅幼嫩，你讓我吸吮那些蜜汁……如今冬天到來，死亡的季節，我們的艱困時刻。

看著那些小無花果從樹枝掉落泥地，你一個一個撿起它們，回到廚房，將這些綠色圓滾的小東西擺在桌上，那張桌子，我們在上面切青菜，你習慣坐那兒看報紙，每晚我利用它來讀英語，寫作業。

一，二，三，四，五，六，七，八，九，十，十一，十二……這會兒總共有十七枚小小的無花果擺在廚房桌上。它們安靜，卑微，平庸，無名無姓。它們有話想要對我講，但終歸無力訴說。它們逃不過季節而凋萎，和你一樣。

眼見你的美麗點滴消磨，都是我害的。日復一日。夜復一夜。

February

contradiction

n. **1.** a combination of statements, ideas, or features which are opposed to one another; **2.** the statement of a position opposite to one already made.

You always live in the middle of two realities. You want to be able to make the art work, but at the same time you don't value it. You want to be away from London, to settle down in a pure and natural place, with mountain and sea, but at the same time you are obsessed to communicate with the society.

Sometimes, we go out for a walk. We walk in the Victoria Park, or we will walk from Broadway Market Street through London Fields. Your pale face is hidden in your old brown leather jacket, and your cheeks tell the pains with no name.

Sometimes I can't help to kiss you, to soften you, to cheer you up. You walk slower than before, slow just like we are a real old aged couple. You are struggling with yourself.

"Do you want to come to China with me?" Again, I invite you. And for the last time, I invite you.

You stop walking and look at me. "Yes. But I don't know if I want to travel anymore. I need to stop *drifting*."

London Fields is in yellow grey. The maple trees are naked. No more children playing around. I wonder if I will be able to see this grass again, coming out in the next spring.

In Hackney Town Hall Library we sit and look at books. Gustave Flaubert said, "In Pericles's time, the Greeks devot-

【矛盾】

〈名詞〉**1.** 相互牴觸的聲明，構想，或特徵；**2.** 立場前後不一致。

　　你永遠活在兩種現實之間。你打算投入藝術創作，但又瞧不起這個工作。你希望遠離倫敦，找個純粹自然的地方安身，擁有山海景觀，但同時又捨不得脫離社會交流往來。

　　偶爾，我們外出散步。我們走進維多利亞公園，或者從布洛德維市場街一路走過倫敦體育場。你蒼白的臉躲在咖啡色老皮夾克裡，兩頰訴說著莫名的痛苦。

　　有時忍不住我會親你，讓你別那麼緊繃，逗你開心。你的腳步比以前緩慢，慢到我們簡直就像一對老夫妻。你就是和自己過不去。

　　「你想跟我一起回中國嗎？」我再度邀請你。這次開口是最後一次了。

　　你停下腳步，看著我。「想。但我不曉得自己還想遠渡重洋嗎？我應該停止漂泊了。」

　　倫敦體育場一片黃灰。楓樹禿光了。見不到那些戲耍的小朋友。我沒把握來春時節，是否能再觀賞這裡的綠地。

　　在哈克尼市立圖書館，我們歇腳瀏覽書籍。

　　古斯塔夫・福樓拜說：「在伯里克利斯的時代，希臘人獻身藝術，不顧明天麵包從何而來。讓我們以希臘人為榜樣！」

ed themselves to art without knowing where the next day's bread might come from. Let us be Greeks!"

I close the Flaubert book, looking at you. You are reading a book with the picture of sculptures. I keep thinking about Flaubert's words: artists should devote themself to the art, like a priest devote to God. But what is so important about art? Why it should be like a devotion?

"How come art can be more important than food?" I ask you in a little voice.

"I agree with you, actually." You close up sculpture book. "I don't think art is so important. But art is fashionable in the West. Everybody wants to be an artist. Artists are like models. That's why I hate it."

You put the book back on shelf.

"But," I protest, "you are like a Chinese saying: *piercing your shield with your spear*. You are contradicting with yourself. You are making art too. So it means art is also a need, a necessary of expression."

"Yes, but if I had better things to do I would give up making art. I would rather do something more solid."

I'm confused.

I'd like to dedicate my life to do something serious, maybe things like writing, or painting, but definitely not making shoes. I don't care what you said about artists. I'd like to write about you, one day. I'd like to write about this country. People say one should separate one's real life from one's art work, and one should protect his real life from his fiction life. So one can has less pain, and be able to see the world soberly. But I think it is a very selfish attitude. I like what Flaubert said about

闔上福樓拜，注視著你。你正閱讀一本雕塑圖集。我心裡反覆尋思福樓拜的話：藝術家應該為藝術獻身，就像神父侍奉上帝一樣。但藝術何以如此重要？為什麼要到奉獻的地步？

「藝術怎麼可能會比食物還重要？」我壓低聲音問你。

「我的看法跟妳一樣，說真的。」你闔上雕塑集。「我不認為藝術有那麼了不起。不過藝術在西方很風行，人人想當藝術家，搞得藝術家就像模特兒。所以我才受不了。」

你將書放回架上。

「可是，」我抗議，「你就像一句中國成語說的：以子之矛攻子之盾。你自相矛盾。你自己就是做藝術的，所以顯然藝術同樣出自一種需要，表達的需要。」

「沒錯，不過要是有其他東西好搞，我就會放棄做藝術。要是有牢靠一點的東西就好了。」

我聽得迷迷糊糊。

我會想要奉獻生命正正經經做點事情，像是寫作，或是繪畫，但絕不會是做鞋。我不在乎你對藝術家的評論。總有一天，我會寫出你的故事。我想寫點這個國家的東西。人家說一個人的真實生活應該和藝術作品分開，而且真實生活也不該和虛構人生混淆。那樣比較能夠避免痛苦，面對世界的時候才能保持清醒。不過，我覺得這種態度其實蠻自私的。我喜歡福樓拜對於希臘人的意見。如果你是真正的藝術家，那人生的一切其實都是你藝術的組成部分。藝術等於生命的紀念碑。藝術是日常存在的抽象表現。

再一次，姥姥口中的佛語告訴我：「包圍我們周遭的現實並非真實。那是生之虛幻。」

Greeks. If you are a real artist, everything in your life is part of your art. The art is a memorial of the life. Art is the abstract way of his daily existence.

Again the Buddhist in my grandmother's voice tells me: "The reality that surrounds us is not real. It is the illusion of life."

fatalism

n. the belief that all events are predetermined and people are powerless to change their destinies.

A film called *Saturday Night and Sunday Morning*, directed by Karel Reisz at 1960s. This is the last film we will see together. This is the last film I will see in London.

The beautiful young man in the film, played by Albert Finney. He is too beautiful for a humble working-class life. He is wild, he wants to play and to have fun. But of course he is also a trouble maker. He gets bored by having an affair with a married woman, and he doesn't want to take any responsibility. So he starts to chase young girls. But after a while he bored again with one young girl, she means nothing to him except for her brief beauty. Womans don't weigh anything in his restless heart. He is bored of physical work, and of unimaginative youth. He becomes frustrated because he gains nothing from searching for the excitements of life. His beauty decays. His youthful energy fades away by the end of the film.

Is your life a bit like him? Have you felt the same way as that young man felt about womans or family? I gaze at your back, your brown hair and your brown leather jacket. We walk along the night street in South Kensington. Again, how familiar, this is the place we first met. It has been one year.

We stop in front of a little corner shop to buy some samosa. The shop is about to close.

【宿命論】

〈名詞〉相信凡事皆已事先注定，人無力改變命運。

　　有部電影叫《週六夜與週日晨》（譯按：台譯《浪子春潮》），卡雷爾‧瑞茲一九六〇年代導的片子。這將是我們共同觀賞的最後一部電影。我在倫敦看的最後一部電影。

　　電影裡頭那個漂亮的青年，亞伯特‧芬尼演的。那股帥勁對底層的工人階級生活而言，委實不太相襯。年少輕狂的他一心只想玩樂，當然免不了闖出大小禍端。他厭倦了和一位人妻的風流韻事，又不想擔負任何責任，便開始追求其他的年輕小姐。但興頭一過，他又對這位小姐厭倦，除了美貌的短暫吸引，她在他眼中其實可有可無。心定不下來，女人再多也救不了他。厭倦了賣力氣的工作，厭倦無聊的青春。一味追求刺激的生活，到頭來抵不過空虛而挫折。他的俊美衰敗，所有的青春活力於片尾終了消逝無蹤。

　　你的人生是否和他有點類似？你對女人或家庭是否和那年輕的主角有同樣的感慨？我注視你的背影，你的棕髮和咖啡色皮夾克。我們沿著南肯辛頓夜晚的街道漫步。再度地，多麼熟悉，這是你我初次相逢的場景。已經一年了。

　　我們在轉角一家小店駐足，買印度炸荸薺吃。小店準備收攤了。

　　「你不覺得他可以愛那個結婚的女人？」我問。

"So you don't think he can love that married woman?" I ask.

I am still living in the film.

"No." You take two cold vegetarian samosa from the shop-keeper.

"And, you don't think he can love that young girl either?"

"No. None of them love each other. No love exists between them," you comment. "They are loveless."

I bite the cold samosa. Ah. Loveless.

"What you will do if you were the man in the film?" I don't let you go.

"I would leave the town, just like I left Lower End Farm. Things are dead and finished in that town."

I stop eating samosa. One more thing I need to know: "Why you don't want to be with that young woman either? She is young, and pretty and simple. They can be together for the rest of their lifes."

"Because she demonstrated how limited she is at the end of the film. Remember the last scene? When they sit on the hill looking down on the suburb, and she says to him that one day they will live in one of those houses? He listens to her and throws the stone down the hill."

"Why a house, or a home, is a boring thing?"

"Because . . ."

You stop. You don't want to explain anymore. Maybe you know you are being unreasonable.

We arrive at home at midnight. The little street is dead quiet, and the house is dead cold. We are so tired; nobody wants to

253

我還沉浸在電影當中。

「不。」你從老闆手中接過兩個涼掉的炸素餃。

「還有，你也不覺得他可以愛那個年輕的小姐？」

「不。他們沒有一個人相愛。他們彼此之間沒有愛情存在，」你下斷語。「他們得不到愛的。」

我咬了口冷餃子。噢，得不到愛。

「如果你是電影裡面那個男的，你會怎麼做？」我不放過你。

「我會離開那小鎮，像我離開低尾農場一樣。那地方的東西都已經死掉，完蛋。」

我放下炸素餃，還有件事想弄清楚：「為什麼你也不想跟那個年輕小姐在一起？她那麼年輕，漂亮又單純。他們可以攜手共度往後的人生。」

「因為電影末尾她已經表現出自己有多麼狹隘。記得最後一幕？他們一起坐在山丘上俯望郊區，她對他說有天他們也會在那些房子裡面有個家？聽了她的話，他朝底下猛力扔石頭。」

「為什麼房子或家，會是無聊的東西？」

「因為……」

你沒往下講，不想再多做解釋。大概你曉得自己也講不出什麼道理。

我們午夜才到家。小小的街道一片死寂，房子冷得要命。我們累壞了；沒人有力氣再費唇舌。愛情和人生的話題再討論下去，結果如何我們心中雪亮。所以放棄就好，不用開口。

接著，我領會到此刻便是週六夜與週日晨。一個命中注定

have further discussion. We know clearly how far we could reach if we carry on the discussion about love and life. We both give up, without saying it.

Then I realise it is indeed Saturday night and Sunday morning. A doom night and a doom morning. An absolutely doom moment in my life. There is a special delivery letter sitting on the kitchen table waiting for me. You got it this morning. My heart is racing, racing badly. No, I shouldn't open this letter. It is from Home Office.

It is you who open it. You read it, and give it to me, without any words.

There is a black stamp on the page twenty-two of my passport, from IMMIGRATION & NATIONALITY DIRECTORATE of Home Office. It is a pentagonal stamp. Pentagon, a strange shape. Only the Pentagon near Washington has that strange shape. It is a doom stamp.

The application for my extension of UK visa has been refused.

Once you told me I am an *agnostic*, or maybe even a sceptic, but now I proof myself that actually I am a *fatalist*, like lots of Asian people are. The result of my visa application is in my expectation. Not because I am being a *pessimist*, just because I know there is no actual reason for both me and authority to extend this visa. I already knew this when I prepared my paperwork. I say there is no reason, I mean even you: you can't be my reason to stay in this country. And you can't save my life. You, a possible Anarchist, always want to be free.

I put my passport back in a drawer. I sit down, switch on the

的夜與晨。不折不扣就是我人生命中注定的時刻。一封掛號信躺在廚房桌上等我。你今天早上收到的。我的心臟狂跳，狂跳不止。不要，我不能拆開這封信。內政部寄來的。

結果信是你拆的。你讀了，遞給我，沒說半句話。

我的護照第二十二頁上頭有個黑印，內政部移民與國籍局蓋的。五角形的戳印。五角形，好怪的形狀。只有華盛頓附近的五角大廈形狀如此奇怪。命中注定的戳印。

我申請延長英國簽證被拒絕。

有一次你說我是不可知論者，或甚至是懷疑論者，但這下我已經證明自己其實是宿命論者，像多數的亞洲人那樣。簽證申請結果早在我的預料之中。並非我已成為悲觀主義者，而是因為我很清楚自己和有關當局都找不到確切的理由延長這份簽證。其實準備文件資料的時候我已經了然於胸。我說沒有任何理由的意思也包括你在內：你沒辦法成為我留在這個國家的理由。而且你沒辦法拯救我的人生。你，一個恰如其分的安那其，永遠想要自由自在。

將護照放回抽屜，我坐下來，開了燈，打開筆記本。我瀏覽上禮拜學到的所有字彙。接著，我將抵達這國家第一天起學過的全部生字和片語逐一讀過：外國人，住宿處，全套英式早餐，妥當，霧，汙水（事實上是氣泡水，現在我知道了）……這麼多的字詞。過去一年我學了好多好多。筆記本裡的字彙，一天天地，變得越來越複雜，越來越通暢。

翻啟新的一頁，空白的頁面；我寫下電影片名《週六夜與週日晨》。手中握住的筆帶有憤怒，和深沉的失望──氣我自己命運如此，怪你讓我失望透頂。

lamp and open my notebook. I look at all the words I learned in the last week. Then I look at all the words I learned since the first day I arrived in this country: *Alien, Hostel, Full English Breakfast, Properly, Fog, Filthy Water* (actually fizzy water, now I know) . . . So many words. So much I learned in the passed year. The vocabularies on my notebook, day by day, become more and more complicated, and more and more sophisticated.

I open a new page, a blank page; I start to write down the film title *Saturday Night and Sunday Morning.* The pen holds in my hand with the anger, and deep disappointment—the anger about my fate, the disappointment about you.

"What are you writing?" You stand in the opposite corner of the room, staring at me.

I don't want to answer.

"I know what you are writing, actually."

You voice sounds vague. Not only vague, but also cold.

You turn your back and throw me the last sentence before we go to bed:

"AT LEAST YOU'RE STILL LEARNING A LOT. EVEN IF EVERYTHING IS BROKEN."

You voice horrifies me.

You leave me, and disappear into the bedroom.

「妳在寫什麼?」你站在對面角落,注視著我。

我不想回答。

「其實,妳寫什麼我知道。」

你的聲音聽起來沒有表情。不只沒有表情,還很冷酷。

你轉身,拋給我睡前最後一句話:

「至少妳還是有學到很多,即使一切破滅。」

你的聲音讓我驚愣。

你離開,消失於臥室當中。

race

n. **1.** a contest of speed; **2.** any competition or rivalry, e.g. the arms race; **3.** a rapid current or channel.

"Life is a race against time." My father always says so: "Wasting time is shameful, just like leave the grain rotten in fields."

"An inch of time is an inch of gold, but you can't buy that inch of time with an inch of gold."

After all these education, I believed time was the most expensive thing in the world. When I was a teenager in the middle school, I dared not waste just even twenty minutes to play around. Staring at blue sky having daydream is a fool. Sleeping on the grass under the sun is a lazy cow, without producing milk for the people. Wasting time will earn nothing back in the future. But here, in this country, people spent whole afternoon having a pot of tea, and spent hours having a piece of cheese cake, and a whole night to drink beers in the pub. If life is a race against time, why people pay so much attention on tea and cake and beer?

"You are too anxious. Try to relax. Try to enjoy life." You say it to me, on the way back from Wales to London.

If life is a race against time, like my father and my teacher said, then life itself must be a very aggressive thing. There is no peace and no relaxation in a race. And one's life would never win anything in the end. Because whatever effort one

【競賽】

〈名詞〉**1.** 速度競賽；**2.** 任何競爭或對抗，如武器競賽；**3.** 急流，水道。

「人活著是在和時間賽跑。」我父親的口頭禪：
「浪費時間最要不得，跟田裡的稻穀放給它爛沒兩樣。」
「一寸光陰一寸金，寸金難買寸光陰。」

經過這番耳提面命，我相信時間是世界上最昂貴的東西。十幾歲唸中學的時候，我連二十分鐘都不敢浪費輕鬆。望著藍天做白日夢的都是傻瓜。躺在草地上晒太陽是條懶母牛，沒盡到產奶餵人的責任。時間一浪費，就別指望將來會有收穫。不過這裡，在這個國家，人們整個下午的時間拿來喝茶，一塊起司蛋糕吃掉兩三個鐘頭，整晚泡在酒吧猛灌啤酒。如果活著是和時間賽跑，大家怎有這許多閒情逸致關心茶和蛋糕和啤酒？

「妳太緊張了。放輕鬆點，享受一下生活。」從威爾斯回倫敦的路上，你對我這麼說。

如果活著是和時間賽跑，如我父親和老師所言，那生命本身想必侵略性十足。比賽當中可沒有時間讓你休息輕鬆。而且，人的一生到頭來什麼東西也贏不到。因為不論如何努力，時間總是在你身邊亦步亦趨。人總有一天會停下腳步，讓時間領頭遠去。我父親錯了，我想。這裡人家可沒有那樣過日子。

而你又如何呢，吾愛？生活於你似乎和競賽沾不上邊。因為你已決定搬離都市人群，住到大自然裡，和山海森林為伍。

makes, time always parallels passing the one. The one will eventually stop racing one day, let time goes by. My father is wrong, I think. People here they don't live like that.

And what about you, my lover? Life to you seems not a race at all. Because you already decide not living in the towns and society, but living in the nature, living with the sea and the mountain and the forest. So there will be no more social struggle to you anymore. So you can achieve peace. You talk slow and walk slow, you let the time pass by you, because you don't want to be in a race. So you won't lose, in the end.

And here it comes to the fate. I met you; a man was born in the year of Rat. A rat never has a stable home, like me, born the year of the goat. Two unstable animals, two homeless things. It won't work. It is our destiny.

In China, we say: *"There are many dreams in a long night."* It has been a long night, but I don't know if I want to continue the dreams. It feels like I am walking on a little path, both sides are dark mountains and valleys. I am walking towards a little light in the distance. Walking, and walking, I am seeing that light diminishing. I am seeing myself walk towards the end of the love, the sad end.

I love you more than I loved you before. I love you more than I should love you. But I must leave. I am losing myself. It is painful that I can't see myself. It is time for me to say those words, those words you kept telling me recently. "Yes, I agree with you. We can't be together."

所以你再也無須和社會拚搏了。你可以得到寧靜。你可以放慢講話和走路的速度，任憑時間從身邊超越，因為你不想參與這場競賽。所以你沒什麼東西好輸的，即便終點到來。

而此刻命運已至。我和你相遇；一個鼠年出生的男人。老鼠不可能安穩成家，就像我，羊年出生的也是。兩隻沒辦法安定的動物，與家無緣的小東西。此路不通，只能說你我命運如此。

在中國，我們說：「夜長夢多。」這真是漫漫長夜，但我不曉得自己是否還想繼續做夢。感覺有如走在一條羊腸小道，兩邊是黑漆漆的高山和溪谷。我向遠處的一絲光線摸索前進。走著走著，眼看那光芒黯淡，熄滅。眼看自己一步步走向愛的盡頭，感傷的終點。

此刻我比以前更愛你，我的愛超過自己的限度。但該走的還是要走，我失魂落魄，疼痛不能自已。時候到了，換我對你說出口，說出你最近不斷對我講的話。「對，你說得沒錯，我們沒辦法在一起。」

departure

n. the action or an instance of departing.

Dear Student, Welcome to London! On finishing our course, you will find yourself speaking and thinking in your new language quite effortlessly. You will be able to communicate in a wide variety of situations, empowered by the ability to create your own sentences and use language naturally.

This is what language school leaflet says. Is it true? Perhaps. Mrs. Margaret tells me she is proud of me speaking English like this among her other students. When our last lesson finished, I finally pluck up my courage and run after her:

"Mrs. Margaret, can I ask you a question?"

"Of course you can." She smiles.

"Where did you normally buying your shoes?"

"Where do I normally buy my shoes?" she corrects me."Why? Do you like them?" She looks down her shoes. It is a coffee-colour, high-heel shoes, with a shining metal buckle in front.

"Yes," I reply.

"Thank you. I bought them from Clarks."

"Oh." I remember there is a shoes shop in Tottenham Court Road called Clarks.

Mrs. Margaret intends to leave.

【離開】

〈名詞〉離開，起程。

親愛的同學，歡迎來到倫敦！完成我們的課程之後，你將發現自己能夠輕鬆自如地使用新的語言來談話及思考。你可以在各種不同的情境下與人溝通，具備足夠的能力創造自己的語句並且靈活運用語言。

　　這是語言學校傳單上面講的。此話當真？或許吧。瑪格麗特小姐誇獎說我講的英語就像這樣，和其他學生相比。當我們最後一堂課結束，我終於鼓起勇氣趕上她：

　　「瑪格麗特小姐，能請教妳一個問題嗎？」

　　「當然可以。」她面露微笑。

　　「妳一直都在哪裡買鞋子？」

　　「我一向都在哪裡買鞋？」她糾正我。「怎麼了？妳喜歡嗎？」她朝下打量她的鞋子。一雙咖啡色高跟鞋，鞋面有個亮眼的金屬釦環。

　　「喜歡，」我回答。

　　「謝謝。我在克拉克買的。」

　　「噢。」想起來了，圖騰罕路有家鞋店就叫克拉克。

　　瑪格麗特小姐準備要走。

　　「跟妳說，瑪格麗特小姐，我父母親是做鞋子的。」

"You know, Mrs. Margaret, my parents are shoemakers."

"Oh, really? Well, I know China produces goods for the whole world . . ." She smiles another time. "Anyway, good luck with your studies. I hope to see you again."

"Thank you." I smile to her as well.

"By the way, it is not right to call me Mrs. Margaret. You should say Mrs. Watkinson, or just Margaret. All right?"

"All right, Margaret." I lower down my voice.

"Bye."

"Bye."

I like her, in the end.

When a woman is leaving her man, when a woman finally decides her departure,

Does she still need to water the plants every day?

Does she still need to wait until the spring, until seeing the flowers come out in his garden, probably in two weeks? Or in three weeks?

Does she still need to wash his shirts, socks and jeans? Check all his pockets before washing them?

Does she still need to cook food every evening before he comes back? Soup, or rice? Or salad? Or noodles? Or just leave everything uncooked in the fridge? Like those days when he was a bachelor?

Does she still need to wash the dishes, and sweep the floor?

Does she still kiss him? When he comes back through the evening door?

Does she still prepare the hot water for him and pour refreshing bath oil in the hot water at night?

「哦，真的？嗯，我知道中國幫全世界生產東西⋯⋯」她再度露出微笑的臉。「不管怎樣，祝妳學的東西帶來好運，希望有機會能再見面。」

「謝謝妳。」我也對她微笑。

「順便一提，叫我瑪格麗特小姐是不對的。妳應該說韋金生小姐，或瑪格麗特就好。好嗎？」

「好的，瑪格麗特。」我聲音壓低。

「再見。」

「再見。」

我喜歡她，最後可以這麼說。

當女人準備離開她的男人，當女人終於下定決心離去。

她還要每天幫植物澆水嗎？

她還得清洗他的襯衫、襪子和牛仔褲嗎？清洗之前還得將口袋一一查看？

每天晚上繼續煮飯等他回家？或者全部東西擱在冰箱別管？就像他以前單身漢的日子？

她還得洗碗掃地嗎？

繼續給他親吻？當他晚上開門進來。

還會想要和他親熱嗎？

她會哭嗎，當她感覺自己的身體需要有人體貼溫暖，但不是這一個，不是此刻躺在她身邊的這個人？

她會說出口嗎，我要離開你了，就在某一天？就在某一時？就在某一刻？

她可會僱車或叫一輛計程車，在他弄清狀況之前將自己的家當全部帶走？

Does she still lie down beside him when he suffers migraine every two days? Or even worse, every single day?

Does she still touch his skinny body? Using her soft hand? Stroke his naked arm? His naked chest? His naked belly? And his naked legs?

Does she still want to make love with him?

Does she, or will she cry, when she feels her body needs somebody to cover it and warm it, but not this one, the one lies beside hers?

Does she, or will she say, I am leaving you, on a particular day? Or at a particular time? Or in a particular moment?

Does she, or will she hire a car or a taxi, to take all her things before he understands what's happening?

Does she, or will she cry, cry loudly, when she starts leading her head to a new life, a life without anybody waiting for her and without anybody lighting a fire for her?

The telephone rings. The Chinatown travel agency tells me my air tickets are ready to pick up. I take all my money and I put on my coat. On the way out, I pass by your sculpture. It is nearly finished. All the pieces of the body lie jumbled at bottom of plastic bath.

I come out from the house, you are standing in the garden and watering the plants. You stand still, holding the hose, with your back towards me. The brown of your leather jacket is refusing me, or maybe avoiding me. I think you don't want to see me leaving. I think you are angry. Water from the hose in hard stream straight on the plants. For a long time you don't move. I am waiting. I look up at the grey sky. I want to tell you

她會哭嗎，放聲大哭，當她孤身踏上新的人生，不再有人等她，不再有人為她生火取暖？

　　電話鈴響。中國城的旅行社來電說我的機票可以過去拿了。我拿好全部的錢，穿上外套。出門時，經過你的雕塑。幾乎快要完工了。全部的身體零件胡亂堆在塑膠澡盆底部。

　　我走出戶外，你正在院子裡幫植物澆水。你站得挺直，手持水管，背對著我。皮夾克的咖啡色對我散發抗拒，或者可能是閃躲。我想你是不願意看著我出門。我想你在生氣。強力的水柱直接沖刷那些植物。良久，你一動不動。我等著，仰望灰濛濛的天空，想對你說這是冬季，或許你今天無須幫它們澆水。但我什麼也沒說，走了出去，腳步遲疑，安靜。正要掩上庭院的門時，我聽見你的聲音。

　　「等等，這個拿去。」

　　我回身，看見你從土裡拔起一小束雪花蓮。你捧著那些白色小花向我走來。

　　「給妳。」

　　我接過雪花蓮，凝視手中的花朵。它們如此嬌嫩，以致在我掌心的溫熱裡便已開始凋萎。

it is winter. I want to tell you maybe you don't need to water the plants today. But I don't say anything. I walk out, hesitate, quiet. When I try to close the garden's door, I hear your voice:

"Here, take these."

I turn back. I see you pulling out a small bunch of snow-drops from the soil. You hold out those little white flowers and walk towards me.

"For you."

I take the snowdrops. I gaze at the flowers in my hand. So delicate, they are already wilting in the heat of my palm.

Afterwards

epilogue

n. a short speech or poem at the end of a literary work, esp. a play.

Day 1

It's a big aeroplane, with so many seats, so many passengers. Air China, with the phoenix tail drawn on the side. This time, it takes me east. Which direction is the wind blowing now, I wonder? Coming to England was not easy, but going back is much harder. I look at the window and it reflects a stranger's face. It's not the same "Z" as one year ago. She will never look at the world in the same way. Her heart is wounded, wounded, wounded, like the nightingale bleeding on the red rose.

The lights are on again. A Chinese steward smiles at me, and serves my second meal: rice with fried pork and some broccoli. It is hot, and sticky. As my body slowly digests the rice, I understand, deeply, in my bones: we are indeed separated.

People say nowadays there are no more boundaries between nations. Really? The boundary between you and me is so broad, so high.

When I first saw you, I felt I saw another me, a me against me, a me which I contradicted all the time. And now I cannot forget you and I cannot stop loving you because you are a part

【尾聲】

〈名詞〉文學作品（特別是戲劇）結尾的短語或詩。

1 天

　　大型航空客機，好多座位，好多乘客。中國航空，機身繪有鳳凰彩尾。這一回，它載我飛向東方。此刻風往哪個方向吹，我納悶？幾經波折來到英國，如今回去更是辛苦。我瞧著窗戶，一張陌生的臉映照。那已經不是一年之前的那個「Z」。她對世界的看法再也無法回到從前。她的心受了傷，一傷再傷，像那夜鶯淌血將玫瑰染紅。

　　燈光再度亮起。一位中國空服員對我微笑，送來第二餐：米飯配紅燒肉和甘藍菜。熱燙，黏稠。米飯在體內慢慢消化，我深深地了解到，打從骨子裡：我們確實已經分離。

　　人家說時至今日，國家與國家之間不再有界限。當真？你和我之間的界限何其寬，何其高。

　　最初和你相遇之時，感覺看見另一個我，一個和自己作對的我，老是和我產生矛盾的我。如今我對你無法忘懷，我無法停止愛你，你已經成為我的一部分。

　　不過，或許這些都是廢話，西洋哲學廢話。你我未能結合純屬命中注定，我們命運如此，緣分盡了。

　　十三個鐘頭之後，我們降落北京。我花了一整天在城裡四處閒逛。蒙古沙漠吹來的風沙襲擊自行車、草木、屋頂車頂。

of me.

But, maybe all this is just nonsense, Western philosophical nonsense. We can't be together just because that is our fate, our destiny. We have no yuan fen.

Thirteen hours later, we touch down in Beijing. I spend day walking around the city. The sandy wind from the Mongol desert drags through bicycles, trees, roofs. No wonder people are much stronger and tougher here. The whole city is dusty and messy. Unfinished skeletons of skyscrapers and naked construction sites fill the horizon. The taxi drivers spit loudly on to the road through their open windows. Torn plastic bags are stuck on trees like strange fruits. Pollution, pollution, great pollution in my great country.

I call my mother. I tell her I have decided to leave my hometown job and move to Beijing. She is desperate. Sometimes I wish I could kill her. Her power control, for ever, is just like this country.

"Are you stupid or something?" she shouts at me in the telephone. "How will you live without a proper job?"

I try to say something:

"But I can speak little bit English now, so maybe I can find a job where I use my English, or perhaps I will try to write something . . ."

She strikes back immediately: "Writing on paper is a piece of nothing compared with a stable job in a government work unit! You think you can reshape your feet to fit new shoes? How are you going to live without government medical insurance? What if I die soon? And what if your father dies as well?"

莫怪這裡的老百姓一個比一個強悍。整個北京城灰撲撲的，亂成一團。放眼望去，盡是尚未完工的摩天大樓鋼骨和裸露的工地。計程車司機開窗使勁啐出響痰。穿洞的塑膠袋黏在樹上，像奇異的果實。汙染，汙染，我的國家偉大，汙染也跟著越來越大。

我打電話給母親，告訴她我已經決定辭掉家鄉的工作，搬到北京來住。她氣瘋了。有時真希望能殺了她。她的權威掌握一切，永遠如此，跟這國家好像。

「妳腦子壞了不成？」她在電話裡吼道。「妳沒像樣的工作靠什麼生活？」

我想辦法分辯幾句：

「可是我現在能講一點英語，或許可以靠英語找個事情來做，要不然也可以寫點東西……」

她馬上回我：「報紙寫個什麼玩意怎麼跟政府工作單位的鐵飯碗比！妳以為腳削一削就塞得進新鞋嗎？少了政府的醫療保險，看妳到時候怎麼活命？如果我有個三長兩短怎麼辦？如果你爸爸也跟著死了呢？」

她老是威脅隔天就要去死。這招一使出來，除了閉嘴我還能怎樣。

「妳就存心等那兔子自己拿頭去撞樹，半點力氣不花就能撿現成便宜？！真不明白現在年輕人怎麼想的。妳爸爸跟我忙得跟狗一樣，妳到現在腦袋還不曉得清醒。妳白日夢也該做完了，幫妳自己找個合適的工作和像樣的男人。趁妳爸爸和我還有一口氣在，趕緊嫁人，孩子生一生！」

當我保持沉默，沒吭聲頂撞之下，她丟下最後一道批評：

「曉得妳的毛病在哪兒：妳從不考慮將來！妳只顧活在當

She always threatens to die the next day. Whenever it comes to this deadly subject, I can only keep my mouth shut.

"Are you waiting for rabbits to knock themselves out on trees, so you can catch them without any effort?! I don't understand young people today. Your father and I have worked like dogs, but you haven't even woken up yet. Well, it's time you stopped daydreaming and found yourself a proper job and a proper man. Get married and have children before your father and I are dead!"

As I keep silent and don't counter her, she throws me her final comment:

"You know what your problem is: you never think of the future! You only live in the present!"

And she bursts into tears.

Day 100

During my year of absence, Beijing has changed as if ten years passed. It has become unrecognisable.

I am sitting in a Starbucks cafe in a brand new shopping centre, a large twenty-two-storey mall with a neon sign in English on its roof: *Oriental Globe*. Everything inside is shining, as if they stole all the lights and jewels from Tiffany's and Harrod's. In the West there is "Nike" and our Chinese factories make "Li Ning", after an Olympic champion. In the West there is "Puma" and we have "Poma". The style and design are exactly the same. The West created "Chanel no. 5" for Marilyn Monroe. For our citizens we make "Chanel no. 6" jasmine perfume. We have everything here, and more.

下！」

說著說著她就哭了。

100 天

我不在的這一年，北京變化之大有如悠悠十年已過，教人難以辨認。

坐在一家新開幕購物中心的星巴克咖啡館裡，二十二層樓的大型賣場，樓頂有座英語的霓虹招牌：東方全球。賣場裡頭全部的東西都閃閃發亮，他們好像把第凡內珠寶和哈洛德百貨的燈光和裝飾品全偷來這了。西方有「耐吉」，我們中國的工廠一次奧林匹克奪冠之後就做出「李寧」。西方有「彪馬」，我們有「波馬」，款式設計絲毫不差。西方為瑪麗蓮·夢露打造「香奈兒五號」，為了廣大的市民群眾我們創造了「香奈兒六號」茉莉香水。我們這裡什麼都有，比別人有的還多。

晚上，幾個朋友帶我去一間卡拉OK。這種地方跟我不合。中國男人對家裡的黃臉婆生厭才跑來這裡找樂子。空盪的房間，緊身迷你裙的年輕小姐半露酥胸，等候無聊人士上門唱歌。昏暗的房間教我想起倫敦的酒吧：煙霧瀰漫，皮椅，矮茶几，吵鬧聲，放肆大笑。我坐著聽那些男士扯喉高歌「長征」或「東方紅」。

我在中國感覺人地不宜。不管去到哪兒，茶館、火鍋店、人民公園、甜甜圈店，甚至長城上頭，人人嘴裡談的都是買車買房，商品投資，抓緊北京奧運的商機大撈一筆，或者從外國人口袋把錢偷過來。他們的談話我沒辦法融入。我的世界似乎太過不切實際，缺乏生產力。

At night, some friends take me to a Karaoke. The place is not made for me. It is for Chinese men who seek freshness when they have grown tired of their old wives. In empty rooms, young women in tight miniskirts with half naked breasts wait for loners to come and sing. The dim rooms remind me of the pubs in London: smoke, leather seats, low tea tables, loud voices and crazy laughing. I sit and listen to men singing songs like The Long March or The East Is Red.

I feel out of place in China. Wherever I go, in tea houses, in hotpot restaurants, in People's parks, in Dunkin Donuts, or even on top of the Great Wall, everybody talks about buying cars and houses, investing in new products, grabbing the opportunity of the 2008 Olympics to make money, or to steal money from the foreigner's pockets. I can't join in their conversations. My world seems too unpractical and nonproductive.

"But you can speak English, that alone should earn you lots of money! Nowadays, anything to do with the West can make money." My friends and my relatives keep telling me this.

Day 500

I think I have received your last letter. It arrived a month and a half ago and there has been nothing since then. I don't know why.

I think maybe I will never go back to England, the country where I became an adult, where I grew into a woman, the country where I also got injured, the country where I had my most confused days and my greatest passion and my brief hap-

「可是妳會講英語，光靠這一點妳就撈不完了！這時機啊，任何跟西方沾上邊的東西都能賺錢。」我的朋友和親戚老是跟我這麼說。

500天

我想我有收到你上一封信。最後一封。一個半月前收到的，然後就沒有消息了。不曉得怎會這樣。

我想，或許再也沒有機會回到英國，那個讓我變成大人的國度。在那兒，我成長為女人，同時也嚐到受傷害的滋味。在那兒，我度過最迷惘的日子，擁有最熱烈的激情，以及短暫的幸福和無言的哀傷。或許，我害怕想到自己依然深愛著你。

不過這千絲萬縷已經不再那麼令人牽掛。只是某些時刻，當我獨自待在北京的公寓，夜色朦朧，窗外的建築工地敲打未休，依稀感覺那疼痛還在。是的，地理的阻隔頗有助益。我明白最好的辦法便是彼此放手，讓我們各自活在不同的星球，平行度日，別再有交集。

親愛的Z，

我從威爾斯寫信給妳。終於搬離倫敦了。我住的石屋後面那座山叫卡寧格里，這是威爾斯語，意指天使之山……

我們院子裡的幾株植物和廚房那張老桌子都跟我搬來此地。我覺得向日葵很想妳，它們的頭害羞低垂——好像做錯事被老師處罰——花瓣的鮮黃已經轉為深褐。不過，我想妳的小竹子快活得很，因為上個月我們這裡的天氣非

piness and my quiet sadness. Perhaps I am scared to think that I am still in love with you.

But all these thoughts don't matter too much anymore. Only sometimes, when I am alone in Beijing in my flat, an obscure night, noisy construction sites outside my window, I still can feel that pain. Yes, the geography helps a lot. I know the best thing to do is to let each other go, to let us each live on a different planet, parallel lives, no more crossing over.

Dear Z,

I am writing to you from Wales. I've finally moved out of London. The mountain behind my stone cottage is called Carningli. It is Welsh, it means Mountain of the Angel. . . .

I brought some of our plants and the old kitchen table here. I think the sunflowers are missing you. Their heads have bowed down in shame—as if they have been punished by their school teacher—and their bright yellow petals have turned deep brown. But I think your little bamboo tree is very happy because we have had Chinese weather for the last month. Last week I planted some climbing roses outside my cottage because I thought it would be good to have more colours around.

Every day I walk through the valley to the sea. It is a long walk. When I look at the sea, I wonder if you have learned to swim. . . .

Your words are soaked in your great peace and happiness, and these words are being stored in my memory. I kiss this letter. I bury my face in the paper, a sheet torn from some exercise book. I try to smell that faraway valley. I picture you standing on your fields, the mountain behind you, and the

常中國。上禮拜我在石屋外頭種了一些蔓性玫瑰，周遭多添一點色彩想來應該很不錯。

　　每天我會穿過溪谷走到海邊。路要走很久。看到海的時候，就會想，不知妳是否已經學會游泳……

　　字字句句浸漬著你無比的寧靜和快樂，這些字句已積存進我的記憶中。我親吻這封信，把臉埋進這一頁從練習簿撕下的信紙。我試著從中聞一聞遠方的那處溪谷，彷彿看見你站在你的田園裡，後面是座山，海濤聲浪來來去去。你描述的畫面何等美妙，這是你給過我的最佳贈禮。

　　信封上的地址很眼熟，一定是在西威爾斯。沒錯，我們一起去過的地方。還記得那裡好多雨水。雨下個不停，覆蓋了整片森林、連綿的山脈，以及放眼望去的大地。

sound of the sea coming and going. It is such a great picture you describe. It is the best gift you ever gave me.

The address on the envelope is familiar. It must be in west Wales. Yes, we went there together. I remember how it rained. The rain was ceaseless, covering the whole forest, the whole mountain, and the whole land.

Acknowledgements

The author wishes to thank
Rebecca Carter, Claire Paterson, Beth Coates, Alison Samuel,
Rachel Cugnoni, Suzanne Dean, Toby Eady, Clara Farmer,
Juliet Brooke, Audrey Brooks, Nan Talese, Lorna Owen
and all the others who have followed this book on its journey.

謝辭

作者誠摯感謝
Rebecca Carter, Claire Paterson, Beth Coates, Alison Samuel,
Rachel Cugnoni, Suzanne Dean, Toby Eady, Clara Farmer,
Juliet Brooke, Audrey Brooks, Nan Talese, Lorna Owen
以及其他所有陪伴這本書一路走來的朋友。

LOCUS

LOCUS